MW01206359

Night and Day

By

Sherrie Hansen

Andy and Sarah, To second chances, Sherrie Hansen

Star-Crossed Books
Published by Indigo Sea Press
Winston-Salem

Star-Crossed Books
Indigo Sea Press
302 Ricks Drive
Winston-Salem, NC 27103

First Star-Crossed Books edition published April, 2016
Star-Crossed Books, Moon Sailor, and all production design are trademarks of Indigo Sea Press, used under license.

For information regarding bulk purchases of this book, digital purchase and special discounts, please contact the publisher at indigoseapress.com

Cover design by Tracy Beltran, Photo by Sherrie Hansen

Manufactured in the United States of America
ISBN 978-1-63066-397-1

To my Grandma Hansen, who was a wonderful storyteller, for the gifts of make-believe, curiosity, and awe. My first stories were written and acted out between the trees in her front yard.

To my Grandma Victoria and her Danish cousin, Boyda, for each letter written, for sharing hearts and history, for keeping our family's legends alive.

Sherrie Hansen

1.

It wasn't just her own life that flashed before Jensen Marie Christiansen's eyes as she watched the ribbon of black smoke curling up from the horizon. It was her mother's, her Grandma Victoria's, and her Great-grandma Maren Jensen's.

Her car fishtailed on the loose gravel and she gripped the steering wheel. A gust of wind rattled the windows and the smoke billowing in the distance scattered in a merry dance that she might have thought pretty if she hadn't been so intent on strangling her brother. The last mile raced by and she roared into the farmyard, careened around the barn on the circular driveway and slid to a halt in front of the house.

Her brother was standing nonchalantly in front of a bonfire, a package tied with pink and blue ribbons clutched in one hand, drawn back like he was ready to lob a baseball.

She leapt from the car. "Peder—no!"

Peder turned at the same moment he released his grip. A cluster of old letters sailed by her face and landed in a pile of smoldering embers at the edge of the fire.

She cringed at the smell of burned hair as she leaned into the flames, grabbed the ribbons holding the bundle of letters together and pulled them from the fire. The heat dried the tears on her cheeks faster than they could form.

Peder grabbed her sweater from behind and yanked her away from the flames. "Are you nuts?"

"Let me go." She shoved him away with one hand.

He'd always been stronger than she was. "Stupid girl. Look at them! They're in Danish. Risking your life to save a bunch of old letters you can't even read."

"So? Someone, somewhere certainly can," she said.

"They've been in the attic for thirty years. If no one's looked at them in all that time, no one's ever going to."

She cradled the sooty stack of letters to her chest and glared up at him. "You said you would wait until I got here."

"You said you would be here first thing in the morning."

"It's only nine-thirty. I left the house at eight. If you wanted me here by six, you should have said so."

"So now it's my fault that you sleep away half the day and work half the night? You're the one marching to a different drummer here, not me," Peder said, sounding strangely like her father had when she was a teenager. He took a rake and stirred the hot part of the fire to spread the flames. "If the world waited to start spinning until you woke up, nothing would ever get done."

She resisted the urge to pull a stack of old Farmer's Elevator calendars from the fire and watched instead as the flames licked away at Grandma's handwritten notes. Maren had kept track of everything that happened on the farm... what day they'd planted corn in 1962, when the beans had turned back in '53, and how many pigs had been born to each of their sows.

She looked at the fire and blinked away tears. Grandpa Frederik's old tube radio was illuminated in a ghostly aura. The charred remains of the carpet that had been her great-grandma's pride and joy were cocked at an odd angle, the bottom half burned and the top half ready to fall back on itself.

"You threw away Grandma's trunks? They came over from Denmark in the bottom of the ship."

"And smelled like it, too," Peder said. "Damp, musty old pieces of junk."

"I would have taken them," she said, another tear slipping down her cheek. "Damn it, Peder. This is our legacy. Our family's history."

"The trunks were built for a purpose. They served it—a hundred years ago. Let them rest in peace."

"If that's all any of this means to you, maybe you should tear down the house, scrap the whole place."

Peder poked his rake deeper into the fire until what was left of Grandma's rug fell into the flames with a poof of red-hot embers. "Don't tempt me."

A chill ran down her spine. "You're not serious."

Peder's body radiated an obstinate stance that had probably come over on the same ship as the Jensens and Christiansens. "This place needs a lot of work."

This place? Her head throbbed. Peder might love the rich, black dirt it sat on, but it was she who loved the house. Images of supper times, birthday celebrations and family reunions set against the house's beautiful quarter-sawn oak pocket doors and leaded glass windows flashed through her head like a slide show. She'd dreamed about living in that house with her husband and children just like her mother had, and her mother before her, and her mother before her.

"Tara's brother is an architect," Peder said, his fair cheeks red from the heat of the fire. "He thinks we should build down on the rise overlooking the creek."

Emotions she'd been holding back—ever since Ed had come home from the outpatient clinic with an ice pack between his legs—poured over her. It wasn't just the fire. It was her mom and dad leaving for Arizona and Peder and Tara moving into the house she'd always wanted for her own and not appreciating it. It was growing up in a family who were research papers to her poetry. It was dreams so rusty and corroded with age that she barely recognized them.

"Enough with the tears already." Peder coughed and looked like he wanted to pat her on the back but didn't know how.

A tear dripped off her chin as she raised her head to look Peder in the eyes. "You have no right to burn or tear down property that's just as much mine as it is yours."

"You can't save the whole world," Peder said, looking irritatingly unfazed. "Your basement is a ten foot square hole of dirt and Mom and Dad's condo is barely big enough for them."

She couldn't even save herself. "I could have sold the radio on eBay," she said, reverting to a language Peder understood. "A friend of mine found one at a garage sale and sold it for over two hundred dollars to some guy in Italy."

"For every musty old artifact I threw in the fire, there are two more still in the attic. Stop griping and come inside. If we get to it, we can be done sorting the stuff by noon."

Unlikely. Peder and Tara's attic was—had been—stuffed to the rafters, not only with mementos of her Great Grandma Jensen's, but boxes full of stuff from when they were kids.

"Do you know how much fuel oil it takes to heat this monstrosity of an old house?" Peder said in a voice that sounded old and cold instead of young and boyish.

"So get the insulation in and put the things back where you found them," she suggested, trying a nice tact this time.

Peder frowned. "You try hauling all Mom's junk up and down these steep stairs. Once it's out, it's staying out. Besides, if we're going to live here, we'd like to be able to use the space to store our own stuff."

It took every ounce of restraint she possessed to keep from pointing out the fact that if it weren't for the people whose 'stuff' was in the attic, the house wouldn't be his. The house wouldn't exist. Neither would Peder for that matter.

The stench of smoke grated on her throat. "Store the boxes in my old room until Thanksgiving when Mom and Dad come."

"Uh, Tara's planning on taking the wallpaper down and painting in there as soon as we finish picking corn."

Okay. So that hurt. She'd spent hours putting up that wallpaper... a tiny calico design on top with blue, pink and green stripes on the bottom and a border of hearts in-between. It was still in perfect condition. She'd even left the quilt and curtains she'd made to match for Tara to use.

"What's she going to...?" She managed.

"Turn it into an exercise area," Peder said.

"You always wanted my room."

"Don't go getting all offended now. Tara's just not into pastels. She wants something bright and peppy. More modern. Whatever. You know me. I leave the decorating stuff to her."

She knew him all right. The one thing she, Peder, and Karl

all had in common was that they were all stubborn as mules. "And this all has to be done today?" She asked wearily. "Tara took a few days off to help combine beans. When we got rained out last night, it just made sense to do it now."

Sense hadn't played any part in the crackling fire blazing in front of her, at least by her definition. She looked up at Peder's face and tried to rein in her anger. The only reason she took any of his guff was because he was her little brother and she remembered how cute he'd been when he was a baby. "I understand you and Tara wanting to make the farmhouse yours. All I'm saying is that I need some time to come up with a plan."

"Time? Funny you should mention time when Tara and I have been working night and day to get the beans in, the sweet corn frozen, the tomatoes canned, the pumpkins picked, the apples dried, and the corn picker ready. It's darn near more work than two people, one of whom works in town full time, can handle."

Jensen clutched Maren's letters and tore her eyes away from the inferno. If she left in a huff, Peder would no doubt burn the whole kit and caboodle.

Peder turned on his heels and strode across the yard. He was halfway to the house when she finally turned to follow him. The home Maren and Frederik Jensen had built so lovingly loomed in front of her, a forsaken dream in which she was supposed to have starred. The house's narrow, white board siding was punctuated with sage green window boxes like it had been for almost a century. Maren had always filled them with bright red geraniums to match the Danish flag she'd kept hanging on the front porch.

If Tara hated pastels so much, why on earth had she switched to pink petunias?

*****

Anders Westerlund rolled over, one arm still bunched

5

around his pillow, the other groping the sleek wood shelves that hugged the wall behind his bed. Eyes still closed, he found the clock and pushed a button to silence the intrusive beep. The noise droned on—a loud, obnoxious whining noise that alternately buzzed and chewed its way through his semi-sleep. He squinted his eyes. Four slivers of sunshine gleamed around the edges of his bedroom windows and fluttered against the marine blue walls. The glossy white and lemon yellow trim pulsed with energy, Star-Crossed him awake. He rubbed the sleep from his eyes and glanced at the clock. He'd worked from two until ten and hadn't gotten to bed until after midnight. It might be the middle of the morning to his energetic young neighbor, but to him, it felt like dawn. Much as he loved Danemark, he had to admit that dawn came much too early in Copenhagen.

Anders pushed back his quilt, stood and stretched. It looked to be another glorious fall day. Trying to focus his eyes, he walked to the window and peered between two wooden slats. *No! Not the lilac bushes.* He stepped into his shorts as quickly as he could shove his legs into the holes and grabbed a polo shirt on his way out the door. He was still trying to stuff his arms into his sleeves when he reached the yard.

"Jesper," he yelled, assuming that anyone else on the street who might have been sleeping had already been awakened by Jesper's chainsaw. Anders leapt over the pile of branches between his yard and Jesper's and got the lad's attention seconds before he lopped off the limb of an apple tree.

"Godmorgen, Mr. Westerlund!" Jesper said, cutting the engine and beaming at Anders with a pleased look on his face.

Anders sighed. Those lilacs had been his only shield from the morning sun and the prying eyes of the whole neighborhood.

"Sorry, Mr. Westerlund. I forgot about your schedule."

He wasn't about to let Jesper deflate his sails just because the boy had grown up playing with his son. "Anders. If you're old enough to be married, have kids, and own a house, you're old enough to call me Anders."

"Sure thing, Mr. Westerlund," Jesper said.

"About those bushes you just hacked down," Anders said, hoping the morning gruffness in his voice made him sound stern. "They might be slightly over your side of our property line, but they provide me with a great deal of shade and privacy. If you had consulted with me before you..."

"My wife's gardening magazine said that getting rid of the dead wood would help keep them healthy. I didn't think..."

"I've trimmed them back a foot or two early every spring for over twenty years. They've always been fine."

"The article said they would surpass their original height in a few years," Jesper said.

The look Anders gave him must have gotten his point across.

"Maybe a wooden shutter for your window," Jesper blathered.

"I'll be fine," Anders said, feeling old and crabby. "But in the future..."

"Certainly," Jesper said. "Please say hi to Bjorn. I hope to buy a computer soon so I can talk to him online."

Anders turned and waved without looking back.

*****

Jensen climbed behind the wheel of her car, started the engine, and watched as a gaggle of geese waddled toward the safety of the pasture. The old red barn where she'd played as a little girl still stood tall and proud in its fresh coat of paint, but the wood-slatted corncrib was listing to the left. It hadn't been used since her father had put up a cluster of galvanized steel grain bins some twenty years ago.

She craned her neck to see over the stack of boxes piled on the seat behind her and looked out the rear view mirror to make sure it was safe to back up. A confetti of tiny, half-burned bits and pieces mixed with embers from Peder's bonfire soared heavenward as she drove down the lane.

She turned out of the driveway and onto a gravel road, skirting potholes and washboards while she punched the dial button on her cell phone.

"Hello." Her mother answered breathlessly.

"Thank goodness you're finally home. I've been trying since first thing this morning."

"Must be important if you were up early." Her mother laughed. "We met Ruth and Jim for breakfast at that place out on the highway north of town—you know, the one that has that all you can eat breakfast buffet for four ninety-five."

No, I don't know, Jensen thought, feeling grumpier with every flick of the odometer. *How would I know?*

"Your dad and Jim played eighteen holes. Ruth and I worked on our cross stitch and talked," her mom said in a rambling tone that was as slow as retired life. "Is something wrong?"

"Not unless you don't care that your son is going to tear down Grandma's house."

"Over my dead body," her mother said. "Charles, get in here and pick up the portable. Your son is making trouble again."

Jensen heard her dad pick up the extension. "Peder? What's he up to now?"

"See," Jensen said. "You knew it was Peder before I even said a word."

"Karl never makes any trouble," her mother said.

"It's always you and..." her father chimed in.

"Good grief," Jensen said. "I know I can be a little stubborn, but I hope you're not lumping me into the same category as that hard-headed little—"

"Calm down and tell us what's the matter, dear."

She switched ears and rounded a corner. "Peder and Tara asked me to help clean out the attic at the farm. They're trying to make the place a little more livable until they can afford to tear it down and build something more energy efficient," she said, knowing that would get a rise out of her mother.

"Well, I hope you reminded them that that house belongs to all three of you," her mother said huffily.

"If I say any more than I have already, he'll just dig his heels in and be all the more unreasonable," Jensen said.

"He'd probably call the demolition crew just to spite you," her father concurred. "You two always did rub each other wrong."

"Exactly," Jensen said. "Which is why you two really need to get back here and have a talk with him."

"You know we're too far away just to jump in the car and run home whenever we want to," her mother said.

"Of course. Peder knows it, too. That's why he's gotten so cocky. He knows with you gone, he can do whatever he wants."

"There's only so much we can do when we're this far away," her father said.

"I know you like it in Arizona," Jensen said, "but..."

"We've talked about this over and over again, dear. We're where we want to be, at least for now."

"And I still don't understand. Minnesota is your home. If you don't want to live in Blooming Prairie anymore you should move to Red Wing. There's a great golf course and all kinds of fun things to do along the Mississippi. Most important, you'd still be close to home." *And to me.*

"You don't want us to end up like the Swensons, do you?"

"Of course not," she said without hesitating. Mr. Swenson had died of a heart attack while shoveling snow on the farm he'd lived on for over eighty years. "You could be like the Larsons."

"The Larsons came home from Florida because their daughter had twins and they didn't want to miss out on being grandparents," her mother said pointedly.

"There you have it," her dad said. "Grandchildren."

"Just one more reason you should talk to Peder," Jensen said, trying to swallow her bitterness. "If he and Tara had a baby, maybe they'd start to appreciate our family history."

"I'm sure they will when the time is right," her mom said.

"Well, I hope their kids like sleeping in an exercise room, a first floor laundry facility, or a state of the art computer room, because their bedrooms are disappearing fast."

"You're a fine one to talk." Her mother laughed. "Your house is so tiny you barely have room for you."

"I told you you needed more closets, a good furnace, and storm windows when you bought the place," her father butted in. "But you were too busy swooning over the stained glass windows and claw-footed bathtub to worry about practical things."

"My house may have faults, but I love it," Jensen said.

"Maybe I should have a talk with Ed," her dad said. "His house would be plenty big enough for the two of you and a baby."

Jensen clamped her jaw shut and made a hard left turn.

"You'd have to look long and hard to find a man that would make a better provider than Ed," her dad continued.

She was still driving, so she couldn't close her eyes and cry, or even curl up in a ball like she wanted to. "I'm sorry to disappoint you. Again. Ed's made it perfectly clear that he doesn't want any more children. He hasn't seen the ones he has in twenty years. Besides, Ed's convinced that he's not going to live beyond sixty," she said, trying to make light of words that were so not funny.

"What on earth?" Her mother said.

"He thinks it would be cruel to have children when he wouldn't even be here to see them through high school."

"Tell him to take out a large insurance policy. You and the children will be fine," her mother said. "Besides, I plan to live to be a hundred, so I'll be there to cheer for them on graduation day even if he's not. The old fuddy dud."

"Damn fool doesn't know what a gem he has in you," her dad said.

She couldn't handle this. She just couldn't.

"I know I've given you a bad time about staying at Ed's when you two hadn't set a date." Her dad's voice revved up. "I know all kinds of people get pregnant out of wedlock these days, but we certainly didn't want that for you if we could help it."

"I didn't want that either," she said. But part of her had, so badly that she hadn't cared if it happened in or out.

"It is frustrating being so far away at moments like this," her mother said. "I'd give you a big hug if I could."

"That's what I was trying to say earlier." Jensen struggled to maintain her composure. "Peder has the home place and Tara and half of the Italians in Philadelphia. Karl has Melody and her whole family. They'll both have kids. Grandkids after that."

Her hands shook as she pulled the car to the shoulder. "You guys, Peder and Karl, and that old house are all I have."

"And you always will." Her mother's voice was stronger now, the matriarch once more.

"Not if Peder keeps having bonfires," Jensen said.

She could hear her mother's sharp intake of breath. "I rescued as much as I could. But who knows about next time?" She looked at the soot-stained letters on the seat beside her. "I found some old letters from Grandma that are written in Danish."

"He was going to throw out Maren's letters?" Her father said angrily. "Aren't they those Boyda mailed from Denmark?"

"Maren wrote them to her cousin, Sophie, in Denmark after Grandpa Frederik brought the family to Minnesota," her mother said. "Sophie's daughter sent them to me after her mother died."

"Does anyone know what they say?" Jensen asked.

"Boyda knows a little English. All we know is that your great-grandmother was a very beautiful woman, and that there was another man in love with her," her mother said. "Your Great-grandfather Frederik moved the whole family to the United States to get her away from this man."

"Wow," Jensen said. "I wonder what happened."

"I'm sure there's more to the story, but that's all I've ever been able to find out," her mother said.

When they'd said all there was to say, Jensen turned back onto the road and slowly crested a hill, her mind whirling so fast the car could barely keep up.

She was too tired to even think about unpacking her car by the time she reached home—besides, she had no place to put the things she'd saved. Her garage was full of antiques she'd picked up at this garage sale or that back in the days when she'd assumed that she would be the one living in Maren's big house. That she would need a big oak dresser for her son, a walnut wardrobe for her daughter, and a basinet for her baby.

Yeah, well, a car full of "junk" and a stack of sooty letters was all that was left of those dreams.

*****

Anders turned to reassess the damage to his hedge when he reached the shadow of the patio. The line of lilacs along the east side of his property joined up with a brick wall at the rear and met a fence that attached to the west side of his home to form a nice, tidy square. The yard was very private. He only closed the blinds at all because the sun came up at four A.M. and he didn't like being awakened so soon after he'd dozed off.

He squinted at the rainbow of colors that hugged the fence. A wave of brilliant, periwinkle blue hydrangeas bobbed in the breeze along the far edge of the yard. His climbing roses clung to the mortar between the bricks in a lacey design he'd orchestrated himself.

He did love his plants. The day before, he'd spent an hour photographing an elusive shadow shifting around the fronds of the maidenhair fern in his bay window, then watched the sunshine slice through the kitchen curtain like a carefully placed spotlight illuminating the African violets on his windowsill.

Sad commentary, having to resort to taking pictures of his foliage. Sadder still that he had no one to show the pictures to. He could imagine his co-workers reactions if he added his garden shots to the family photos they passed around at work. He had scanned a few and sent them to Bjorn. It served the kid right if he had to look at flower photos—if Bjorn had stayed in Danemark, gotten married, and started a family instead of running off to America, Anders might have had grandchildren to take pictures of.

His day had already gotten off to a bad start. The last thing in the world he needed to be thinking about was the many evils good old America had wreaked upon his life. He went back in the house, slipped his arms from his shirt and tried to refocus his thoughts on something more pleasant.

His plants might not provide the companionship he'd craved since Bjorn had moved to Seattle, but tending to their needs made him feel necessary. They responded to his touch and appreciated his endeavors. He gave them the gift of life. They added some color and a little bit of wonder to his life. It wasn't much, but it was something.

*****

Jensen woke with a start. The room was wrapped in shadows, broken only by the slivers of moonlight wafting through the Venetian blinds. The lack of lace took a second to register—Ed's house.

She could feel Ed's chest rising and falling, the weight of his knee pinning her to the bed. Until now, she'd always thought the way he wrapped himself around her while she slept was sweet.

"Ed?" She wove her fingers through his hair.

He didn't open his eyes, but she felt his fingers stroking her thigh and knew he was awake.

"Mmmm. Twice in one night? Baby..."

"No. Not that. I just wanted to ask you something."

13

Ed exhaled slowly. "The alarm goes off at five."

"It doesn't have to. You don't have to go in until eight."

He rolled away from her. "We can talk tomorrow."

"I can't forget about Peder's bonfire."

"How could you when those stupid letters are stinking up the whole house?"

Twice in one day, she'd rescued the letters. First from the fire. Then from the trash.

"I got the soot off the counter and put them in a baggie."

"The edges are all singed. What good are they that way?"

She ignored him. "The thought of Peder tearing down Grandma's house really bothers me," she said, rubbing Ed's back to keep him awake.

Ed sighed. Well, really, it was more of a huff, but she could ignore a sigh.

"It breaks my heart that he and Tara don't appreciate the treasure they have in Gram's house, say nothing about all the memories wrapped up in those thick, plaster walls."

Ed rolled over. "You can stay up until midnight and sleep until noon if you want to. I can't."

The part of her body that wasn't near Ed's shivered. She reached for the corner of Ed's bedspread and tried to ignore the scratchy pills that dotted the surface. She'd made Ed a "Trip Around the World" quilt when they first started dating. She hadn't intended it to be a disparaging comment on his lackluster bedroom or colorless surroundings.

She'd stitched it with the same passion she'd felt for him. She'd dreamed of evenings tucked under it, whispering, cuddling. Ed had put it in the cedar chest so it wouldn't wear out.

She lay without moving while minutes stretched into an hour. It was almost eleven. She couldn't bear to stay another second, yet she couldn't seem to move. She needed to think, to let her mind sort through her feelings without the distraction of Ed's body to muddle her thoughts.

Ed didn't understand what it felt like to have an inborn,

night-loving, second wind that kicked in whether you wanted it to or not. Ed saw nothing strange about starting his day in the middle of the night or needing four cups of coffee to wake up, but thought she was odd because she was wide awake at midnight.

When her Great-grandmother, Maren Jensen, had still been alive, she'd claimed it was Jensen's Danish blood—a theory that made perfect sense. After all, daylight dawned in Denmark about the same time the clock struck twelve in Minnesota.

She crept out of the bed, being careful not to jiggle the mattress, tiptoed toward the living room, and found a spot on Ed's box-like couch. Thank goodness Ed's floors didn't creak like hers did.

She scanned the naked white walls of Ed's living room. At least he wouldn't have to spackle if he moved. She wiggled her toes against the stiff Berber that carpeted the floors. It was the same flat shade as the walls, flecked with brown to camouflage any specks of dirt that might accumulate between the frequent vacuumings Ed was careful to give his house. Her quilt would have looked lovely mounted on the west wall. Ed had been afraid it would fade.

Okay. That was it. She had to get out. She was an artist. She needed spontaneity, color, a little disarray in her life.

She left the chilly patch of sofa, found her clothes, bundled up the quilt top she'd been working on, and took the plastic bag with the letters in it from the hook by the back door where Ed had hung it earlier.

She was able to ease out the back door without so much as a squeak. Ed faithfully oiled the hinges in his house once a month. Her car was in the driveway, still piled high with boxes, her bike on the rack. She certainly hadn't brought her Schwinn cruiser along so she could ride home in the middle of the night, but it seemed like the best choice for a quiet get-away. The moon was bright, almost full, and she had a headlight. Her battery pack was freshly charged and ready to go, thanks to Ed. Silently, she lifted the bike from the rack and tucked her quilt top and the letters in the big, wicker basket Ed had mounted on the front. Using her shirttail to wipe the dew off the seat, she swung one leg over the crossbar and pushed off with the other. Fresh air penetrated her lungs. She felt a tug of relief as she finally faced the truth. Ed had made her feel beautiful, secure, and cared-about at a time when she'd been very lonely. She'd loved him for that, at the beginning. But sexual camaraderie just wasn't enough anymore. She needed someone who cherished her, heart and soul, someone who understood the way her mind worked, someone who shared her hopes and passions. Someone who shared her dream of having a family of her own.

She pedaled away from the tract homes in Ed's subdivision as fast as she could, relaxing only when she heard the familiar click of her bicycle tires on the slightly warped ribbon of boardwalk that sliced through the swampland running along the Mississippi just north of Red Wing.

A loud splash interrupted the chorus of frogs singing to her right. Jensen braked and resisted the urge to peer into the darkness. It was probably only an otter, or maybe a muskrat. If she didn't keep her eyes on the narrow ribbon of dimly-lit boards splitting the swamp, she'd be the one taking a dip.

2.

The night air should have cleared her head, but all she could think about was Ed and the words they'd exchanged a few hours earlier.

After leaving Peder's, she'd stopped at her house in Welch long enough to shower, grab the quilt she was working on, and put her bike on the back of her car. She'd arrived about four and busied herself with adding some lemon-colored French knots to a flower on a quilt she called Daffodil Daze.

She'd heard Ed come in from outdoors, stopping to wipe his feet on the rag rug just inside the back door like he always did so as not to track dirt onto the newly waxed kitchen floor.

Her mind conjured up Ed's image—steel blue eyes, thick, brown hair, and shoulders that were perpetually rigid, at least when she was around.

"What's with the junk in your car?" Ed had said.

It had taken her a second to shift from one world to the other. She always did feel like she was caught in a time warp when she was quilting.

"I need your keys so I can change your oil," Ed had said, adding "I can drive the car down to the Goodwill store and unload it for you in the morning if you want me to."

"It's not junk. It's stuff from Grandma's attic and I need a place to store it." She'd untangled herself from the spot she was appliquéing as quickly as she could. "I was hoping—"

"Forget it. It's not going in the basement," Ed said, giving her a disgusted look as she rounded the corner. "I need to hurry if I'm going to finish your car before dark."

"I've only had it out of the garage six times all summer."

"In-town driving is hard on an engine," Ed had started to expound. "Frequent starting and stopping..."

Jensen squeezed her brakes in time to avoid a chipmunk that skittered across the trail and headed west toward Welch. She was on the straightaway now; a smooth stretch of asphalt built on an abandoned railroad track that followed the Cannon River.

She really hadn't been aiming at Ed's mouth when she'd thrown him her keys.

"If I didn't know better I'd think you managed an apartment complex," Ed had grumbled as he caught the cluster mid-air.

"Right," she'd said, knowing there was no point in trying to defend the rationale behind keeping her junior high diary key on her ring. Besides, there was no need to go down that road again. The ruts were deep enough already.

"Sorry, Ed. I really do appreciate..."

He'd snorted.

"Why don't we bike down to the river and get a bite to eat when you're done?" She'd said. "It's been a stressful day. Don't you feel like stretching your legs?"

"I've got venison thawing," Ed had said. "I'd have the steaks on the coals already but someone distracted me the other night before I got the grill cleaned." He'd smiled and lifted his left eyebrow. All the man ever thought about was sex. Her bicycle surged forward.

"I called earlier about the play that's showing at the Chippewa Theatre," she'd said, idiotically imagining that he might agree to go. "It starts at eight. If we hurry..."

Ed's jaw had stiffened—a sure sign that any further cajoling was pointless.

"I just thought it would help me get my mind off things," she'd persisted. "It's called 'The Crazy Quilt Club'."

"Well they got one thing right." Ed had frowned.

Her pedals spun angrily under her feet as she remembered Ed's hands skimming the dip at the small of her back.

That was when she'd resorted to whining, which was downright humiliating, especially considering it hadn't worked. "You promised me we could do some fun things before the summer was out. It's September already and our big excitement has been watching reruns on TV and trying to use up our venison so we've got space in the freezer if the neighbor gives us more."

She ducked to clear a low branch dangling over the trail. She could still see the hurt look that had glazed Ed's eyes. "Well, I can't speak for you, but I've had a pretty good summer. Nice and mellow and laid back the way summers are supposed to be." Ed had said, touching her in the spot he knew would make her body melt. "All I really want to do tonight is to stay home and enjoy you, be with you. Love you."

Her bike slowed. So Ed wasn't exactly the man of her dreams—he had his good points. The night air nipped at her ears as she changed gears, then raced forward once more.

She knew every twist and turn of the trail, but that didn't mean she could anticipate what was around the next bend. The moon disappeared behind a cloud and the headlight mounted under her handlebars strained to cut a swath through the black canyon. She'd ridden the narrow chute at dusk enough times to know that all kinds of creatures lived in the trees and caves along the bluffs. She tried not to think about the bats that were probably swooping mere inches over her head and pumped her pedals a little harder.

A moonbeam momentarily illuminated the white stripe on the back of a skunk. *Whew. Close call.*

She took a deep breath and tried to dispel her jitters. She'd missed the skunk by at least five feet. It hadn't sprayed. It wasn't going to. A sense of relief was finally starting to replace the echo of her pounding heart when something—something big—moved in the darkness in front of her. Jensen gripped her hand brakes and hung on for dear life.

Whatever—or whomever —was blocking the trail was big. What she'd glimpsed—or sensed—wasn't light and feathery like the shadow of a bat. It was thick, dense, and ominous. Terrifying. All she could see at first was that the path was blocked. The night was too deep, and her headlight not quite strong enough to see by what. She looked over her shoulder and tried not to give in to her nerves. It had been over a half hour since she'd passed the edge of the swamp and turned west on the old railroad straight-away. She had to be close to Welch. A tail. A bushy tail swung once at the very edge of her headlight. That was when she saw the eyes, gleaming in the moonlight. Big, yellow eyes.

"Don't come any closer," a woman's voice, full of false cheerfulness, said from her left, about ten feet ahead. She'd been so mesmerized by the eyes she hadn't even noticed the woman. "There's a big bobcat just a few feet from me," the woman said, her voice as smooth and silky as honey. "Big pussycat is just a little hungry, that's all. She was stalking a rabbit when Ginger and I startled her. But she knows there are a lot of rabbits to be had with much less effort than it would take to eat a tough old crow like me."

Jensen gulped. So did the bobcat. He licked his lips with a massive, pinkish gray tongue.

Jensen looked at the woman. A small cocker spaniel sat frozen at her side, his tail twitching nervously.

"I've never seen one up close," Jensen whispered, not knowing what to do or say.

"You don't happen to have some raw chicken in that basket of yours, do you?" the woman said.

"Sorry."

"You and me both," the woman said.

The cat's eyes gleamed from the darkness, the twin points of light staring into her eyes.

"Aren't you the woman who used to baby-sit Justin and Molly LaValley?" the woman said. "The quilter?"

"Yes," Jensen said, recognizing the woman as a new neighbor to a family she had been a dear friend to for years.

She had to do something. "Scat," she said, her voice husky, strong, spitting out the word as forcefully as she could. "Get," she threatened, in the same stern voice she'd heard her Great-grandma Jensen use years earlier when she'd shamed a coyote from the chicken coop. "There's plenty of food for you in the forest." Her voice grew even louder. "Leave us alone."

The bobcat stared at her for what seemed like an eternity, sizing her up, trying to decide if she meant business. Well she did. She'd taken about all the guff she could stand in one short day. First Peder, then Ed. Enough was enough. "Scat!"

The cat turned and slunk into the woods.

"Thank you!" The woman said, visibly shaking. "I don't know what would have happened if you hadn't come along when you did."

They hurriedly made their way into town, making their introductions, speculating in hushed tones, looking over their shoulders. Adrenalin was still pulsing through Jensen's veins when she arrived at home. Her little cottage looked cozy and inviting even in the dark. She wasn't at all tired, but she'd certainly had enough "nightlife" for one evening.

She cocked her knee and lifted her ankle to dismount. Her leg was almost free of the bar when she realized she didn't have her keys. Damn. That would mean they were still in the front pocket of Ed's blue jeans.

*****

Anders looked over his shoulder one last time and tried to banish all thoughts of his now two-foot high hedge of lilacs from his mind. With the bushes gone, his roses would get far more light. Maybe they would have more blossoms next year.

He was naked again within seconds of stepping into the house. He went to the shower, pulled the circular curtain around his body, and let the water run down his torso in rivulets.

As soon as he'd dried himself and slipped into a pair of shorts, he went to his computer. It was nine A.M. in Danemark. If he hurried, he could catch Bjorn in time to say goodnight before he went to bed, a habit he indulged in two or three times a week; a ritual he needed more than his son did.

He'd used computers at work for years; a good working

knowledge of the systems his fledgling air traffic controllers used was essential to his job. But the main frames he had learned on bore little resemblance to this PC and its fancy software. He'd conquer the creature one day, but for the time being, it was enough that he knew how to log on and find Bjorn.

His software alerted Bjorn that he had joined the twenty-five occupants of the room entitled Thirty-Something Romance. Bjorn's first message flashed up on his screen.

Boy_Wonder: Hey, Ugly_Duckling. I thought I talked you into changing your name. You'll never catch a woman like this.

Anders typed his response with nimble fingers.

Ugly_Duckling: We are both stubborn, ja? Because I thought I had talked you into looking for a woman your own age.

Boy_Wonder: You can always tell a Dane, but you can't tell him much.

Anders smiled. At least something he'd told his son had sunk in. Hmm. With a little effort he could make Bjorn wish he were typing in Danish. The boy had always been fun to tease.

Ugly_Duckling: Don't they check ID's in these rooms?

Boy_Wonder: Quit it, Ugly. They'll think I'm a teenager.

Ugly_Duckling: It's not that long ago you were.

Boy_Wonder: Women in their twenties come here to look for older men. I just have to convince them that youthful exuberance is way more cool than maturity.

Anders envisioned his son's devil-may-care smile, and wished he could see Bjorn in the flesh. He was proud of the boy even if he had regressed to hanging out in chat rooms and using grammatically incorrect American slang.

*****

Jensen leaned her bicycle against the side of her house and started through the narrow slot between her house and the thick hedge of lilacs that hugged her yard. The lacey, fragile-looking branches slapped and scratched her face without mercy as she squeezed along the side of the house. Not that she would ever give Ed the pleasure of saying so. Ed had been griping about her lilac bushes all summer. "They're half dead wood," he'd said in a patient tone that irritated the hell out of her. "Trimming them now would encourage new growth next spring. Besides, overgrown yards like yours are exactly the kind of set-up burglars look for." He was probably right, but she hated the thought of his chainsaw anywhere near her bushes. Not only did she appreciate the privacy the hedge gave her, she loved looking out at the fluttering leaves in the summer, and in the spring, smelling the scent of lilac perfume in the wind when the bushes blossomed.

She stood on her tiptoes and groped for the key she'd hidden above the door, refusing to feel one bit guilty. People hid spare keys all the time, for situations just like this one. No need for Ed to make her feel foolish because she saw the world a little differently than he did.

Besides, according to Ed, her delicately constructed French doors, complete with skeleton keys, were so flimsy that she might as well leave them hanging wide open for anyone to get in.

"All it would take is one swift kick and those pretty glass panes would be laying in a million pieces," Ed had said, trying to convince her to replace them with a set of solid, steel-case cookie cutters with deadbolts from the lumberyard.

She pulled her hand away from the sticky paste of cobwebs and old dust on top of the door. What business was it of Ed's? She shouldn't have to act contrite just because she liked a little color in her life. Its old-fashioned idiosyncrasies were the very reason she loved her house.

She could have sworn this was where she'd hidden the key. Wait. She squatted, brushed away the pink geraniums and blue lobelia cascading over the sides of a large terra cotta pot and hoped the grating noise the clay made as she slid it across the cement wouldn't wake the neighbors.

A white envelope zipped inside a plastic bag shone in the moonlight. The smudge of ink scrawled in the center was in Ed's handwriting. She ripped the note open. "This had better be good."

Well, if you're reading this note, you've probably locked yourself out of your house again.

Again? That was hardly fair. It had been at least six months since she'd lost her keys. And that was only because her skirt had had shallow pockets. Besides, she'd retraced her route and found them eventually, which just proved that having a large, easy to see cluster of keys like hers was a good thing.

It obviously does no good to lecture you, so I won't. Your key is in a magnetic box hidden under your car. Ed

She was going to kill him—right after she found a stick or a rock to use to pry her way into her house. Ed had made sure all her windows were locked except for the one over her bed, which was unreachable without a ladder. Which she didn't have because Ed had padlocked it in the storage shed after he'd cleaned out her gutters last week. Damn. She hated that she'd let him make love to her. Her body flushed with humiliation at every point Ed had touched her.

But that was beside the point. If she wanted to get into the house, she was going to have to break one of the panes in the French doors. She stood and watched the moon glint off the original, hand-blown glass panes. Leave it to her to ruin a piece of artistic workmanship that had lasted a hundred years.

She took a rock from beside the walk and smashed it through the glass. The sound of the window cracking and breaking echoed in her mind as she reached in to open the door and stepped around the shards of glass to flip on a light. She was fishing a jagged chunk out from under the radiator when her phone rang.

24

Her first thought was that Ed had woken up, her second, that it would never happen. Ed had had his fill of venison and sex. Without her there to bother him, he wouldn't stir until his alarm went off.

It was her mother, and she sounded ridiculously cheery, even for her. Jensen groaned. She needed to talk to someone, but the subject of Ed was a little too close at the moment. And she definitely knew better than to tell her mother about her encounter with a bobcat.

"Good grief, Mom. Do you know what time it is?"

"I knew you'd be awake. Your father is asleep and I felt like talking." Her mother paused dramatically. "Are you alone?"

"Yes," Jensen said, feeling as if she was in the eighth grade again. "Does that make you happy?"

"Yes. No. I've been thinking about what we talked about earlier. I know how much you've always wanted children. And you know we love Ed. We've always assumed, wished, I mean, we always thought that eventually you and Ed would get married and start a family... I mean, your father and I didn't fall off the turnip truck yesterday. We know times have changed, but, still..."

"Mother, you do remember that I'm thirty-nine, don't you?"

"I do," her mother said emphatically. "I wouldn't give your love life a thought if you were still in your twenties and had time to spare. But as Grandpa Jensen used to say, time's a wastin'. If there's any hope of you marrying while you can still have a baby, you need to get a move on. Give old Ed a wristwatch and tell him to take the hint."

Tears leaped to her eyes and started to stream down her cheeks so quickly that she barely had time to reach for a tissue. "There aren't going to be any grandkids, Mom. At least not from me. Ed had a vasectomy last month."

"Oh, sweetheart." Her mother sounded as shocked as Jensen had been when she'd heard the news. "You never said a thing. Did the two of you decide this together?"

Her throat was so tight she could barely force out a sound. "Ed made the appointment and went in one day when I thought he was at work. I didn't know about it until it was done."

"You're such a cute couple. You would have had darling babies," her mom said quietly.

Jensen dabbed at her face. "I know."

"You should go to a sperm bank then," her mother said. "If you really want a child, you should just do it."

"I do want a child. I never thought it would come to this. I mean, I want someone to love me, too, you know?"

"A child would love you, sweetheart," her mom said.

"I wouldn't know how or where to start," Jensen said, choking back tears.

"Use your computer," her mother said in a reverent voice, like Jensen's PC could mysteriously and magically solve any problem, anywhere, any time, with the simple act of flipping a switch.

"You hate computers," Jensen reminded her.

"They use computers for everything else," her mother said, undaunted. "You tell them you want some nice Scandinavian sperm from someone who's smart and funny and musical and hard-working. I'll bet they can match you up in no time."

"So if I'm going to use the computer to find love, why not just look for a nice Danish man and get pregnant the old-fashioned way?"

"Because it takes too much time. You're in a hurry."

Jensen suppressed a giggle. The last twenty-four hours had been bizarre beyond words. Nothing could surprise her anymore.

"So you'll go on the computer and see what you can find?"

"It's something to think about," Jensen said. "I don't know if I could, or want to raise a child by myself."

Her mother paused like she often did when trying to choose the right words. "Ed is very good to you, sweetheart. I'm sure he'll come around in time. Do you really think he would walk away from a cute, snuggly, little baby if you went ahead and..."

She really did.

"Maybe if your father talked to him..."

"No, Mom. Really. That would not help." She could hear her mother's sigh as clearly as if she was still at home in Blooming Prairie and not half a hemisphere away.

"You and Ed would be good parents. I know you're very different in some ways, but Ed helps you keep your feet on the ground. You know what they say about too much of a good thing."

Her mother would know. Over the years, her family had seen her through one crush after another with boys she'd met in choir or art classes—all just like she was. Spacey. Artistic. Poetic. She sighed. Something about the sight of a man strumming a guitar... She took the phone and headed for the kitchen to find chocolate.

Ed didn't have a creative bone in his body. Never had. Never would. Of course, she could make the argument that Ed's efficiency complemented her technical ineptness. But that would require that she listen to her head instead of her heart. Or her body. If she'd done that, she wouldn't be in this mess.

She sighed. "Good thing the nearest Krispy Kreme is almost fifty miles away."

"Definitely," her mother said.

The airwaves between Arizona and Minnesota were quiet as they contemplated Glazed Krispy Kremes with cream filling.

"Don't tell Dad about Ed, okay? You know how much Dad likes him. I don't want Dad to take it personally when I break up with him." Jensen eased a handful of milk chocolate into her mouth.

"He won't," her mother said. "Chocolate?"

"Yes," she said. "How can he not? You're always telling him how much Ed reminds you of Dad when he was Ed's age."

"Oh. That. Give me a week to start dropping some innuendos. By the time I tell him you've broken up, he'll be thanking his lucky stars that you didn't end up with the man."

27

She sighed. She'd grown up with a father and brothers who were basically just like Ed. She might not always appreciate the ways in which their outlook varied from hers, but they signified a way of thinking and living she'd learned to endure gracefully, and in some ways envied.

"Your father is very proud of you, Jensen."

A fact she knew, but rarely felt. She'd learned long ago that her inclination for the lovely was destined to be an unappreciated gift amongst those whose praise she wished for the most. Her stylish, nouveau quilts had earned her respect in every corner of the world, yet her own family still shook their heads at the lengths people were willing to go to own one of her creations, say nothing about the prices they were willing to pay. Her dad had once said that despite all Jensen's brains, she didn't have the common sense a horse was born with. Maybe he'd been right. She'd grown up on a farm. She knew that there were far more important things in life to worry about than creating beauty or expressing one's heart. "Tell Daddy I love him."

"Your dad and I were Depression babies," her mother said, picking up on a recurring thread they'd talked about many times over. "Any quilts we were lucky enough to have were made from old clothes. If they happened to be pretty, it was an added bonus. If not, it made little difference. They warmed our bones at the end of the day. Nothing more."

"I know how hard you and Dad worked when I was little. Sunup until sundown."

"My eyes got so chafed from the wind and sun that I could barely see, let alone dawdle long enough to make a fancy coverlet," her mother said, her voice a little defensive.

"You must have had a favorite quilt, didn't you, Mom?"

"I was always fond of the one that was on the bed when your father and I were newlyweds, and I still can't use that Log Cabin my mother made without thinking about the time Peder had the mumps. I was so relieved when his fever finally broke.

To me, it's not the pretty top, but the living that went on under them that makes them special."

Jensen felt a quick stab of regret. Her mother had been blessed with a good husband, three children, a full, rich life. Was it so far-fetched for her to want the same things? She'd have given anything—would still give anything—to know what it felt like to look at a quilt and have memories of a baby nursing at her breast under its soft cover.

"I envy you your memories, Mom. Which is why I don't understand how you can leave them all behind. You hardly know a soul in Arizona. No one there loves you the way we do."

She listened as her mother's soft laughter tinkled across five state lines and two time zones.

"Each day is a new beginning, dear. You make new memories. They enable you to treasure and appreciate the old even more."

There was much more she would have loved to talk to her mother about, but rehashing her concerns about Peder and Tara's plans for the farmhouse seemed futile. She wanted her parents to be happy. She wanted them to be free from day to day worries so they could relax and enjoy their retirement. She just wished things could have stayed the way they were.

She listened to her mother's accounts of retirement for a few more minutes, said goodnight, and went to look for duct tape. She'd solved a lot of problems with duct tape before she met Ed. Assuming he hadn't put the roll away in some logical new spot that she'd never be able to find, she was sure she could use it and some cardboard to seal her broken window pane.

*****

Anders reread Bjorn's message and searched for an answer that would put an end to the subject of Juletide in Seattle once and for all. Much as he loved his son, there was no way he was going to leave behind the cherished traditions of his beloved Danemark and fly off to participate in a glitzy, gaudy, overly-commercialized American Christmas. Of course, he'd love to spend the holiday with Bjorn, but not if it meant going to America. He'd ignored his son's previous attempts to get him to come to Seattle. He should have known Bjorn wouldn't give up.

Ugly_Duckling: Who would take care of my plants?
Boy_Wonder: That's a lame excuse if I ever heard one.
Ugly_Duckling: Lame?
Boy_Wonder: Flimsy, lacking substance.

Anders watched his screen as Bjorn answered a somewhat suggestive message from a woman named SweetYoungThing.

Ugly_Duckling: They were looking for single people who didn't have any plans to work over Juletide so those who have families could go to their celebrations. I volunteered to work.
Boy_Wonder: But you have family. Hey. Check it out.

Anders diverted his eyes to the other messages scrolling down his screen. Someone named Wild_Rose had messaged him. Nice name, but he still wasn't interested in engaging in conversation with anyone but Bjorn. The only reason he came here to talk to his son instead of using a direct communication program was because glimpsing a little of what Bjorn was up to made him feel more connected to his son. As far as he was concerned, the others in the room might well have been invisible.

Anders leaned back in his chair. He and Bjorn routinely chatted about everyday things in open view of whoever happened to be watching, just as they had during the twenty years they'd lived under the same roof. The fact that they happened to be in a chat room instead of the living room was part of the territory.

But then, he hadn't chosen the terrain. He understood why Bjorn enjoyed the carefree banter that occurred in these places. That didn't mean he shared the sentiment.

Ugly_Duckling: It is time for me to go. I have much gardening to do before I go to work. The sunshine is bright and the sky is clear. A perfect day to spend in my garden.

He added the latter knowing it was very probably cool, foggy, and drizzling in Seattle.

Bjorn had diverted his attention to SweetYoungThing and didn't appear to notice his last comment. He supposed he should be pleased that Bjorn had stopped trying to talk him into coming to Seattle. Especially since he had no intention of going. Ever.

He waited a moment longer—still no response from Bjorn. As eager as he was to be on his way so he could begin working on his garden, he hated to disappear without saying good-bye.

*****

The slivers of glass were gone. A ring of duct tape surrounded a tidy rectangle of cardboard stuck in the windowpane of Jensen's French door.

Of course, she still had to deal with the problems that couldn't be fixed with duct tape. Like talking to Ed. Once he discovered her keys in his pocket he was bound to figure out that she had either broken into her house or spent the night on her porch swing. It would serve him right if he was worried, but not communicating with him would only bring him to her door, and she really, really didn't want to see him just now.

She flicked the switch on her computer, feeling bold and fearless and unsettled and anxious all at once. Much as she dreaded facing Ed, the thought of ending things with an emailed "Dear John" letter seemed terribly tacky. On the other hand, a brief, mildly reassuring email message could buy her time until she found the guts to tell Ed how she was feeling face to face.

She sat down, rubbed the smooth wood arms of her desk chair, and wrote a vaguely heartening yet non-specific email that made no sense at all. Just what Ed would expect from her.

31

She clicked on the "Cheery Chat" icon as an afterthought. Meeting up with a bobcat had exhilarated her senses to the point that sleep wasn't an option—she thought she might as well try something new. She'd downloaded the software because a friend had told her the program gave its users the option of typing messages in rainbow hues. "Very Jensen," her friend had written in an email comprised of shaded blue words that undulated through the letter like waves.

She'd never chatted online, but she was just antsy enough that the thought of diddling around with a palate full of computerized colors sounded like fun—it wasn't like she'd have to actually talk to anyone. She'd heard what went on in chat rooms, especially this time of night. Watching from the sidelines couldn't be any different than blending into the woodwork at a party, could it?

The set-up wizard prompted her to pick a name. She liked Creature_of_the_Night but thought it might attract the wrong kind of attention. In the end, she choose The_Little_Mermaid, which made no reference to the fact that she was a night owl, but seemed appropriate given she was Danish and very curious.

Jensen lifted her head and watched the moonlight shine through the lace panels hanging at her bedroom windows. At least here, she was in her element. She selected a color scheme, sliding the mouse up, down and around the circles that determined brightness, tone and intensity until each shade was perfect. It was almost as fun as perusing the aisles at A Stitch in Time in search of the right fabric for her latest quilt.

The prompt advised her to select the chat room she wanted to enter. She scrolled down to romance. She sure as heck wasn't going to get an objective opinion on her dilemma with Ed from her family. Maybe she could find the anonymity she needed online. It was Friday night in America. Not long past midnight in California. There had to be someone out there who was as lonely for meaningful interaction as she was.

She shivered and grabbed a quilt to throw across her lap,

not wanting to miss a second of the action unraveling on her screen. Her enthusiasm faded quickly. With the exception of a few obligatory greetings, no one seemed to realize she was even in the chat room. If she were going to see the effect of the colors she had chosen on her screen, she was going to have to jump into the melee and try to engage someone in conversation.

She looked over the list of people occupying the room. Studly_Stephen no doubt lived with his mother, drove a Ford Pinto and worked at the photo mart at the mall. Looking4HotBabes was probably five foot one and bald. Ugly_Duckling sounded a bit more modest.

So you like fairy tales, she thought. *Why not Prince Charming or Knight in Shining Armor, or something that sounds a bit more dashing?*

"Type," she reminded herself, directing her pointer to her screen, transferring her words to print, and pressing send.

Her question to Ugly_Duckling appeared on the screen a scant second before a message from someone named Boy_Wonder that also looked like it was directed to the Duck. Maybe she shouldn't have assumed that Ugly_Duckling was a man. She crossed her ankles and tucked the edges of her quilt around her legs as she read the discourse scrolling down her monitor.

Boy_Wonder: So—will you come to visit me over Juletide, Dad? The flight to Seattle isn't all that awful. I'm sure you have plenty of vacation time saved up.

Cool. The Duck was a man. Not that it mattered. Finding someone who understood the way she felt seemed like too much of a miracle even for the most marvelous piece of technology in the universe.

3.

Anders adjusted his chair so the sun was shining squarely on his chest and leaned back to bask in the light. He should have logged off ten minutes ago when he'd had the chance.

Boy_Wonder: Incoming approaching the runway, Dad. Looks like someone you should get to know.

He'd seen someone named The_Little_Mermaid enter the chat room and ignored the prompt just as he had ignored the others. Her desire to chit-chat, find romance, or do whatever people did in these rooms did not concern him.

The_Little_Mermaid: I like your name, Ugly_Duck-ling.

Anders rolled his eyes. Were the women of the world so desperate that they had nothing better to do with their time than to badger men who obviously had no desire to be disturbed? He'd specifically chosen his name to discourage the attentions of the women who frequented the chat rooms. The fact that his moniker was unique amongst the sea of crass vulgarities chosen by the other men in the room made him a rarity, and thus, he supposed, noteworthy to some. His eyes settled in on a second message from The_Little_Mermaid, then looked away.

Unfortunately, The_Little_Mermaid appeared to be as persistent as his son. A few seconds later, her words lit up his screen in another display of hues no less vibrant than the splash of colors along his garden wall.

The_Little_Mermaid: Juletide...You must be Dan-ish!

Hmm. She could not be all bad if she was a Dane. He'd assumed her name was a tribute to Disney's horrid aberration of a movie, but given she was Scandinavian; she could conceivably be a Hans Christian Andersen fan. He shrugged and typed a response. He didn't want to be rude to a fellow European.

Ugly_Duckling: Ja, I am a Dane.

Boy_Wonder: Go Dad! ☺

Anders glared at the screen as though Bjorn could actually

see him. A new message flashed across his screen.

The_Little_Mermaid: My Great-Grandma Jensen loved to tell stories about her Juletide traditions.

Ugly_Duckling: You're fortunate to remember her. My great-grandparents all died before I was born.

The_Little_Mermaid: I knew my Great-Grandma Jensen until I was a teenager. One of my favorite things in the whole world is a quilt that she made to give my Grandma on her wedding day.

Ugly_Duckling: I also have a quilt. My mother made it for me when I was a boy. She has died too, some years ago.

Why on earth had he told her that? He had no intention of getting personal with this woman. He was about to excuse himself when another ripple of colored letters floated onto his screen.

The_Little_Mermaid: I found the quilt I have buried in a cedar chest at my Grandma Victoria's house. The edges had gotten a little tattered, so she'd stopped using it.

It was those vibrant colors. If she had used the same stark, lifeless black fonts everyone else did, he wouldn't have looked twice. The colors made her seem almost real.

Anders scanned his screen to see if Bjorn was still talking to SweetYoungThing before he started to type.

Ugly_Duckling: Mine will be threadbare one day soon if I persist in using it so much. I keep it at the foot of the bed so I can pull it up when the night air is cold.

Great. Now she had him describing his bed linens for the whole world to see. He was ready to say goodbye to Bjorn and leave when the Little Mermaid's reply appeared on his screen in another glowing array of color.

The_Little_Mermaid: Do you know what pattern it is? I make quilts. Sometimes I'm able to recreate old designs.

Anders sighed and started to type.

Ugly_Duckling: It has a blue or yellow sailboat centered in every block. My ex-wife thought it was... foolish for me to keep the quilt all these years.

Was foolish the word he wanted? He wasn't used to conversing about this topic in English—or any other language. He put his fingers to the keyboard and plowed on, figuring out what the new words meant from the context she used them in and reusing them as needed.

Ugly_Duckling: When she left, I decided to do as I pleased and rearranged my bedroom to match my quilt.

Now he'd dragged Bjorn's mother into it. What was wrong with him? He didn't even speak of her to Bjorn. She was the farthest thing from his mind.

The_Little_Mermaid: When I found this quilt, Grandma said, "What on earth would you want with that old thing? It was beautiful when it was new, but it's seen better days."

Anders chuckled in spite of himself.

Ugly_Duckling: That could be said about a lot of us.

The_Little_Mermaid: My grandma says this quilt was tucked around my grandpa when he died. She didn't have the heart to bury him in it because my mother was just a baby and Grandma liked to put it around her to soothe her when she cried in the night. She snuggled up in it herself when she was lonely.

Anders smiled in spite of the melancholy tone of her words, amazed at how quickly he'd conjured up an image of this woman based on the things she'd chosen to reveal about herself.

Ugly_Duckling: The sentiments I associate with my quilt take on more significance with every year that passes.

The_Little_Mermaid: Quilts shelter us through many storms.

Ugly_Duckling: Yes. That is why I love mine so much—it preserves a tangible memory of my family's legacy.

The_Little_Mermaid: You put my brothers to shame. They could care less about "Grandma's junk". Once I'm gone...

Ugly_Duckling: That's why each new generation is so important. We're the link between what was and what will be.

The_Little_Mermaid: One of my biggest regrets is that I have no one to pass on my family's stories and traditions to.

His heart went out to her. He and Bjorn might be separated by an ocean—for the time being—but he still had his son's love. Life without Bjorn would be very empty indeed.

Ugly_Duckling: One of my biggest fears is that my son will like it in Seattle so much that he will never come home. If he marries someone from the West Coast and has babies, I will likely see his children only once a year. They will know me from photographs and the things Bjorn may tell them, but they will have lost their connection to our family's rich Danish legacy.

The_Little_Mermaid: So few people seem to care about their family's history anymore. The majority of twenty and thirty-somethings I know don't put any stock in 'old things'.

Ugly_Duckling: Ja. Like my ex-wife. The only old thing she values is 'old money'.

Was he imagining things, or could he almost see her smile?

Ugly_Duckling: I've never spoken to a stranger here. It is very limiting not to be able to envision your expressions. Please tell me about your quilts.

What he really wanted to know was what she looked like, where she lived, how old she was. But he didn't know how to ask without seeming as forward and inappropriate as the others.

Listen to yourself, he thought scornfully—spinning fairy tales about a woman you know absolutely nothing about except that she's colorful. What kind of sticky web had he fallen into?

The_Little_Mermaid: I make quilts that resemble landscapes except that they're 'painted' with bits and pieces of fabric instead of oils.

Ugly_Duckling: If you are as good at painting these quilts with fabric as you are painting pictures with your words, I am sure they are beautiful.

He almost deleted what he'd written, but in the end, he pressed send and shot up a quick prayer that Bjorn wasn't still around. He would hate to see his son witness the cliché truisms oozing out of his mouth. Or in this case, his fingers.

He would never hear the end of it if Bjorn were watching.

Sherrie Hansen

And rightly so—he was doing the same inane things he'd chided Bjorn about, and worse. He was suddenly infuriated... at The_Little_Mermaid for luring him into doing something that he'd sworn he'd never do, at Bjorn, for dragging him into the setting and situation in the first place, and at himself, for being such a foolish old ass.

*****

Jensen felt as giddy as a ten-year-old sitting at the grown-up table... finally, someone who understood! Duckling truly seemed to enjoy bantering with her. She could hardly believe her good fortune. At last, someone who appreciated what she was saying and agreed with her way of looking at the world.

Ugly_Duckling: The fact that you're an artist would explain your colorful letters. Please tell me how it is done. I am curious to know how one paints with scraps of fabric.

Her fingers flew over the keyboard as she told him about her quilts. A sun-parched garden surprised by a shower couldn't have soaked up any more of his admiration.

Ugly_Duckling: It must take a great deal of skill to make these creations. Are the fabrics woven together or layered?

At Duckling's prompting, she told him about the quilt she'd just finished—a snowy mountainside in purples, periwinkle blues and teal greens with a flurry of white snowflakes appliquéd over the top in a lacy design. Her soul was singing with jubilation so heartfelt that it almost hurt.

She sat back in her chair and waited for the Duck to respond. Might as well enjoy the attention while you can, she thought. Once Duckling got to know her better, he'd find out what a pain in the butt she could be when she was in one of her creative moods.

A chill washed over her as she realized the significance of her thoughts. Ed. She'd let the man stomp on her artistic instincts so often that the light inside her soul had flickered and dimmed to near darkness. If she were Tinker Bell, and Ed, the last child on earth, Ed wouldn't hesitate for a second before saying "I don't believe in fairies."

She let him do it every time she listened to his subtle criticisms of the way she was, the ideals she valued, the things she liked to do. She hadn't dated anyone for almost five years when Ed had come along. She'd been so hungry for a little affection, so hopeful that Ed would give her the home and children she'd always dreamed of, that she'd settled for the first man who...

Duckling's next message appeared on her screen before she had a chance to finish analyzing her revelation.

Ugly_Duckling: It must be satisfying to create things, to have the power to change what does not seem right to your eye.

The_Little_Mermaid: Yes, very. Although there are times when my imagination fails me, times that I just can't see what the quilt needs until it's done. If that means getting the ripper out and starting all over again, that's what I do.

Ugly_Duckling: There is nothing wrong with aspiring to do your best.

The_Little_Mermaid: The quilt I've been working on has dark blues and greens in both the lake and the trees. The colors are so similar that everything started to run together into one big, uninteresting blob. So I added a log cabin with window boxes full of pink geraniums peeking through the shade of the forest, some wild roses and sweet peas growing in a jumble at the lake's edge, and a tiny little snippet of yellow just above the skyline to look like a goldfinch in flight. A few cattails and blue herons hovering in the shallow marsh waters by the lake, and voila! It's amazing how much dimension a few dark, vertical lines can add to a landscape that's primarily horizontal.

She stopped typing and waited for Duckling's response, feeling a little embarrassed that she'd gotten so carried away.

There was no response.

The_Little_Mermaid: Duckling?

She waited; assuming that the message he was typing must be a lengthy one if it was taking him this long to type.

Nothing. The part of her that had been so puffed up with excitement began to droop.

The_Little_Mermaid: Are you still out there, Duck-ling?

The four walls of the empty room in which she sat stared mockingly back at her. He had seemed so real.

She scrolled back as far as her computer would let her to see if she had missed a message. She found notices a page or two back indicating that Boy_Wonder and SweetYoungThing had left for a private room. Several others had logged off, but there was no such signal that Ugly_Duckling had left.

She found his last few messages, and waited until a flood of new messages had swallowed up any evidence that Ugly_Duckling and she had ever met and carried on a conversation.

What could have happened? Was it something she'd said? Something she'd not said? He'd seemed so polite, so gentlemanly, so interested. How could he have left without saying goodbye? Her fingers, suddenly shy, flicked timidly over the keyboard.

The_Little_Mermaid: Duckling, are you there?

Studly_Stephen: What's wrong, Mermaid? Lost your lover?

Her cheeks flushed hot with humiliation. Which made no sense. No one here knew or cared that she was a Christiansen from Blooming Prairie. No one here would ever know who she was, what she did, or where she was from. Including Ugly_Duckling.

The_Little_Mermaid: We were just talking.

Studly_Stephen: That's all anybody ever does, babe. Welcome to Cyberland. Talk is a hot commodity here.

HungLikeaHorse: Talk is all we got.

WisconsinWonder: Yah—we're all talk and no action, and mighty proud of it.

Studly_Stephen: So Mermaid, how'd you like to retire to a private room and tell each other 'bedtime stories'?

WisconsinWonder: Can I come, too? You can sit on my lap.

Jensen shook her head wearily. She didn't know where Duckling had gone, or where he was from for that matter. She assumed somewhere on the East Coast. He'd acted like Seattle was half a world away. She looked at the clock. It was the middle of the night in Minnesota, almost daybreak in New York. She'd waited almost a half hour. It was obvious Ugly_Duckling wasn't coming back.

*****

Anders drummed his fingers on his desk and resisted the urge to knock somebody's head off. A good thing, since the only other person in the room was Bob, his new boss from California.

Not a thing had gone right all day. First, the lilac bushes, second, a computer crash at the most inopportune time in the world, and third, the dismally low performance of his students on the navigation simulator.

Bob had been ranting on the other side of his desk for over ten minutes. "These kids think that just because they can pilot a starship without crashing into the moon on some stupid video game, they can handle an air traffic control simulator."

Anders loosened his tie and tried to relax. He couldn't believe he was in agreement with an American. "Their generation has no respect for the intricacies of the job or the emotional fortitude it takes to stay focused in a crisis."

"Their minds have been so over-stimulated that they can't concentrate on anything for longer than two seconds," Bob said.

"With all the lunatics out there, one would think they'd realize the importance of diligence on the job," Anders said.

"That's the problem—they just don't get it. They have no concept of what a true emergency is. It's those damn video games. One minute, the Jeep they're riding in explodes and their bodies are blown to smithereens, the next, they're back in the game as a different character." His boss railed on. "Or on a different side. They don't care whether they're the terrorist or the hero, or whether they're serving under Roosevelt or Hitler as long as they're having fun. It's all a game to them."

Anders understood what the problem was, but was at a loss as to how to correct it. "They've been desensitized to horror." Anders shifted in his chair, loosened his tie a little more, and wished Bob would get to the point. Everyone he worked with had been on edge since American Aeronautics had bought out Copenhagen International's air traffic division.

"Jason, my supervisor, is twenty-eight-years-old," Bob said. "In his book, maturity and wisdom count for very little."

Anders supposed that would be him.

"The way Jason sees it, he's spending a big chunk of his budget retraining old guys to use new equipment, then paying them a hefty salary to train young recruits who were weaned on computers and already know twice as much as they do."

Anders tried to swallow without letting his nervousness show. "Being a competent air traffic controller involves much more than knowing how to use the fancy equipment."

"I know that, and you know that," Bob said, "but all Jason and the company heads see is the bottom line."

That's the way it always was with Americans. It always came down to money. Anders tried to conceal his frustration. It seemed like just yesterday that he'd been a struggling, young, single parent. He'd passed over several promotions so he could be there after school to be with Bjorn. Now, when his job was all he had, he was suddenly one of the dreaded older generation and in danger of being downsized or, worse yet, outsourced by some smart-mouthed American kid who was Bjorn's age.

"For the record, I am willing to take whatever classes they want me to—computer science or whatever other area they might think I'm lacking in," Anders said, swallowing his pride.

"I like you, Anders," Bob said. "I've looked at your record, and you've got a couple of things on your side. One is your secondary degree in counseling. The other is your command of the English language."

"Thank you," Anders said, sensing he was about to hear the flipside of the equation.

"The only red flag I see in your file is your involvement in *Danes for Denmark*," Bob said, sitting up in his chair.

Anders stiffened. His old boss had seen that as an asset.

"I do sympathize with your efforts. When I first visited Copenhagen thirty years ago, I ate at Danish restaurants, shopped in Danish department stores, and bought souvenirs made by Danes. Now it's Burger King on one corner and Kodak on the next. Tourist shops sell Danish-looking trinkets marked 'Made in China' just like half the stuff you buy in America," Bob said. "It's easier to find pizza or Szechwan chicken than it is to find a Danish ham dinner. Same problem we have at home."

Anders sincerely doubted that, but now wasn't the time to challenge his boss. "We're attempting to preserve our identity," he said. "The effects of globalization make it very difficult for a small country to hold their own against the superpowers and their all-pervasive moral, economic, and political agendas."

"I know what you're saying," Bob said, "but when you start using words like 'against' and 'agendas', people get nervous."

"I won't curtail my involvement with the organization," Anders said quietly. "I'm a charter member, and very proud of what we've accomplished in the past ten years."

"Jason will be looking over each employee's file. If he thinks you're unhappy working for an American company..."

"Thanks," Anders said gruffly, finding it ironic that *Danes for Danemark* could cost him his job. Well he'd be damned before he'd let the Americans run the Danes out of their own airport.

4.

It may have been the rain that woke her. The wind was coming from the east, sweeping huge sheets of rain against the window behind her bed. Her lips curved into a smile when she realized she was in her own bed, then thinned back to a worried line as she remembered what had transpired the night before.

Yes, she'd finally had the nerve to leave Ed. But she'd hardly earned the right to feel delighted with herself. She had, after all, departed after they'd made love, and not before. Yes, she'd written him a note, but she'd given him a flimsy excuse instead of confronting him like she should have.

At least he'd been considerate enough not to wake her. Yet.

The jarring sound of the telephone was a balm compared to Ed's voice. With no hello, he said, "What did you expect me to think when you just up and left in the middle of the night?"

"That I couldn't sleep and I didn't want to wake you up."

There was a long silence. She could almost see Ed fuming.

"I don't know whether to be relieved or furious that you rode that damn trail in the middle of the night. For God's sake, there are bears and bobcats in those woods," Ed said. "What the hell were you thinking? You could have been killed. A woman in Pennsylvania died last year when a squirrel got caught in the spokes of her bicycle. She was catapulted over the top of her handlebars and hurled more than thirty feet before she landed. And that was a squirrel. You could have run into an elk."

Jensen rolled her eyes and clamped the receiver in her hand. No way was she going to confirm Ed's offhand suggestion or give him a reason to gloat. The bobcat would remain her little secret. "People hit deer with their cars all the time. There are even fatalities. You don't expect people to stop driving at night because there's danger lurking around every corner."

"That's not the point and you know it. You just don't think, Jensen."

"I was careful. I wore my helmet."

"Well, there's no sense paying long distance for the privilege of arguing," Ed said. "We can talk tonight."

"Except we won't talk. We'll just put another couple of steaks on the grill, watch reruns on TV, and make love again."

"There's something wrong with that?"

"If it's all we ever do."

"So what are you saying?"

"That I'd like to go for a walk," Jensen said. "Go out to dinner, go on a picnic... do anything, go anyplace where we can have a nice, quiet evening together, talking and listening."

"There are a lot of women out there who would give anything to spend a quiet evening at home with the man they love."

"Well, they're not me. If you took the time to listen, and tried to understand me a little better, you'd know that."

"I may not know what's on your mind, but I sure know..."

Finally. He'd hit the nail on the head. Ed knew how to make her body sing. He hadn't a clue when it came to her heart and soul. If he had, he would never have had a vasectomy.

Her mind reeled with the fact that he had done something so... definitive... so final... without telling her.

"I left your keys on the counter," Ed was saying, "but you'll have to wait until tonight to get them."

Her key to his house was on the same ring. "I think I need some time to myself tonight," she said.

"Whatever you want."

If only that were true. She put the phone back on its cradle, her mind a cauldron of emotions. Was it so wrong of her to wish for a man who would share her passion for life, her love of art and beauty, travel and adventure? Maybe she couldn't share her heart with Ed; maybe they saw things a little differently when it came to having a family... But Ed was a good man, cut from the same dependable, hard-working, trustworthy, reliable cloth as her father, brothers and neighbors.

She understood more than ever at that moment that her

heritage was both a bane and a blessing. She took her Grandma's letters from their bag, blotted the soot away from them, and put them in a woven basket. The smell of smoke would disappear quickly enough once they'd had a chance to air out.

She spent the rest of the day sketching a new quilt, thinking all the while about a man whose name she didn't even know, a man who had appeared, then disappeared. A man she would probably never meet again.

At least she could count on Ed. Ed would never disappear. Hell, he never went anywhere but work.

It was still well before the time when Ed was due home when the rain stopped. She found the extra keys to her car, rode her bike to Red Wing, and retrieved her car, boxes and all.

Her thoughts were a jumble. The only thing she knew for sure was that driving a car in broad daylight when you were all but blinded by tears had to be infinitely more dangerous than a peaceful bike ride through the forest in the dark. Well, almost peaceful.

It was ten o'clock when she connected to the internet, this time consciously foregoing the reality she shared with Ed to pursue a fantasy with a man she knew only as the Ugly_Duckling.

*****

Anders set aside what was left of his pride and reset the prompts that he usually used to find Bjorn to take him to whatever chat room The_Little_Mermaid might surface in. Just how did one appear nonchalant in a chat room? Bjorn was nowhere in sight, so he couldn't pretend he was there to see his son.

He felt awful about the night before. What must she have thought when he disappeared? He'd seen others in the chat room send cyber roses and thought them absurd. But now that he needed to make an apology, it seemed like an appropriate thing to do. It took him almost an hour to figure out how to do the colors and key in the strokes. He was all thumbs as he set about making pink blossoms from ampersands, green leaves from comparatives and brown stems from dashes, but he had a dozen flowers ready to give to her when she arrived.

The moment he saw The_Little_Mermaid appear on his screen, he pressed 'send' and watched his greeting blossom on the screen, feeling ridiculously proud.

How he wished he could see her for just a minute. But he couldn't. The roses were the best he could do—that and an explanation of what had happened. He never had mastered the art of being coy.

The_Little_Mermaid: They're beautiful, Duckling.

He explained what had happened and asked her forgiveness.

The_Little_Mermaid: I thought perhaps I had put you to sleep in your computer chair, but there was no way to tell.

Anders knew what she meant. He hated the sense of helplessness he felt, and being at the mercy of something as skittish as the internet. His inability to see, sense, and gage her reactions already haunted him and he barely knew her.

For all he knew, Mermaid was a grandmother from Iceland who kept herself busy sewing quilts for her grandchildren. They were in a room for thirty-somethings, but he was over forty, and Bjorn barely into his twenties. Nothing could be assumed in a chat room.

He needed to find some subtle way of getting her to talk about herself, to get a little more personal with her answers. He was curious to know where she lived but didn't want to endanger her by asking her where in Danemark she lived—the eyes of many who didn't share his sense of integrity were on them.

Ugly_Duckling: I have always admired creative people, and wondered where they get their inspiration.

The_Little_Mermaid: It can come from anywhere, even the least likely places! One of the shops where I display my work did a promo last spring called *The View From Your Front Porch*. Their customers submitted a photo and an essay for a chance to win a custom designed quilt featuring their view. I took all kinds of special orders as a result of the publicity.

Ugly_Duckling: You would have great fun re-creating the textures of the flower garden I look out at from my porch. It has a brick wall with pink cabbage roses climbing up the center.

The_Little_Mermaid: Delphiniums, too?

Ugly_Duckling: Some brilliant blue ones. Why do you ask?

The_Little_Mermaid: No reason. I've been sketching a garden scene for a quilt I've just begun and the blues and pinks look so perfect together.

Ugly_Duckling: This design is from your imagination?

The_Little_Mermaid: To be honest, I'm not entirely sure. I feel like I've been there, but I can't place where or when. It's probably something I just dreamed up—except that it sounds eerily like your garden.

Ugly_Duckling: I don't remember discussing my flowers.

The_Little_Mermaid: Neither do I. It was late. I was probably thinking about gardens when I dozed off. I have a friend who thinks my lilac bushes need to be trimmed back. We had argued about it earlier.

Ugly_Duckling: I awoke yesterday to find that my young neighbor had trimmed back a hedge of lilacs that is between my yard and his. He cut them nearly to the ground.

Their messages appeared on his screen as close to simultaneously as was technically possible. He laughed aloud when he read what she had written.

The_Little_Mermaid: We think alike.

Ugly_Duckling: We think alike.

The_Little_Mermaid: We did it again.

Ugly_Duckling: We did it again.

Ugly_Duckling: I knew there was a reason I liked you.

The_Little_Mermaid: Why, thank you, kind sir.

He was enjoying their banter, but he knew nothing more about her than when he'd started. Maybe if he led the way...

Ugly_Duckling: My garden is relaxing, whereas my profession can be very stressful—I'm an air traffic controller. I spend my evenings teaching stress management and crisis counseling at the airport.

The_Little_Mermaid: No wonder you're so easy to talk to.

Anders felt a flush of red creeping across his jaw. He felt at once flattered and uncomfortable with her compliment.

Ugly_Duckling: I come here only to speak to my son. He is young and away from home for the first time. He is in Seattle.

It still shocked him to see the words in black and white. It had been three months since Bjorn moved to the United States. He'd harbored resentment toward America long before Bjorn had abdicated, from the time Benta had run off with Kirk, the arrogant American entrepreneur to whom she was now married. Well, America could have his ex-wife. But now it looked as though he might lose his son, perhaps even his job to the good old USA. No wonder he had little time for America or Americans.

The_Little_Mermaid would very likely understand how he felt. The sympathetic prime minister of Danemark aside, Americans were not popular in Europe given the current situation in the Middle East. He started to type, then changed his mind. They were in an open chat room, and he didn't want to start World War III. Besides, their conversation had been so relaxing—why risk alienating her with talk of ugly American politics when things were so congenial between them?

Ugly_Duckling: May I ask what brings you to this place?

The_Little_Mermaid: Last night was my first time. I had a lot on my mind and thought it would be fun to let my hair down in a place where no one knows me.

Anders felt an overwhelming sense of disappointment.

Ugly_Duckling: Like Rapunzel? You came here to find a man to take to your tower?

The_Little_Mermaid: If that is what I wanted, I could have found it very quickly.

He'd offended her. If only he could see her face.

Ugly_Duckling: I am sorry. The confusion is my fault.

The_Little_Mermaid: I only meant that I wanted to relax.

Ugly_Duckling: I misunderstood. "Letting one's hair down" is an expression I had not heard.

Anders paused and waited for a response. Other messages scrolled by, but nothing from the The_Little_Mermaid. What he wouldn't give to have use of the full range of his senses.

Ugly_Duckling: I am wishing I could see your face and know what you are thinking, Mermaid. If you would, help me to see you with these words you are so good at arranging. Will you join me in a private room so we can talk more freely?

He tried to conjure up an image of how she must look while he created a room, invited her to join him, and waited until she had entered. He'd mocked others in the chat room who started conversations with the standard, "Tell me what you're wearing," judging them to be voyeurs. Perhaps he had been too harsh.

The_Little_Mermaid: Well... I'm thirty-nine, with shoulder length, reddish blond hair, and blue-green eyes, I'm tall and slender, and I've been told I look like Maren Jensen, the great-grandma who made the quilt I love, which is appropriate since I'm named after her. You can call me Jensen if you like.

Ugly_Duckling: Jensen is a lovely name. Anders here.

The_Little_Mermaid: Pleased to meet you, Anders. Now you must return the favor and tell me about you.

Ugly_Duckling: I hope you are not disappointed, given your deft imagination. I am told I am very average—two meters tall, blond hair, blue eyes—except for my weight, which, unfortunately is a little above average. I have gained a few pounds since I turned forty. I ride my bike to work every day. The exercise is a good thing for me. If I had enough hair to let down, that is where it would be.

The_Little_Mermaid: Your words give me goose bumps. I also love riding my bike and go nearly everywhere on it.

His heart pounded as he read her words.

The_Little_Mermaid: In such a big world, what are the odds that two people with as much as we have in common would just happen to stumble across each other? Is it just me, Anders, or do you feel like we were meant to meet?

Ugly_Duckling: We are a miracle of modern technology, ja?

The_Little_Mermaid: The timing—both of us being here, me ending up in the very chat room you and your son—it has to be more than mere coincidence.

He read what they had written. He was making a fool of himself, typing each thought that flitted through his mind before he even realized he was doing it, talking about fate, and things that were meant to be. It made him very uncomfortable.

Bjorn had come online and hooked up with SweetYoungThing again. Anders felt a sudden need to excuse himself—before things got any more out of control than they already were.

He had just started to type when his phone rang through and bumped him off the internet.

It was Helmut, a co-worker from his division at work. "We've got a commuter plane down in the North Sea. They're assembling the families of the passengers."

"I'll be right there." He grabbed his car keys and cast a quick glance over his shoulder. Every second counted in an emergency. There was no time to reboot and reconnect. Reluctantly, he headed out the door. He may have intended to say goodbye; he had not meant to do it like this.

*****

Jensen uncurled her legs and stretched her arms over her head. The air creeping through her open windows was cool, yet she felt deliciously warm.

She didn't know why Anders had disappeared, but she was not going to overreact like she had the night before. Part of

51

Anders' allure was the thrill of the unknown. If she wanted a man who posed no mysteries, a man whose schedule she knew in precise, unalterable detail, a man who had no interests, friends or obligations other than her, she need look no further than Ed.

She got out of bed and checked the duct tape and cardboard she'd used to cover her broken pane of glass. The glass company from Red Wing had wanted a king's ransom to drive to Welch. The handy man she'd used before she met Ed had acted like she'd been unfaithful to him when she'd started dating someone who could fix things and didn't seem interested in the job. She probably should have swallowed her pride and asked Ed to do it.

No. She'd wait a month and pay a fortune before she asked Ed for anything—except for her keys, and possibly the pink bathrobe she'd left in his closet. It was her favorite.

She smiled. Maybe it was the nip of autumn in the air. Maybe it was Anders. She really didn't know except that she felt more chipper and wide-awake than she had in months.

Her parents would call it a bunch of foolish nonsense, but for the first time in years, she felt a real sense of purpose—like she mattered. She'd arrived at Peder's at precisely the right moment to save Maren's letters. A few seconds later and they would have been ashes. Gone forever.

She'd come upon the woman and her dog in the forest just when she was needed the most. She shivered. Who knew what the bobcat might have done if she hadn't happened along?

Things were changing, and much as she liked everything to stay exactly the way it was, for once, she was glad she was in the middle of the maelstrom. She looked up at her Grandma's quilt, then the letters, and let the clutter of fabric, sketchbooks, and mementos littering her room embrace her like a balm.

The sound of the phone interrupted her thoughts. Jensen glanced at her caller ID and felt her heart give a little leap. It was unusual for her mother to call at this time of day. She reached for the portable.

"Sweetheart, I need to talk to you," her mother said, her voice carefully modulated, the way it always was when she had bad news to impart.

"Is something wrong?"

"Not in the way you're thinking. I spoke to Peder and Tara this morning," her mother said, acting like everything was just fine.

"And?"

"They're very excited about the possibility of building a new house down by the creek," her mother said, with false cheeriness.

Jensen's heart nearly stopped cold. "You aren't going to let them do it!"

"They're adults. I can't tell them where to live."

"You tell me what to do all the time."

"Little good it does me."

Jensen let that one go. What could she say? It was pretty much true. "So what did you say to Peder? Did you tell him the house goes with the farm? That if he's going to farm the land he has to live in the house?"

Her mother sighed.

"Houses only last so long," her mother said. "The land is the important thing."

"Now you sound like Dad."

"Your father is thrilled that either of the boys wants to farm. Why do you think Peder and Karl are able to rent so much land?"

"All the other farm kids our age went away to college and never came back."

"Peder and Tara both have degrees in Computer Science," her mother said. "If they moved back to Philadelphia they could make twice as much as they do here, and be close to Tara's parents."

Yeah, because Tara's parents still live in the house Tara grew up in, Jensen thought but didn't say.

"You know, it wouldn't hurt Peder to show a little appreciation for everything Grandma and Grandpa Jensen sacrificed to build the house," Jensen said.

"Grandpa Jensen died the year Peder was born. Peder barely remembers Grandma Jensen. What, was he five the year she passed?"

"He must have been," Jensen said, calculating their age differences in her head. "It was the summer before I turned seventeen."

"You can't expect Peder and Karl to feel the same way you do about Grandma and Grandpa," her mother said. "They don't have the same memories that you do."

"So you let them build a new house," Jensen theorized out loud. "They've already done a lot of remodeling on our place." Her heart quickened in her chest as she imagined the flipside. The positive ramifications. She'd always suspected that deep down, her parents regretted moving out of the farmhouse. They'd only turned over the house to Peder and Tara in the first place because in their minds, it went with the farm. "You and Dad could build an addition onto the back and have a first floor master suite so you wouldn't have to go up and down..."

"We're not moving back to the farm, Jensen. It was a hard decision at the time, but what's done is done."

Her hopes crumbled just as quickly as they'd soared.

"I can't bear the thought of strangers in Grandma's house— not being able to have Thanksgiving or Christmas..." Her voice broke.

"There are several machine shops in Owatonna," her mother said. "If you and Ed..."

No way would Ed move or switch jobs for her. He'd already gone to painstaking lengths to demonstrate how determined he was that nothing about his life would change until the day he died.

"But the barn, and the grain bins, and the augers... It makes sense to have whoever is farming the land living in the house."

"It doesn't make sense if Tara's not happy."

"I guess I should have married Alvin Gustavson when I had the chance," Jensen said.

"Our land and his combined would have made quite the farm," her mother said, chuckling quietly.

"You know I would have loved to live there."

"Getting your own place was what you wanted at the time."

"And being close to Justin and Molly," Jensen said.

"You were very attached to them. When they moved to Welch, it made sense to follow them."

"The money I made doing daycare and teaching piano lessons paid the bills until I started selling quilts."

"I know you love Maren's house, but you couldn't wait to get away from the farm," her mother reminded her, being fairly tactful, for her mother.

"Maybe if the timing had been different," Jensen said.

Her mother paused. "Peder wants to expand the farm, rent another thousand acres from the Oldhams, and bring on a full time hired man."

Jensen's stomach did a flip flop. More changes.

Her mother ploughed on. "With any luck, whomever he hires would be willing to accept the house as partial compensation for their duties."

Jensen choked back tears. Maren's precious house reduced to a bargaining chip in a business deal. No more family gatherings around Maren's big, quarter-sawn oak table. No more Sunday night trips to the farm for raspberries still warm from the sun served on Dad's homemade ice cream. No more dreams of...

"I always thought I'd get married in front of the fireplace in the parlor just like Grandma Victoria did."

"Just like I did," her mother said, finally letting a hint of sadness creep into her stoic voice. "There's nothing else we can do. We want Tara to be happy. If a new house will keep Peder and Tara on the farm, then..."

"Mom? There's another call coming through," Jensen said, desperate to end the call, desperate to deny reality.

"I'll talk to you soon, then," her mother said.

"Goodbye," Jensen said. Something she'd been saying entirely too much of as of late.

She went to the computer as soon as she was off the phone. She'd always clung to the past, always tried to preserve whatever bits and pieces of it that she could. And why not? The future had never looked all that promising.

But this time, things were different. She'd found a kindred spirit in Anders. Her heart fluttered with anticipation. The idea that they had stumbled upon one another purely by accident was preposterous. Suddenly, the past didn't seem quite as important as it had before. Something new and good had been set in motion the second Anders had responded to her post. Something was different, better, this time. She could feel it.

Of course, that's what she'd thought when she met Ed.

5.

Anders was back at his office, sitting with his elbows propped on his desk and his face in his hands when Helmut slipped in the door.

"You as exhausted as I am?" Helmut asked.

Anders nodded, so tired he didn't want to waste what little energy he had left on words.

"Hard night," Helmut said.

"It always is."

"The daughter of that businessman who had lost her mother to cancer a few months ago really got to me. Must be an awful feeling to be all alone in the world."

The businessman that Helmut was so objectively referring to was microscopic bits of fish food now, but Anders' mind couldn't handle thinking about the reality of his demise any more than Helmut could.

"She's young," Anders said. "Hopefully she'll marry and have a family of her own one day."

He endured the silence as long as he could before he trumped the dead air space and played another round of words. "The one who got to me was the woman who lost both of her sons."

"She have any other kids?" Helmut asked woodenly.

"No, just the two. They were going to backpack in the mountains west of Oslo. She said they'd been close as kids and tried to do something like this every few years."

I saw Bob coming out of your office yesterday afternoon," Helmut said. "He have anything exciting to say?"

He gratefully followed Helmut's lead. He'd said, done, and absorbed all the grief he could for now. "You probably already know if you were hovering outside my door like you usually do."

"Nah. Couldn't hear a thing this time. Bob's voice doesn't carry the way old Lars' used to." Helmut laughed. "So. You in trouble again?" He asked, the joke being that Anders never got in trouble whereas he often did.

"We were discussing the disciplinary problems with the new class," Anders said, not wanting to go into detail.

"You'll do what you have to. You always pull the rabbit out of the hat," Helmut said.

Anders wasn't sure if it was admiration or envy he heard in Helmut's voice. "My students may think they know everything, but their youthful bravado won't last long when it comes to dealing with an angry family member who's just lost a loved one. They need me to teach them how to handle that."

"They may be computer whizzes, but they don't know diddlysquat when it comes to the sensitivity and finesse it takes to counsel someone," Helmut said.

"I don't know how to get through to them. What do I know about talking to the younger generation? I can't even get my own son to listen to me," Anders said.

"Ja, well Bjorn's not only yours, he's his mother's."

Anders clenched his fist. "He was five when Benta left. I raised him. He knows better than to put his stock in America's glitter and glamour."

The shock of it slapped him in the face as hard as it had eighteen years ago. He could accept the fact that Benta and Kirk had fallen in love, but leaving behind a five-year-old—who loved his mother with all his heart—to run off to New York City? Anders would never understand, or forgive Benta for that.

Helmut slumped into the chair that faced his desk. "Bjorn spent plenty of summers with Benta over the years."

"Never more than two weeks at a stretch. How much influence could she have had?"

"Enough to plant the seed." Helmut picked up Anders' copy of *Europe Today* and flipped through the pages. "You're a nice guy, Anders, but you're a little stuck in the mud. You put down deep roots. You bloom where you're planted, and all that muckity muck. Which is a good thing. But not everyone is like you."

"You think Bjorn left to get away from me?"

"That's not what I'm saying. Think about it. Your ex was a stewardess. From what I remember of her, she barely stayed in one place long enough to change clothes before she was headed out the door again. It's the legacy of the Vikings. Wanderlust. Some Danes just have it in their veins. And like it or not, Bjorn's blood is half hers."

"So you think I've lost him for good?"

"No. I think you have to quit beating yourself up over something you have no control over and move on with your life. Bjorn is all grown up. He lives his life the way he sees fit; you live yours. Quit moping around, kick up your heels and live a little. Half of your life is still ahead."

*****

Jensen's whole body felt like it was buzzing with a newly discovered source of renewable energy. By ten that morning, she'd washed and folded two weeks' worth of laundry, made a batch of cookies, and finished sketching a quilt design made from a photograph she'd received in the mail the week before.

She took a break when she finished and rode her bicycle to A Stitch in Time in Cannon Falls to search for a pale yellow fabric she needed to blend with the blue skies over the walled garden she'd sketched the day before.

She could feel her cheeks flushing with pleasure as she picked through the new winter colors. She was so preoccupied she almost ran into Mrs. Ryan, the owner of the shop.

"I'm glad you got to be the first to see the new shipment." Mrs. Ryan looked at her with a satisfied smile. "I'm afraid it may be the last one I'll be getting, unless..."

Jensen looked up and tried to suppress the cloud of worrisome thoughts flitting through her mind. "Is something wrong?" She certainly hoped Mrs. Ryan wasn't ill, or having financial difficulties.

"I've been trying to sell the store for over a year now, and just haven't had any luck." Mrs. Ryan folded and smoothed the edge of a recently cut bolt of fabric and put it back on the shelf. "If I don't find a buyer soon, I'm afraid I'll have to close the doors. I'm moving to North Carolina to be nearer my grandchildren."

"I don't know what to say."

"I almost came to you to see if you were interested in buying the store," Mrs. Ryan said. "I used to do a lot of quilting myself, but after I bought the store all I ever got done besides helping customers was ordering, bookkeeping, and working on my advertising budget," Mrs. Ryan had said. "I couldn't bear to see someone as talented as you are wasting their gift on administrative duties."

Jensen gave her a quick hug. "I'll miss you!" She was heartbroken, but she didn't want to make the woman feel guilty about what had to have been a hard decision. "It will be a change not having a store within bike riding distance."

"There's not even a fabric store in Red Wing since So-Fro closed. I'm afraid you'll have to go to Rochester or the Twin Cities to find fabrics from now on," Mrs. Ryan had said. "If you're active on the internet, you may want to check for fabric stores online—a friend of mine has been buying remnants on eBay, of all places."

"It seems like it would be awfully hard to see if the colors are right on a computer screen," Jensen said.

"Well, Ethel's not the perfectionist you are, that's for sure. She's one who thinks yellow is yellow and blue is blue."

"I suppose I am pickier than most," Jensen admitted.

"It's something to check into," Mrs. Ryan said. "Although, speaking for myself, I can't imagine buying a piece of fabric I couldn't see with my own two eyes or touch with my own two fingers. There are too many fine nuances of color and texture that come into play. That's why I always did my buying personally at market instead of ordering from catalogs. How could you possibly tell if a piece of fabric is what you really want just by looking at a tiny little swatch on your screen?"

"I agree." *How could you tell from a few conversations on a computer if someone really is the man of your dreams?*

"The Realtor warned me I would have trouble finding a buyer," Mrs. Ryan said. "I guess we all have to face the fact that sewing, quilting, and crafting just aren't as popular as they used to be. With the economy the way it is, and so many women working full-time jobs nowadays, I'm afraid small town quilt shops may soon be a thing of the past."

"It breaks my heart," Jensen said. "People think quilting is something they don't have time for until they're retired."

"Except nowadays, even old grandmas like me have to work," Mrs. Ryan said. "Sadder still is the fact that no one even bothers to teach young people how to sew anymore. My sister's daughter has two girls in 4-H. They call the old sewing category 'Clothing,' and instead of showing them how to pin a pattern and put in a zipper, they teach them how to shop for store-bought clothes that are flattering and a good value for the dollar."

"They give out ribbons for that?" Jensen had been in 4-H for years and had won several purple championship ribbons. It was mind boggling to realize how much the world had changed.

Jensen forced herself to smile. "You've made such a difference in so many lives in the years you've been open. You've always had such a beautiful selection of fabrics— you've inspired many people to sew who wouldn't have otherwise."

Mrs. Ryan patted her hand. "Thank you, dear. It is hard to go, but I always said I wanted to see the world someday, and this seems like my chance after being so tied down all these years. I've wished I lived closer to my daughter ever since my husband died. With her husband's career, it's obvious she won't be moving back here anytime soon, so that leaves it up to me to follow them around the world if I want to see them."

"Do they move a lot?"

"Oh my, yes. Her husband is a captain in the army. They

move to a new duty assignment every three years or so. They've already lived in Oklahoma, Germany and Kansas. They've only been in North Carolina for a month, and expect to be there awhile, so this is a good time for me to join them, especially if Ron gets sent to the Middle East again."

"I can't imagine moving halfway across the world." Jensen slid her fingers over the newly unwrapped bolts. Some of the fabrics were starched stiff, others flowed smooth as water under her fingertips. Some were laced together with fine weaves and crowned with printed designs, others were flecked with nubs and threaded through with homespun irregularities. "My Grandma Victoria always said that I put down deeper roots than most people. I guess she was right. I could never live in a place that was totally new and unfamiliar."

Mrs. Ryan laughed. "With a last name like Christiansen, I'd have thought you would have inherited a smidgen of Viking wanderlust."

"Not me. I like it when things stay just the way they are."

A bell chimed at the front of the store and Mrs. Ryan went to see to another customer. Jensen went back to looking for the fabric she needed and scoping out the new fabrics. Imagining which pieces would make bricks, stones, or a winding gravel road was one of her favorite things to do. But today, all she could think about was the fact that one more cherished thing in her life was coming to an end.

A half hour later, she'd located the pieces she needed plus some and packed up her purchases in the basket of her bicycle.

Soon, she was back in the safe haven of her cozy little bungalow, pouring her frustrations into her work until angst had become beauty, and rancor, creativity. By mid-afternoon, she was done drawing and designing and on to piecing a quilt she now thought of as Anders' Garden. She wasn't going to let the Amish women who usually quilted her designs touch it. This quilt would be hers from start to finish.

It was invigorating. This was why she had devoted her life to quilting in the first place. Ed might think she was a total ditz, all but incapable of taking care of herself. He was wrong. Her Grandma Victoria had always said that Jensen had inherited the best of both worlds—Maren's creative flair and artistic spirit and Frederik's hardworking hands and shrewd business savvy. "The talent to go places and the smarts to know what to do with it."

Screw Ed. Screw upheaval and instability and the roller coaster ride her life had become. Screw mixed messages and uncertainty and men who made decisions that affected her without talking to her first. Screw the ever-changing world in general. From now on, she was an island. She had her memories. She had very deep roots. And she believed in herself. That was all that mattered.

*****

Anders settled back into his chair and looked out at a garden filled with sunshine and color. Perhaps he had gotten a little too comfortable with his life. Maybe now that Bjorn was off pursuing his youthful ambitions, he needed to start dreaming a few dreams of his own.

He'd spent the last two days comforting people whose dreams for the future had come to an end. Not just thwarted, but gone forever—wives who had lost husbands, daughters who had lost fathers, mothers who had lost sons.

How could he be content to waste another day? Somewhere in Danemark, a woman who called herself The_Little_Mermaid seemed to honestly care about him, to believe their fates were connected. The least he could do was to open himself up to the possibility.

He went to the computer and typed her name into the chat system's search feature, but found no sign of her. He tried Bjorn next and found him talking to SweetYoungThing.

Ugly_Duckling: Hi, Bjorn. Hello, Jessica.

Boy_Wonder: No Mermaid tonight? I saw her yesterday, but she hasn't been around this evening.

Ugly_Duckling: You spoke to her?

Boy_Wonder: Briefly. She was busy talking to some guy.

Great. She had probably met someone else. The miracle of the rapport he and she had shared was due to her openness, not his. If she had chosen to favor someone else with her kind words and thought-provoking questions, he had to assume they would have been as taken with her as he had been. And vice versa. He certainly was no virtuoso when it came to conversation, especially the online variety.

He retyped her name, compelled for the first time in months.

Ugly_Duckling: Was she talking to someone she just met or someone she already knew?

Boy_Wonder: No clue. His name was PrinceEric.

SweetYoungThing: Hey, I get it. Cool. Prince Eric from The_Little_Mermaid. I love that movie. The music is so awesome.

Anders winced.

Ugly_Duckling: *The Little Mermaid* isn't a movie. It is a fairy tale, and it mentions neither Ariel nor Prince Eric.

Boy_Wonder: Don't get him going. He's been down on Disney ever since they took a few liberties with Hans Christian Andersen's version of *The Little Mermaid*.

Ugly_Duckling: Hans Christian Andersen's story is not a version. And Disney did a lot more than 'take liberties'. They changed half the story. They gave it a happy ending.

Boy_Wonder: God forbid someone in a fairy tale should live happily ever after.

Ugly_Duckling: Andersen's story ends with a meaningful moral—there are repercussions for your actions. Once a decision is made; it can't be undone. You have to live with the consequences. Children need to learn to appreciate what they have instead of thinking the grass is greener on the other side of the fence. Disney took something deep and insightful and made a travesty out of it. Don't even get me going on their gaudy merchandising and obnoxious plastic figurines.

Boy_Wonder: Well, I hate to break it to you, Dad, but with net revenues of almost a hundred mil and zillions of copies sold, it appears that you're the only one who feels that way.

SweetYoungThing: Wow, Mr. W. I've never met someone who didn't like Disney. Barney, the big purple dinosaur, I could understand, but Disney? Disneyland is an American institution.

Boy_Wonder: Exactly. Dad can't stand the thought that an American thought of something that a Dane didn't. Hans Christian Andersen was a great storyteller. Disney took a nice idea and made it even better. It drives Dad nuts that the story only catapulted to fame when Disney got a hold of it.

Anders could feel his blood pressure mounting as he tapped out one furious word after another.

Ugly_Duckling: All America does is take. The Almighty Americans use their power and influence to take whatever they want. Practically everything the Americans call their own is a cheap rip-off or shoddy imitation of somebody else's idea. Your precious America stole pizza from the Italians, Volkswagen Beetles from the Germans, golf from the Scots— even their famous hamburgers and French fries have European origins.

Boy_Wonder: The Americans have come up with a few good ideas of their own—they did go to the moon.

Ugly_Duckling: With the help of a few dozen German scientists they stole from der Fuhrer. Because they couldn't stand to be shown up by the Russians. Even the auto industry the Americans are so proud of is little more than a handful of companies trying to keep their plants afloat by making cars that look like Hondas or Toyotas.

SweetYoungThing: Um... I hate to break up the party, but it's getting late. I have to be at work early.

Boy_Wonder: Don't leave now. I'm sure Dad has to go water his plants. Or something.

Ugly_Duckling: I am sorry. I did not mean to force my opinions on you, Jess.

SweetYoungThing: No problem, Mr. W. I'm sure it's different living in Europe. I mean, I've heard that all the European newscasters ever show people over there is all the awful stuff that happens in America.

Of which there never seems to be a shortage, he thought.

Ugly_Duckling: That may be true. At any rate, I am sorry to appear so gruff. Jess, I hope you can get to work on time and that you feel well rested. Bjorn has not mentioned what you do.

Boy_Wonder: She teaches junior high math.

Ugly_Duckling: A very admirable profession.

SweetYoungThing: Thanks. This is only my second year, and trying to hold their attention is a daily battle. Apparently what I have to teach them is not nearly as exciting as X-Box.

Or Walt Disney videos, Anders refrained from adding.

Boy_Wonder: It's been swell, Dad, but, ah...

Ugly_Duckling: I will say goodbye as well. I am going to take some pictures of my petunias, and I must hurry, or the angle of the sun will be wrong and I will have lost my chance.

So he was a curmudgeonly, sarcastic old fool. Everyone in the chat room already knew it—no sense pretending now.

SweetYoungThing: Sorry you weren't able to hook up with your friend.

Is that what this woman who occupied so much of his thoughts was to him?

Ugly_Duckling: We have only spoken twice.

Boy_Wonder: Better luck next time.

Until three days ago he hadn't even known who Jensen was; now he was acting like a fool because he thought he'd lost her.

6.

It was time to take care of some old business. Jensen packed up some of the cookies she'd baked that morning and took off on her bike again—this time in the direction of Red Wing.

In the sunlight, the wooded bluff that had seemed so menacing in the dark hugged her comfortingly on one side, the lacy tree branches lining the water on the other. She pedaled effortlessly along the river's edge until she reached town, then veered away from the Mississippi to turn into the well-manicured loops of Ed's subdivision.

Things didn't bode well from the start. It was odd knocking on Ed's door at all, odder still finding she could predict the precise number of seconds it took Ed to walk from the television in his living room to the door off the kitchen where she stood waiting, odder yet being outside rather than in.

Ed's face was a mixture of defensiveness and regret when he opened the door. "So you finally decided to show up."

"I've missed you, too." She handed him some cookies, which hopefully made the fact that she didn't hug him less noticeable.

Ed handed her the keys. "I left my key on the ring. You'll have to take it off yourself if you don't want it anymore."

"You're still upset with me," she said.

Ed leaned against the doorframe, effectively blocking her entrance. His muscular arms were deeply tanned and sprinkled with fine brown hairs bleached by the sun. He squinted his eyes. She could tell by the twitch in his cheek that he was struggling to maintain the control that she'd assumed came easily to him.

Her knees felt shaky and her stomach lurched as her bravado started to fade. "Do you want your key back?"

"If I did, I'd have kept it when I had the chance."

She looked down at the neatly trimmed, box-shaped shrubs

that circled Ed's foundation and felt very cold. The tendrils of hair that had fallen down around her face while she was riding her bike stuck to her temples in clammy clumps. "I don't understand why you're being this way."

"What am I supposed to do? You obviously don't want me to touch you."

"I didn't want that to be the only thing there was between us," she stammered hesitantly, her eyes locked on his.

Ed gritted his perfectly spaced white teeth. "Yeah, well, you and I both know I can't give you the one thing you really want. And I'm not sure I have the rest to give."

She searched his face for some remnant of the affection they'd shared, the companionship they'd enjoyed. She was the one who had been going to break things off with him—gently, kindly. Instead, it was as though he had severed the link that connected them with one harsh slash of a knife. "I didn't mean to hurt you, Ed."

"You're the one who wanted this, not me," he said.

She never did quite remember how she made it home. The last thing she recalled was Ed telling her that he had updated the sticker inside her car door so she would have a record of when her oil had last been changed. The rest was a blur.

*****

There would be no roses, no fanfare, today. Anders was not going to get caught up with wondering when or if Jensen would come back to talk to him. He was eager to see her again, but he was not going to let a cold, hard piece of machinery, or the relationship that had sprung up from it, rule his life.

When she finally showed up, he thought at first that his attitude was to blame for the anti-climactic tone of their meeting. Although he could not see her face, he could tell by her words, or lack of them, that she was feeling subdued, less exuberant, than before—somehow wounded in her demeanor. He had no idea why, or if it was he, PrinceEric, or someone or something else that had precipitated the change.

Bottom line, he simply didn't know her well enough to gauge the lengthy pauses between her responses.

Ugly_Duckling: Is something bothering you?

The_Little_Mermaid: I don't want to burden you with my problems, Anders. They're no doing of yours.

Her words should have come as a relief, but for reasons he couldn't decipher, they stung.

Ugly_Duckling: You can say what you wish to me, Jensen. I am a good listener.

For the first time, he caught a glimpse of why people flocked to chat rooms. There was an appealing anonymity here, a freedom to confide to relative strangers things you could not, or would not, share with people you knew.

The_Little_Mermaid: It started last week. I got an invitation to enter an on-line contest asking me to describe my dream in fifty words. The prize was a hundred dollars. I was at my boyfriend's house that night, so I mentioned the contest and asked him what his dream was. He said he'd fulfilled them all long ago and didn't have any anymore.

Ah. So there it was. She had a boyfriend. Anders felt his muscles sag. It wasn't just that he was disappointed. His irrational hopes had been just that. In part, it was that he did not want to be put in the role of listener again. He had listened to enough disillusioned wives and husbands complaining about their spouses at work to last him a lifetime. Good old Anders was the perfect one to gripe to. Not only was he a trained counselor, he'd been dumped himself. Years ago, granted, but then one never forgets what it feels like to have the life sucked out of you by someone you trust.

The_Little_Mermaid: Ed's response shocked me. I can't imagine feeling that way. I tried to draw him out by asking about his goals for the future, thinking that maybe the word *dreams* was what was putting him off. Still nothing. He showed no passion about anything. Finally I asked him where that left us—if he didn't have some sort of dream that revolved around me, something he'd like to do together, somewhere he'd like to go with me, anything. He couldn't answer.

This Ed was an idiot. For the first time, Anders was glad he couldn't see Jensen's face. Glad she couldn't see his. He reined in his frustration and typed.

Ugly_Duckling: You impress me as a woman who would inspire many dreams in a man, Jensen.

The_Little_Mermaid: I suppose we all like to believe that we're capable of inspiring a few fantasies.

Ugly_Duckling: A fantasy is very different from a dream.

The_Little_Mermaid: Right now I'd settle for being the impetus for either.

Ugly_Duckling: I may not know you well, but I do know that you deserve all that you dream of. Compromise is required in some areas when you enter into a relationship, but a person should never have to sacrifice their dreams. A man and a woman should encourage and empower one another to be the best they can be, to follow their dreams and act on their ideas.

A minute or two went by; she said nothing.

Ugly_Duckling: What is it that you dream of besides a man who understands how you feel?

It was several minutes more before she responded.

The_Little_Mermaid: You make me feel absolutely and totally naked, Anders. It's as though you can read my mind.

Ugly_Duckling: Tell me what you are feeling, sweet woman.

Her answer came quickly, followed by a second before he'd even finished reading the first.

The_Little_Mermaid: Of course I dream of being loved. Really loved. Being treasured by someone who can see inside my heart. Being confidante and friend and lover to someone who knows me inside and out. Seeing the world with someone who finds beauty in the same things I do, but who will open my eyes to things I would have overlooked on my own.

The_Little_Mermaid: I've probably gone over my word limit already. I'll never win the prize now.

Anders indicated to her that she had made him laugh.

Ugly_Duckling: I do not mean to put a damper on things, but have you ever stopped to think that the dreams you just listed are all dependent on someone else?

The_Little_Mermaid: No, I hadn't. But you're right.

Ugly_Duckling: I don't mean to deflate you. I used to dream of sharing my life with a woman, and all that it entails, but when it was not to be, I took comfort in raising a son and pursuing other things that brought me pleasure. However simple, they were at least things that lay within my own control to bring about. Some would say I gave up, but I disagree. I still have dreams; I simply learned not to hold my nose while waiting for them to come true.

The_Little_Mermaid: My Great-Grandma Jensen once told me that we all have to bloom where we're planted. I admire people who have the courage to realign their dreams with the reality of their lives. Maybe that's what I did when I started seeing Ed. But I never stopped hoping that I would find my heart's desire.

Ugly_Duckling: It is good to dream, and it is good to be content with what you have. We have only to find a good balance.

The_Little_Mermaid: I wish I could give you a hug.

Ugly_Duckling: I have seen people here do it like this. (((((Jensen))))

The_Little_Mermaid: The modern version of the XOXO marks my Grandma put at the end of her letters for hugs and kisses.

It shocked him to realize how much he really did want to hug her. To kiss her, too. There. He'd admitted it. He'd never felt so connected to a woman as he did to her. He felt his heartbeat quicken, and his neck getting hot and scratchy. He needed to get some fresh air, to clear his head.

Ugly_Duckling: It's been a pleasure talking to you, Jensen, but I should say farewell to Bjorn and do a little gardening before I go to work. The sun is so bright it would be a sin not to spend at least part of the day outside. If you would agree to meet me here again tomorrow I would like to have the opportunity to talk to you more.

The_Little_Mermaid: The sun?

Her question didn't sound at all peculiar at first. After more than a decade of directing planes through the airspace over the Danish peninsula, Anders knew that the shifting weather patterns dictated by the North Sea often resulted in vast variations in the weather from one part of Danemark to another.

Ugly_Duckling: Is it cloudy where you are?

The_Little_Mermaid: It's pitch dark—it's the middle of the night.

Anders watched as Jensen's words came to a brief halt, then scrolled forward in a frantic gush.

The_Little_Mermaid: I'm doing a quick mental calculation of the time on both the East and West Coast (which is no easy feat at this time of night). I know it's late, but it will be hours before the sun rises anywhere in the United States.

Anders groaned aloud.

Ugly_Duckling: You said you were Danish. Where do you live?

The_Little_Mermaid: I am Danish. I live in Minnesota. Where do you live?

The nerve endings that had been tingling a moment ago went numb with disbelief. Damn! It was bad enough that he had wasted his time nurturing an ill-advised infatuation with someone he'd met on the internet, someone who already had a boyfriend. But she was an American. She lived on the other side of the world.

Ugly_Duckling: I hate to dash your dreams, Jensen, but like most Americans, your world perspective is severely out of kilter. The honor of being Danish is reserved for those of us who were born in Danemark. If you were born and live in America, you are an American, not a Dane.

The_Little_Mermaid: You're from Denmark?

Ugly_Duckling: I told you I was Danish from the start.

The_Little_Mermaid: Fine. Touché. We're proud of our heritage in Minnesota. We refer to people as being Danish, German, Norwegian or Bohemian depending on which country their ancestors came from. I didn't stop to think that it might be a bone of contention among those who are native to the countries. I guess we Americans do tend to think the world revolves around us. I just never dreamed... You speak (or should I say type?) English perfectly.

He couldn't be angry with her. She was too endearing. Still, he couldn't quell his disappointment.

Ugly_Duckling: I am sorry to be so touchy. I have been feeling somewhat resentful toward Americans since Bjorn decided to leave Danemark.

So it was a bit of an understatement. It was bad enough that he'd spewed his Anti-American thoughts in front of Bjorn's friend. He didn't need to dump his feelings on Jensen. Besides, it was nothing personal. He tried not to harbor bitterness against anyone or anything, but it just seemed to him that the good old USA had taken much from him and given nothing back.

The_Little_Mermaid: I'm sorry you feel that way, Anders.

He was suddenly at a loss for words. He appreciated America's generosity and its commitment to freedom. Thousands of Danes would have perished had America's arms not been held wide when famine, war, persecution and strife had plagued Europe. But in his opinion, what had started out as a noble coming-together of the needy, adventurous, and poor had mutated into a greedy, arrogant giant that took what it wished and left the rest behind. In Anders' case, the light of his life—his only son.

His head clouded with impassioned fury. Jensen seemed like a nice woman, and he sincerely wished her the best life had to offer. But as for him... he could offer her nothing.

Jensen felt a rising sense of panic as she waited for Anders to respond—had she finally met the man of her dreams only to lose him again over something so silly as whether the sun was shining or the stars were out? She struggled to find words that would reestablish their connection.

The_Little_Mermaid: You probably thought Bjorn would always live nearby. It's a perfectly natural assumption.

Ugly_Duckling: I was a fool to presume that Bjorn would marry a nice Danish girl, settle down in Copenhagen and make me a grandfather. I may have considered slight variations on the theme, but none of them included visions of my grown son and I frequenting chat rooms, separated by an ocean and the whole continent of America.

He sounded so resigned, so bitter.

The_Little_Mermaid: I know I live a bit further away from you than you first thought, but I hope that we can still talk.

How she wished she could see his face! She could understand why he was disappointed. She had already fantasized about meeting him, perhaps even having some sort of real relationship when they'd gotten to know each other better. That would be all but impossible now.

Ugly_Duckling: I will watch for you when I am here.

The_Little_Mermaid: Leaving it to chance seems a little risky. I mean, lightning isn't supposed to strike twice in the same place and all. What if our paths never cross again?

Ugly_Duckling: I will find you if I feel like talking.

Oh, Anders. Please, please don't shut me out. Your friendship, your words have meant so much to me already. She was losing him and there wasn't a damn thing she could do about it.

Ugly_Duckling: I really must get out to the garden.

The_Little_Mermaid: I suppose I should be getting to bed. Enjoy your sunshine, Anders.

Ugly_Duckling: Sweet dreams, Jensen.

The_Little_Mermaid: Now that I know we're half a world apart, I don't know whether to say goodnight or good-day.

Ugly_Duckling: The Bavarians use *Grüß Gott* to greet one

another whether it is daytime or night. Loosely translated, it means 'God be with you'. Perhaps it would be appropriate.

The_Little_Mermaid: Then *Grüß Gott* until we meet again.

If they met again. It sounded like Anders hoped God would watch over her because he sure wasn't going to be around to do it himself.

7.

Anders secured his backpack in the basket mounted on the back of his bicycle and rolled his bike out of the garage. He took note of the overcast sky and checked to make sure he had his slicker in case he encountered rain. His patch repair kit and portable tire pump were at the ready. He was sick of being surprised. From now on, he was going to be on guard; prepared for any contingency, no matter how unexpected.

"Godmorgen, Mr. Westerlund." Jesper was leaning out his front door. "I see you are up and about."

Ja, Jesper probably had his schedule memorized by now. Without the lilac branches to shield his movements, everything he did was in clear view of half the neighborhood.

Jesper sprinted over. "I am glad I caught you."

"I am on my way to do some errands," Anders said, mustering a smile that he hoped looked more sincere than he felt.

"We have relatives visiting from America," Jesper said. "You are so good with the English that I thought you might join us at our house in order to help us understand them."

Ja, well, if Jesper was looking for someone who understood Americans, he'd come to the wrong place. "I see." Anders tried to think of an excuse. "I wish I could help, but I am out of eggs, and must go to the store. It closes before I am off work."

"I have plenty of eggs to share with you. We stocked up since we were expecting company. My mother had the same idea. Our icebox is now so crowded we barely have room for milk. Come." Jesper urged him toward the house. "You will love Betsy and Casey. They are six and eight. They are my third cousins on my father's side."

The next thing Anders knew he was sitting between the two little girls at a high, tile-topped coffee table drinking coffee, nibbling on Jarlsburg and rye, and thinking he would rather be any place on earth than in Jesper's living room with a bunch of

American tourists. They even looked the part in their Nike tennis shoes, neon colored windbreakers, and baseball caps.

"My favorite thing so far was seeing the Little Mermaid," Betsy jabbered, so happy to have found someone besides her parents to talk to that she could barely contain her exuberance. Both girls seemed oblivious to Anders' discomfort, although he did catch their father glancing at him sympathetically.

"You'll have to excuse the girls," their mother whispered when Betsy had gone to the kitchen for a refill of milk. "They've heard about the Little Mermaid in school, so seeing her in real life was very exciting for them."

"I suppose they were disappointed when they saw what a plain little creature she is," Anders said. "As opposed to the flashy, sequin-covered, animated version they are used to."

Betsy's mother smiled. "They've never seen the Disney version if that's what you're referring to. Girls, Mr. Westerlund would like to know what you thought of the Little Mermaid."

"She looked just like I imagined she would." Betsy shuffled between his leg and the coffee table on her way back from the kitchen. "From now on, when I stand at the beach and watch the waves on the shore, I'll look at the foam of the sea and wonder if it's the Little Mermaid."

Anders arched one eyebrow and nodded at her mother.

"I got to sit on Hans Christian Andersen's lap at the park while my mother took my picture," Casey said. "He's so tall that I couldn't even climb up there by myself. I had to stand on my daddy's shoulders." Casey moved closer to him and slipped her hand in his. "Hans Christian Andersen must have been a giant."

Betsy plopped on the sofa on his other side. "Hans Christian Andersen has a very high hat."

Casey leaned her head on his arm. "Sir, would you please read us the *Little Mermaid*?"

"I am so used to how the story sounds in my own tongue that I'm not sure I can find the words fast enough in English."

"We want to hear what the story sounds like in Danish," the little one said.

Sherrie Hansen

"Please, Mr. Westerlund?" Betsy said.

"You will not understand a word I am saying," Anders said.

"We know the story by heart. If we close our eyes, it will almost be like Hans Christian Andersen himself is telling us a story," Betsy said.

Fine. So all Americans aren't ugly.

"I can't wait to tell my friend at school that we got to have a real Danish person read to us," Casey said, her round little cheeks glowing with excitement. "May I sit on your lap?"

*****

Jensen could see Ed's pick-up sitting in front of her house from two blocks down the road. Her tires screeched as she pulled up behind him. She'd just gotten off the telephone with Peder and she was itching for a fight. If Ed had so much as touched her lilac trees...

She rounded the corner to the back yard. "What are you doing here?" She asked, her voice still mad with pent up frustration. Ed was holding a tube of caulk.

"Isn't it obvious?" Ed said condescendingly. "You have a window that needs to be fixed. I'm fixing it."

"I didn't ask you to fix anything."

"You just hadn't gotten around to it. I didn't want the rain to leak in and ruin your hardwood floors."

"I called a handyman. He said he would come as soon as he had a free afternoon."

"As in never. Use your head, Jen. Handymen are in higher demand than doctors. They have better things to do with their time than to drive ten miles one way to do a five minute job."

"I not only didn't ask you to fix my window, I didn't tell you I had a window that needed fixing," she sputtered, trying to regain the upper hand.

"I'm not an idiot. You didn't have a key, and I know you."

"You don't have a clue."

"Oh yeah?" Ed said, looking peeved. "I know you a lot

better than you think I do."

"You don't know anything!" she said loudly, not caring that bare lilac branches were no hedge against sound.

"You think I don't know why you left?" Ed said in a voice she hardly recognized. "You think I don't know that I destroyed all your perfect little dreams when I got snipped?"

She felt her jaw drop in an involuntary reflex.

"I've been laying odds on how long you'd stick around once you knew I'd be shooting blanks. The doc said you could still get pregnant for a month after the procedure. I figured once my thirty days was up, you'd be out of here."

"Number one, I couldn't have known that. I wasn't there when the doctor talked to you. I didn't know you were having a vasectomy," she said, shaking. "Number two, we've always used condoms, so what difference would it have made if I had?"

"You can't tell me that you haven't had friends whose husbands have had vasectomies. And you most certainly know that condoms aren't a hundred percent safe."

"I wouldn't have slept with you in the first place if I hadn't been willing to accept the possibility that I might..."

"You were trying to get pregnant. You hoped..."

"I was not trying! I've always hoped..."

"What? That if you got pregnant I'd ask you to marry me?"

She looked away. It was too embarrassing to admit that that was exactly what she'd thought. "I thought it was possible that God might use the situation to bring about a miracle."

"See? I was right." Ed glared at her. "Not only were you plotting to get pregnant, you were bringing God into it."

"So now I can't hope, can't pray?"

"You do whatever you want to," Ed said. "You always do anyway. If you'd gone on the pill, I wouldn't have had to have a vasectomy in the first place. You wanted a baby from day one."

"Which I freely admitted. I never once asked you not to use a condom, but I wasn't going to do something to my body that would prevent me from getting pregnant when having a baby is the one thing I want more than anything in the world. I'm too old to play those kind of games."

"Oh, it was a game, all right—Russian roulette, using my sperm. The only reason you stuck around as long as you did is because I have good DNA."

She was sick of being nice. She was always nice. No more. He'd hurt her one too many times. "There are sperm banks for women like that, Ed. They drive down to a nice, colorful clinic and browse through the files until they find their perfect match. Nice and tidy. They don't have to pretend to like Monday night football, watch Terminator movies, or eat venison."

"That would never work for you though, would it, babe?"

She shifted uncomfortably, waiting. He'd never called her babe before.

"You're too into your perfect little scenarios. You're too traditional. You're too into sex. Having a baby wouldn't *feel right* unless you'd gotten pregnant the old-fashioned way. Under your grandmother's precious quilt, or maybe one that you'd made just for the occasion. Oh, and don't forget the orgasm. The pretty little picture wouldn't be perfect unless you conceived right after you had the best orgasm of your life."

Her cheeks felt flaming hot; her heart was pounding in her chest. Why in heaven's name had she ever let him touch her?

"So if you know me so well that you had all this figured out, why in hell's name did you waste a precious year of my life? If you'd been honest with me about the fact that you had no intention of marrying me, if you'd told me how much you loathed the idea of fathering my child and what lengths you were willing to go to prevent it, I would have left a long time ago."

Ed grabbed his toolbox and a handful of loose tools he'd used to fix the window and stormed away.

Her head felt like it was about to explode. She waited until she heard Ed's pick-up start, picked up the nearest rock, and bashed it against the windowpane he had just fixed. She might not have her pride, but she still had her duct tape.

*****

Anders waved to Betsy and Casey as he tooled down the street past Jesper's house. He was going to have to be quick about his errands if he was going to make it to work on time.

He rounded the corner with a graceful swoop to the left and turned hard onto the main thoroughfare that connected his neighborhood to Copenhagen. He had to admit that Jesper's relatives seemed like good people. He was very impressed with the fact that they had exposed their daughters to the great children's classics of each country they'd visited. In Germany, the Olsen's had taken Betsy and Casey to the opera to see *Hansel and Gretel*; in England, to see Mr. MacGregor's garden at Beatrix Potter's home. Bjorn had loved the story of Peter Cottontail when he was little.

He coasted for a second, reveling in the memory of Bjorn snuggling in his lap; needing him. He resumed pedaling; loving the way the wind rifled through his hair as he raced along the side of the street. A car was approaching, traveling the same direction he was. He looked over his shoulder to make sure they weren't signaling. They weren't. He pumped down on his pedals and let his bike surge toward the intersection. It was a rush, feeling the power he was generating propel him forward.

In a flash the car passed him and turned right into his path. His front wheel had just cleared the slope of the cutaway in the curb. He was inches from the car's passenger door, barreling ahead at full speed, unable to stop. Instinctively, he turned his handlebar to the right as hard as his shaking arms could manage and twisted his front wheel back onto itself. His bike crumpled under him as he crashed into the curb, his bones jarring into each other, joints popping and tendons stretching to their limits. His shoulder ploughed into a lamppost at the side of the road. The car sped off.

He lay still and looked up at the sky. His elbow stung with

grit from the concrete gutter, but thankfully, he had landed in the grass. He didn't move, unsure if he could, paralyzed by shock if not injury. He could hear drums braking and wheels crunching as car after car rounded the corner, accelerated, and drove away, assaulting his ears with their indifference.

How could they not see him? He was only a few blocks from home. These were his neighbors, the parents of Bjorn's schoolmates, the people he rubbed shoulders with at the grocery. At least one in the string of cars must have seen what happened.

"You okay?" someone yelled, presumably out a car window. He tried to nod. His head begin to throb. The car drove on. Had someone at least used their cell phone to call the police?

Silence. The light two blocks back must have turned red. He groaned and tried to lift a leg. At least it moved. He rolled to his side. His sleeve was torn and his forearm was bleeding, although the wound looked to be only skin-deep. He sat, ignoring his aches, and reached for his bike. The front wheel was bent.

He could hear another car approaching just as he was trying to stand and was relieved when the car pulled over. The prospect of limping over a mile to get home, dragging his bike behind him, was not a pleasant one.

A large, older man and a younger woman leaped out of the car simultaneously, one from each side.

"Are you hurt?" the woman asked in English.

"Not seriously," Anders replied, so surprised to hear English that he didn't switch languages until mid-sentence. "At least I don't think so."

"It looks like you had a pretty good upset there," the man said. "Can we give you a lift?"

Anders nodded, and gingerly stood.

"We'd be happy to take you to the doctor if you need to get checked out," the man said.

"I think I'll be all right," Anders said. "But my bike..."

The man already had the trunk open when Anders turned around. "Mother, I told you you shouldn't have bought so much china at that Royal Copenhagen place."

"If we move the packages and the suitcases to the back seat with me his bike can go in the trunk," an older woman said. "Jenny, you don't mind waiting here for a few minutes while we run him home, do you? I don't think there's room for him and his bike and all three of us in the car."

"Sure," the younger woman said without hesitating. "Toss me my book, would you, Mom?" She helped move some bags to the trunk, then crouched and sat cross-legged in the grass, her back against the same lamppost he'd smashed into.

"We probably should have rented a bigger car," the man said, "but we're not used to paying so much for gas in Iowa."

"That is part of the reason I am on my bicycle," Anders said. Minnesota wasn't far from Iowa. He looked at the woman who had given up her seat for him. "I hate to inconvenience you."

"Nonsense," the man said.

"I'm fine," his daughter said. "Take care of that arm. I hope the rest of you doesn't feel too bad in the morning."

"I am sure I will feel every little bruise by then."

"I hope not," she said, looking earnest. "*Grüß Gott.*"

That's when the dizziness hit him. He steadied himself against the car and slowly lowered himself to the seat. A torrent of thoughts was cascading through his brain. Why had no Dane stopped to help him? What odd quirk of chance had dictated that this kindly American family would happen by at the precise moment he needed help? Perhaps Jensen was right. Perhaps the fates were conspiring to get them together.

Bjorn kept telling him Americans weren't such a bad lot. At the very least, it was increasingly hard to justify his long-seated resentment of the people as a whole. He'd hated Benta's Kirk so much that it had been easy to buy into the media's portrayal of the ugly American. He'd never even questioned if it had been a fair assessment.

Another thought cloyed its way into consciousness. What if he had been badly hurt? Who would have taken care of him while he healed? Whom would he have called to help? A fresh awareness of what it meant to be alone in the world washed over him. Goodness, his arm hurt. And his hip, and his neck, and his head.

The Americans helped him get his bicycle into the garage, never once making him feel guilty for inconveniencing them. He offered them money for their trouble. They refused.

Anders collapsed into a chair as soon as they'd left. It was too late to call a substitute teacher. He would have to shower, bandage his abrasions, and hope he could get to work before his class started by making up for lost time in his car.

*****

Jensen was still fuming when she turned on her computer to check her email. She'd obviously been dissatisfied with her relationship with Ed—she would be lying if she claimed otherwise. But she really hadn't wanted Ed to end their relationship altogether; she'd wanted him to meet her halfway. She'd made compromises during the time they'd shared their lives—couldn't he do the same?

Her life was a litany of hardheaded, unyielding men. First Peder, who would probably never appreciate her great-grandmother Maren's house; then Ed, who didn't appreciate her; now Anders, who appeared to be another case in point. Granted, meeting someone halfway wasn't easy when one of you was in Denmark and the other was in Minnesota, but from the sound of things, Anders was ready to forget they'd ever met just because they were from different countries. She hadn't thought Anders would be a go-to-the-movies, grab-a-bite-to-eat-afterwards kind of friend anyway, so the revelation that he was further away than she'd first imagined didn't change all that much.

She still craved his words—his mind, his thoughts, his

encouragement. She needed a friend, someone to confide in, someone with whom she could share her deepest fears and wildest dreams. Anders had been more of that to her in the last few days than Ed had been in a whole year. She'd been so happy to find him online again, now, only a few hours later, she was afraid she would never see him again, that he was gone for good, as unexpectedly as he had come in the first place.

It was hours later when she woke up sitting upright in the chair in front of her desk. She'd dozed off from sheer exhaustion. She was in such a foul mood that she toyed with the idea of going right to bed. Her head was pounding and her eyes felt like peeled grapes wrapped in sandpaper.

When she finally connected to the internet, it was only because she knew no one would be able to see her blotchy cheeks or hear from her voice that her nose was stuffed up from crying. It certainly wasn't because she desired contact with anyone resembling the male species, but because she felt obligated to check and see if any of her customers had sent messages. It was still too early for Anders to be online. That was fine with her. She really didn't feel like talking to anyone, not even him.

The first message in her box was an inquiry regarding matching twin sized quilts for a customer in Vail, Colorado. Her eyes opened wide as she spotted the second, an email from Anders Westerlund. She had no idea how he'd gotten her address—all she knew is that the whole room lit up at the thought of Anders sitting at his desk, thinking of her, and composing a letter.

Dearest Jensen, I know we left it to fate, where and when we would meet again, but after I got over the surprise of learning you were from the United States, I found I was not content to leave things so "up in the air". (Of all the American phrases I have heard, that is the one we in the aviation industry think is the most funny.) After you left, Bjorn urged me to Google your name and "quilts" to see if you had a website, or if there was an article about your work that would have information on how to contact you. As it turns out, you are quite famous; thus I had no trouble finding your email address.

Jensen, I also sense that you and I are connected in some way. We think alike and dream alike. We wonder about the same things at the same time. You are in limbo regarding another relationship that may or may not be continuing. I am unsure of the depths of your feelings for this man and wish only that whatever happens with him, that you will not be hurt. While you are sorting through the complexities of your feelings and establishing what is real and what is not, please know that while part of our relationship may be limited to the fantasy realm of the cyber world, the friendship and understanding I feel for you are genuine.

The sun has come out, and the weather in Copenhagen is perfect for riding bicycles. I know of a secluded little cove where a hidden creek flows through the woods— would you join me there for a picnic? I will pack smørrebrød and a blanket to spread on the grassy banks. The creek makes a bubbling noise that is very soothing. You will love it.

I have never 'met' you, yet I can envision the way your eyes shine. Imagine that I am feeding you grapes, one by one, lifting your chin to meet my fingers, perhaps even tasting the sweetness of your lips. Forgive me if I am too forward, but I can see the beauty that is inside of you even though the splendor of your physical self has not yet been revealed to me. You have uncovered yourself to me through your words, and I am most taken

*with the creature I have glimpsed. Good day, my little
mermaid. XOXOXOX Anders*

She melted back into her chair, took a deep breath, and
blinked her eyes. She was still groggy from her nap, but she
wasn't dreaming. She was sure of that much. What she couldn't
begin to fathom was how well Anders seemed to know her. She
sat up straight and let her fingers fly over her keyboard,
frantically trying to express the wonder she felt.

> *Dear Anders, Thank you for writing! I awoke to
> your letter just a few minutes ago. (You caught me
> taking a nap.) Even before I knew you had written, I
> was snuggled up with you in my dreams, your sweet
> words resounding through my sub-conscious, the
> memory of our time together wrapped around me
> like loving arms. You have a magic touch. Finding
> you is one of the most delightful surprises life has
> bestowed on me in years... I look forward to
> spending more time with you in our fantasy world.
> XOXOXOX Jensen*

8.

By ten-thirty that night, she'd taken a bubble bath, painted her toenails, and dressed in a soft pink T-shirt she slept in when it was cold. She'd felt an overwhelming sense of rapport as she read Anders' words. Maybe it was midnight in Minnesota and daylight in Denmark, but the way their minds worked was anything but night and day.

When Peder and Karl were babies, she'd hovered over their cribs for hours while they napped, waiting for them to wake up and reach their chubby little arms up to her. She was no less eager for the sun to rise in Denmark so Anders would wake up and come to her now.

Anders finally appeared, and with his first words, the world was swathed in roses once again.

The_Little_Mermaid: I was hoping you'd be up early today! I was so excited to talk to you that I could hardly wait for night to come.

Ugly_Duckling: I could barely sleep for thinking of you. I am sorry I behaved so rigidly when I found out where you lived.

Jensen smiled, wishing there were some way she could feign a Scandinavian accent in typeset.

The_Little_Mermaid: Ja, if the subject of time hadn't come up, you still wouldn't know I wasn't born in Danemark.

Ugly_Duckling: Ja, right. I'll bet you've never even been to the motherland.

The_Little_Mermaid: I've flown into København twice. We may have passed each other on the tarmac for all we know.

Ugly_Duckling: It makes me feel closer to you—knowing we've shared the same space in time for however brief a moment.

The_Little_Mermaid: I loved Denmark. The people were friendly and the sights were beautiful. I felt very at home.

Ugly_Duckling: Do you have relatives here?

The_Little_Mermaid: Some third and fourth cousins in a little town called Slangerup.

Ugly_Duckling: That is only sixty kilometers from here.

The_Little_Mermaid: They are descendants of my Great-Grandma Jensen's cousin Sophie. I have been thinking of Sophie and her daughter, Boyda, all week. I rescued a stack of letters my Great-Grandma Jensen sent back to Denmark after Frederik and Maren immigrated to America from my brother Peder's bonfire.

She went on to tell him about her clash with Peder.

Ugly_Duckling: So none of you has been able to read them?

The_Little_Mermaid: No. They're in Danish. All I've been told is that they hold the secret of why my great-grandparents left Denmark and came to America.

Ugly_Duckling: Maybe your mother knows the solution to the mystery.

The_Little_Mermaid: Boyda told my mother that my Great-Grandma Jensen was a very beautiful woman, and that her husband brought her and their children to America because there was another man who was in love with her.

Ugly_Duckling: Ah. A love story. A scandalous one.

The_Little_Mermaid: My great-grandmother was seventy-seven-years-old when I was born and ninety-five when she died. It's hard for me to imagine her being involved in a scandal so momentous that her husband would pack up and relocate their whole family to another continent.

Ugly_Duckling: What things do you remember about her?

Jensen let her mind wander back through dozens of twenty-year-old memories.

The_Little_Mermaid: Her name was Maren Jensen. We called her Grandma Jenny. She raised a large family and made lovely quilts. She had an aura of great strength. She was very independent - just as renowned for her stubborn streak as she was her faith. I have an old autograph book she signed when I was ten. She wrote 'keep looking up'. I've tried never to forget her advice.

Ugly_Duckling: Life's defining moments come in many different ways. Your relationship with her helped make you who you are.

She glanced around her bedroom at her quilts and the family photographs she kept nestled in antique frames on her bureau. They were her most obvious connections to the past, but other treasures of her heart were in abundance as well. A photograph taken from the top of Pike's Peak when she'd climbed her first and only "fourteener" summit... a tea cup with bluebells on it that she'd gotten at a boot sale in Wales... a dream catcher given to her by an old Indian woman from Canada... a painting of a rainbow she'd found at the Art Sail in Clear Lake, Iowa when she and a friend had ridden their bikes around the lake. Each brought back memories of her proudest, most bittersweet or memorable moments—moments that had defined who and what she was today.

Ugly_Duckling: I'm looking at photos of Bjorn's first time on the Ferris wheel at Tivoli, the two of us with giant pretzels strung around our necks at Oktoberfest in München, Bjorn and I silhouetted against the skyline of Bergen, Norway the day we got up at dawn and climbed the mountain behind our hotel. Seemingly insignificant moments in the grand scheme of things, but without a doubt the building blocks that shaped me into who I am.

The_Little_Mermaid: I feel the same. Each little adventure and event is a stepping-stone that takes us closer and closer to our calling.

Ugly_Duckling: Not just the good things either. I wouldn't wish my marital woes on anyone, but when I think back on the man I was when I was first married to Benta and compare him to the man I am now, I can honestly say that my moder was right when she used to say "all things work together for good".

The_Little_Mermaid: My Grandma Victoria used to quote the same verse.

Not that Jensen hadn't taken issue with the passage at times. What was good about God knitting her together with such a great capacity for mother love, then denying her a baby to nurture and love? Maybe she'd see the good in it someday, but Bible or no, she couldn't just yet.

Ugly_Duckling: Ja, it is. My moder also used to tell me about a Good Samaritan who helped a Jew laying hurt along the roadside that others had passed by without a thought.

She read Anders' words with horror and relief as he related the story of what had happened to him the afternoon before. A chill ran down her spine when she realized how differently his bike ride might have ended.

The_Little_Mermaid: I wish I were there to help patch you up.

He could have been killed—disappeared from her screen without a poof. She would've never known what became of him.

Ugly_Duckling: I will be fine. I am just sore, and humbled to realize my bicycle and I are not as invincible as I thought.

The_Little_Mermaid: Maybe they were angels. It would have served you right if God had sent a band of angels from the USA to save you when you've been so judgmental about we Americans.

Ugly_Duckling: Ja. My moder would have had a thing or two to say about my bad attitude if she was here.

The_Little_Mermaid: I'll bet she was a good Lutheran, your mother.

Ugly_Duckling: Ja, always down at the church tending the flowers on my father's grave. She planted a tiny boxwood hedge in a heart shape over the spot where he lay and filled the center with rose begonias every spring until she died. I don't think she ever got over losing him.

The_Little_Mermaid: She must have been very proud that she passed her love of flowers on to you.

There was a longer than usual pause while she waited for Anders' response.

Ugly_Duckling: If you could hear me speak, you would know you have made my throat gruff. I am not an emotional person, but you have made me understand why I take such comfort in gardening. You also make me realize that if Bjorn stays in America, there will be no one to tend the flowers on my mother and father's graves when I am gone.

The_Little_Mermaid: Oh, Anders. I wish I could hug you.

Ugly_Duckling: We take so many influences from our past for granted. Bjorn's getting a job in Seattle will change the course of my family's history for all time. Years ago, some thing or someone resulted in your great-grandfather making a decision that redefined the destiny of yours. I wonder if Maren or this unidentified man who loved her had any concept of the chain of events that were set in motion the day they first met?

Her mind whirled as she read his words.

The_Little_Mermaid: I've never stopped to think how pivotal certain moments are, or how their repercussions ripple through time. I just wish I'd heard this story when Grandma Jensen was still alive to shed some light on things.

Ugly_Duckling: These letters were written to her best friend in the passion of the moment—they're likely to be more revealing than anything she might have shared with you anyway.

The_Little_Mermaid: I'm still having a hard time linking my Grandma Jenny to the sort of scandalous scenarios that are running through my mind.

Ugly_Duckling: If you wish to solve the mystery, you must stop thinking of her as your great-grandmother and envision a beautiful young woman with an intriguing history. Would you trust me to read the letters and translate them for you?

The_Little_Mermaid: I'd be delighted to let you read them if it's not too much trouble.

She took down the basket of letters from the shelf by Maren's quilt and held one in her hand. In addition to being sooty, the envelopes they were tucked in and the paper they were written on were yellowed and fragile with age, rubbed smooth by longing fingers, even tearstained in places. The scrolling sweeps of ink that made up the script they were penned in was as foreign to Jensen's eyes as the language they were written in.

The_Little_Mermaid: I should warn you that unless you're big on flowery embellishments, they might be hard to decipher.

Ugly_Duckling: If you have a scanner and a fax machine, we'll soon find out.

The_Little_Mermaid: Perfect. I'd rather not risk losing them in the mail.

Jensen looked at the quilt that had always linked her so tangibly to Maren Jensen.

The_Little_Mermaid: You don't think she would see this as a betrayal of her confidence, do you?

Ugly_Duckling: If you think it's better not to know what is in the letters, I would understand, but I have always thought there is much to be learned by studying history and unlocking the lessons contained in past events.

The_Little_Mermaid: If we do this, you must tell me about your family, too. If I'm going to trust you to unlock my family's secrets, turn-about is only fair.

Ugly_Duckling: According to my mother, my great, great-grandmother was a chambermaid for the Royal Prince of Danemark before she left the palace to marry my great, great-grandfather. Her first child, a big baby boy who was my great-grandfather, was born only six months after she married. A good story, ja?

The_Little_Mermaid: Are you saying what I think you are?

Ugly_Duckling: That's *Your Royal Illegitimate Highness* to you, miss.

The_Little_Mermaid: Wow! Ill-begotten royal blood flowing through your veins. Just think...

Ugly_Duckling: I am thinking—of the great beauty that runs in your family—and wishing I could see you.

The_Little_Mermaid: You already know me better than anyone except for my mother. I'm curious about what you look like, too, but not being about to see you is kind of like knowing you from the inside out. I don't want to lose that.

Ugly_Duckling: In some ways, I feel like we have known each other forever, in other ways, you are a mystery. One of two I hope to unravel.

A sequence of shivers tingled its way down her spine.

The_Little_Mermaid: I can't speak for Maren, but the thought of being 'unraveled' by a dashing, though illegitimate, descendant of the crown prince of Denmark is very tantalizing.

Ugly_Duckling: I've been called many things in my forty-five years, but never dashing.

She smiled and wished again that she could touch him.

The_Little_Mermaid: Okay, Prince Charming. Give me your fax number and I'll send you a photo and one of Maren's letters before I go to sleep.

She suddenly realized that she hadn't thought of Peder's bonfire or Ed and the horrible things they'd said to each other even once since she'd gotten Anders' email.

Ugly_Duckling: I'll look forward to it. Now I must limp off to the shower and get to work. I have an early meeting. I'll leave my fax machine on while I'm showering and fixing my breakfast and check it before I leave. Sweet dreams, Jensen.

The_Little_Mermaid: XOXOXOXOXOX, Anders.

9.

Anders went to work with a bounce in his step he hadn't felt in years. The meeting he had to sit through was punctuated with images of Jensen. But instead of being a distraction, his thoughts of her had an energizing affect. When the meeting was done, it was still a few hours before he normally started his workday, so he used the gap time to look at Maren's letters. But not before he'd scrutinized the cover letter Jensen had addressed to him.

Unimportant as the words she'd written were in and of themselves, they were real, tangible, a part of her that he could hold in his hands. He shut the door to his office, and for the tenth time that morning, examined her words.

> *Hi, sweet man. I didn't go into detail when we talked, but there have been some other developments here, too. Suffice it to say that Ed and I are over. I'll explain when I'm not so tired. Thank you for being there for me. Receiving your kind email was just what I needed given the hostility I've experienced in the last few days. You're a Godsend, Anders. Love, Jensen*

He drew in a ragged breath. The paper Jensen's handwriting was printed on was nothing special—plain white, multi-purpose computer paper from the new American mega store just down the street. The ink that formed her slow curls and bold strokes was from a plain black cartridge. But the handwriting was hers. She had formed each word by her own hand.

She couldn't have felt any more real to him at that moment had she stood before him in the flesh. Knowing he was being ridiculous didn't make it any better. He held the paper in his hands and tried to imagine the scent of the perfume she wore, the way her hair and eyelashes would feel brushing against his cheek. Admitting he was an old fool didn't put an end to the daydreams he was entertaining either.

Reading Maren's letters to Sophie only fanned the fire. He read quickly at first, from curiosity rather than boredom, and then slowly, to decipher the varied connections between Maren and the other names mentioned in the letters. Maren's relationship to each of them slowly became clear. Her husband, Frederik Jensen, and their three children, Mathilda, Karl, and baby Victoria, were the first to take shape. He paid little attention to the names of the cousins that rounded out Sophie and Maren's extended family in Danemark. Although Maren inquired as to their well-being and implored Sophie to pass her greetings to them, they had little bearing on the story.

The script the letters were penned in was at the same time lovely and frustrating. Even the way the thoughts flowed was archaic. A word-for-word translation seemed futile; there were too many phrases he couldn't find exact translations for. After struggling through several pages that bore interesting accounts of Maren and Frederik's shipboard journey to America, the trip by train to Blooming Prairie, Minnesota, and the rigors of building a small shanty where they could live until there was time to make the house bigger and more modern, he felt like he was starting to get a feel for who Maren Jensen was.

He smiled with satisfaction when Maren referred to a man named Leif in response to Sophie's questions about a Herr Unterschlag. A hastily jotted note at the end of one of the letters, an added sentence that looked as though it had been dashed in haste just before the letter was sealed, was his first clue that Leif might be the one who had been in love with Maren.

If you can do so discreetly, Sophie, please send word of me to Leif. Oh, how I miss him!

Maren's perfect penmanship took a lopsided loop at his

name. Perhaps she had looked over her shoulder before she wrote his name to make sure no one was watching. Perhaps the depth of her emotion had made her hand shake ever so slightly as she penned the words.

Anders glanced down at his wristwatch before taking the next page from the leather briefcase he'd brought from home. He sensed no guilt or shame in Maren's tone; no need to defend her feelings for Leif or excuse her obvious frustration toward Frederik. The letters were descriptive, well written and passionate; her musings candid, honest, and unaffected.

He didn't have benefit of the letters Sophie had written to Maren, but it was obvious at times that Maren was attempting to answer questions posed by her cousin. The letters were lengthy—he could only suppose that Maren desperately needed someone to talk to. Separated from her family and friends not only by an ocean, but miles of virtual wilderness, alone in a new country, cooped up in a farmhouse distanced from both village and neighbors, Maren had been lonely.

Maren's image appeared in Anders' mind's eye as it had so many times that morning. Jensen had promised to send a photograph, and she had. Unfortunately, it hadn't been of her.

The photo was in sepia tones, taken in Danemark when Maren was a young woman, perhaps when she had finished her schooling. The barely tamed curls that framed Maren's face appeared to be soft and light in color. Jensen said she'd had Maren's blond locks as a child, but that they had straightened to light, reddish brown waves as she'd grown older.

Anders took the facsimile likeness of Maren's photo in his hands and brushed his thumbs across her cheeks. Her features were perfectly formed, with lush, full lips and a heart-shaped face lovely enough to melt the heart of any beau. Her dress was a wispy creation of organdy and hand-tatted lace. She wore a broach at the throat, from which a high lace collar rose to cover an inch of her neck, a long, gracefully tilted neck that beckoned to be touched. No surprise, given it was the only part of her body that was exposed. Soft pleats lined the bodice of the sheer-sleeved dress, and a deep waistband accentuated the swell of her breasts above a dainty waist (a feature Jensen claimed not to have inherited).

Anders gazed into her eyes and let the picture fill his whole frame of reference. Legend had not exaggerated Maren's beauty. With her image fresh in his mind, Anders could almost hear the longing in her voice as she described her life in the New World and lamented leaving the Old.

You should see them snuggled up on the sofa together, Sophie, Maren wrote. *Victoria's little head is framed in golden curls just like my first two babies.*

Mathilda is growing like a weed and looking more like her father every day—tall and slender as a reed like the Jensens. Such a serious little thing for age five. She loves to set the table, dry dishes, and sew on buttons. With another baby on the way and me feeling queasy at times, I do not know how I would manage without her!

"Mathilda, would you mind giving Victoria her bottle? I am trying to finish this letter to Sophie so I can send it with Mr. Jenkins when he comes to pick up the milk tomorrow morning."

"Yes, Momma," Mathilda said.

"Baby Victoria is lucky to have a big sister like you."

Frederik has been taking Karl to the fields with him, Maren wrote, *a blessing since I have been prone to morning sickness with this pregnancy. I worried that Fred would get little accomplished with Karl getting into mischief, but from what he tells me, Karl is no trouble. Fred is rarely around the house, and so stern-faced when he is, that I think Karl is frightened of him and thus amiss to do anything that might rile the man.*

As fate would have it, I believe Karl to have inherited my artistic inclinations, a potentially sad fate for the son of a dirt farmer. If we had stayed in Danemark I would have loved to send him in to Leif to learn the bakery business, assuming Frederik would have allowed it.

Anders made a notation beside the paraphrased script he was jotting to share with Jensen as he read. So Leif was a baker. He stroked his chin and let his eyes drift back to the letter.

Perhaps if the child I'm carrying is another son, one who shares his father's love of farming, Frederik might yet be persuaded to seek an apprenticeship for Karl when the time is right. (The new baby will be Wilfred if it is a boy and Agnes if it is a girl.) I'm confident there are tremendous opportunities for Karl here in America, perhaps even more than if we were still at home. Mercy me. Karl may even go on to the university or teacher's college! One can never predict what the future will hold, especially in this progressive time we live in.

Do you ever wonder, Sophie, what might have happened if a certain circumstance had happened differently, or not at all? I try not to get caught up in such musings. My life is what it is. I am truly blessed to have been given so much. Still, I cannot help thinking back on the events that precipitated our move.

I would never have met Leif in the first place if old Dame Schmidt had bore a child to take over the bakery. If Leif had spent his holiday in Sweden instead of coming to Copenhagen, he never would have seen the flier advertising the bakery for sale. If there had not been so many weddings that summer, Leif would never have sought an assistant to help bake the Danish wedding cakes... Oh, how different things might have been!

It breaks my heart to think of all that has transpired because of a few fateful decisions, most of which I had no part in. And yet, the thought I might never have met Leif... Sadly, that would have been the greater tragedy.

"Momma, Baby Victoria won't sit still."

"Come to Momma, little one." Maren set the letter aside and sprung to her feet. She put one arm around Mathilda and cradled the squirming Victoria in the crook of the other. "Do not fear, sweet barn, your moder is here." She smiled at Mathilda and spoke the words again in English, this time slowly, and with the best pronunciation she could manage.

She had tried to do as Frederik wished and speak the foreign tongue so the children would learn English, but Mathilda already knew far more words than she did, and more often than not translated for her when Mr. Jenkins came for the milk.

Mathilda's curls bobbed up and down as she nodded at her mother. "Very good, Momma."

Maren mussed her oldest daughter's hair and pulled her close for a quick hug. "If it weren't for your curls, I would think it was your father's face before me." Maren smiled brightly as Mathilda continued to look up at her, wide-eyed and solemn. "Your father has good reason to wear a serious face; three children to support and another on the way, a wife, a farm in need of clearing, cows in need of milking and a loan from the bank. But you, my sweet—you have no need to be so somber."

Mathilda seemed to understand that she was trying to make her smile, but evidently saw nothing humorous in their exchange. "I only want to learn my English well so I will get high marks in school, Momma."

"You will, Mathilda. You are a smart girl. But you must learn not to worry so. You must enjoy life, open your eyes to the beauty around you, and take pleasure in the mysteries of life. There is much more to life than doing what is expected of you and memorizing facts to recite back to your teacher."

The way Mathilda watched her, acting like she understood

every word she was saying, was a case in point. She might as well be talking to herself! But she couldn't stop. After months with only Frederik's droll humor and a houseful of babies to challenge her mind, she needed to remind herself what was important in life.

"Reciting memorized facts has its place, but you must also learn to think for yourself, to defend what you know to be right in your heart, and to express yourself creatively. You must remember to smile, and that the things you see along the side of the road you are traveling on are often more important than what you find once you have reached your destination. Learning to see beauty, and to process information so you may apply it to finding solutions to problems is more important than neatness and always having the correct answers. My mama called it following your instincts. Papa called it old-fashioned common sense."

"I miss Grandma and Grandpa Andersen."

Maren smiled. It was from her parents that she had learned to love art and beauty, gardening and cookery. And she didn't mean the meat and potatoes Frederik wanted every night for dinner, or the doubled up American sandwiches she packed in her husband's lunch pail for him to take to the field every morning.

"Ja. My mama taught me to make the prettiest smørrebrød in all of Danemark. Each one a work of art." Maren flushed with happiness at the memory of sitting with her mother in front of the hearth, chattering like magpies while they spread, cut, and decorated the delicate open-faced sandwiches.

"And butter cookies, Mama. Grandma made the prettiest Melting Moments. She showed me how to swirl the frosting just so." Mathilda pretended she held a butter knife in her right hand and a cookie in her left and demonstrated the lifting motions her Grandma had taught her. "And Danish wedding cakes! Leif said you make the best wedding cakes in all of Danemark." Mathilda's eyes sparkled with excitement.

Tears pooled in the corners of Maren's eyes. Leif had been

a part of Mathilda's life from the time she was tiny. He had held her daughter in his arms and rocked her to sleep on many an occasion. Her daughter loved the man as much as she did. Leif was the one person in the world who had never had any trouble getting Mathilda to smile.

Maren turned quickly before Mathilda noticed her tears, set the baby in her high chair, and busied herself with scrubbing potatoes. "When I was a little girl, Grandma and Grandpa took me to see many great castles and cathedrals. We went on holiday to the mainland and took the ferry to Sweden to attend the May Day festivals. We heard guest musicians playing the pipe organ at church and traveled to Tivoli to see the traveling minstrels perform their magic."

Maren dried her hands, leaned over baby Victoria, and gave her a quick kiss. "It is harder for me to teach you of history, art and music here in America." Maren sighed quietly. "There are no castles in Blooming Prairie. But there are streams in the meadow, rainbows, wildflowers, and a sky filled with fluffy white clouds."

"We can still make smørrebrød," Mathilda piped in.

"Yes, when the radishes and carrots are ready to dig, and the herbs we planted in the garden start to bloom, we can make all manner of lovely smørrebrød." Maren smiled reassuringly, as much for her benefit as Mathilda's. "Mama and I spent hours working together in the garden, planting and hoeing."

"And not just onions and potatoes," Mathilda filled in the words of the story she'd heard so many times she knew it by heart. "But roses and hollyhocks and sweet peas and coral bells and all kinds of pretty things that are not at all useful!"

Maren couldn't help giggling at that. She swirled Mathilda around the room, thrilled to see her daughter smiling at last. Baby Victoria gurgled and clapped her hands.

"My mama told me to read everything I could," she told her daughter. "Keep a journal. Jot down anything that strikes your fancy, makes you smile, or causes you to raise your eyebrows."

Mathilda raised one eyebrow and gave her mother a look.

"Ja! That is it!" Maren said. "Use your own words, my mother told me. You do not learn anything by copying exact phrases or sentences from the textbooks. Read. When you are done, close the book and take your journal to a quiet place."

"And use the mind the good Lord gave you. Let your imagination go wild!" Mathilda said, stumbling over her pronunciation just a little.

"Yes, my dear, you have memorized the story well." Maren doubted her daughter realized the irony of the fact that by being able to repeat her mother's tale back to her word for word; she had missed the whole moral of the story. Still, Maren had high hopes that if she told the story often enough, Mathilda might one day understand the meaning of her words.

"May I play with grandpa's button box, Momma?"

Maren smiled. She had spent hours playing with the bangles in her father's button box when she was a child; sorting the precious buttons by shape, size and color and arranging them in beautiful designs on her mother's mahogany side table. Her father, a tailor by trade, had collected extra buttons from the clothing of many people over the years, rich and poor, soldier and farmer, handmaiden and princess. There were buttons made of bone, smooth black glass, and mother of pearl. There were metal military buttons with dates long past etched into their tinny surfaces. There were shiny gold buttons cast with the shape of royal crests and rough-hewn buttons carved of wood or woven of leather. There were huge buttons from outerwear and dainty crystal buttons in every color of the rainbow that must certainly have adorned the gowns of princesses.

"Ja, my love. See if you can imagine what kind of garment the buttons were sewn on and who might have worn them." Maren, who had never needed to be urged to use her imagination, would happily have spent her every waking hour pursuing her fantasies. That same gift of intuition told her now that her daughter needed to be given the task of daydreaming, else she would never be able to give herself over to the sheer silliness of it.

Maren folded the pages of her letter and tucked them inside a small wooden box. "It is long past time I was building a fire in the cook stove and putting dinner on."

And time for me to get to work. Anders tucked his pen in his shirt pocket and hurriedly glanced at his wristwatch. He could hardly wait till morning when he could share his findings with Jensen.

10.

Anders woke with a start. His room was dark—not a sliver of light peeked through the slats of his blinds. He had slept for only a couple of hours, just an hour since the last time he'd awakened. His body ached for more sleep, yet he was wide-awake. He rolled out of bed gingerly, went to his computer, and started to type.

My dear Jensen. It is the middle of the night here in Danemark. I know you are not expecting to hear from me for a couple of hours. I was trying to sleep when I had the strangest sensation that something was wrong. The feeling was so intense I got out of bed and checked for smoke, made sure I'd turned the iron off, and looked to see that both of my doors were locked. I ignored my instincts and went back to bed for a time, but I continued to be awakened by thoughts of you. If you are there, please email me as soon as this arrives.

She was half a world away, living in a time frame that was out of synch with his, but thanks to the magic of the internet, she was at his side just seconds after he'd pressed send.

He reassured her that his bumps and bruises were healing just fine. Then it was her turn to talk about the beating her heart had taken. It took him only a few minutes to get her to tell him what was wrong.

The_Little_Mermaid: I've been trying to let it go, forget all the awful things Ed and I said to each other, but I can't.

Ugly_Duckling: You knew Ed was not right for you. It was a matter of time. You just forced his hand. You initiated the end.

The_Little_Mermaid: Part of me didn't want it to end. Part of me wanted to start over, to make our relationship better than it was, to move forward. Was that such an impossible dream?

Ugly_Duckling: It is hard for you to let go and move on. You are the kind of person who puts down deep roots, even when the soil is hard and rocky.

The_Little_Mermaid: You know me so well.

Ugly_Duckling: Bjorn told me an American saying one of his friends at work shared with him after he had had his heart stomped on: 'Burned and learned, not scarred and scared'.

The_Little_Mermaid: It sounds like good advice.

Ugly_Duckling: You have sampled life with this man. That doesn't mean it was meant to last forever. When a relationship ends, you have to take the good, forget the bad, and move on.

The_Little_Mermaid: I know what you're saying.

Ugly_Duckling: Each experience we have in life makes us richer and wiser.

He loosened his bathrobe and rubbed his fingers over the rough line of scabs that ran the length of his arm and down one leg. His bones and muscles screamed with residual pain from his near catastrophe.

Ugly_Duckling: I know from what you've told me that by dating this man you've learned much about what you want in life.

The_Little_Mermaid: But not how to get it.

He ignored her sarcasm and continued.

Ugly_Duckling: You've learned that you need deep mental affection. You've learned what is meaningful, how to communicate in all ways. You're a package, Jen, beautiful inside and out. You will meet someone who appreciates every facet of you.

The_Little_Mermaid: I'm honored that you think so, Anders.

Ugly_Duckling: You can be accepted and cared about, and be *you* all at the same time. The sun had climbed high while he typed. He was sitting in a pool of light that illuminated his desk, soothed his pain, and warmed him to the point of feeling flushed.

The_Little_Mermaid: Was it like this when your marriage ended?

His fingers fell in terse staccato strokes that belied only a fraction of the emotions he remembered as he typed. He was quick and concise in his description of the events that led to the downfall of his marriage.

Ugly_Duckling: Yes, my pride was hurt, but it was more than that. The thought of such a pompous ass raising Bjorn tortured me. I still don't understand how Benta could have betrayed our marriage vows with such a person.

Anders pulled at the waist of his robe until the belt un-cinched and the side panels slipped over the sides of his thighs to pool on the floor.

The_Little_Mermaid: How did you find out about the affair?

Ugly_Duckling: Something Bjorn said made me suspicious. When I confronted Benta, she did not lie to me. She asked for my forgiveness and I gave it. For a time, it seemed like everything might be fine. We worked hard to restore the lines of communication between us. I gave it my best.

Anders stopped typing and took a second to search for Boy_Wonder in the chat system. Benta might be many things, but she was also Bjorn's mother. Anders had no wish to air his opinions on certain matters in front of the boy. He continued to type only when he was sure his son was not logged on.

Ugly_Duckling: By that time Benta had learned to like the things Kirk could give her—the special attention she was shown when she was on his arm, the perks she was privy to by virtue of his being one of the rich and famous. Kirk is nothing if not cunning. He played to her vulnerabilities, plied her with every kind of luxurious invitation, and showered her with exotic gifts. He is a man who knows how to get what he wants.

The_Little_Mermaid: I'm so sorry, Anders.

Ugly_Duckling: All that mattered to me at that point was Bjorn. And for whatever reasons, Kirk did not want my boy. I felt much hate for the man. But for Bjorn's sake, I laid my adversarial instincts aside and walked away.

The_Little_Mermaid: I keep thinking about what you said earlier—that there are no wrong answers when it comes to my feelings. That's a sentiment I needed to hear, and one that you must take to heart as well.

He could almost see her sitting at her computer. Despite her brave words, he could tell she was feeling hurt and dejected— the biggest clue being that her usually gregarious chatter had been replaced with long silences. It was an awful feeling, being so far from her that he couldn't touch or hug her.

Ugly_Duckling: If I were there, I would take you in my arms, hold you. Will you let me do that for you, here, as best I can?

The_Little_Mermaid: I'm not sure what you mean.

Ugly_Duckling: I feel an intense urge to protect you, shelter you. What would you like me to do if I were there?

The_Little_Mermaid: If you were here, our actions would come naturally. We wouldn't talk about what to do; we would just do it.

Ugly_Duckling: You are right, of course. All we have here are our words. That is why I wish you to tell me how you are feeling, how your body is reacting, what you are thinking. It is the only way I can touch you.

He knew what he was asking was difficult, awkward. He took the initiative to create a private room and issue an invitation for her to follow him there, which, thankfully, she did.

The_Little_Mermaid: I can feel heat rushing to my face, so most likely I'm blushing. I feel vulnerable and a little scared. At the same time, I can't think of any reason not to tell you what I'm feeling. I mean, what could be safer than confiding in someone I've never met and probably never will? How can someone halfway across the world possibly hurt me?

Her words pierced his soul. But he understood that he must win her trust just as completely as if they were together.

Ugly_Duckling: If I were there with you, would you feel

comfortable letting me put my arms around you?

The_Little_Mermaid: I'd like to snuggle on the sofa, maybe fall asleep with my head on your chest. You seem so strong, and it would be nice to feel safe and warm and loved again.

Anders took a deep breath.

Ugly_Duckling: Then imagine me propped up on one elbow beside you, listening to your thoughts and watching your eyelashes flutter against your cheek.

The_Little_Mermaid: You have a way of chasing every trouble from my mind.

Ugly_Duckling: You make me feel good about me, Jensen.

The_Little_Mermaid: Ed called me 'Beautiful'. But I feel beautiful when I'm with you. I love the way you talk to me.

Ugly_Duckling: You are very real to me, Jensen.

The_Little_Mermaid: You make me feel relaxed, and so very drowsy that I can almost feel your caresses.

Ugly_Duckling: Then go to sleep, sweet angel. Go to sleep, my love.

The_Little_Mermaid: Did you see that last lazy yawn?

Ugly_Duckling: I love being with you, Jensen.

The_Little_Mermaid: Me too. You're a sweetheart, Anders.

He sighed.

Ugly_Duckling: You are beautiful. So desirable. So female. Close your eyes, love.

The_Little_Mermaid: Not too tight, or I won't be able to see your words.

Ugly_Duckling: You should sleep while you can. May I wake you with a kiss and hold you again later on?

The_Little_Mermaid: Yes. You too, I hope.

Ugly_Duckling: I'll try my best.

The_Little_Mermaid: Anders?

Ugly_Duckling: Yes?

The_Little_Mermaid: I can't believe you made me smile. Thank you.

Ugly_Duckling: Anytime, sweetheart.

Anders pulled his robe closed and switched off the light. He could only imagine what a fool this Ed must be. It infuriated him to witness what a year of the man's subtle disapproval and unappreciative manner had done to her. She didn't come close to realizing what a way she had about her.

He plumped his pillow to fit his neck, lay down and tucked his quilt around his shoulders, realizing that in all the time he and Jensen had talked, he'd never told her what he'd learned about Maren. "Ah, sweet Jensen." He said to the darkness. "If you and Maren are cut from the same cloth, and I believe you are, poor Leif never stood a chance." He flipped onto his back, resituated his quilt and stared up at the ceiling.

*****

Jensen woke up from her nap feeling gloriously alive. She could feel the delight of what it meant to be admired and respected in the tips of her breasts, warm and soft and full in the cocoon under her covers. She could feel it in the heated flush of her cheeks as they defied the chilly air enveloping her pillow. She could feel it in her thighs, relaxed enough to melt, tense enough to bounce. She was positively glowing.

She tried not to compare Ed to Anders. They were different men, with different strengths and gifts—Anders had the gift of self-awareness. His ability to communicate and relate his feelings outshone that of any man she had known. Ed was a man's man, a good provider and a caretaker. She'd lain in bed with Ed night after night longing for the kind of intimacy she felt toward Anders until she'd ceased to believe that men like Anders still existed, or ever had. She was no less surprised to find him than she would have been to see a knight in shining armor riding down the Cannon Valley bike trail. That didn't mean she didn't care for and appreciate Ed, or recognize his unique gifts just as much as she did Anders'. It just meant...

That was when she caught sight of the clock. In all the excitement she'd almost forgotten she was scheduled to teach a class at A Stitch in Time.

She brushed her teeth, threw on some clothes, and drove to Cannon Falls to make up for lost time. A few minutes later she was laying her notes on the counter at A Stitch in Time and unfolding the quilt she'd grabbed on the way out the door.

"You can spread your quilt over here, Jensen. Sorry I don't have a spot free on the wall. I didn't have time to drag out the ladder and rearrange like I'd planned to this morning."

"No problem. My morning was a little rushed as well." She was lucky that this was a repeat of a class she'd taught a month ago, and not a new topic. She wasn't in the mood to be winging anything today.

"We're so excited to have you here again." Mrs. Ryan took one end of the quilt and helped Jensen spread it over the fortress-like wall of fabric at the far end of the long, narrow room. A circle of small tables topped with sewing machines faced the area where they stood.

"We have a full house again. Your classes are always popular. I think half of these people tried to get into the last class and couldn't. They were delighted when the new flier came out announcing we were doing a repeat."

"The classes are a lot more fun the second time around." Jensen laid her notes and the handouts she'd prepared a month ago on the slightly larger table at the front of the room and tried to glance down at them as inconspicuously as she could.

Her stomach was rumbling by the time she'd finished her presentation, passed out the instructions and made sure each student was progressing on their project. A snack sufficed for the lunch she'd missed; soon after, the ladies settled down to chat and stitch. Jensen answered periodic questions and worked on her own quilt while the conversation took off around her in a tornadic whirl.

Their chatter touched on everything from one woman's neighbor's labor pains, another's frustrations with trying to train a puppy, and another still whose mother-in-law had Alzheimer's. Before long, topics were flittering back and forth without rhyme or reason, gathering momentum as they went.

Some had opinions or a suggestion or two; others simply listened or chuckled to themselves now and again while they worked.

"So, Jensen," Mrs. Ryan said, "What are you going to do when the weather changes and you can't ride your bike back and forth to your boyfriend's house in Red Wing anymore?"

The three or four ladies sitting closest to her chuckled.

"Actually, we're not seeing each other anymore."

"Oh." Mrs. Ryan's mouth pinched into a crease. "I'm sorry."

"Hey, Jensen," a woman from St. Paul spoke up. "I've got an adorable younger brother I'd love to set you up with. He's been divorced for a year now and he's finally ready to be back in a relationship. It's just so hard for him to meet anyone when he's working all the time. You two would make a great pair."

"Go for it, Jensen," the woman's friend piped up. "This guy is a hunk, and as sweet as they come. If I weren't married I'd be tempted to snatch him up for myself."

A round of knowing smiles flew around the circle of women, their heads only half bent over their sewing.

Jensen hated to dash their efforts at matchmaking, but she felt she had to set the record straight since they had brought it up. "To be honest, I'm seeing someone else." *Kind of.* They were doing something—even if just talking, it was much more meaningful than anything she and Ed had done.

"Well, that's wonderful!" Mrs. Ryan said. "Is he someone I know or isn't he from around here?"

Jensen looked down at her quilt to hide her reddening cheeks. "Um... Well, actually, he's from Copenhagen."

"Copenhagen as in Copenhagen, Denmark?" the lady with the adorable brother asked incredulously.

"How on earth did you meet him?" another queried.

She was more than slightly mortified to realize the room had grown quiet. She looked down at her quilt and mumbled, "We met on the internet. We were in the same chat room, we both had names from Hans Christian Anderson and he thought

I was Danish." Her voice trailed off. She felt herself blushing furiously.

The room was dead quiet.

One finally decided to speak her mind. "You didn't see *60 Minutes* last week, did you?"

"Or *48 Hours* last month," another chimed in, her voice filled with genuine concern.

"I don't watch a lot of TV," Jensen said.

"We just hate to see you get hurt, dear," one of the older women said kindly.

"I really don't think..." Jensen hated it when her voice faltered. "He seems wonderful." She glanced around the circle. They were all staring at her now. "What exactly did they say?"

"Of course, they always have the worst possible scenarios on *60 Minutes*," one said. "But the gist of it was that there's a whole new breed of con men that are using the internet to prey on unsuspecting women."

Jensen looked from worried face to worried face as the women shared what they knew.

"They target women from small towns or rural areas because they're naturally more trusting and naive," a woman wearing a quilted vest with bears and pine trees on the front added.

Jensen nodded helplessly.

"They claim to be good, Christian men with respectable jobs and money to spare. They do and say whatever it takes to gain your trust. The really crafty ones find out what's important to the lady they're pursuing so they can take advantage of her vulnerabilities by telling her exactly what she wants to hear.

"And being you've met them on the internet, there's no way to verify that what they're saying is true—or not."

"But what if what they're saying *is* true?" Jensen asked.

Ten pair of cynical eyes turned to her in unison. They shook their heads in barely feigned sympathy.

"That's the whole point. We friendly, church-going Midwesterners always want to believe the best of a person.

We're honest, so we assume everyone else is, too."

"That's why people like us are so easy to scam. That kind of out and out-lying is just inconceivable to us."

She couldn't believe that any of what they were saying applied to her and Anders. She busied herself with her quilt and hoped someone would change the subject.

A woman about her mother's age that Jensen recognized as a Mrs. Hughes from Cannon Falls cleared her throat and started to speak in a tone that brought an immediate hush to the circle. "My daughter would kill me if she knew I was sharing this, but I think it needs to be said, especially if it's going to keep someone else from getting hurt."

A friend who had accompanied her to the class patted her arm and nodded.

"My daughter had been divorced for ten years and hadn't dated anyone seriously in all that time."

"It's hard for a young gal to meet someone in these little towns," her friend added.

"So she went on the internet and signed up for a single's service. It wasn't long before men were emailing her, asking her to meet them online to chat, or worse yet, trying to get her to agree to an illicit rendezvous."

The ruddy complexioned woman set her quilting aside and continued to speak. "What the man Christine met did to her was nothing compared to the women they featured on *60 Minutes*. Her life was never in danger. All I can do is to say thank goodness she learned the truth before she got on that airplane to California and did something she'd always regret."

"What he did do was bad enough."

"He broke her heart, poor thing."

"She had no reason not to believe him."

"He lied to her?" Jensen asked, more in deference to the fact that the woman was obviously sincere than out of any fear that Anders was dishonest.

"Well, for starters, he made himself out to be quite a looker. Told her he was 6'2", blond, wealthy, thirty-six-years-old, and a surfer. He said he'd just gotten his computer and was trying it out for the first time that night. He told her he was not officially divorced, but that he'd been separated for almost a year after his wife ran off with a man she worked with and left him to care for his two young sons. Of course, he made his estranged wife out to be some sort of Jezebel and painted himself as the poor, put-upon hero."

"He even mailed her photos of his little boys. Cutest little towheads you've ever seen," her friend inserted.

"Of course, Christine's heart went out to him and his boys, not having children of her own and always having wanted them the way she did." Christine's mother sighed and wiped her eyes. "Christine thought he was the answer to her prayers. Of course it was less than ideal, being separated by so many miles, but she had his cell phone and work numbers, so she could call and leave a message whenever she needed to talk to him. Then he invited her out to California and offered to put her up in some swank hotel near Knott's Berry Farm; all but asked her to marry him. The whole thing seemed like a fairy tale romance to her after not having had a man in her life for so many years."

Jensen was starting to feel slightly nauseous. "How did she find out he was lying?"

"Well, some of it he confessed to her as time went by, I supposed figuring she'd find out soon enough since they were planning to meet in person. Oh, he played her like a fiddle. The poor girl was in love with him by that time, and he knew it. Of course, it would have made her look like she was pretty shallow if she rejected him just because he was fat, bald, and 5'7" instead of 6'2" and muscular."

"He counted on the fact that she was too nice to hold his little exaggerations of the truth against him," her friend added knowingly.

"Then it was fifty-one years old instead of thirty-six. Suddenly there were financial problems because he'd had a car accident and the other driver was suing. Of course she was a little worried, but what kind of a woman would she have been if she'd made a fuss about staying at the Motel 6 instead of the Marriott?"

The two women looked at each other. "Isn't that when he disappeared for a couple of days and told her he'd been hospitalized with some sort of heart problem?"

"I think you're right. Only God knows if that was the truth or just one more ploy to keep her from breaking things off with him. By that time he knew good and well that she wasn't the type of woman who would kick a man when he was down. What choice did she have but to stick with him?"

"Then he almost lost his job at Martin-Marietta because some sizzling hot love letter he sent to Christine not only went to her email but everyone he worked with whose last name began with H, including the big boss himself."

Jensen glanced around the room. The women were shaking their heads in unison.

"But the clincher was when Christine got a call from his wife. Come to find out the woman had been right there under the same roof with him, sharing his bed, cooking his meals and cleaning his house the whole time he'd been carrying on with Christine and telling her his sob stories about raising those sweet little boys by himself."

Mrs. Hughes' face was beet red by the time she'd reached her end of the story.

"The whole thing was an outrage."

"And not a thing illegal about what he did," her friend added with a disgusted tone.

"Happens every day, the authorities say."

"She's just lucky he didn't con her into loaning him money or investing in some get rich scheme and losing everything like those women and their families did on *60 Minutes*."

"If she'd gone out to meet him she could have ended up catching some disease or committing adultery without even knowing it," another of Jensen's students commented dryly.

"Who knows how many women he carried on with before he got caught?"

"His wife was a fountain of information about his goings on once she discovered Christine was just another innocent victim like herself. The poor woman found files and files of love letters and photographs on his computer once she gained access to his personal files. Seems he'd been quite the busy boy," Mrs. Hughes said, chagrin written all over her face.

"Poor Christine," said the woman in the quilted vest. "She must have been mortified."

"How humiliating," another said, shaking her head.

"And it all came about because of something so innocent," Mrs. Hughes finished. "Christine had just purchased some aquatic plants for the pond she installed in her back yard last year. That's why she happened to choose the nickname Waterlily. His online name was Froggy Pond. Christine thought it was a match made in heaven."

Jensen's head was swimming. She dared not try to defend herself or Anders in light of the mountain of evidence the women had presented. She simply couldn't believe the things they were saying could be true of Anders. She had no reason to think he was anything less than he claimed. She looked around the circle at the concerned faces encompassing the room. Then again, she had no proof that Anders was who he said he was.

She wanted to cry. Her feelings for Anders had intensified to the point that she couldn't bear to think about losing him. It was inconceivable to her that he would do anything to hurt her. Unfortunately, it would seem that Waterlily had felt the same way about her Froggy Pond as the Little Mermaid did about her Ugly Duckling. And look where it had gotten her.

11.

She went online and spoke to Anders as usual that night, but the words that had flown so fluidly between them felt as wooden as her fingers. Jensen blamed it on the fact that she was sleepy, Anders on another new rotation of freshmen air traffic controllers he'd just been assigned. Bottom line, she didn't trust him the way she had before her imagination had been filled with the dangers of the internet. For all she knew—and she felt like she knew nothing for sure—her subconscious mind was trying to make him slip up so she could catch him in a lie.

The_Little_Mermaid: It's hard to understand how a mother could walk away from her only child.

Ugly_Duckling: In retrospect, I'm thankful she did. I don't know what would have become of me if I'd lost Bjorn.

The_Little_Mermaid: You'd have become like Ed.

She'd typed the words without even thinking.

Ugly_Duckling: Ed?

The_Little_Mermaid: Ed has two children. He's been divorced for twenty years and hasn't seen his son or daughter in eighteen. He won't discuss them or try to make contact with them. I know. I made the mistake of encouraging him to try. He hardly spoke to me for days, and soon after, had a vasectomy.

Ugly_Duckling: Did he do this with your permission? Do you not want to be a mother? If you had stayed with him you would never have had a child.

The_Little_Mermaid: He knew I've always dreamed of having a baby. He didn't even discuss it with me.

Damn. He had a way of making her talk about the very thoughts and emotions she was determined not to. She was supposed to be prying the truth out of him, not vice versa.

Ugly_Duckling: You mentioned brothers. Maybe you will be an aunt someday.

The_Little_Mermaid: Maybe. I haven't totally given up on being a mother yet.

But she pretty much had. She'd been working through her disappointment by sewing a baby quilt. She didn't tell Anders. She'd revealed enough of her vulnerabilities without telling him she was making a receiving blanket for a child she'd never have.

Ugly_Duckling: And you shouldn't. Ever.

The_Little_Mermaid: Yesterday you said there would be no one to tend your parent's graves when you are gone. It breaks my heart to think how many of my family's traditions will end with me if I never have a child.

Ugly_Duckling: You must have loved this man very much if you were willing to give up so many dreams for him.

The_Little_Mermaid: But I wasn't willing. That's why I left. I wanted more and apparently, Ed was giving all he had to give.

She was talking to someone she'd probably never meet, someone who didn't know Ed from Adam, but she still felt guilty.

The_Little_Mermaid: Ed is a wonderful man in many ways. He's just asleep emotionally.

Oh, this was great. If Anders was lying, she'd just given him the green light. She'd as much as painted a decoy on her forehead. 'Hey, over here! Con me! I'm a pushover!'

Ugly_Duckling: Jensen, the fact that you are so eternally whimsical and sure that fairy tales come true is the very thing about you that makes you so wonderful.

The_Little_Mermaid: And dumb. What was I thinking? That all I'd have to do is kiss Ed and he'd wake up?

Ugly_Duckling: I don't know the man, but I think your love and optimism was wasted on Ed. It is a dangerous thing, turning off your emotions. Once a person does it, a part of them dies. I have known women and men over the years who have been hurt so deeply that something inside them just snapped.

The_Little_Mermaid: Losing his children must have been awful for Ed.

Ugly_Duckling: What probably started out as a conscious effort on his part to ensure he would never be vulnerable to that kind of pain again might well have manifested itself in an inability to love. It is a very fine line.

The_Little_Mermaid: Ed isn't very self-aware, or good at expressing himself, but he does have a good heart.

Ugly_Duckling: And good taste if he chose you.

Flattery. Did he mean it, or was he buttering her up so he could dupe her, bilk her of her money and her pride?

The_Little_Mermaid: I wonder if you and I would be able to talk this freely if we were face to face. Do you think our seeming ability to be honest with one another is really something special between us, or part of the fantasy that happens because this place isn't real?

Okay. So she'd thrown the bit about being honest in there to see if he started acting guilty.

Ugly_Duckling: I don't want to minimize that I think the way we talk to one another is very unique. I have rarely felt so at ease with a woman. And I do not feel at all compelled to defend your Ed. But I will urge you not to be too hard on him. No matter what country we're from or what cultural influences mold us, men are not taught to communicate like women are, especially when it comes to expressing their emotions.

The_Little_Mermaid: Then how did you get to be so good?

Ugly_Duckling: I am a counselor. I teach classes in stress management. I train people to counsel crash survivors, comfort grieving loved ones, and support traumatized aviation and rescue personnel after air disasters. Good communication is critical to what I do.

So he was a professional. He'd been trained to be emotionally supportive, to help people feel a desired way. A person with that kind of background, twisted just a little in the wrong direction, would be the consummate manipulator.

But he made her feel so cared for. How could that be a lie?

The_Little_Mermaid: You make me feel very appreciated. I know I'm a little different from the average person, and that Ed and my family have had to put up with a few idiosyncrasies over the years.

Ugly_Duckling: Do not ever let anyone accuse you of being average, Jensen.

The_Little_Mermaid: Ed and I are so different. When I was with him, it was almost as though I forgot to feel proud of who I am.

Ugly_Duckling: There's nothing wrong with asking for forgiveness when you make a mistake, but never apologize for who you are.

She looked around at the cozy quilts that encircled her bedroom. She'd always felt safe and comfortable with her life; confident in her own judgment. If Anders were lying, it would come as a shock to her.

Ugly_Duckling: Jensen, you are a beautiful woman on the inside, where it matters. I know it has only been a short time since we have met, but because of you, I am seeing things through a different set of perceptions. Forget Ed. Let me be real to you. I want to be your dream and your reality.

She started to shake when she read his words. She had to be right about him; he had to be real. He had to be speaking the truth. She couldn't bear it if he wasn't.

The_Little_Mermaid: Oh, Anders. I want to believe you.

Ugly_Duckling: I mean every word.

She tried to swallow and wiped a tear from her eye.

Ugly_Duckling: So what do you say, my little mermaid? We have the technology to send photographs across the pond. Let's be brave and exchange pictures.

The_Little_Mermaid: I'd like that.

Ugly_Duckling: You're getting sleepy, aren't you?

The_Little_Mermaid: How can you tell?

Ugly_Duckling: Your answers are getting shorter and shorter. And more agreeable.

The_Little_Mermaid: They are? ☺

Ugly_Duckling: You just agreed to scan a photo of yourself and send it to me.

The_Little_Mermaid: I did? ☺

Ugly_Duckling: You are not getting out of it that easily!

She laughed out loud even though she knew there was no one to hear. Her skepticism had only made her more confident that Anders was all he claimed to be. But it wasn't just that she was convinced he was being honest. It went far beyond that. It was as though he was the nameless man she'd made love to in her fantasies, the one she'd prayed God would send to her, the one she'd been looking for all these years, the one designed with her in mind. She didn't know how it could be, but in her heart, she knew that he was the one.

*****

Anders glanced down and tried to focus his eyes on the scribbled notes he had jotted alongside his outline. His students were role-playing in small groups, trying to perfect their skills in counseling survivors and loved ones after an air emergency. He moved from one group to another, nodding encouragement here, making a suggestion there, making note of which students seemed to have mastered the techniques and who needed more help.

Anders tried to clear his head, but the anvils pounding at his temples refused to give way to reasonable thought. Steeling himself against the pain, he flanked his grimace with a smile, thanked his students for their efforts and gave them an assignment to complete before their next session. His shoulders slumped uncharacteristically as he made his way to his desk.

Thank God the day was almost over. Anders loosened his tie and logged on to check his interoffice email one last time before he called it a day.

"Hey Anders, how goes it?" His buddy Erik poked his head around the corner of his office door and nodded a greeting.

Anders grunted.

His co-worker stepped around the corner and glanced at Anders' computer screen. "So you got the cartoon everyone has been passing around. Funny, ja?"

Anders glanced at the carton. A grotesquely obese man who

looked as though he hadn't shaved or bathed in weeks was sitting in front of a computer screen in his underwear. The caption in the first box said, "I work as a lifeguard on the weekends to keep my tan up. It's a nice switch from the hectic pace of the corporate office." The second box showed an unkempt old woman in ratty slippers and a threadbare housecoat, also sitting in front of a computer screen, saying, "I was a cheerleader for the Dallas Cowboys until a few weeks ago, but I had to give it up when I got hired as an airline stewardess."

Anders eyes were blazing as he turned to his friend. "Sad."

"So what's eating you?" Erik came right to the point.

"I met a woman on the internet."

"Oh, man." Erik grinned lecherously. "I didn't think you were into that stuff."

"I'm not."

"So you afraid she looks like the chick in the cartoon or why the gloomy expression?"

"I don't know what she looks like and I don't really care. It's not about that. What worries me is that I'm really starting to like her. A lot."

"And this is a bad thing because?"

"She's from Minnesota. A town on the Mississippi River."

"The way you feel about Americans? Oh, this is rich." Erik chuckled and slugged him in the arm.

"She may have been born in America, but her heritage is Danish." Anders stared listlessly at the cartoon on his screen, not really seeing it, or anything else.

Erik crossed his arms. "You really have it bad, don't you?"

Anders tried to think of a snazzy comeback, but couldn't.

"Don't let her get to you, man." Erik stood, closed the door, and faced Anders head on. "I know you didn't ask for my advice, but I'm going to interject a friendly piece of it anyway. I know you've been lonely since Bjorn left for Seattle, and I'm sure this woman is wonderful, but I can't see this relationship doing anything to enhance your reputation—I mean if word ever got out that you're doing the cybersex thing."

"We're not doing..."

Erik cut him off mid-sentence. "Whatever. There's been a lot of bad publicity on the whole internet gig lately."

"It's not like that," Anders said, crumpling back into his chair with the dead weight of a sack of soggy potting soil.

"Hey, I'm not saying I think any less of you, I just wouldn't be bragging about your little liaisons around the office." Erik gestured toward his computer. "Have you seen a photo of her?"

"No, but... "

"I've heard people clip photos out of magazines, scan them into their computers, and say it's them."

"She wouldn't do that. I know her."

"You think you know her. The reality is you know exactly what she chooses to tell you and that's it. If you haven't seen a photo of her, there's a reason why."

"It doesn't matter to me what she's like on the outside."

"Even if she looks like her?" Erik gestured to the figure on Anders' screen. "The cartoon pretty much says it all."

"Fine." Anders shut down his computer with a quick series of jabs. "I'll keep my private business to myself."

"Good idea." Erik said brightly, ignoring Anders' implication that he was overstepping his bounds.

Anders pounded his mouse on the side of his desk. "Damn thing keeps locking up on me."

"Don't do anything stupid," Erik said. "Make sure she's who she says she is. You've got too much to lose."

A sharp rap on the door interrupted them.

"You still here, Anders?"

"Come on in, Bob." Anders sprung to his feet and reached out to shake his supervisor's hand. Erik followed suit.

"I'm glad I caught you, Anders. You too, Erik."

The three men stood in a loose circle with their hands in their pockets, each rocking back and forth on their heels, their knees locked, elbows jutting out. Anders quickly deemed his shirt to be the more rumpled of the three and cursed himself for loosening his tie before he'd left the office.

Bob cut to the quick. "The wife is planning a little get together a week from this Sunday and asked me to invite the two of you." He looked at Erik. "Helle, too, of course. Uh, nothing fancy. Brunch in the backyard. We may putt a few balls around before the day is out."

"We'd love to attend," Erik said in a polished voice.

The pleats in Erik's pants were crisp and sharply pressed, the fabric wrinkle free. Anders had scuffed the toe of his left shoe on his bicycle pedal in his rush to get to work on time. The bike was one that Bjorn had ridden when he was going to college, and he wasn't used to it. Had he even combed his hair?

Erik smiled confidently, his every action accentuating Anders' discomfort. "Helle will want to know if she can bring something."

"No need. Sonja has everything planned."

Anders managed a smile.

"We've invited a new friend of Sonja's to come on Sunday as well. Someone she wants you to meet, Anders. Nice gal. Very pretty. Sonja thinks the world of her."

Anders couldn't have loosed his tongue from his teeth if his life had depended on it.

Erik punched his arm. "Now there's a deal, Anders. Sounds like Sonja thought of everything."

Bob and Erik chuckled in unison.

Anders nodded. "I'll mark the date on my calendar." He dragged his fingers through his hair, suddenly feeling more like eighty than his forty-five young years.

12.

You have not sent your picture yet.
Do not forget to send your picture! You promised!
I am still waiting.

Jensen's eyes scanned the last few emails she'd received from Anders, then settled on the new arrivals.

Aren't you just a little bit curious?

That was when she spied the paperclip. She held her breath and scrolled down. No need to panic. She hoped.

A wisp of blue delphiniums came into view first, then a close-up of a cabbage rose in full bloom. To her relief, there were no people in the picture—unless you counted the stone statue in the right-hand corner of Anders' garden.

Are you familiar with the expression 'Curiosity killed the cat'? She responded.

She wasn't sure why she hadn't just gotten it over with. Her latest excuse was that she wanted to do it while they were both online so she could actually hear his reaction. The fear that he might not like what he saw, that seeing her would somehow change the feeling of total and utter acceptance she felt from him, was something she hadn't felt ready to risk.

She added one more line before she pressed send. *I'll feel exactly the same about you no matter what you look like.*

She wasn't willing to let anything negatively impact the honesty and openness that was flourishing between them. Now that she'd recovered from the shock of finding out Anders was from Denmark, she was kind of enjoying the hazy perimeters of their trans-Atlantic relationship. No need to rush when it came to bridging the span. For the time being, it was pleasure enough to join their minds.

Her eyes latched onto a new email from Peder.

We finished the beans last night and have decided to let the corn dry out a little more before we start picking.

Tara would like to get some painting done while it's still warm enough to have the windows open. If you can get the rest of Gran's boxes sometime in the next few days (today or tomorrow would be even better), it would be a big help. We'll keep the trunks here until I have time to bring them over in the pick-up. Thanks, Your little bro.

She punched Peder's number into her cell phone. "There's no place else you can keep Gram's boxes?" She said without saying hello.

"There's always the dumpster."

"Do I have to call Mom?"

"That line may have worked when I was four and scared of getting spanked, but it's a little meaningless now that we're adults, don't you think?"

"Just put them back in the attic. The steps aren't that steep."

"No room at the inn. Tara's parents sold their house and moved into a condo last month. Different family, same story."

"What do you expect me to do—stack them in the middle of my living room?"

Which is exactly where they were eight long hours later. She grunted as she climbed up the step stool, her hands wrapped around one last box, and stacked it in the small space left between her and the ceiling.

She hadn't gotten to work on her quilt or read the latest of Anders' translated letters. Worse yet, she'd missed her bike ride, which she hated almost as much as having her living room half full of boxes.

She hadn't been in such a bad mood since she'd walked out of Ed's. The whole world had seemed different since she'd met Anders. Today made it clear nothing had really changed. She still missed her parents, she was still fighting with Peder, and she was still basically alone. The only thing that had really changed was that when she rode the Cannon Valley Bike Trail, she steered clear of Ed's street and the places they'd frequented—in this case, blessedly few.

For the first time since she'd met Anders, she felt intensely lonely. The two of them had settled into such a comfortable pattern—Anders going to bed early so they could spend her evenings—his mornings together while she rushed to finish her day's work before it was time to meet Anders on-line. Until now, she'd been having more fun with her new, imaginary boyfriend than she'd had with her old, real one.

After complaining for months about not having anyone to go places with, she'd been truly content with she and Anders' long distance relationship. Last Sunday, she'd gone to church, joined a group of couples about her age for coffee and brunch at a restaurant afterwards, and then gone to a matinee—alone. She hadn't felt a bit uncomfortable. In a way, it was easier going to activities by herself now than it had been to be there alone, knowing she was part of a couple whose partner wouldn't or didn't want to accompany her.

She jiggled a stack of boxes a little closer to the wall to make room for a chair. Maybe it was odd that she felt happier with Anders than she had with Ed. Friends who had been married for years claimed they had no trouble imagining it—all of the magic and romance, none of the disgusting realities. According to her friend, it was a no-brainer—endearing love letters or dirty toilets. Which would you choose?

Just yesterday, she'd gotten a letter from Anders saying, *Maren's letters are providing the perfect backdrop for getting to know both of you. I don't know who is more intriguing— Maren with her insightful word pictures, or you, with your complex reactions.*

Bottom line, Ed, her father, and her brothers just didn't "get" her. Anders made her feel intriguing, sensuous, and adored. They talked for hours, sometimes discussing the world and its woes, sometimes simply holding each other with their words. In the end, Anders' simple willingness to listen endeared him to her more than a million nights of lovemaking could have.

*****

Anders examined the last of the photographs he'd taken at Frederiksborg Castle and clicked open a program he would use to crop them before emailing them to Jensen and Bjorn. Bjorn had seen the castle dozens of times. Frederiksborg was only forty kilometers from their house and had been one of their favorite places to spend the day. This time, Anders had gone alone to hear a guest performer play the great Compenius organ. Not only had the music been superb, the gardens had been resplendent with color, the sunshine glorious as it shone off the moat.

The only thing that could have made it more perfect was to have had Jensen at his side. He smoldered with the desire to match her thoughts to her face, to show her how beautiful Danemark was in the flesh. He tried to content himself with the few intimacies that were within their power to enjoy. He had come to regard his computer as both cold and sterile and magical and miraculous, for it both brought him together and kept him apart from Jensen.

He tweaked the size and sharpness of another photo. Bjorn had teased him more than once about his camera. His excuse for taking it along was to capture the ever-changing scenery in case Bjorn grew homesick. He now had the added motivation of trying to convince Jensen of Danemark's desirability. But Bjorn was right—the camera was a kind of companion. He was perfectly at ease wandering about on his own as long as he had his telephoto lens to occupy his thoughts and keep his hands busy.

He replied to Jensen's latest email and chuckled, understanding now what Jensen meant when she talked about getting a "second wind". If the efforts she described were any indication of what she could accomplish late at night when she was already weary from a full day's work, it was no wonder that it took a dozen quilters to match the pace she set piecing the tops. Just knowing her had infused his attitude with passion.

He worked more intently by day and slept better by night. Superiors and co-workers who had worried about him since Bjorn moved to America took note of the invigorating spring to his step and wondered what or who was behind his sudden revitalization. Even his students chuckled with him over the never-ending supply of American expressions he was suddenly interjecting into his lessons, in his words, to "keep them on their toes."

He turned his attention back to the letter he was working on as soon as he'd sent the last of his photographs. Curled up under the lamplight in his favorite reading chair with the warmth from the fireplace stroking his legs, he could almost imagine that it was a sunny day in July in southern Minnesota.

I am sorry it has been so long since I have last written, Sophie. The days are full to the brim now that Frederik has started to put up hay. Farmers live by a predictable cycle here just as they do at home. I was reminiscing about the old country yesterday when I realized that Frederik's life has changed very little since we moved to America. Of course, a new herd of cows means new quirks to grow accustomed to. (He tells me every night how much he misses old Bessie). A different farm means locating new wet spots, accessing new types of soil, and learning about new weather patterns. But all in all, Frederik spends his days exactly the same way he did back in Danemark—outside from sunup to sundown, milking cows twice a day, and in between, never-ending work. We may have moved half way around the world, but a farmer is a farmer no matter where he plants himself.

My morning sickness has nearly passed, but I have grown large and cumbersome and cannot seem to muster enough energy to do anything except seeing to the girls and keeping supper warm until Frederik comes in from the fields. But the seasons go on for the husmoder just as they do for the farmer, and so I gather up my stubborn Danish will and put it to good use until all the work is done. Mathilda and I have been putting up strawberry jam and canning tomatoes. Even Victoria has learned to snap beans and shell peas. She has such fun helping that I see no reason to tell her that some consider the tasks work and not play.

When Frederik has all the hay in the barn, we will invite the neighbors over to make apple cider with the new press. I hope to have time to butcher before the baby comes so we will have mincemeat and rolapulsa this winter.

There was a little gap in the letter, a slight change of slant in Maren's handwriting that led Anders to believe she had left the letter for a time, then returned to it.

You asked how it happened that I befriended Leif when he first moved to Slangerup. Ironically, it was my husband who cooked his own goose in that department. I was pregnant with Victoria, but only my moder and Frederik knew. It had not been that long since Karl, so no one had guessed, thinking my belly was left from my first.

Leif had just purchased the village bakery and moved to town. He came from Sweden; no one knew quite why or how he came to settle in Danemark. He created a stir when he first came to town, but it was clear from the beginning that he was more taken with his bakery than with opportunities to socialize, preferring to keep to himself. Still, he had many a young woman swooning—no wonder, with hair the color of spun gold, robust, pink cheeks, and sun-washed eyes of blue.

As fate would have it, something must have caused a sudden increase in the population, for there were more marriageable daughters in town that year than I had ever known there to be—all of them planning spring or summer weddings. Ha! Maybe there was a particularly cold winter about sixteen years ago. Or a border skirmish that took the men away for a time before they returned, very happy to see their wives?

Leif was busy learning the business, modernizing his kitchen and changing an old storage room to the west of the display counter into an eating area where travelers and shoppers could have soup and smørrebrød when they were in town over the noontime meal. No wonder Leif was taken aback when advance orders for Danish wedding cakes started coming in droves.

Being Swedish, Leif did not have a clear concept of our specific traditions regarding the cakes, or a recipe of his own. As spring grew near and business continued to boom, Leif became convinced he needed help at the bakery.

Maren took a moment to resettle herself in the overstuffed chair she had situated just inside the parlor door. Not only was the seat cushion soft and the arms the perfect height upon which to perch her stationary, but she could see both the door to the bedroom where Victoria was napping and the kitchen table where Mathilda was drawing a picture for Karl, who was in his father's care in the field.

She smoothed the soft cotton of her dress over her bulging belly and waited for the now familiar kicks. Frederik was hoping for another son. It mattered not to her. Smiling contentedly, she turned back to her parchment and resumed writing.

Forgive me if I seem to speak highly of myself, Sophie, but upon completing his survey, Leif was compelled to approach me about making wedding cakes for his bakery. Of course I was flattered, that day he first drove out to the farm to discuss the possibilities with Frederik and I, but with Mathilda still so young, Karl still a babe, and another on the way, there was no possibility that I could accept employment in town.

Leif impressed both Frederik and I as an honorable man. We learned he was from a family of highly accomplished bakers. As the youngest of four sons, however, he was relegated to little else than forever washing dishes and minding the till.

My heart went out to him when he told us he had come to Copenhagen on holiday some weeks after losing his wife and what would have been their firstborn in childbirth. His voice quavered when he spoke of his family, whose well-meaning sympathies only served to continuously reopen the wound in his heart. His desire for a fresh start in new surroundings became a reality when he saw the placard advertising the bakery for sale in Slangerup.

As I listened to his tale, I found myself searching for a workable solution, truly wishing to give him every advantage in his new venture. Frederik suggested that I might make the cakes at home, at my leisure, so as not to slight my duties to my family. Leif was most appreciative of his offer, assuming the details and terms could be arranged to both of our satisfaction.

It was appealing to me to bake in the comfort of my own kitchen, using my own cook stove. The almond pastry and delicate sugarwork used for wedding cakes are so touchy!

Frederik agreed that he would deliver the cakes and other confections I might make at home to Leif's bakery in town on the agreed upon days. And so he did, transporting my creations promptly and with the utmost of care—until it was time to start mowing the hay. We had settled into a comfortable routine by then, Leif and I, working together when the need was there, and communicating through the notes that we sent back and forth with Frederik in the wagon.

Word spread quickly and Leif was soon famed for his pumpernickel, cardamom and onion cheese breads, even in the near-by villages of Lillerod and Lynge. He mastered the art of making Danish pastries, apple strudel, and almond kringle to perfection—crisp and flaky on the outside and melt-in-your-mouth moist on the inside. I rounded things out with Kransekage for all the weddings, Seven Sister's Butter Rings, and a host of little butter cookies like your mother's Melting Moments that Leif marketed in tins filled with an assortment of goodies he called Danish Delights.

As I said, all was well until Frederik started mowing the first cutting of hay. By that time, I was too far along for all the jouncing and jostling of frequent wagon rides to town, so there was no option but to end our arrangement—unless Leif were to come to the farm and get the baked goods himself.

I need not have worried. Leif was accommodating and gracious. He baked in the early hours of the morning, served lunch and adjusted his schedule to allow for the twice-weekly, afternoon trip to the farm. I told him he should not have to pay so much for my baking when he was being forced to drive so far to get it. He refused, said it was no trouble and offered to bring me the dry goods I needed on his next trip. I was so grateful that I invited him to join the children and I for dinner.

Our friendship grew from there. The children adored him. Mathilda, who still hides behind my skirts when her father comes in from the barn, took to climbing up into Leif's lap and asking him to read her a story. Karl lay in his arms and crooned the whole time I fluttered about.

Having a home-cooked meal was a great treat for Leif, who had been separated from his family for months by that time. He made such a fuss over the simple suppers I fixed for the children and myself. How can I say it? The way he complimented me on the baked goods I made for the bakery and expressed his appreciation for the simple things I did around the house made me feel like a person who is greatly valued.

One afternoon I decided I would teach him how to make the wedding cakes himself, knowing that there was at least one wedding planned for the time I would be laid up with the new baby. He resisted, preferring to convince me that no one, least of all him, could rival my expertise, but in the end he turned out to be a quick learner, and I showed him how to assemble the cakes from start to finish.

We started from scratch, making the pastilage and marzipan and piping the almond cake batter into eighteen rings in graduated sizes. We assembled the rings around a special bottle of wine I had been saving until after the baby was born. I showed him how to drizzle icing and make scallops on the top and sides of each ring to hold the tiers together. I did the eight-inch ring, being careful to handle it delicately. After I had placed the largest ring, he placed the next largest ring on top of mine while the icing was still soft, and we continued on, tier by tier, giggling like children while we worked. We were having great fun, dabbing the icing here and there on each tier to keep the rings from slipping, and arguing about how we would decorate the cake—with flags or marzipan medallions or candied sugar bells or fresh fruit from the garden—when Leif shocked me by grabbing the top ring of the cake and eating it in one quick gulp. I laughed so hard I cried! That alarmed the children, so we broke the next ring into pieces and fed it to them to pacify them. Before we knew it, the four of us had devoured the whole cake from top to bottom. We were having so much fun we didn't realize how late it had gotten until Frederik appeared and said it was too dark to work.

If it bothered Frederik to find us acting silly and talking a mile a minute, the children flecked with dabs of frosting and me with my hair falling down around my shoulders from laughing, he gave no indication. The next time Leif drove the wagon out from town Frederik was working in the field adjacent to the house. He could have joined us for dinner if he had wished. Leif's wagon was in clear view the whole time Frederik was traversing the field with the horses, raking up the hay into stacks.

Later that night, after Frederik had taken his bath, we spoke of the day's events. I told him what I had fixed for dinner and that Mathilda had asked Leif to read her the same storybook four times; worse yet that he would have complied had I not jumped in and rescued him by telling her she must help me dry the dishes. Frederik laughed, said Mathilda didn't get her persistence from strangers, and held me in his arms like he always does as he drifts off to sleep.

Maren was nearly ready to drift off to sleep herself when she heard a gut-wrenching shout.

13.

"Momma!" Mathilda shrieked. "Come quickly! It's Karl!"

Maren could hear Mathilda's voice fading as she raced back through the door and down the walk to the barnyard.

The letter flew forgotten to the floor. Maren jumped up from the chair as fast as her large girth would allow and made her way to the door. The sight that greeted her made her blood run cold.

Mathilda was halfway across the yard, her braids flying out from behind her head. Frederik, covered with sweat, dirt, and chaff from the fields, was running toward her with Karl hanging limply from his arms.

Maren clutched her stomach and collapsed against the doorframe. "Karl?" She cried, frantically grasping for her child, her hysteria rising with every second she waited.

"He's been stung." Frederik was just a few feet away from her now. Mathilda trailed behind, unable to keep up with his long legs. "A hornet. A wasp. I don't know. He was looking for four-leaf clovers." He looked at Maren, his face ashen, and spread Karl out on the quilt that topped their bed. "He was playing one minute, the next..." A sob escaped his lips as he loosened the button at the top of his son's shirt and stripped off his boots. "He is such a good boy."

Maren fell to the bed and brushed the hair from Karl's face. His face and neck were covered in hives. She could hear rasping noises coming from his chest. "Breathe slowly." She forced her voice to remain calm. "Just one little breath at a time, Karl," she crooned reassuringly.

"We unhooked the horse so one of the neighbors could go for the doctor."

"Ja. That is good." Maren forced herself to take a deep breath and exhaled slowly as another pain ripped through her abdomen. They were only a mile from town. *Please be in your office*, she prayed. "Did you hear that, honey? The doctor is on his way. We will take good care of you until he comes." She spoke to them in Danish now. She could feel the comforting words wrapping around her tongue like her own mother's arms. "Mathilda, will you get the cider vinegar and some cotton?" She rolled onto her side and tried to ignore the pain that clutched at her mid-section as she cradled her son in her arms. "Frederik, there's some plantain growing along the far side of the garden next to the rhubarb. I need some leaves crushed or chewed to make a poultice." She ran her fingers from Karl's hand to his shoulder, pressing gently with her fingertips. "Where did he get stung?"

His legs were swollen to twice their normally spindly size. His eyes looked large in his face, even though it, too, was puffy and red.

"He said his left ankle hurt."

"Go quickly," she begged him.

Frederik flew out the door, his long legs pumping like pistons. Karl's eyes followed his father; a mewing noise escaped his throat. He could not speak. Maren could see his poor little tongue was swollen.

A shudder passed through his ravaged little form. Maren pulled the edge of the quilt to cover him and stretched out beside him. She kissed his swollen cheeks and petted his hair, staying far enough from his face to make sure he had plenty of air. It was important that he not be scared. If she was going to lose her little boy, he was going to pass into the Father's arms feeling loved and safe and cared for with every fiber of his heart.

"Momma will take care of you, Karl. You are such a brave, strong boy. You will be fine."

Karl stared up at her, his eyes wide and emotionless. Mathilda handed her a cup of cider vinegar and some cotton, which she proceeded to daub over the bite and the hives on his face until the cotton was black with dust and chaff. She took another piece and continued to wipe him clean.

Karl tried to cough. She mustered the strength in her arms

to lift his upper torso until he was leaning against her arms; Mathilda propped up his back with pillows. "Climb up on the quilt with me, honey," she urged Mathilda. "Sit behind him like this and put your arms around him." She helped Mathilda hike up her dress and spread her legs in a V around her brother to support him from the rear. "If he is sick, we must not let him choke on the bile in his throat." Maren shifted her weight in a series of cumbersome movements until she felt the baby drifting back into a comfortable position inside her body. If there was ever a time she wished she was lithe and limber as a girl, this was it.

She was leaning toward Karl, a cider-dampened wad of cotton still clutched in her hand, when the pain struck again. Everything went black.

She awoke to the sound of Victoria sobbing, and the hushed tones of two men's voices conferring over the din. She tried to sit up. "Karl?"

"Lay down." Frederik stepped to her side and took her hand in his. "The doctor is here. Karl is going to be fine."

Maren fell back against the stack of pillows Mathilda had propped up for Karl a few minutes ago. Or had it been longer than that? She struggled to focus her eyes. Her memory was fuzzy and she felt an overwhelming sense of fatigue.

"Where is he?" She mumbled, unconvinced that they were telling her the truth. She groped the quilt on either side of her body. "Where is Karl?"

"Everything is fine, Maren. You must relax. The doctor has worries for our baby. You must lie still."

"But Karl?"

"He is right here in the rocking chair."

Maren turned her head and saw Karl in the chair, looking pale and blotchy, but otherwise fine. Mathilda was at her little brother's side, crouched beside the chair, petting his hair and caressing his cheek just as she'd seen her mother do.

Maren burst into tears. "Oh, Frederik. I was so scared. You are sure he will recover?"

Frederik translated her words from Danish to English, then repeated the doctor's response back to Maren, stumbling over a few of the words. "Karl will be fine. He has had an allergic reaction. He must be careful not to run into another hornet, ja?"

The doctor said a few words to Karl in English. Maren could see Karl's head bob up and down.

Frederik knew she would not be content until she heard every detail of the doctor's diagnosis. "The anaphylaxis is a severe allergic reaction that occurs when you are exposed to a substance that your body was sensitized to during a previous exposure. I told the doctor I did not know of a time when Karl had been stung before today, but it is possible he was. You cannot have an anaphylactic reaction to an insect's venom the first time you are stung. Karl will be in great danger if he is stung again."

Maren strained to look at Karl.

"The doctor asks me to tell you that you did well to ask for plantain and the vinegar, too. But if he is stung again, we must call the doctor very quickly."

Maren nodded and tried to keep her chin from quivering. "We will kill every hornet between here and Danemark if that is what we need to do to keep him safe."

The doctor seemed to comprehend the gist of what she was saying, waved his hand to let Frederik know he understood.

"You will take good care of the boy." He spoke directly to Maren, his shaggy eyebrows bent in consternation. "But now you must take care of yourself and your baby," he said sternly. "You will stay in bed for one week. I will examine you then to determine if you may get up or if you must continue to rest until the baby comes."

Frederik nodded seriously. "We feared you were starting your labor. The doctor believes it is much too soon. You must do what he says."

"But the children, and the hay."

"Our neighbor has gone to fetch his daughter. Anna Marie will stay with us until you are up and about. She is fourteen-years-old. Klaus says she is a good worker and a fine cook and has learned the English well. Mathilda will help her with the baby. It will be fine."

Maren's eyes filled with tears of frustration, of relief, of... she did not quite know what. She had not let herself cry in all the months since they had left Danemark. She had not cried when she said goodbye to her mother and father. She had not cried in all the weeks since she had seen Leif, or her cousin, Sophie. She had been strong, and brave, but now she needed to cry, and cry she did.

It was hours later when Mathilda fetched her letter from the parlor floor and brought it to her bed.

"Are you still sad, Momma?"

Maren smiled down at her oldest daughter, fingered the letter and let her thoughts return to Danemark for a precious few moments. "I am fine, sweet Tildy. I only wish I had my mother to kiss me and make it all better."

"Like you do to me." Mathilda reached up and cuddled her mother's face with her hand. "And Karl and Victoria."

"Yes. Sometimes we all need our mother."

"I miss Grandma, too. And Leif."

"Ja, Tildy. Me too."

She finished the letter while Anna Marie served the supper she'd prepared before Karl's accident.

Oh, Sophie. I am so sorry to send off such a disjointed letter. You must think we American Jensens rende rundt som skoldede grise all day long. Maren shook her head and smiled as she penned the words of the old Danish expression. Anna Marie had told her the English did not 'run around like scalded pigs, they 'bounced off the walls.' Whatever one chose to call her feeling of helplessness in the face of pandemonium, and whether they said the words in English or Danish, made little difference. Either set of words was an apt description of the last twenty-four hours of her life.

Karl is getting better already, she penned hurriedly. *He must stay in the house until Frederik is done churning up the hornet's nests in the hay fields. Anna Marie will look after him. I am assured I will be fine as long as I do what the doctor says. And since it appears that I will have plenty of time to catch up on my letter writing in the week to come, I will close for now to make sure my letter is posted and write you more in the week ahead. If you should happen to travel to Slangerup to see my mother, you may tell her of our adventures of late and mention that I will write her soon. With love, Maren*

*****

Jensen wiped her eyes, refolded Maren's letter and set it on her nightstand with the others she'd received from Anders. Jensen had never stopped to think about how her great-grandmother must have felt leaving her family behind when she traveled to America, knowing that it was unlikely she would ever see them again. Her heart ached for Maren, alone with her husband in a strange land, left to rely on strangers in times of trouble, with only an occasional letter that often took months to arrive.

She knew Maren's words would touch her mother's heart, too. But she couldn't tell them about the letters until she told them about Anders, and she wasn't ready to do that just yet.

She looked out the French doors to the dark night beyond. Her mother would be gratified to know how dearly Maren had loved her husband. And it was obvious she had, different as they'd been. Despite the friendship she'd shared with Leif, Maren had clearly relied on and appreciated Frederik's silent strength and consistent care on behalf of she and their children.

Maren's accounts of her great-grandfather Frederik reminded her of Ed. It was like she'd discovered a parallel universe where her practical and creative needs clashed just like they did in her own world. It made her shiver to think that Maren's letters might give her an insight or a realization that would alter the course of her own life. Maybe she was better off with someone like Ed. The fabric of her family's history would have been vastly different if Maren had refused to leave Denmark, and stayed with Leif. Or hadn't she had the option? How she wished she could have her Grandma Jensen back just long enough to ask her.

She hadn't spoken to Ed since the day they'd argued. She'd called his house once during the day when she knew he'd be at work and left a message on his machine about getting back the things she'd left at his house. She'd made sure her voice sounded pleasant, and let him know there was no hurry. She hadn't been surprised when Ed had followed suit and called her when he knew she'd probably be out riding, claiming that next week would be better for him, citing long hours at work and massive amounts of laundry needing to be done.

She'd since discovered she'd left one of her sketchbooks at Ed's. Unfortunately, she needed the graphs she'd done to begin a project whose deadline was sneaking up.

Ed answered the phone on the third ring, just as she'd known he would. Her "Hi" was greeted with silence. Which meant he was still angry.

"I'm sorry to bother you," she said, determined to finish what she'd finally had nerve enough to start, "but I need some of the things I left at your place, and wondered if I could stop by and get the stuff sometime this week."

"Whenever," Ed said. "You've still got a key, don't you?"

"Yes, but..." She felt no desire for another confrontation, especially not about keys, but the unresolved emotions dangling over the phone line felt like a noose around her neck. Somebody needed to say something.

"I thought for sure you'd bring up the article that was in the paper last week about the mountain lion that attacked and tried to eat a man while he was riding his bicycle down a country road in British Columbia," she said.

"What do you want me to say, Jensen? I could say I told you so, but I'm not one to gloat."

"Maybe the lion was hungry for fast food," she said, still hoping on some level that if she could only make him laugh, they could forget all the horrid things they'd said to each other and find a way to move forward.

"I obviously didn't find the article as amusing as you did," Ed said.

"I might think twice before I take another midnight ride along the river," she said.

"You can do or not do whatever you damn well please now that I'm not around to nag you," Ed replied.

She felt awful by the time they said their good-byes. The worst of it had been hearing the tension in his voice, knowing she was responsible, and that she could do nothing to comfort him. Not when she was the one who had hurt him.

14.

Jensen splashed down into a hot bathtub full of bubbles. It was almost time to meet Anders. He'd said he'd be waiting for her in a private chat room—a room that existed in thin air and was furnished only with their imaginations. She touched the shiny porcelain glaze coating her cast iron tub, which weighed a ton, and was as real as you could get, and tried to forget reality for a second.

The image of Peder and Tara stripping the quaint, old-fashioned wallpaper from the walls of her childhood sanctuary popped back into her head unwanted. She sank down into the tub, tried to relax, and wondered if Maren had loved bubble baths as much as she did. She liked to think she'd inherited much from her namesake. Although she suspected her great-grandmother would have thought the color of her tub more appropriate for a lady of the night than a Jensen. Six months ago, after several days at Ed's house had brought on an intense episode of color craving, she'd painted the outside of the bathtub raspberry rose and circled it with a bright teal, rose and navy wallpaper border with a peacock design. She'd found fabric that matched for the window above the tub and set a conglomeration of vases filled with shimmering peacock feathers mounted on low pedestals of varying heights to give the room an exotic, relaxing, other-worldly feel.

A haze of chilly air clashed with the steamy heat radiating from her bath water and hovered over the tub. Her windows were notoriously drafty and the night air had a definite nip to it. It was time to put her storm windows on and have the furnace inspected—tasks Ed had taken care of the past two autumns.

Jensen leaned back to rest her shoulders on the slanted back of the tub. Ed had probably told her if he had put anti-freeze in her car when he changed her oil and added windshield wiper fluid, but she wouldn't have considered the information important enough to remember since it had been assumed that

Ed would be around to remind her if the need ever arose.

She made a mental note to check the sticker on her car door, and sank back into the tub. Ed had stored all of her storm windows and snow shovels in the carriage house. Much as she dreaded it, she was going to have to brave the bats and do some winterizing before the month was out.

Relax. She looked up at the ceiling and imagined herself cavorting with Anders, somewhere far, far away from Peder and Tara's new exercise room. Which made her think about her stationary bike adapter. Last year, Ed had helped her wrestle her bike onto the trainer that allowed her to ride inside over the winter. Aligning the rear axle of her heavy Schwinn Cruiser with the frame's unwieldy lug nuts and tightening them until the bike was secure was a job that almost required four hands and a lot of patience. Her face settled into a frown. She hated having to worry about these things.

Determined to relax, she ran her palms over her breasts, sent a million, tiny, symbolic little droplets scattering, and sunk deeper into the water. The almond-scented oil she'd put in the water beaded on the tops of her breasts and made her hair cling to her shoulders in wavy tendrils. What she wouldn't give if Anders were near.

She felt a pang of longing as she sank deeper into the steamy abyss. There was something very reassuring about having someone nearby to help you take care of everyday tasks. For all his faults, she knew that Ed had truly enjoyed pampering her. She'd taken a lot about Ed for granted.

Deciding that trying to relax was pointless, she sat up in the tub and rinsed out her hair with the hand-held sprayer Ed had connected to her faucet with an ingenious metal device that prevented it from slipping off even when the water pressure was on at full blast. She yanked the chain attached to the stopper and rose from the water, spraying her breasts, her thighs and finally her toes. The water drained from the tub in a gurgling swirl of deflated bubbles as she swathed herself in a towel.

A few minutes later she was dressed in a cream-colored lace teddy that accentuated the last of a suntan she hadn't thought about all summer, but coveted now that it was cold outside. Satisfied that she looked her best, which was completely ridiculous under the circumstances, she wrapped her robe around her waist and smoothed the periwinkle blue chenille against her arms. The fabric was dotted with twinkling stars and the words Sweet Dreams.

She felt aglow with rosy cheeks and soft, just shaved legs, her thighs still flushed with heat from her bath. She looped her bare feet over the legs of her chair and tried to un-tense her shoulders. She had a clear image of Anders in her mind even though she'd yet to see his picture; broad shoulders, thick blond hair, his eyes heavy with slumber. She envisioned him stirring in his bed, his naked skin radiating heat like the sunshine in June.

"Wake up, my love," she whispered to her screen.

Within seconds, the room was filled with his presence. She could feel her heart thumping inside her chest. Sure, it defied reason; sure it was irrational, but her responses to him couldn't have been any more intense if he'd actually been in the room.

Her day was nearly over, his was just starting. She raised her hands to her keyboard and chose a soft blue hue for her words, one she thought must certainly be the color of a whisper.

The_Little_Mermaid: Good morning.

Ugly_Duckling: Godmorgen.

The_Little_Mermaid: Trying to teach me Danish again?

Ugly_Duckling: Is it working?

The_Little_Mermaid: Maybe a little.

Ugly_Duckling: If my students can learn English so well that it rolls off their tongues in an emergency, there's no reason you can't absorb Danish. It's in your blood.

She laughed out loud as she typed.

The_Little_Mermaid: I love the way your brain works. Speaking of, I appreciate the time you're spending on translating Maren's letters.

Ugly_Duckling: I may have been trying to be gallant when I first made the offer, but now I'm as tied into this as you are.

The_Little_Mermaid: We're close to finding out the truth. I can feel it

Ugly_Duckling: Some of the letters are so intense I can't put them down. Do you know what became of Karl, Jensen? He would have been your Grandma Victoria's older brother, correct?

The_Little_Mermaid: Yes. My great-uncle. I remember hearing of him, but he must have died before I was born or when I was young, which means Maren lost at least one child during her lifetime. I wish I could recall how, or when he died.

Ugly_Duckling: It must have broken her heart. I can't imagine what it would be like to lose Bjorn. Would your mother know what became of him?

The_Little_Mermaid: Yes, but suddenly asking about her Uncle Karl would make her suspicious. I haven't told her that we're translating the letters.

Or about you, she thought guiltily.

Ugly_Duckling: Will she not be excited when she finds out?

The_Little_Mermaid: Oh, yes. She'll think it's wonderful to know what happened after all these years.

Ugly_Duckling: You will love the letter I just finished. I will not spoil the surprise for you, but I will say that I slept like a baby when I was done. You'll understand once you read it.

Maybe. The image of Anders sleeping was far more interesting than anything Maren might have had to say. She felt her lips flow into the teasing smile Ed had claimed could melt his heart, then felt silly to think that she was wasting her wiles on no one.

The_Little_Mermaid: I'm envious that you slept so soundly. Judging from my bedcovers, I spent a lot of time thrashing around looking for someone to warm me up.

Ugly_Duckling: If I didn't know better I'd think you were flirting with me.

The_Little_Mermaid: You know nothing.

And everything, she thought.

Ugly_Duckling: There's nothing I'd love more than to find you cuddled up against me in the middle of the night.

Something stirred deep inside her.

The_Little_Mermaid: What a pair we'd make... you, a snuggler, and me, a light sleeper.

Ugly_Duckling: Even now, when I can't sleep, I dream of touching you. The more I get to know you, the lustier my thoughts become.

"I know," she whispered aloud as she typed, breathless with anticipation, her fingers tentatively caressing each key.

Ugly_Duckling: You give me such pleasure with your words, The thought of being with you in the flesh is extremely tantalizing.

The_Little_Mermaid: I feel the same.

Ugly_Duckling: If I were there I would take your face in my hands and kiss you, Jensen. A lingering, tender kiss.

Silly as it might seem, sitting alone in her room, she felt an undeniable flutter of feeling.

The_Little_Mermaid: If I were there, I'd gaze into your eyes and tell you how much you excite me.

Ugly_Duckling: I would snuggle you into a long, long hug that would not end for hours.

Her senses soared at the mere suggestion.

The_Little_Mermaid: I'd open the front of your robe and run my hands over your chest, up and down, from your belly to your shoulders.

Ugly_Duckling: Do you have any idea what you are doing to me?

The_Little_Mermaid: Tell me what my hands would feel if I slipped them inside your robe, Anders. Touch your hand to your chest and tell me what you feel.

She waited impatiently.

Ugly_Duckling: Hot. Toned. Smooth in some spots, crinkly with hair in others. My nipples have tightened up into two, rock hard beads that stand out from my pectorals.

"Yes." Her own were so hard they hurt, jutting against the lace of her teddy.

Ugly_Duckling: Another part of my anatomy is just as hard—hard and thick.

Thick. A simple word not normally associated with one's anatomy. His word. Their word. She would blush and think of him from that moment forward whenever she heard the word. Through thick and thin. Stir over medium heat until thick and creamy. Thick or thin crust on your pizza, ma'am? The context wouldn't matter. She would think of him, hard and thick with wanting her.

It wasn't long before she'd shed enough of her inhibitions to admit that she was wet from thinking about him. She wasn't teasing him. It was true. Her fingers flew over her keyboard, telling him what she would do to him if she were there, his candid responses spurring her on, emboldening her descriptions, and catapulting her higher and higher in her instinctive desire to give him pleasure and satisfy her need. Sensations raced through her body like a flame struck to dry brush. She tensed with need as the reverberations from his words swept over her.

His responses flew back in English phrases peppered with Danish endearments; grammar, sentence structure and reason were forgotten as their enjoyment intensified, their need to please each other grew more frenzied.

Ugly_Duckling: You have me so knotted up with emotion I can barely type. I can feel you, your heat, the actual sensation, when I read your words. Do you understand?

The_Little_Mermaid: I feel it, too.

Ugly_Duckling: I am stunned by the effect you have on me. You are ladylike and proper, and purely sensual and utterly beguiling all at once. If you are half as expressive a lover when using your body to communicate, as you are fluent in the ability to please me with your words, I am in awe.

The_Little_Mermaid: Ja, well, I guess what I lack in

aptitude for foreign languages, I make up for in other ways.

Licking, stroking, tasting, touching... the imagined sensations were so exquisitely real, her pleasure so vivid she could have sworn he was beside her, arms wrapped around her, the weight of his body pressing against hers, his hands caressing her.

The_Little_Mermaid: Oh, Anders.

She realized later that she had whimpered the words aloud, inexplicably overcome by emotion.

The_Little_Mermaid: I've never in my life felt so intimately connected with anyone.

Ugly_Duckling: You are so, so beautiful! I want to be able to look into your eyes and touch you. I am totally mesmerized by the energy you transmit with your words.

Her whole body was glowing; she could feel it from the crux of her thighs to the small of her back. Relaxing her shoulders, she fell limply into the cradle of her chair. She'd never imagined a person could feel so loved, so adored, so desirable, least of all by a person she'd never seen, met, or touched.

The_Little_Mermaid: You've touched a part of me no one else ever has. I can't even explain how that can be. All I know is that I feel utterly content. I know we can't be together in real life, yet you still make me complete.

Ugly_Duckling: Don't be so sure that I'm not real, Jensen. I would do almost anything to have you in the flesh, even momentarily.

Her heart skipped a beat.

The_Little_Mermaid: You have my heart, Anders.

Her reality changed in the space of a second. The bat flew directly at her, its two-foot long, dark brown wings sweeping perilously close to her face as it swooped over the top of her computer.

She shrieked. No one heard her scream except the bat, which circled for a second, heart-stopping loop. She clutched her bathrobe and tried to shield her face with a piece of paper she grabbed from the printer tray, alternately screaming and whimpering each time the bat circled to her corner of the room.

The bat was unfazed. She cowered helplessly as the dark, hair-covered rodent flew directly over her head.

"Help!" she sobbed, crouching lower still until she was trembling beneath her keyboard. She fumbled for her purse and found her cell phone with one hand, the other frozen with sheer terror over her head, still clutching the flimsy white paper. She couldn't get to either of the doors exiting her bedroom without walking directly into its path.

She autodialed Ed's number without thinking, keeping one eye on the bat. Her heart shaking like it was about to pound out of her chest.

"Hello?" Irritation registered first. Then alarm. It was after midnight. He would have been sleeping for over two hours.

Her teeth were chattering so hard she could hardly speak. "It's me, Ed. There's a bat in my room." It was all she had to say. He knew how terrified she was of the things.

"I'll be right there."

He hung up, and she was alone again. Her arm trembled with fatigue. She shrieked again as the bat's shadow slid between her head and the light. She couldn't stop shaking. How long had this thing been in her house? How had it gotten in? What if there were others? She gulped frantically to choke down the bile rising in her throat.

"Anders." It seemed like hours since she'd sat basking in his attentions. Only a few minutes had elapsed, but she knew he must be frantic with wondering what had become of her.

She tilted the piece of typing paper clutched in her fingers and tried to see the computer screen. The bat was flying in compact loops around the perimeters of her room, rising and dipping at intervals just low enough to keep her skin etched in goose bumps. If she'd been watching him outdoors, from a safe distance, she might have appreciated the grace with which the bat navigated such a confined space.

She arched her neck until she could see the screen. There

was no sign of the last line she'd typed. Anders had filled a whole screen with worried attempts to rouse her.

Ugly_Duckling: Just say something! Anything. Is something wrong?

She inched her free hand toward the keyboard, but the bat chose that moment to descend only inches from her desktop. She screamed involuntarily and tried again, watching the slimy wings out of the corner of her eye. Her fingers curled around the edge of her mouse pad, scudded against the keys, then jerked back in the nick of time as the bat swooped even lower.

The_Little_Mermaid: bsc,v

"Go away!" She screamed at the bat.

Ugly_Duckling: Okay, sweetheart. I know you're there. Can you tell me what's wrong?

She was ready by the bat's next orbit. She envisioned the placement of the keys just before the bat flew by, ducked up the second he'd passed, and punched in the letters.

The_Little_Mermaid: bat

Ugly_Duckling: Bat? Baseball bat? What do you mean? Did someone break into your house and hit you with a baseball bat? I have visions of you lying in a pool of blood, half-conscious. I don't know what to do. I can't stand feeling so helpless. I know something is wrong and I can't do a damn thing about it!

She wanted to cry, laugh, scream. Leave it to someone from Europe to assume she'd been the victim of a crime. Anders had to know that the exaggerated reports of violence in the United States were a sensationalistic ploy by the European media. Didn't he?

It seemed like hours had passed since she'd phoned Ed. It took almost as long to drive from Red Wing to Welch as it did to ride the same distance on bike—the road went the long way around the base of the hills instead of following the river valley like the bike trail did. Still, it seemed like he should have arrived by now.

She glanced at the bat, and shivered. Did they even have

bats in Denmark? They did in Transylvania, probably all of the old European castles. She raised her fingers once more, then ducked. The bat was getting braver and braver.

The_Little_Mermaid: fly

Her scream must have muffled Ed's arrival. Thank God he still had a key or she'd have had another broken window.

"Are you okay?"

"I'm in my bedroom. Please catch it before it gets out into the rest of the house. I'm afraid we'll never find it if it gets into the living room."

The curses Ed muttered about "no shortage of places to hide" was a thinly veiled comment on what he considered to be the enormous amount of clutter strewn about her house. She caught a glimpse of his face in the crack of the door leading in from the hallway. He didn't look happy.

"Do you have a tennis racket?"

"In the closet by the front door. At least I think that's where it is."

She could hear Ed grunt as he rummaged through her coats.

"I'm sorry I woke you up. I didn't know who else to call." Her thoughts drifted back to Anders. He might feel an instinctual urge to protect her, but there was no way he could. No way on earth.

She clutched her bathrobe shut around the front of her teddy. She was stiff and cold and still terrified, although it certainly helped knowing her savior was at hand. "Is it there?"

She heard a resounding crash, then a muffled explicative. "Where did all the boxes come from?"

"It seemed like it took forever for you to get here. I was so scared." She always rambled when she was wound up.

"I hit a deer."

She cringed at the hostility in his voice. "On the way over here? Oh, Ed."

"My insurance should cover everything but the deductible."

"Is the truck bad?"

His voice was stronger now. She looked up and saw that he

had opened the door. "He's a big sucker, isn't he?"

"The deer or the bat?" Jensen peeked out from under the desk. She could see the lower half of Ed's plaid flannel shirt weaving back and forth as he rocked in harmony with the bat, his hand gripped tightly around the handle of the tennis racket, waiting for his chance to strike.

"I meant the bat, but the deer was big, too. It took out the headlight, grill and bumper on my side and cracked the windshield when it bounced on top of the truck from the impact."

"Oh, I'm so sorry!"

"It's not your fault."

"You wouldn't have been out driving around in the middle of the night if it hadn't been for me."

The argument they'd had over her midnight bike ride flashed through her brain.

"It must be a big brown. You don't see them around much. Mostly the little guys."

She heard a mild thwack as the strings of the tennis racket sliced through the air and made contact with the bat. "Got it."

"Is it dead?"

"Dead or stunned. Do you have a trash bag?"

"In the kitchen." She could hear him walking away. "Ed?"

"Yah?"

"Maybe you should put something over it, just in case."

"It's not going to hurt you now."

She peeked around the corner of her desk and got a glimpse of what now looked like a wilted pile of wet leaves someone had tracked in from the garden. "I just want to be sure." She almost felt foolish to have been so afraid of the tiny pile of fur. Ed left for the kitchen.

She raised herself to her knees and started typing without reading what Anders had added since she'd last looked.

Ugly_Duckling: Sounds like you had a slight air traffic control problem there, Red Wing.

The_Little_Mermaid: Sure did, Copenhagen. A UFO now

confirmed to be a big brown bat. Give me a minute. Ed is here.

Ed reappeared with a paper sack from the Piggly Wiggly and scooped the bat into the bag with an old newspaper.

Jensen stood, cinched the belt of her robe, and looked at Ed appreciatively. "Thank you," she said with real sincerity.

"You should be able to sleep now." He stretched out his arm and handed her the tennis racket from where he stood. "You should probably keep this close by just in case."

"Do you think...?"

"No." He was quick to reassure her. "It probably came in in one of these boxes. But you should call a chimney sweep and have someone look over your chimney cap and those screens I attached to your roof to keep the pigeons from roosting last year. Sometimes a squirrel will loosen one up. Make sure you have them check the metal liner down inside your chimney, too. It was fine last time I checked it, but it may have rusted out with all the snow we had last year."

It seemed so final; Ed standing there like he was afraid he'd catch the plague if he came any nearer, recommending a professional repair service instead of offering to take a look at it when he got off work the next day.

"Thanks again. I don't know what I would have done if you hadn't come to my rescue."

"No problem." Ed looked at her and let his eyes slowly scan her before he settled in on her face. "Are you sure you'll be okay?"

"I'll be fine." At least she hoped she would be. If she'd ever needed a hug, it was now.

"Well, if you're sure." He shuffled his feet nervously. "Morning's going to come pretty early."

"I'm really sorry about all of this." She waved her arm as though to encompass the totality of her existence. "If it's going to hurt your truck to drive it, you can take my car."

"Thanks. There doesn't seem to be any damage to the axle."

"Okay then. Well, thanks again, Ed." The air between them

was as heavy as the fog that hugged the marshes along the Mississippi. "Thick as pea soup," her mother always used to say.

Her face started to turn red before the thought was even fully formed. She glanced at the computer.

"Well, I guess I'd better get going." Ed looked over his shoulder on his way out the door. "Don't forget to call the chimney sweep in the morning. This is the time of year when bats are looking for a nice warm place to spend the winter."

She rushed to the computer to reassure Anders that she was safe and well as soon as she'd locked the door behind Ed.

Having gone from sublime pleasure to stark terror in a matter of minutes had exhausted her. The irony of it was so acute it was painful. To have been loved so exquisitely by one man, and then, within seconds, been forced to turn to another for help.

It must have been hard on Anders, too, because he insisted on calling, something he'd never done before. He told her to get ready for bed first, but she couldn't bear the thought of being alone in the dark. She'd heard that bats fly toward light, so she compromised by leaving the hall light on and her door open a crack, just enough so she could see in the shadowy darkness. She truly doubted she would sleep a wink. Her whole body felt tense.

She was snuggled under the covers when the phone rang, her tennis racket gripped tightly in one hand.

Anders' voice was low and sultry, with only the slightest hint of an accent, his English as flawlessly spoken as it was typed. She felt instantly at ease, as comfortable as if she'd known him and his voice forever.

He spent the next hour calming her fears with his soothing endearments, hugging her with understanding expressions, and holding her with gentle words while she talked away her tension. His words kissed the lips she pressed to the phone as they said goodnight. It seemed that Anders always knew just what to say.

15.

When she finally crawled out of bed the next morning, her whole body was stiff from tension. Pulling on the robe she'd left at the foot of her bed, she took her tennis racket in hand and made her way to her computer.

Anders had had to rush off to work soon after they'd finished talking—sometime in the wee hours of her night—so she was surprised when the first thing to appear before her fatigue-weary eyes was a letter from Denmark.

> *My dear Jensen, if the world was a fair place, you would have awakened this morning with your best friend by your side, a kiss on your lips, a cup of hot chocolate served to you in bed, and quiet, intimate conversation to start your day. Unfortunately, I cannot do anything to bring that about. But I can tell you what I would do if I were there.*
>
> *In the fantasy world we shared last night, you were awakened to more love making very early this morning. You were held and kissed until you drifted back into a deep contented sleep. You awoke to warm sunshine streaming through your bedroom window and a note on the pillow next to you. You showered and worked for the rest of the morning. Early in the afternoon, flowers arrived with a note asking you to join me for dinner tonight. You were amazing and left me wanting more. Take care of you today, Jensen. XOXOXOX Anders*

Her heart swelled to twice its normal size.

She was glad no one was there to witness what she did next. Maybe she was a fool, but she needed to feel the reality of Anders' presence in whatever way was available to her—and she didn't have many options. She copied and pasted his letter into Word, changed the font to one that looked like handwriting, and printed it on a piece of parchment paper, which she laid on the pillow next to hers with a single pink rose from her garden.

She perched her tennis racket on the edge of her desk and went to her computer, keeping watch with one eye while she tried to dwell on the magical moments she'd spent with Anders before and after the bat had intruded. She told Anders how much she'd enjoyed hearing his voice and reassured him that she'd made it through the remainder of the night unscathed.

And then she took a moment to thank Ed. It was the least she could do when she'd woken him in the middle of the night; say nothing about the fact that he'd damaged his truck in his hurry to reach her. She knew Ed would never take money from her, but she felt like she had to do something to show her appreciation.

She was still edgy and taut as a guitar string ready to spring. To Anders' credit, she'd slept three or four hours. The rest of the night, she'd lain awake, imagining she'd heard (maybe she had) numerous flutters and squeaks. She'd lain with the covers pulled over her head, her heart pounding, imagining her attic was full of the creatures, hundreds of them hanging from the rafters, looking for the tiniest of holes to squeeze through, intent on invading her bedroom and extracting revenge.

She called chimney sweeps, roof repairmen and a man who specialized in caulking to implore them to come to her house the second they could free themselves. Night would soon come again, and with it, darkness, and the possibility of more bats.

The better part of the morning had passed and she was still in her teddy and robe because she was afraid to open her closet and find something to wear. She finally remembered some jeans and a sweatshirt she'd stored in a drawer, peered down the sleeves and legs, and dared to slide her arms and legs in.

She bumped the edge of a tissue she'd left on her desk and

jerked her hand back like she'd been bitten. Okay. Time to take a deep breath, unclench her hands, and stop being paranoid.

Again, Anders provided the perfect distraction—a second email, this one with an attachment. But instead of looking, she paced the room, her tennis racket cocked and ready to swing. The beauty of her relationship with Anders was that it was limited to their hearts. Their minds. Their souls. Limited, but freeing. She was free to be herself with him; free to say what she thought, free to let him glimpse the parts of her heart she'd never let anyone see.

Seeing each other opened a whole can of worms. Meryl Streep and Clint Eastwood had ruined the fanciful images of Francesca and Robert Kincaid she'd painted in her mind while reading *The Bridges of Madison County*. Kevin Costner was adorable, but she still wished she'd never gone to the movie version of *Message in a Bottle*.

What if she was repulsed by the way Anders looked? Or he, by her? What if the fantasy died once they came face to face? There was no need to be self-conscious with someone you'd never seen, no reason to feel intimidated or less than, no basis to feel ill-suited or not right for. Seeing Anders, for better or worse, could destroy everything she'd come to cherish about him.

She tried to imagine how she would feel if she'd sent him her photo. In the end, that settled it. She'd be waiting on pins and needles to hear what he thought. She couldn't leave him dangling when he'd been brave enough to send his picture. She needed to affirm him.

Her hand shook as she scrolled down and looked. A tingling sensation ran from her temples to her toes. She felt as though every molecule in her body had been rearranged, her universe at once eternally altered and permanently fused.

She knew him. It would sound crazy to anyone she might tell, and likely she wouldn't, unless one day to a child in the same fairy tale voice her Grandma Victoria had used to spur on her own belief in magic. Anders was the man she'd wished for since she first started to think about boys, the one she'd dreamed of holding in her arms when she was too young to know about heartache, the one whose picture she'd drawn when a teacher had asked the class to write and illustrate a fairy tale, the one she'd written about in Creative Writing class when she was sixteen and had longed to know what it felt like to be in love.

She trembled, thoughts of bats forgotten as she gazed into Anders' deep brown eyes and saw for the first time his blond hair, rugged jaw line, and broad shoulders. His legs were as tanned and shapely from riding bike as hers were. He was perfect for her. And he lived in Denmark. She typed a few approving words to Anders, then lifted her eyes, intent on having a little talk with God on the subject of latitude and longitude.

*****

Anders had been out of sorts ever since he'd talked to Jensen on the phone that morning. He'd loved hearing her voice, but he'd had an unsettled feeling ever since, and only in part because they'd talked so long he'd almost been late to work.

He wasn't quite sure what was bothering him. Jensen was the one that had lived through the trauma of having a bat fly out at her, not him. Sure, he'd been a little stressed out, first wondering what was wrong, then knowing and not being able to help. But he'd done everything he could, certainly more than she'd expected when he'd insisted on calling her.

Anders turned his back on his class and stretched out his arms, trying to rid himself of the malaise that had settled around him. Okay. So he'd admit it. It was Ed. He hated the thought that she'd had to call Ed to rescue her.

He didn't get a chance to check his email until his next break. Why he'd chosen to send his photo now, when he was in a bad mood already, he didn't know, but he was eager to find out if he'd met with her approval or if she really did think him an ugly duckling.

He sighed with relief when he read her words. But he was still peeved about Ed. He hated the thought that he'd let his anger diminish the joy of sharing his picture and seeing hers. The photo she'd sent was beautiful, but all he could think about was how small and vulnerable she looked, standing beside her favorite quilt. The slightly self-conscious way she held her shoulders, the hesitant curve of her smile, the look in her eyes—everything about her made him want to take her in his arms and never let her go. Which only intensified his desire to be with her in the flesh.

He wrote and expressed his approval as best he could. But in his heart, he knew this was a time when words were not enough. He needed, wanted to show her how he felt with a touch, a glance, a hug. The elegance of the words they shared, even in passion, was suddenly, irreparably insufficient. He didn't want to know what she was feeling. He wanted to feel her. He didn't want to hear that she was wet with desire for him, he wanted to feel it—not simply in his heart, but with his hands, his tongue, his cock.

His rational, responsible side said to get out while he could. Their relationship was a no-win situation. He would never move to America; she would never leave. He could not be content without her; he could not be content within the limitations of their current situation. He was caught in the most treacherous of traps.

*****

Jensen let out a yelp and pulled the broken tip of the sewing machine's needle from her finger. A bead of blood oozed up from her skin as she snipped the thread that connected her finger to the bobbin, then pulled the other end out of her finger. Ouch. She hadn't sewn over her own finger since 7th grade Home Ec class.

Everything had changed since they'd seen each other's photos. Anders was driving her crazy. She was all for the idea of communicating more effectively, but this was insane. Had he no idea how deep the ocean that separated them was? Evidently not, because he seemed to think he personally had power to circumvent every obstacle in their path.

He'd started by enlisting Bjorn and some buddies from Microsoft to introduce them to the latest technological advances in internet communications. He'd ordered a microphone and video cam for each of them and found programs that enabled them to talk computer to computer without paying long distance charges. He'd downloaded programs that let them see each other's image in the corner of their screens while they were chatting, and secured web access via video calls, instant messaging, and premium PC-to-phone forwarding. He'd mastered the art of recording music files so he could serenade her with his favorite songs. He'd spent hours getting complicated advice from Bjorn, reading help files, and tutoring her in the various devices he found to enhance their means of communicating.

It all added up to one thing in the end. He couldn't touch her and she couldn't touch him. Anders said his discoveries inspired him with hope that an internet relationship might actually lead to long-term fulfillment.

All she really wanted from Anders were the words he wove together with such poetic grace. But she smiled prettily at her video cam while they talked and pretended she enjoyed the crackling online phone conversations they attempted. She did like being serenaded and found the music Anders liked very pleasing. She loved seeing the photographs he'd taken of various points of interest around Denmark. But by the end of the week, she was starting to feel a familiar dissatisfaction. She was lonely for the simple conversations she'd shared with Anders when they first met. To put it bluntly, she felt she might have stayed at Ed's and watched television every night if she'd wanted a machine to rule their time together.

No matter how ingenious the premises behind the latest technological fads were, they were downright frustrating in her inexperienced hands. She didn't want to hurt Anders, but she finally lost it when he asked her to try some software that was supposed to create scents capable of being transferred online.

That was when he branched into finding and forwarding web sites with Danish-American themes. First, an online dictionary where all she had to do was punch in a word to find the Danish equivalent, next, a deluge of information on a Danish Immigrant Museum in Elk Horn, Iowa, Danish Yahoo, Explore Denmark, a Danish bakery in Solvang, California, and a page that listed Danish idioms with their American counterparts he thought she'd find interesting given the number of times they'd laughed over amusing American expressions.

Her favorite link had a sky cam looking out on Copenhagen and the North Sea. It was almost as good as being there. She'd liked the idea that she'd be able to see the sunrise or sunset where Anders lived, to know by sight whether it was raining or snowing, whether the traffic was dense or the fog, thick.

16.

Either the room was too damn small or his legs were too damn long. All Anders knew for sure was that he was tired of being holed up in front of his computer. His legs were cramped, his eyes strained, and his wrists stiff. He grabbed a sweater and strode out the patio door to his yard. The night was on the nippy side; the wind blowing off the North Sea was downright cold. Not a good night for a bike ride. He walked.

He was fine with the fact that Jensen was technologically challenged and uninterested in mastering her computer—those weren't her gifts. It was her love of colors that had attracted him to her, not her hi-tech savvy. He stepped down off the low curb with a little more momentum than he had intended and winced with pain.

Anders ignored the pinch in his ankle, shoved his hands in his pockets and lengthened his stride. Jensen might have been a little more appreciative of his efforts. Maybe she could live in some fantasy world, cut off from the reality of touch and taste and smell, but he could not. Knowing what she looked like only made it worse.

He rounded a corner and noticed for the first time that his neighbor's yard was newly landscaped. He hadn't even known they were working on it. He'd walked down these streets thousands of times to fetch Bjorn for supper, chat with a neighbor, or join a friend for a game of horseshoes in the back yard. These days he barely ventured out of his house except to go to work and come home again.

He gazed appreciatively at the small plot of land. Land in Danemark was at a premium, and his neighbors had designed and utilized each inch to its maximum potential. Danes were a resourceful bunch. Anders frowned. He'd been ignoring his garden and his house, which hadn't been dusted in a month. His work schedule was getting more and more demanding, and he'd hardly talked to Bjorn, their quick tutorials of the past week aside.

This was insane. There were plenty of productive things he could do with his time besides obsessing about the hopeless task of trying to turn a fantasy into reality. Worse yet, he'd very nearly ruined what basis of reality they did share. Jensen had tried to understand what he was attempting to accomplish and dispel the tension that had sprung up between them, but by the time they'd finished talking on Friday night she'd been downright vocal in her insistence that the next time they spoke they should set aside their attempts to understand the intricacies of the technological revolution and simply spend some time together.

He'd taken a lot of pleasure in the conversations they'd shared. But right now, he was sick of words.

*****

Maybe Anders' technological rampage was the reason she felt such a strong need to take a break from the computer and spend some time immersed in Maren's letters. She'd been itching to get back to them all week, but her time had been divvied up between chimney sweeps, roof repairmen, energy efficiency experts, trips to the dry cleaners and Anders. She'd hardly even touched her quilts.

A few minutes later she was sprawled on a blanket laid out on the lush carpet of grass in her back yard, tilting the letter she held in her hand to catch the full sweep of the sun. The leaves were almost gone, and sunshine was flooding her yard. It was one of those autumn days when the weather is so glorious that it's impossible to believe winter is almost upon you.

My dearest Sophie,
I have been flat on my back for three days now and am nearly fit to be tied. If it were winter, I might be content to snuggle in the warm cocoon of my bed for days on end, stitching on the little quilt I am making for the new baby and penning letters. But it is summertime

and I feel as though I should be making hay while the sun shines.

Anna Marie is a godsend, although I must admit it makes me weary to watch the speed at which she goes about her tasks. Was I really and truly that young and full of energy just a few short years ago? She is not even a decade younger than I. To think how my life has changed in these last ten years!

Oh, Sophie. I miss you so dearly. It would seem that little Karl's harrowing escapade has brought all my emotions to the surface. Perhaps it is just the pregnancy, but I have been missing you and my moder and papa and Leif so terribly that I can scarcely bear it. Frederik has done his best to be helpful and has been working in the fields closest to the house in case the labor pains should start again.

Why is it, Sophie, that with some people we can bare our hearts and souls without effort and receive the same in return, almost as though the whole exchange was pre-ordained, when with others, the bridge simply cannot be crossed?

I can remember how thrilled I was the first time I noticed Frederik smiling shyly at me from across the room. My heart thudded in my chest. He was very handsome, but I think it was his strength that drew me to him. No matter that we did little more than smile and blush at one another when we were in the same room. I had my moder and papa and grandma and grandpa and you to chatter to, all of us full of stories to tell and ideas to share.

I know you will not think less of me when I say what I am about to say, Sophie. When I met Frederik, my life was full and blessed with good fortune in every way but one. The only thing missing from the rich life I shared with my family and friends was romance. When Frederik came along, he was the icing on the cake. He made everything perfect—until the time came when Frederik and I married and moved out to the farm and I suddenly found myself alone with no one with whom I could tease or laugh or cry, no one to talk to, no one to fill the hollow spot in my heart.

The first year was the worst and the best. It seemed the only way my strong, silent husband knew how to communicate his love for me was with his body (and no, I do not mean what you are thinking, Sophie, at least not only that). Frederik may have had little to say, but he loved me with his whole body, from his tender eyes to his hardworking hands to his warm feet keeping my cold toes warm under the covers. (And everything that fell in between.) I have never doubted his love. It has been that way since the first time Frederik came courting. We said very little to one another, but when he helped me into my coat I found his touch to be so thrilling and intensely hot that I thought his fingers would burn a hole in my new Sunday coat. The sensation was so real that I imagined my moder would be angry because she would have to mend my coat after I had only worn it once.

Truth be known, I still love what happens between Frederik and me once we are under our quilt. Yet I lament, especially at times like these, that he cannot speak the words I long to hear, that Frederik cannot touch my soul the way he touches my body.

Jensen flipped over on her back and let the sun beat down on her. It both thrilled and distressed her to hear Maren's thoughts, to realize afresh that she and Maren were cut from the same cloth. Maren's feelings for Frederik were a case in point. It was all a little too close to home. Which reminded her that she needed to do something for Ed to thank him for rescuing her from the bat.

Food seemed the best way to express her gratitude. What

duct tape couldn't fix, food usually did. Ed's favorite meal was fried chicken with homemade biscuits and gravy, and apple pie made with real apples, not the kind that came in a can.

Her only regret as she took the cinnamon-scented pie out of the oven an hour or two later was that she hadn't made two. Maybe Ed would invite her to share a piece. She'd been a total recluse since she met Anders—a strong dose of the real world would probably do her good.

She packed the chicken in the bottom of the basket on her bicycle and topped it with two plastic containers, one filled with biscuits, the other with gravy. She tucked carrot and celery sticks bundled in Ziploc bags around the edges to make a solid surface on which to perch the pie, making sure the rim of the tin was securely inside the basket.

She dressed in blue jeans and low heeled, lace-up boots, a lavender, soft-to-the-touch, sweater, and a plum-colored, hooded jacket in case it got chilly, then set out on the bike trail.

She thought about calling ahead, but she knew Ed worked until three-thirty Saturday afternoons and was home by four. She timed her arrival for five to make sure he had time to shower, dress, check his email, and glance at the paper before she came. Ed's habit was to go to the kitchen and look for something to put on the grill as soon as he'd finished the paper. Her plan was to be there before he went to the bother of getting the coals ready, and home again by the time she was slated to meet Anders online.

It went without saying that he wouldn't be going out. Ed spent Saturday nights at home like he did every other evening. It had been less than a month since she'd been part of the schedule. So little time had passed that she could still recite the Saturday night television line-up by memory.

Riding her bike was pure pleasure, especially this time of year, when sadly, her days were numbered. Here there were no judgments asked or given, no need for approval or condemnation, no customers to please or disappoint, no expectations to adhere to. The only challenges were those she set for herself—to decrease the time it took her to get from point A to point B, to make it to the top of the hill without shifting down a gear, to feel her strength and flexibility grow and improve.

Her face was glistening with a thin sheen of sweat when she finally came to a halt in Ed's driveway. She glanced at her watch. Perfect timing. The food tucked in her basket should still be warm. She smiled, anticipating Ed's surprise. The thought of making him happy was a nice change after the guilt she'd been feeling over his wrecked truck and their wrecked relationship.

She rang the doorbell, removed her helmet, and eased the legs of her jeans down where they'd crept up. She stood at the door at least a minute longer than it should have taken Ed to get from the kitchen table where he always sat while he thumbed through the mail. She glanced at the garage. She could see the top of his pick-up cab through the windows on the garage door from her vantage point on the top step.

She rang the bell again. Maybe Ed had the television on so loud that he hadn't heard it the first time. Seconds later, the door gave way. A chagrinned looking Ed stood in the doorway dressed only in his bathrobe.

"I decided to surprise you with some of your favorite goodies as a thank you for rescuing me the other night. Everything is warm from the oven."

The fact that Ed looked so absolutely awkward was a mystery to her. It wasn't as if she'd never seen him in his robe.

"Sorry I didn't call first. I thought I'd catch you before you started dinner." She looked down just long enough to notice that Ed wasn't wearing any slippers. Hmm. That was odd.

Ed lowered his eyes and folded his arms across his chest. "My schedule is off. I didn't go to work today—had some shopping to do down at the mall in La Crosse."

Ed had driven all the way to Wisconsin to shop? Granted, it had been a beautiful day for a drive along the river, but the whole thing sounded so unlike him. What could he have possibly wanted from La Crosse that he couldn't have gotten in Red Wing?

She was staring at him, already slightly stupefied, when a second bathrobe-clad figure stepped out from behind Ed and slipped her arm around his waist.

"What's the matter, hon?" The woman tried to smooth the tousled red hair framing her face and looked from Ed to Jensen, seemingly unaware that there was cause for embarrassment.

Ed's eyes rolled back in his head.

"Uh, Jensen, this is Charlotte. Charlotte, Jensen."

"Oh. The one with the bat." Charlotte's face turned a tone just slightly less red than her hair. "Nice to meet you."

Jensen felt as though she'd been plunged feet first into the Mississippi in March. The one with the bat? That's what Ed had chosen to tell his new girlfriend about her? She fastened her eyes on the redhead and backed up a step. Charlotte was petite everywhere but her breasts, which were so huge her bathrobe barely closed. Oh, God.

"That's my bathrobe."

Ed gave her a disapproving look. "Jensen."

"Well it is," she said, starting to tremble. "How dare you?"

Ed grabbed her elbow and escorted her down the steps, his feet shrinking away from the stone-cold sidewalk.

"I'll be right back," he told Charlotte, who reluctantly shut the door behind them.

Ed glared at Jensen, propelling her away from the door with a none-too-gentle twist of her arm. "What did you expect me to do? Become a monk?"

"You took her to La Crosse?" Tears filled Jensen's eyes. "You took a Saturday off to go shopping?"

"The radiator in her car has a hole in it and she can't afford to get it fixed right now. She needed some things."

"Like a new bathrobe?"

"It was hanging on the hook in the closet. She must have grabbed it. I'll wash it as soon as she leaves."

"Burn it. Or maybe she'd like to keep it. She fills it out

much better than I do."

"Jensen." Ed clenched his jaw.

She turned and started toward her bike. "Excuse me if I take my apple pie and go." She batted away a tear with one hand and grabbed a handle bar with the other, her head held high in a fruitless attempt to salvage what pride she still had left.

"She means nothing to me, Jensen. You said yourself that when it's only physical it doesn't mean anything."

"I didn't say it didn't mean anything. I said it wasn't all there was. I said it wasn't enough."

"Nothing ever was when it came to you."

She glared at him a second and lopped her leg over the bar of her bicycle. "I was everything you'd ever wanted as long as I kept my mouth shut and my side of the bed warm."

"You know that's not true."

"You said you loved me."

"I do."

She put her foot on a pedal and prepared to shove off. "You have a funny way of showing it."

Ed cinched the belt of his robe with a yank. "Jensen!" She could still hear him yelling her name as she careened around the end of his driveway and pedaled down the street.

*****

Anders jabbed the sharp end of a trowel into the already loose dirt at the edge of his garden. The blade sunk into the soil with a satisfying thud. He repeated the exercise, thrusting and scooping with one hand and dropping bulbs into the hollows he'd created with the other. The shriveled brown bulbs would be beautiful come spring. Crimson tulips, blue hyacinth and yellow daffodils, ready to blossom at the first sign of warmth. He and Bjorn had planted bulbs every fall; a tradition Anders refused to give up even though Bjorn was not here to help him.

He stabbed the trowel through a clump of roots from the

summer geraniums he'd planted on the side of the garden wall. It had never been his intent to be dishonest with Jensen. He simply didn't know what rules of etiquette governed a relationship such as theirs. Was he expected to be faithful to a fantasy? Could he commit to a dream? He couldn't be accused of physically betraying someone he had never seen or touched, could he?

Anders straightened his back and stretched, his hand still clenching the trowel. His attempt to relieve the tension in his shoulders was unsuccessful. He muttered under his breath. He had no reason to feel guilty except that he'd known about the picnic at his boss's house for two weeks and had neglected to tell her that he would be at the picnic Sunday morning at the precise time he usually met her online.

Anders swiveled his neck as much as his taut muscles would allow. He would have told her about the picnic sooner had it been a real date. He stood back to survey his work, circling the yard, his footsteps terse and clipped. It wasn't like he was going to leave Jensen sitting at some bar thinking something had happened to him. They met when they could. He couldn't make it today. Just because they usually met in the morning shouldn't mean he was expected to be there every single day.

It wasn't like he had anything to hide. Why arouse suspicion over some ridiculous blind date that wouldn't amount to anything anyway? The chances that he would hit it off with this woman, or she with him, were one in a million. There was no reason to bother Jensen with the details of a date he hadn't asked for, didn't want, and had no intention of consummating with anything other than polite conversation.

He sent Jensen an email before he went to bed, briefly mentioning Bob and Sonja's picnic and his friends Erik and Helle. He even told her when he expected to be home in case she wanted to spend some time chatting after she'd awakened. Case closed.

17.

Jensen pumped her legs furiously and willed her bike to go faster with every ounce of strength she possessed. A car honked at her as she wove her way through the traffic. *Damn Saturday night tourists.* She scowled threateningly at the driver of a Mercedes Benz who was obviously a looky-loo, and a second later, narrowly avoided sideswiping a Dodge minivan full of children when she attempted to turn toward the bike trail.

She had never felt so humiliated. Sure, she'd talked to Anders about sex, but she hadn't done it. Ed had been in bed with Charlotte. She may have fantasized about touching her lips to Anders', but all she'd really shared with him were words and emotions. She may have wished he was there to share her bed, but he hadn't been. Bottom line, she and Anders had spent twice as much time talking about Ed than they had sex.

The fact that Ed had done what she never could have, even if an ocean hadn't separated her and Anders, filled her with bitterness. She wanted to weep. Had being inside the warm recesses of her body meant nothing to Ed? Had she meant so little to him? Had he forgotten her that quickly? Had she been that easy to replace?

Damn him! The wind snatched the curse from her lips as quickly as she uttered it. A simple phone call from Ed, telling her he was seeing someone else and asking when he could return the things she'd left at his house could have saved her a lot of embarrassment. But it wasn't just Ed's insensitivity that hurt. It was knowing that Charlotte had succeeded where she had failed.

Ed might not have feelings, but Jensen did, and she couldn't turn them on and off like a water faucet.

There was no stopping her once she was north of the heavily trafficked downtown area. She kept her mouth shut against the shower of bugs that pelted her face and breathed through her nose, her nostrils flared with angst as though they could somehow vent the frustration that raged in her midsection. Faster and faster she flew, instinctively dodging potholes and puddles, her eyes straining against the sharp wind and slanted rays of sunlight that penetrated the forest.

All she wanted was to be home, safe and sound in her own house, surrounded by the things that comforted her; a long hot soak in her bathtub, Maren's quilt wrapped around her, a piece of the homemade apple pie still tucked in her basket. And Anders. She wanted Anders. Anders always knew what to say.

Tears streamed down her cheeks, cheeks chapped from the wind, now pink with shame, cheeks that needed to be cupped by a tender hand to soothe the tears away. The only thing that kept her going was the thought of Anders' loving voice wrapped around her, Anders holding her until her hurts went away.

When she finally cleared the woods, the sun was shining almost parallel to the ground, hurrying on its way to the horizon. The last few blocks to her house were along the streets of Welch.

An eerie sensation slithered past her neck and down her back as she glided up to the walk in front of her house. The chill in the air was so sudden that Jensen looked to see if a cloud had blocked the sun before she realized she was standing in the shadow of her own house. The sun was cutting out earlier with every day that passed.

At least she hadn't handed over the pie before Miss Charlotte appeared. That was something. If she'd paid more attention to Anders' hands-free communication wizardry she could have eaten it while she was on the computer without worrying about greasy fingerprints.

She was lifting the pie from the basket when something in the window of her living room caught her eye. Tilting her head, she looked past the lacy shadows made by tree branches reflected in the glass and tried to see inside.

Her mouth opened. Something was different. She couldn't

quite place what it was. Her lips narrowed. The mini-blinds in the front parlor were down. In all the time she'd lived in her house, she could only think of two times she'd pulled the blinds. Once on her birthday, when her mother had given her a gift certificate for a massage from a masseuse with a portable table. Another, when she and Ed had been watching a sexy movie and things had gotten a little out of control.

Granted, she'd been a little tired ever since the whole bat episode, but she couldn't remember pulling down the blinds. The more she thought about it, the more she was sure that she hadn't.

The chill that had descended on her when she first pulled into the yard deepened with intensifying clarity. Someone was in, or had been in her house. She set the pie on the bottom step of the porch and backed slowly down the walk, flipping her freshly oiled, guaranteed-not-to-make-a-squeak-thanks-to-Ed kickstand up with her foot, and wheeling her bike back to the street. When she reached the row of lilac trees, she pulled the seat of her bike tightly against her, using the hedge as a shield. Scarcely breathing, she reached into her fanny pack, took out her cell phone, and dialed 911, keeping her eyes trained on the house and yard.

Welch was too small to have its own policeman. Her call went through to the Goodhue County Sheriff's office. The dispatcher said they would send an officer to check things out.

She waited in the trees for what seemed like forever, half-frozen, half-dazed, waiting and watching. She was reasonably sure no one was still in the house, and worried one minute about being thought a fool should there be no signs of forced entry when the deputy arrived, the next, about what a perpetrator might have done, or taken if someone had indeed been inside.

She thought about going to a neighbor's house, but it was dusk, and the lights weren't on in any of the houses in her block. The LaValley's were out of town. She pulled her hood up, looked at the pie on the front steps, and felt very alone. If ever she'd needed comfort food, it was now. She'd still had Ed to call when the bat got in the house. Now, she had no one.

*****

Anders stood in the entry to Bob and Sonja's kitchen, his frame filling the door from shoulder to shoulder. The morning light felt good on his back and the warmth from Sonja's kitchen just as wonderful on his face.

He smiled and took a deep breath. Occasional office politics and pressures notwithstanding, he'd learned to respect Bob. He'd worked with Erik for almost twenty years. The two of them had started out within a week of each other—two young, inexperienced air traffic controllers working their way up through the trenches. In later years they'd been a part of the team that redefined the industry, writing their own job descriptions at a pace dictated by a myriad of technological advances, increased air traffic, and the infrequent but tragic accidents that occasionally plagued the industry.

He would trust Erik with his life. He and Helle cared about him. They'd been there for him when Benta had run off with Kirk, and covered for him when he'd had to miss work to take care of Bjorn. He respected their judgment and had relied on their counsel more than once over the years. They were his friends. They wanted the best life had to offer for him.

Anders eyed Sonja's friend. She was leaning against the counter at right angles to the door where he stood, saying little, but following the conversation with her eyes, smiling up at whomever happened to be talking. Anders helped himself to another diet soda. The woman had a nonchalant grace about her that was very appealing, and she was certainly pretty enough if you liked long, dark, silky curls. Anders had never been one to go gaga over a dimple, or the long, shapely legs so many men were suckers for, but she did have a sweet smile, and the mid-calf length shorts and tight, scoop necked T-shirt she was wearing were certainly flattering. The way the lacey white cutwork of her blouse stood out against the deeply tanned tops of her breasts was stunning.

He was wondering if Jensen had a blouse like hers when she looked up and met his glance. *Great. Caught in the act of breast gazing.* He smiled. Her teeth were pearly white against the ruby lips that smiled back at him, her waist small and rimmed in a thin leather belt that matched her blouse. Her jacket and shorts were smartly tailored, a color that was a cross between his delphiniums and roses. He imagined Jensen would have several suitable ideas for naming the color—something whimsical like raspberry sherbet or pink champagne. He smiled and let his thoughts drift in the direction of Minnesota.

"Anders, if you wouldn't mind giving Laila a hand with the drinks, we'll move the party outside to the patio so we can enjoy a little of this sunshine."

Bob and Sonja disappeared around the corner, their hands full of covered dishes. Erik and Helle had gone outside a few minutes before with silverware, napkins and plates. Their voices wafted in from the yard.

Anders nodded at Laila. She certainly did have an exotic beauty about her. "Do you want the pitcher and the coffee server or the cups and glasses?"

Laila smiled up at him. He looked down, intending to meet her glance. His eyes honed in on her breasts again. He could feel his neck coloring as he pulled his head upright. "Why don't I take the tray with the cups and glasses? It looks like the heaviest of the two."

Laila simply smiled as she exited the kitchen.

Anders lagged behind just long to chide himself for responding to her flirtations. She had a subtlety about her that affected him more than a blatant come on would have. A sensual look, a smoldering glance... it had been a long while since Anders had participated in sexual flirtations, but her message was loud and clear.

"You get lost in there, Anders?" Erik asked in a voice just loud enough to get his attention. He turned to the others and laughed as Anders stepped out the door with the tray full of glassware. "And we trust this guy to direct the routes of million dollar aircraft."

Four pairs of eyes focused on Anders, their smiles kindly, but knowing. The men looked envious, the women, bemused. Laila had the good grace to start filling coffee cups.

Anders may not have been the most experienced person in the room when it came to modern day relationships, but his instincts told him Laila would be a willing partner if he chose to fulfill the desires he'd had on hold for so many years.

He felt a momentary pang of guilt, which quickly dissipated. This whole situation was Jensen's fault. She'd awakened a raging beast. Her little notes and teasing words had heightened his sexual awareness to all but unbearable levels. He didn't know whether to thank her or curse her for waking him from the boring malice he'd settled into over the years, but if anything did happen with Laila, Jensen was to blame.

Laila was beautiful, available, obviously willing, and so close he could smell her. He thought of Jensen, thousands of miles away. Would they ever meet? Would he ever be more to her than a voice in the night? He shifted uncomfortably in his seat and looked up to find Laila smiling up at him, a cup of freshly poured coffee in her outstretched hands.

Anders winced and forced a smile. He was damned if he did and damned if he didn't.

*****

Jensen looked around the disheveled mess that used to be her parlor and tried to hold back her tears. She'd already humiliated herself once that day when she'd cried in front of Ed. She didn't want to add insult to injury by crying in front of the sheriff.

The heavyset deputy wheezed as he hammered a piece of plywood over the broken panes in her kitchen window. "You'll want to call someone first thing in the morning about this window. I got it up there best I could, but it's definitely not tight enough to keep the mosquitoes out. Or the bats for that matter." The sheriff stood back, pushed his hat back on his forehead and surveyed his work. "Not very secure either."

Jensen shot him a cynical look.

"By golly," he said. "If they want in, they'll find a way."

"Maybe we could stuff a couple of towels behind the plywood to make it a little tighter." Jensen suggested. It went without saying she wasn't looking to repeat her experience with a bat.

He looked at her warily, as though he still expected her to become hysterical, and tugged on the bottom of his shirt. "You sure there's no one I can call for you?"

Jensen shook her head. Her parents were too far away and her brothers, too busy milking cows and tending to their own troubles to be bothered with hers. It wasn't like someone had died. They'd think she was a big baby if she called them over something so trivial.

The deputy chomped down on a fresh wad of gum. "I can call over to the bed and breakfast in Cannon Falls to see if they have a room open if you're uneasy about spending the night here. Looks like it's going to take a lot of elbow grease to get this place put back together."

Her bottom lip quivered. Yes, she was afraid. Afraid to stay, afraid to go, afraid to be alone. "Shouldn't I be here in case they come back?"

The sheriff gave a condescending snort. "Believe me, miss, you don't wanna be here if they come back. A cell phone ain't much protection against some strung-out junkie."

Jensen sucked in her breath and tried to swallow the lump in her throat.

He held up his hand as if to ward off her impending panic. "It could have been kids, but I doubt it. My guess is they were looking for cash. Drug money's what we usually figure. There's been a rash of this type of incident in every small town between here and the Cities ever since all that hype about the new millennium. Damn fanatics said the city people would head out to the country to steal and loot when the power grid collapsed. Everything would have been fine if they hadn't of gone and planted the idea in the head of every scumbag between here and the Cities."

Jensen looked out the window at the black night. "What if I scared them away before they got everything they wanted? They didn't get my computer. Won't they come back?"

The officer puffed out his chest, clearly proud of his expertise in the matter, and strutted to the other side of the room, stepping over a pile of broken pottery pieces and a now filthy fern that had been inside the planter. "I can't believe they'd be stupid enough to come back. Especially not at night when there are neighbors around. Seems they were running a little behind schedule as it was, hitting your place so late in the afternoon. There ain't hardly nobody around in these little bedroom communities during the day when people are at work. By golly, they got it all figured out, too. Small town with no police equals easy pickings."

Jensen felt, and probably looked, like she'd been run over by a truck.

"You sure you're okay?" He asked her again.

She wanted to scream. She'd always been independent. That came with the territory. But she'd also grown to rely on Ed to handle certain things over the many months they'd been together. She'd felt safe with him. It was damn ironic that she couldn't think of one single time she'd actually needed Ed's protection in all the months they'd dated.

Jensen picked up the broken ends of the wires that had connected her telephone lines to her computer modem and phone. "I'll be fine," she said resolutely.

Her entire house looked like a tornado had hit it. The contents of her file cabinet, dresser drawers, and closets were thrown around the room. The floor was covered with trash and debris. Her stereo, television, VCR/DVD player, CD player, scanner, and microwave were gone. The thieves had stolen some jewelry, her credit cards, and a little over a hundred dollars from her purse.

"Better call your bank before you do anything else," the deputy reminded her as she signed the police report.

"I will," Jensen said, her eyes feeling dull with stress.

She retrieved the fried chicken and apple pie before she locked the door, then used her cell phone to dial her bank, credit card companies, and insurance agent. The evening was close to being gone when she finally crawled under the covers, still dressed in the same clothes she'd worn to Ed's hours earlier. The night was still warm, but she felt too vulnerable to be naked.

Jensen lay back on a pile of pillows, balanced a dish of apple pie on her nightstand and picked up the piece of paper on which she'd written Anders' phone number. It was barely daylight in Denmark. She hated to wake Anders up, and she felt so tired she could barely hold her head up. She fingered her cell phone, trying not to worry about how much the roaming charges on an international call might be, and came to the conclusion she should doze a little before she phoned.

She woke with a start a few hours later, feeling foolish for having fallen sound asleep when she'd only intended to nap. It didn't take long for the events of earlier that evening to re-assault her memory. Every light in the house was on. She was fully dressed, and had a wicked crick in her neck. The contents of her house were just as disheveled as they had been when she fell asleep.

Jensen lay still and listened to the sounds of her house—the refrigerator coming on, a car driving by—until she was sure she was still alone.

She looked around the room. Thank goodness they hadn't taken any of her quilts, especially not the wedding ring Maren had made. The papers on her nightstand and most of her personal items were intact as well. She continued to survey her belongings with a vague detachment while she dialed Copenhagen and waited for Anders to pick up the phone.

The telephone rang and rang. Maybe he was in the shower. She dialed again a few minutes later. With her modem disconnected, she had no way to retrieve her email or contact Anders online until Monday morning when she could get someone to repair the telephone wire. She redialed. So much time had slipped by in all the commotion that it was past the time when they normally met online. Surely he wouldn't have given up on her that easily. She wracked her brains, trying to remember if he'd mentioned anything about having to go into work early, then remembered it was Sunday morning in Denmark.

She tried again and again. When she still wasn't able to reach him, she climbed out of bed, slipped on her slippers and padded in to look at her bathtub. The top half of the room looked as serene and inviting as it always did. The bottom half, including the porcelain interiors of the sink and bathtub, were littered with the contents of her medicine chest and a million tiny shards from a vase that had held peacock feathers.

She found a bottle of disinfectant and sprayed the few clear surfaces she found in the bathroom, brushed her teeth and climbed back into bed. She simply did not have the energy to start putting her house back together. Dialing Anders again seemed like an exercise in futility, but she continued to try, too dazed to work, too scared to sleep.

A piece of paper poking out from under the dust ruffle caught her eye as she was putting the cell phone down—the letter from Maren she'd left half-finished hours earlier, before she'd had the inane idea to fix Ed dinner. Jensen picked up the papers and held them clenched in her hand. She didn't know if she should even try to read the rest of the letter in her present state of mind.

*****

Anders looked up at the sky and hoped Jensen had looked at the sky cam of Copenhagen before she went to bed. If she had, she'd seen what a picture-perfect afternoon it was.

He scooted his stool a little closer to the lawn chair where Laila was reclining. He'd spent the morning trying to keep his distance, but it was too cool in the shade and he felt compelled to enjoy as much sunshine as he could before winter's rainy days and foggy nights descended.

"The sun feels so glorious," Laila purred in a sensual voice. "You look like you spend a lot of time outdoors."

Anders could feel her eyes searing a path up his legs. He cleared his throat, leaned back, and crossed both his arms and his ankles. "I ride my bike to work and do some gardening in my spare time."

"I lounge by the pool." Laila smiled and slid her fingertips from her neck to her breasts. Her dimple twinkled beguilingly as she sought out his eyes, silently compelling him to meet her glance. "Bob says you've been under a lot of stress since the new owners took over at work. I'm sure it feels good to get out on your bike and work off some of the tension."

Anders tried to look away from the rounded swells peering out from the top of her blouse. "We've spent a lot of time updating our training curriculum. I'm convinced what we're doing will make the airways substantially safer. Of course, we're also trying to prove ourselves indispensable so we don't get fired."

Laila tilted her head and smiled. "It sounds very intriguing. Tell me more."

It had been a long time since anyone acted so eager to hear what he had to say. Except for Jensen of course. He lifted his chin as if to defend himself against the pang of guilt that washed over him. "It's nothing that hasn't already been done in a number of other countries. British Airways was the first to install computers in their whole fleet. They've had such amazing results that the rest of the world is starting to take notice."

"Bob mentioned that it utilizes the same software they use to simulate flight training exercises for new pilots."

Anders nodded and kept his eyes trained straight ahead.

"Exactly. The same technology with a different application. This software will record each and every turn, bank, and adjustment a pilot makes during his flight as well as recording the takeoff and landing sequence for analysis by independent examiners."

She raised an eyebrow. "Sounds a little like big brother. What does the pilot's union think of this new practice?"

"They're less than thrilled. I believe it's a matter of the bigger good being more important than the rights of a few," Anders said. "We've been analyzing this kind of data for years, but only after a crash landing or problem has occurred. Doing it as a preventative measure should help us identify mechanical troubles or pilot errors before they cause a problem."

Laila tilted her head to expose a little more of her long, svelte neck. "And you train people to analyze the data?"

"We've been working with the lab for several months now. The first team has almost completed their technical training."

Anders paused to raise a beer to his lips. "It's been a challenging class. The program itself is very comprehensive and overlaps with the regular course my air traffic controllers are required to take. Many of the students are fully trained pilots. To be honest, I've learned a lot from them."

"You were brave to take on such a challenge."

Anders flushed at her words. He wasn't used to being gushed over. "It's been a busy few weeks. This week we're scheduled to do real life simulations on land and water. Assuming we don't get called out on an actual emergency."

He could feel Laila's eyes as he tilted his head back to take another slug of beer. He rued the fact that his neck turned red when he was embarrassed.

He stammered in his hurry to distract her eyes from their lingering perusal of his body. "We have twelve trained emergency protocol groups in Denmark that are always on call for national air emergencies. Each group is also on call for international disasters for one month out of the year. This is my team's month."

Laila slid into an upright position and perched on the side of her lounger, facing him. "So your team could get sent anywhere in the world if there happened to be an air emergency?"

"There are a few hostile nations who don't participate in the program, but yes, almost anywhere, especially if international waters or air space are involved." He smiled down at her awkwardly, wishing she weren't sitting quite so near. "Enough about me." He leaned back on the rear legs of the stool he was seated on. "Sonja says you're a psycho-therapist. Do you practice alone or with a group?"

"Alone." Laila leaned a little closer. "When my parents died, I inherited an estate on the North Sea that's been in my family for years." A lock of her silky hair slipped over her shoulder as she sipped from her wine. "I converted the caretaker's cottage to an office. It makes a delightful setting for my work."

"I imagine it does." Anders lifted one eyebrow. "Do you have a specialty?"

Laila swirled her straw in a sultry circle-eight before taking another sip. "Family and marriage. Perhaps you've heard of my 'Growing Through Grief' seminars, or my 'Light at the End of the Tunnel' workshop on caring for elderly parents. The response has been so positive that I've begun to develop a third series geared toward dysfunctional families."

A light clicked on in his head. "You're Dr. Svensen?"

She smiled enticingly. "In the flesh."

Anders nodded appreciatively. Dr. Svensen had garnered countless accolades for her research on the stages of grief and healing. He'd read some of her articles. Never had he imagined her to be so young—or so beautiful.

"Let me guess. You had me pictured along the lines of a Dr. Ruth," she said in a thick accent. "Or was it Joyce Brothers?"

Anders flashed her a grin that probably looked as sheepish as he felt. "You don't fit the image of either."

She laughed quietly.

His hands suddenly seemed too large for his body. "Bob has been talking about asking you to do a presentation for a class I teach on Grief Counseling and Survivor Guilt."

"He's mentioned it a couple of times." She surveyed him silently but frankly. "I was hesitant to say yes—my schedule is so busy. But having met you, I think I might enjoy working on something together." She brushed her fingers ever so lightly over his lower arm. "If you're interested."

"I'm sure my students would love the chance to learn from someone with such extensive training. As would I," he added huskily.

"I'm sure we could learn a great deal from each other."

The silence that followed was laden with insinuations.

Laila sat back in her chair and fingered her wine glass with slow, precise movements of her fingers. "I've enjoyed hearing about Anders the air traffic controller." She flashed him another of her dimpled smiles. "Forgive me if I'm being brash, but I'd love to hear more about Anders, the man." She laid her palm on his bare leg and brushed one finger over the bed of curly hairs that grazed his thigh. "Tell me, Anders. Who takes care of you when you need comforting?"

18.

It was hard to say at what exact moment Jensen became angry with Anders. It may have been the fifteenth time she dialed his number; maybe it wasn't until the twentieth. All she knew was that every time she redialed his ridiculously long number, she got more annoyed.

She supposed it was selfish of her to be angry with someone for not being there when you needed them. Not being home to answer your phone certainly wasn't a crime. Anders was hardly at her beck and call. He had a life, for goodness sake. Errands to run, laundry to do, friends to see. She knew that; still, every time she heard the unanswered ring, ring, ring, she felt more ignored and angry.

She knew it was unreasonable to direct her anger toward Anders. He wasn't the one who had stolen from her, desecrated her sanctuary, or wrapped his voluptuous body in her bathrobe after having sex with Ed. He wasn't the one who had invited another woman to his bed just to satisfy his insatiable itch.

He was probably out doing errands or riding his bike. She tried to go back to sleep, but could not, driven to panic by the unreasonable fear that she had lost him.

There was absolutely no reason whatsoever to think Anders had been in a car accident, died of a heart attack in his sleep, decided he didn't want to talk to her anymore, or found someone else, but she couldn't get the notions out of her head. Given the nature of the last twenty-four hours of her life, it was no wonder she jumped to a list of worst possible scenarios.

She rearranged the pillows propped against her headboard in a vain attempt to ease the tension in her neck. It wasn't Anders' fault he wasn't there to help her clean up the mess the burglars had made or be there to hold her in his arms and whisper that it didn't matter, that the things she'd lost were only things, that they still had each other. She raked her eyes over the shattered remnants of a Red Wing pottery vase that had been a gift from her parents. If nothing else, Anders should have had the good sense or common courtesy to buy a damn answering machine.

*****

Anders ignored the pain in his groin and thrust his legs up and down in time with the pedals of his bike, forcing the wheels to churn faster and faster. He skirted a Mercedes to his left, passed a Volvo to his right and squeezed between an Audi and Renault as he rounded the curve just past the stop light at the main gate of Tivoli. Pausing for a fraction of a second, he pumped down on the pedals and propelled the bike forward, narrowly missing a Toyota changing lanes. His only salvation was that it was Sunday afternoon and not rush hour.

Sweat glistened on his neck. A vein throbbed in his temple. On some conscious level he knew he was risking life and limb by racing down H.C. Andersen Boulevard at break-neck speed, but he didn't care. His anger had no logical basis. He knew that. It wasn't Jensen who had meddled in his once orderly life by playing matchmaker. Nor was it she who had blatantly come on to him at Bob's party despite his clear intent to keep to himself. It wasn't Jensen who'd used her knowledge of psychology to push every one of his buttons, including some he hadn't known he had.

Yet he was furious with her. She'd occupied his every waking thought and dallied with his senses so mercilessly that he felt like he would explode if he couldn't make love to her in the very, very foreseeable future. He gripped his handbrakes, barely avoided a collision with a Mercedes truck, and glared at the driver of a motorcycle that was speeding across his path.

*****

Jensen still couldn't get back to sleep. She'd been up most of the night and she was exhausted. But that wasn't the

189

problem. The problem was Anders. She'd been dialing his number at intervals all through the night. After getting no answer for hours, she was getting a busy signal. She wanted to scream.

She looked around the room. She needed something to distract her—something less messy than a house gone to hell, something less fattening than leftover apple pie, something less hair-raising than big brown bats, something less nerve-wracking than suspicious creaks in the night. She picked up the letter lying on her nightstand and started to read. She had to stop thinking about Anders or she'd lose her mind. Maren's words floated in front of her eyes with an almost mesmerizing effect.

> *Sophie, I will be honest and tell you that there were times I thought I would lose my mind in the days that immediately preceded our departure for America. If only I could have talked to you then, or moder, or Leif, to work out the feelings trapped in my heart, to say my goodbyes, to find some peace after all that had happened.*
>
> *Instead, I was kept in virtual seclusion while Frederik made his plans in secret, left to dissolve my grief with tears. At the time, I was wracked with guilt over what Frederik wrongly perceived to be my betrayal. In retrospect, I realize his pride was wounded, and for that I am sorrowful. But I feel no shame for my actions. I did no wrong. Nor do I apologize for my reactions to the edicts that followed, as I firmly believe they were fitting for a woman who knows she is about to be torn from her family and friends and dragged halfway around the world against her will.*
>
> *I do not mean to sound like a mollycoddled infant fussing for no reason. I have known many brave people to leave for America over the course*

of my short lifetime. Friends and neighbors of my moder and fader left Danemark for the New World from the time I was a child, but always there was a good reason for leaving, something that prompted them to want or need to go, perhaps a time of hardship or grief that made them dream of a better place, a fresh start, or a new opportunity in America.

My moder tells me some went to escape starvation during the great droughts and the famine that followed. Some left because they had lost so much they had nothing more to lose, even had they died on the perilous journey across the sea. Some went to escape the constant reminder of a loved one lost; some, for the pure adventure of it; some, wishing to seek their fortunes in a new land. Whatever the reason, they wanted to make the journey and prepared for their departure months in advance.

The new baby, my precious Victoria, was my only balm. Frederik still does not know that Victoria was the name Leif and his wife had chosen for the baby they were expecting. In a very profound sense, Victoria will always connect me to Leif.

I can still remember Leif standing beside me on that fateful day, his eyes filled with tears as he mourned anew the wife and daughter he'd so recently lost to childbirth. His only concern was for the safety of little Victoria and I; his only thought the wonder and joy of the miracle he had just witnessed. Little did either of us anticipate (nor would it have made any difference) that Frederik would come charging into the house like a bull loose from the pasture at that precise moment, condemning what was beautiful, making ugly an act of pure love.

I have made my peace with Frederik, but it has not been easy. I shall always miss my life, my family, and my friends in Danemark. I am still working on the wedding quilt I started back in Slangerup. Sophie, my heart cries out for all of you as I sew the tiny pieces together... a bit of white from moder's old nightdress, a scrap of blue left over from my sister's Sunday best, a snippet from the apron my grandmother wore as she sat at the sink peeling apples. I swear before heaven that when I hold the fabrics in my hands I can still smell those apples, my moder's perfume, the soap we used to scrub my little sister's face. I can hear their voices, see their faces, feel their arms embracing me as I hold this quilt in my lap. I shall lament their absence from my life and the lives of my children forever, just as I shall always miss Leif with my whole heart and soul.

I must close now, as I can hear the clatter of dishes from the kitchen and know it is almost time for supper. It is up to Mathilda and Karl to set the table (I fear Karl is the noisy one, and pray my dishes survive his gallant attempts to be a good helper.)

I know I have asked before, Sophie, but if you hear word of Leif, or have occasion to see him, please tell him of me, and send word of how he has fared since my hasty departure. I fear for him, Sophie. It breaks my heart to know that I hurt him when he was already wounded so deeply.

I will close now, and wish this letter Godspeed. I will let you know when the baby has arrived, and pray this delivery is not so heart wrenching as the last.

All my love, Maren

Jensen set the letter aside and sniffled into a tissue. Her understanding of why Frederik had brought his family to America was clearer with every letter, although she still felt somewhat mystified by Maren's elusive words. Had Frederik walked in to find Maren and Leif embracing? Had Leif rescued Maren and baby Victoria from some predicament? Even with all she knew, it was hard to understand what had prompted Frederik to bring Maren and their children to America against his wife's wishes.

Her gaze went to the beloved wedding ring quilt hanging on the wall opposite her bed. She breathed a sigh of relief when she thought about how close she had come to losing Maren's quilt. The burglars that robbed her of her electronic equipment obviously didn't have any knowledge in regard to the value of antiques. No matter the reason, she was thankful they had deemed Maren's quilt unworthy of stealing. It meant more to her now than ever before.

She smiled. Now she knew what Anders had been alluding to when he'd promised her she would love the contents of this particular letter. He knew her well and understood what the quilt meant to her.

It was sweet of him not to have spoiled the surprise. She pulled her knees up and wrapped her arms around her legs. She was still frustrated as hell with him, but being reminded of his thoughtfulness made it much harder to be angry.

She tucked an extra quilt around her, leaned back against the headboard, and glanced at the telephone. Now that she'd calmed down, she was ready to admit that her anger toward Anders had been vastly disproportionate to his "crime".

What had come over her, anyway? It had been years since she'd felt so angry with anyone—maybe her mother when she was a teenager; she honestly couldn't recall. She and Ed had had their differences, but she didn't remember ever feeling so angry at him, not in the whole time she'd dated him; not even now, after finding another woman in his bed. She'd certainly been frustrated with him on occasion, but never had she felt the kind of seething, all-consuming anger she'd felt toward Anders.

Maybe she'd never cared enough to get mad at Ed. Their relationship had been convenient, handy, and mutually satisfying in many ways, but she'd never loved him enough to feel truly threatened by the thought of losing him, never invested enough of herself in him to warrant being afraid that he wouldn't be a part of her life forever.

Jensen yawned. The tension in her neck was gone. Her eyes felt fuzzy, her limbs numb and cumbersome. She looked up at Maren's quilt. Its delicately faded, worn-thin-with-love colors seemed to shine in the rosy hue of the sunrise. She slid back under the covers and laid her head against her pillow. No sooner had she closed her eyes than she was asleep.

*****

Anders plunked down on his bed and stretched out on top of his quilt. He was still out of breath and he knew he could use a shower, but he'd always found that once he reached a decision about something, it was best to act on it immediately. He was typically Dane in that he liked to think things over thoroughly before he jumped in. On the other hand, Anders knew that Danes could be very indecisive, and although his instincts told him to *se tiden an,* or *Watch the time a bit first,* he knew in his heart that he could not afford to put this off.

He looked out the window and dialed Bjorn's phone number. He'd made it home just as the sun was setting. Not that he'd had to rush. He was used to riding down the brightly lit boulevards on his way home every night. The difference being he usually didn't ride like such a maniac.

It was Sunday morning in Seattle. Anders hoped it would be a good time to catch Bjorn at home. He cleared his throat as the phone rang once, then twice, and hoped he wasn't going to regret the conversation he was about to initiate.

His son answered on the third ring.

Anders wasted no words. "How would you like to have

company for Juletide?" He asked in flawless English.

"Dad?" Bjorn exclaimed sleepily. "Wow! It's good to hear your voice. Are you serious?"

"As a heart attack." Anders reached back and plumped the pillows behind his neck. His muscles were taut with leftover adrenalin. "I'm not interrupting anything am I?"

"Dad." Bjorn drew out the syllable, then laughed. He followed Anders' lead and switched to Danish. "Like I would tell you if you were."

"Like I could do anything about it if you did," Anders bantered back. "Just had to check. Dads will be dads."

"I'm glad you're coming for Christmas. This doesn't have anything to do with the Little Mermaid does it?"

Anders stammered a few words, stopped, and started over. "Well, since you brought it up, I had thought it might be nice for Jensen and I to meet on neutral ground. I was thinking of asking her to fly out to Seattle and join us for a day or two sometime during my visit—assuming you wouldn't mind. Maybe she could come a few days before or after Juletide if you would rather it was just the two of us over the holiday."

Bjorn laughed. "No offense, Dad, but our Juletide celebrations could use a little livening up."

"Sure, you tell me that now that you're grown up and it's too late for me to do anything about it." Anders feigned hurt feelings in his inflections. "Worse yet, you wait to tell me this when you're so far away I can't even take a swat at you."

"Sorry, Dad, but you don't scare me. I know what an old softie you are."

"Now that hurts."

"Being called a softie?" Bjorn asked.

"No. Old."

Bjorn laughed into the receiver. "I just calls 'em like I sees 'em," he quipped in English.

"Even with all the American expressions I am picking up from Jensen I still can't keep up with you."

"I'll give you a crash course when you get here. I can't wait to show you Seattle. You'll love it, Dad. Bainbridge Island looks like Danemark in so many ways. I know you'll be as taken with this place as I am once you see it."

Anders detected a note of longing in Bjorn's voice and thought it best to nip his wishful thinking in the bud. "Don't get your hopes up, Bjorn. I'm just coming for a visit."

"I know that," he said, sounding irritated that his father could so easily tell what he was thinking. "I know what you think of America. That doesn't stop me from wanting you to have a good first impression of the place where I live."

Anders sighed with the fresh realization that his son had matured into a competent young man.

"At the very least, I keep hoping that someday you might come to understand why I want to live here."

Anders found himself at a loss for words. Bjorn was right. Anders didn't understand, had never understood, and probably never would. But much as he loved Danemark, much as he missed his son and resented the fact that he had left home, he knew he owed it to Bjorn to try.

Bjorn broke the silence. "I guess I thought if things are as serious as they sound with this Jensen that maybe your view of America had softened a bit."

Anders took the defensive. "I care about her despite the fact that she lives in America. Besides, she is Danish."

Bjorn's momentary silence said more than words ever could.

"If we had visual phones you could see me scowling at you, and I, you rolling your eyes at me." Anders was jesting, but his voice had a defensive edge to it and he knew it.

"I forgot there for a minute how stubborn you can be," Bjorn said.

"Ja, look who's talking."

"I didn't inherit it from strangers." Bjorn admitted. "Actually, I've found it can be an asset at work. My boss says that's why I'm so good at what I do. Once I get my teeth around something, I won't let go until I've got the problem licked."

"Sounds like a wise man, your boss."

"Ja. Some Americans really aren't all that bad." Bjorn couldn't resist taking one more jibe. "So does Jensen know how you feel about her country? And assuming she does, is she willing to consider moving to Danemark, or are you two heading for a disaster before you even lay eyes on each other?"

"We haven't discussed it." He heard Bjorn's sigh loud and clear. Bjorn knew he wasn't the type to fly halfway around the world to indulge in a one-night stand.

"Don't say I didn't warn you," Bjorn said.

"So now the son is giving the father advice."

"Hey, I'm not dumb, and I'm not a kid anymore. You've had the chance to hop in the sack with some pretty phenomenal women over the years. If you didn't do it in Danemark with a Dane, you're sure as hell not going to come all the way to Seattle to do it with an American."

"Thank you, I think."

"The way I see it, if you're going to all the trouble of meeting this woman, you must really be in love with her."

"What do you expect me to say to such an accusation?" Anders said gruffly.

"Just be careful. I may be younger and a lot less wise than you are, but I know what it feels like to make a fool of myself. And to get my heart broken."

He'd had nothing to say to Bjorn's advice, but he loved him all the more for it.

When he and Bjorn had finished their heart to heart, he checked his email. There was nothing from Jensen. Not that she had needed to respond to his note about Bob and Sonja's party. He had just thought she would.

He opened a new message and started typing.

Dear Jensen, We did not spend last night together. We are new to each other and this morning feel concerned because we have missed a night of loving. No note or rose on the pillow. No rumpled sheets on the other side of the bed. No masculine scent on you. The phone rings... "Good morning, Jensen. Will you do me the honor of having a cup of coffee and a Danish with me before work? Can you shower and be ready in a half hour? I will be out front waiting for you!"

I want to show you that I value your company. You are an extraordinary lover, but I want you to understand that you are appreciated for more than that. I want you to understand that you are a delightful companion in all settings. Sometimes words don't have to be spoken, conversation does not have to flow. Sometimes a reassuring touch and an understanding silence gives both of us deep fulfillment. But today that is not the case. I need to talk to you, Jensen. I need to tell you what's in my heart.

Now we part company, as it is time for me to be off to bed and you on to your day's business. We will communicate somehow during the day. I hope you feel the growing trust in our relationship that I do and the faith that we will find each other soon. I hope you're having a wonderful day, Jensen. Love, Anders

19.

Jensen eventually woke up and found the strength to start dealing with the mess the burglars had left. First, she rode her bike to the gas station and bought a disposable camera to document the damage for her insurance claim. A tip from the clerk enabled her to find a handyman who was kind enough to move her to the top of his list. He agreed to start as soon as he'd had a bite of dinner.

When he arrived, she swallowed her pride and asked him if it would be possible to install deadbolts on her three entry doors.

His eyes were crinkled and kindly, and he spoke with the faint trace of an Irish brogue. "I understand your fear, miss, but I can see you're not too keen on the idea." He rubbed his free hand over the glass panes of the curved top door at the rear of the house. "I don't mean to scare you, but if they've set their minds to it, they're going to get in, deadbolt or no."

It wasn't exactly what she wanted to hear, but the bright side was she probably didn't need to ruin her doors installing deadbolts.

Mr. Finnegan gestured toward the plywood that the sheriff had nailed over the window. "The burglars choose to come in this way because the next house to the north is quite some distance away. It was less likely your neighbors would hear the glass breaking, if they'd happened to be home. You've got a cluster of big trees on that side of the lot, so it's very dark and shaded from both sides. That nice, private little strip of ground in between the hedgerow and the house just big enough for a man to do his dirty work undetected."

Jensen's face creased with worry.

"You cannot change any of that, darlin'. They'd have used one of your doors to exit the house either way seeing as their arms were full of stolen goods by that time. Granted, it takes a swifter kick to open a bolted door than a latched one, but open it they will. And by the time they do, your pretty doors would be splintered to smithereens. May as well make it easy for them so the door's less likely to be ruined when they're done," he said matter-of-factly. "T'would be a shame to see a beautiful old door like this kicked in."

"So you don't think they chose my house because they could see I didn't have deadbolts on my doors?"

"Nah, missy. Don't be blaming yourself now. They chose your house because pretty out is pretty in." He waved his arm toward the front door. "Window boxes full of geraniums, pink and green gingerbread lining the eaves, a porch swing with a flowery cushion, and a hand-painted house number with flowers to match." He stopped and cocked his head, looking for all the world like a leprechaun. "You're sure you're not Irish?"

She smiled. "Danish through and through except for a smidgen of Swedish on my dad's side."

"A house so nice on the outside is bound to be full of treasures on the inside. Doesn't take a thief to know that."

"Thanks. I'm not sure if I feel better or worse."

He cleared his throat. "You can't stop making your house beautiful just 'cause someone might take notice. It comes down to living your life the way you see fit and knowing that what will be will be in the end."

Jensen nodded. "It would be a sad world if we all took to living in drab houses just so the burglars would be less likely to pick on us." But she knew in her heart that the world was already a bit sadder. She'd always felt so safe, so insulated from the horrors of the big city in her tiny little town.

She felt it very keenly while she was making her list of broken and stolen items, their estimated purchase price, and current value, per her insurance agent's directions. When she was done, she scanned the advertising fliers in her Sunday paper for sales prices on items she hoped to replace immediately.

Mr. Finnegan rewired the telephone wires the burglars had cut while she worked. He left with a promise to return with a new piece of glass for her window on Monday evening as soon as he was done with work and had had a bite of supper.

She spent the remainder of the night cleaning up the mess the burglars had made. By late that evening, the house was at least clean, although bare looking in the spots where her missing or broken things had been. She rewarded herself by climbing into the hot bubble bath she'd been craving ever since she'd raced home from her embarrassing confrontation with Ed and Charlotte twenty-four hours earlier.

She'd retrieved her email before her bath, so she wasn't surprised when she found Anders up bright and early, waiting for her online.

*****

Anders delayed asking Jensen to meet him in Seattle until they'd chatted for some time. It was harder than he'd thought it would be. But he needn't have feared her response.

The_Little_Mermaid: December seems like an eternity from now.

Ugly_Duckling: That's because you're in denial. Winter is right around the corner. You will not admit it because you hate the thought of not being able to ride your bike.

The_Little_Mermaid: You know me too well.

The carelessly uttered words rang in his ears like the punch line of a joke.

Ugly_Duckling: Think about what you just said, Jen.

The_Little_Mermaid: Well you do! Even in the short time we've been friends, you've gotten to know me better than anyone ever has.

Anders typed slowly, giving his thoughts a chance to form.

Ugly_Duckling: In many ways, we are better at communicating than if we had met face-to-face.

The_Little_Mermaid: It's very easy to be open and honest when physical appearance issues aren't there to get in the way.

Ugly_Duckling: We've gotten to know each other with our hearts instead of our bodies.

The_Little_Mermaid: Our relationship feels so intimate because it was built on things of substance instead of a fleeting physical response.

The words she was typing stopped scrolling down his screen—as though she sensed something was bothering him.

Ugly_Duckling: What if I disappoint you? I don't want you to feel let down if the magic that happens between us here doesn't materialize in the real world.

The_Little_Mermaid: Is that how you think it will be?

Ugly_Duckling: I want all of your fantasies about us to be lived out in real life.

He hoped she understood what he was saying. On some level she must be as nervous about trying to bridge the gap between the cyber world and the real world as he was. He had typed the words he had to reassure himself as much as her.

The_Little_Mermaid: How could I be disappointed? With every day that passes I'm more convinced you're everything I've imagined and more. How could meeting the flesh and blood man I've fantasized about, alive and strong and real, be anything less than a dream come true?

Ugly_Duckling: Thank you, Jen.

The_Little_Mermaid: There's nothing to thank me for. I adore you, Anders.

The feelings of unworthiness he'd felt ever since Benta choose to leave him for Kirk vanished as the reality of his feelings clutched at his heart.

Ugly_Duckling: I wanted to say it in person, but you need to know now. I love you, Jen.

The_Little_Mermaid: I love you, too.

Ugly_Duckling: I want to be what you want, what you need; to nourish the beautiful person inside you, to make you feel worshipped, and cherished, to rip whatever hurt has been in your life out of it and heal you.

The_Little_Mermaid: That's what you do each time we come here. I feel savored and respected and cared for after I've been with you.

Ugly_Duckling: I want you to feel... to know that you are truly loved and cared about.

The_Little_Mermaid: You tell me very eloquently every time we're together.

Ugly_Duckling: If I were there I would love you tonight. You would wake up with the scent of our love under your covers.

The_Little_Mermaid: Oh, Anders.

Ugly_Duckling: So many hidden desires and feelings awaiting expression. I'll always have you in my heart and imagination, but I also want you in my arms.

The_Little_Mermaid: It will be everything we hope.

Ugly_Duckling: Call the airlines first thing tomorrow. I will do the same. Juletide will be here before we know it.

The_Little_Mermaid: I hope you'll feel the same way about the real me as you do the "me" you know here.

Ugly_Duckling: I know the real you.

The_Little_Mermaid: You always say the right thing.

Ugly_Duckling: I hope my words tell you how loved you are.

The_Little_Mermaid: They do. That's what I like about you—the tender way you love me. You make me feel like a treasure.

Ugly_Duckling: You make me feel good, too. It is wonderful to feel needed and appreciated again.

The_Little_Mermaid: You are. Very much so.

Ugly_Duckling: Sometimes when I close my eyes I swear I can feel you, smell you, taste you. It is so real it takes my breath away.

The_Little_Mermaid: If you only knew how many nights I've lain under the covers, wanting you, wondering what it would be like to really be with you.

Ugly_Duckling: I had you in the bathtub last night. You sat in front with your back to me. I caressed you and poured warm water over you. We talked and touched but we did not make love. It was very erotic.

The_Little_Mermaid: I feel soft and slippery just thinking about it. I can feel your muscles rippling under my hands in the water.

Ugly_Duckling: And I, the warm water lapping at my chin as I suck your nipples.

The_Little_Mermaid: I imagined your hands cupped under my breasts tonight when I was rinsing off after my bath.

Ugly_Duckling: In my dream you're sitting in front of me, leaning back on me, your head on my shoulder while we talk, sipping Asti Spumante, the candle's light shimmering over the surface of the water as I squeeze warm water over your skin.

The_Little_Mermaid: I dream of riding with you until we're bone tired, then laying in each other's arms talking, kissing, exploring. Where would you touch me first?"

Ugly_Duckling: I would caress your cheek, then your neck.

The_Little_Mermaid: I'd nuzzle your jaw; touch you behind your ears.

He could almost feel her sigh fanning his cheek.

Ugly_Duckling: You're making me thick.

The_Little_Mermaid: That word drives me wild. I feel absolutely breathless every time you say it.

Ugly_Duckling: I dream of tasting you, Jensen. Everywhere.

The_Little_Mermaid: Just the thought of you bending over me and touching me with your tongue makes me tingle.

Ugly_Duckling: Licking your sweet liquid, searching for buried treasure, touching you until I made you bark like a fox. I stir just thinking of drinking your nectar.

The_Little_Mermaid: I can feel your thighs tensing up and relaxing as I explore you with my lips.

The muscles in his legs throbbed with sensation as he read her words. His awareness of her was so acute it almost hurt.

The_Little_Mermaid: I can feel the shape of you over me, your weight, your fingers probing and searching while I stroke you, nuzzling my nose to your chest, licking your nipples.

Ugly_Duckling: I could make love to you all night long.

First lying on our sides, my face to your breast, suckling gently while my fingers caress you.

The_Little_Mermaid: It's so intimate, being face-to-face, so gentle and loving.

Ugly_Duckling: I love being with you.

The_Little_Mermaid: So warm and cozy and wonderful.

His screen remained blank as they lay basking in a contented silence that transcended the miles between them.

Ugly_Duckling: Are you still there, sweetheart?

The_Little_Mermaid: You do know how much you mean to me, don't you, Anders?

Ugly_Duckling: I'm flattered by the way you respond to me.

The_Little_Mermaid: I could snuggle and lay naked in your arms forever. Talking a bit and then cuddling some more.

Ugly_Duckling: If we were together we would snuggle for a few minutes and then start in all over again.

The_Little_Mermaid: I love the thought of our legs all twisted together.

Ugly_Duckling: We are a good fit. This will sound vain, but I am beginning to believe that the only man you could possibly feel totally fulfilled with is the man that I am when with you.

The_Little_Mermaid: You're the only one who has taken the time to really know me... what I like, what excites me, what pleases me, what makes me cry. You are a rare treasure, Anders.

Ugly_Duckling: I am just thinking what it will be like to really touch you. An encounter to satisfy curiosity. To hold no emotion back. To pour out our souls.

The_Little_Mermaid: To feel you on every level.

Ugly_Duckling: I'm thick again at the thought. I am hot and hard, Jensen, as smooth as satin.

The_Little_Mermaid: You'd glide inside me in a heartbeat. I can feel you, hard against my softness. So hot.

Ugly_Duckling: I love you, Jensen.

The_Little_Mermaid: My heart is skipping. Can you feel the palm of my hand? Massaging you gently at first.

Reverently. Then harder. Stronger.

Ugly_Duckling: And me kissing you, your face between my hands, your eyes locked on mine.

The_Little_Mermaid: I love feeling you, Anders; so purposeful and strong, yet gentle and oh, so tender.

Ugly_Duckling: Demanding when the time comes.

The_Little_Mermaid: Not just wanting me, but needing me so intensely...

Ugly_Duckling: You are so warm. So wet.

The_Little_Mermaid: I'm kissing you and touching you from behind. Where you're soft and fleshy like me.

Ugly_Duckling: I like fleshy. I like soft...

The_Little_Mermaid: I like hard.

Ugly_Duckling: I like you. Your words are caresses.

The_Little_Mermaid: Are you still thick, Anders?

Ugly_Duckling: Yes, whenever I think of you.

The_Little_Mermaid: I'm pulling the quilt up around me to keep from shivering now—not from the cold, but from the wonder of being with you. We are so good together.

Ugly_Duckling: Relax with me before I go, Jensen.

He ran his fingers over her photograph.

The_Little_Mermaid: My eyelids are heavy. I feel totally relaxed. My breathing has slowed. It is as though all the angst of the weekend is melting away. I'm cuddling closer to you, covering a yawn with my fingers and nuzzling my backside to your lap. Thank you for making me feel so loved.

Ugly_Duckling: You are precious.

The_Little_Mermaid: Clinging to you... so much love in my heart.

Ugly_Duckling: Holding you tight. Sleep well, dear princess of the night.

20.

Ed knew immediately that something was wrong. There were three extra sacks of trash, double bagged, sitting at the curb outside Jensen's bungalow. He could tell by the looks of them—the misshapen way they bulged, the lumpy texture of their contents, the way their weight settled heavily on the ground—that they weren't filled with empty food containers, toiletries and junk mail like they usually were.

He also knew that Jensen rarely threw anything away. She saved piles of magazines she was sure she would get around to reading someday, catalogs, newspaper clippings about her or anyone she knew, and a slew of those infernal scraps of leftover fabric that floated around her house, clinging to everything they touched. Ed shook his head. The trash bags had to mean a construction project, a major disaster, or at the very least, a housecleaning blitz like she'd never seen the likes of.

He looked to each side of the house as he neared the front door. Not counting the midnight bat escapade, it had been awhile since he'd been at her house. He'd never felt all that comfortable at Jensen's. They'd spent most of their time hanging out at his place.

He looked at the porch swing. She could have tossed the frilly, flowered cushion she'd made for the top and it wouldn't have hurt his feelings any. Nothing else had changed that he could see. Her window boxes were still dripping with pink geraniums. She must have been covering them on the nights the temperatures dipped below freezing. Knowing the way she hated to part with anything, she'd probably winter them over in one of the sunny windows in the room she liked to call her parlor.

He made a mental note to tell her to check under the leaves before she brought them inside. Last fall, a woman he worked with had brought in a bat that was hiding in a big hanging pot she'd moved from her balcony to a sunroom.

He reached for the doorbell and looked down while he waited for her to come to the door. In all the time they'd been together, he'd never once sat on the porch swing with her.

He refocused his attentions on the painted slate welcome sign she'd hung just to the left of the door. If you asked him, the whole place was a little two cutesy. He'd told her when they painted the house last summer that her choices of colors made the house look like something from *Hansel and Gretel*. She'd been so jazzed about the way the new colors looked; she'd missed his point entirely. She'd teasingly called it the Gingerbread House a couple of times since then.

He shifted the weight of the cardboard box in his arms from one hand to the other and looked in the front window. There were no signs of life inside the house, so he started around to the back to see if her bicycle was gone.

She didn't see him at first. She was dressed in a hooded gray sweatshirt and jeans, and her hair was tousled, the ends whipped into thin strands by the wind. She was half-inside a lilac tree, batting the branches and dead growth with one arm while she tried to lift the branch clippers over her head with the other. He could see the branches fighting back from where he stood, whipping her face and clawing mercilessly at her clothes. She moved her hand to protect her eyes and the branches closed in around her again.

She leaned forward, stood on her tiptoes, and tried to lift the clippers again as he watched. He knew from experience that she was waging an unbeatable war. He moved to intercept.

"You're going to poke an eye out if you're not careful."

"Ed." She spun around, startled by his voice. The uplifted shears caught in a tangle of branches as she spun.

"Don't move," he said. "Here. Let me help."

He set the package in the grass and parted the branches so she could escape. "So you're trimming the hedge, huh?"

"Trying to."

He probably looked stumped. He sure felt that way.

"What's wrong?" Her voice was apprehensive. "You've

wanted me to do this since the first time you saw my yard."

"I'm surprised."

She gave him a scathing look.

"I've been wanting to trim these with the electric hedge trimmer for months. Now I find you out here hacking away with this rusty, dull old thing. You don't even have a ladder."

"I do so. It's in the garage."

Ed stuck his hand in his pockets. "With the bats."

"Yes. Are you happy now?"

"No. I'm not happy. Nothing about this situation makes me happy."

She looked like it hurt her to look at him. "Charlotte looked like she was making you plenty ecstatic the other day."

"Damn it, Jensen. Let it go. I just came over to bring you your things. Tell me where you want the box and I'll be on my way." He pulled out a smaller, flat, white box from Marshall Field's and handed it to her. "Your make-up and toothbrush and stuff are in the box. I got you a new bathrobe."

She looked suspicious. "Thanks." She opened the box and pulled out a brushed cotton robe with a small imprint of Winnie the Pooh on the front.

"Thanks." Her lips curved into a faint smile. "It's Classic Pooh."

"I remembered you didn't like the bright Disney version."

"The colors are nice. Did Charlotte help you pick it out?"

Damn. His face always gave him away. He let his shoulder's slump. "Yah. Right before she said she didn't want to see me anymore. She makes it her policy not to date guys who are still hung up on their old girlfriends."

"Sorry." Jensen looked toward the house. "When I got home from your place the other night I found my house had been broken into. They came through the kitchen window and got most of my electronic stuff."

Ed shook his head. "You should have called."

She sounded resigned, not accusing. "You seemed kind of busy at the time."

"Yah, well..."

"Oh, Ed." She sighed. "You and I both know I've relied on you to do a lot of things for me. You've taken good care of me for a long time," she added. "I appreciate it more than you'll ever know. But I've got to start standing on my own two feet at some point or you'll be married to someone else and I'll still be calling you to come rescue me in the middle of the night."

"Except I'm not the marrying kind."

"Regardless. There are dozens of Charlottes out there. You'll find someone. Things will change."

He tried to keep the glum look off his face. Damn. She looked like she was going to hug him.

"I found a handyman to make some repairs for me. A Mr. Finnegan. He's near retirement, kind of the fatherly type," she added graciously. "He fixed my telephone wires yesterday. He'll be by in a bit to put new glass in the window they broke." She looked away. "He's the one who suggested I trim the lilacs back."

Ed said nothing for a minute. "I may as well run home and get my hedge trimmer and stick around and help him for a while."

"It's nice of you to offer." She met his eyes tentatively. "I still have some fried chicken and apple pie left in the fridge. I could make a new batch of biscuits if you want to have a bite to eat when you're done."

"I'd like that."

*****

Anders was sound asleep when the call came. His thoughts were a jumbled mass of questions as he threw his clothes on and raced out the door. It had been three years since he'd been called to report to the site of an international air emergency. It was the hope and the scourge of airplane crashes—infrequent enough that you almost forget they happen, but so devastatingly cruel in their severity and massive in their impact that when they did occur, you never forgot.

He said a quick prayer as he threw his suitcase into his car, fastened the seat belt and turned the key. The engine sputtered once as Anders backed out his driveway and headed for the airport. His tiny car felt uncomfortable and confining—he shifted gears impatiently and alternately gripped and loosened his hands from the steering wheel, wishing he could weave through traffic as efficiently as he did on his bicycle. If he were on his bike, he could vent the nervous energy cramped in his arms and legs.

The gruesome image of bloated arms and legs floating in clusters on the North Sea, tossed to and fro by waves and currents, appeared briefly before his eyes. It had been years, but he would never forget.

He reported directly to Bob's office where he was told their plane would leave for Nova Scotia within the hour. The people who comprised the passenger list would be diverse: accident investigators to review the salvaged wreckage, Viking Airways public relations specialists to handle the press, grief counselors to work with survivors and the families of the deceased in the airport chapel at Halifax and at the scene of the disaster, representatives from the Transportation Safety Board and many others who, with Anders, comprised Danemark's disaster team.

Forty-five minutes later he boarded the plane. They had called in all the major players for this one—Viking Airway's legal team, some top-notch independent flight analysts, an environmental impact engineer, divers from the Danish Royal Navy, and a variety of clergy representing the Jewish, Muslim, Catholic and Protestant faiths.

Efforts made by teams like Anders' were always deemed to be Rescue Operations for the first twenty-four hours following a crash, but Anders knew, as did everyone on the plane, that the chances of there being any survivors after an impact of this magnitude were next to zero. Their main function would be to recover bodies, the flight recorder, and pieces from the wreckage so they could patch together what had caused the crash and deal with the aftermath. A similar team was already on duty at Copenhagen International, talking to family members who were congregating to await word of their loved ones and fielding questions from the media.

The airplane was abuzz with the faint hum of voices, voices hushed with equal parts of dread and adrenalin. The soft echoes pulsed through the cabin with a respectful calm, uninterrupted except for the periodic punctuations of a voice issuing a request. Anders sat alone, next to the window. Helmut and Erik sat immediately across the aisle; their heads leaned inward in quiet consultation. Anders made no effort to engage them in conversation.

The details, sketchy at first, were now crystal clear. Viking Airways Flight 4021 had originated in New York, made a scheduled stopover in Nova Scotia and departed from Halifax at eleven o'clock Sunday evening, bound for Copenhagen. The Boeing 767 was over open water just northeast of Prince Edward Island when the first distress call came in. The pilot reported a minor problem with his instruments, then, a few minutes later, requested permission to make an emergency course change and return to the nearest landing strip.

The pilot had requested clearance for a possible emergency landing at the short, seven thousand foot runway at Charlottetown Airport on Prince Edward Island, the nearest reasonably suitable airport in the vicinity. Anders could imagine the panic that had ensued at the pilot's request. The runway wasn't big enough for a large aircraft to land on under the best of circumstances, say nothing about an airplane partially crippled or operating with inaccurate sensor information or contorted data from a faulty instrument. Such a landing would have been dramatic at best, tragic at worst. Short runways allowed no margin for error.

Anders knew the pilot and most of the members of the crew of the downed plane professionally but not socially. The pilot was a man he respected. He could only guess at the anguish the man must have felt given the choice of landing on a too short runway in a populated area, thereby risking not only a greater chance of injury to his passengers, but endangering the lives of hundreds of civilians. He'd tried to make it to Halifax's longer runway, where emergency crews were also better prepared to deal with a possible crash landing. The plane had crashed into the ocean twenty miles off the coast of Nova Scotia.

A crewmember seated directly behind Anders tapped him on the shoulder and imparted the latest information that had filtered down through their on-site colleagues. Confirmation had just come in that the pilot had dumped his fuel over the Atlantic, a maneuver commonly used to get the plane's weight down to a point where the landing gear and structure could handle the stress of a jolting impact. The pilot had clearly anticipated a difficult landing.

He remembered an incident when a Boeing 747 had made a successful emergency landing on a short runway in northern Norway, near the Arctic Circle. Once repairs had been completed, the crews had been forced to gut the insides of the plane, stripping it of every unessential piece of equipment just to get it back into the air.

A trio of stewardesses clustered near their station moved aside to let a pair of well-known investigative reporters pass by. An entourage of cameramen laden with backpacks, tripods, and a plethora of photo equipment followed the two men down the aisle. Anders mouthed another prayer for the families of the victims and turned his head to watch the ground crews loading the last of the equipment and luggage.

He heard a familiar voice and looked up.

"Mind if I have a seat?" Laila asked sweetly, her sultry voice unaffected by the change of scenery.

"W-what are you doing here?" He stammered rudely.

"I volunteered to help counsel the families of the victims." She smiled, as if pleased by his discomfort.

"Don't you have clients?" He watched as she swung her carry-on bag into the overhead compartment with the lithe grace of a cat jumping unbidden from its intended place on the floor to a table heaped with food.

"My secretary is rescheduling my appointments." Laila crossed her legs and swirled one scantily clad ankle until the tip of her fine leather shoe brushed his shin. "I've been hoping for an opportunity to test some of my theories in the field."

His eyes must have revealed some fraction of the animosity he felt.

"No need to feel threatened, darling. I have no desire to interfere." She smiled engagingly. "Nor do I mean to imply that your team is in any way ill-equipped to handle the situation on your own."

"I'm sure we'll be able to use all the help we can get." Anders leaned toward the window and resumed looking out at the landscape.

"I was thrilled when the call came out for extra counselors willing to work with the victim's families," she said a trifle too cheerily.

Anders looked at her sharply and watched as her perfectly sculpted nails skimmed over her silk-shrouded thigh to brush away a piece of lint she'd found clinging to her leg.

The woman was oblivious to the horrors that awaited them. He closed his eyes against images of twisted pieces of metal, jagged shards of steel, the sodden remains of suitcases and bodies. He shuddered as a wave of revulsion swept over him. He could taste the bile in the back of his mouth. "I'm going to try to get some sleep. It's going to be a long day."

He thought of Jensen, and assumed she'd heard news of the crash. Special reports were already interrupting the regular programming of television stations around the world, updating viewers with news of estimated casualties and rescue attempts.

Laila rubbed her palm over his thigh. "Sweet dreams, love."

He shifted his weight toward the window and wadded up a pillow to place between his head and the glass. A few minutes later Laila snuggled quietly into his arm and let her head droop ubiquitously on his shoulder.

*****

Jensen was at home working on a quilt top she'd promised to mail to a customer in Aspen before the end of the week. It was eerily quiet—she hadn't had a chance to replace her radio, television, or CD player.

She lopped one hand under the quilt and flipped the fabric over to examine the right side of the seam she'd just sewn. The pieces were perfectly aligned.

She intended to go shopping as soon as she finished piecing the blue sky and maroon mountain peaks that formed the backdrop of the quilt. That was when the phone rang.

Her mother's voice was so clear and strong she might have been in the next room. Jensen hadn't talked to her since she and Anders had gotten close. Which had been somewhat intentional—she was a grown woman for heaven's sake. She shouldn't have to justify her actions to her parents. At the same time, she was eager to tell them about Maren's letters.

She was able to keep certain things from her mother in the emails they traded back and forth—it would be next to impossible to shield the truth from her now that her mother could hear her voice.

Ja, the same computer that elicited such honest expression could just as easily be used to hide the truth. That was the double-edged sword when it came to emailing. You could speak about things you might never be able to say face to face. You could also tell a bald-faced lie without the risk that your body language or voice would give you away.

Jensen squirmed in her chair. There was no denying that she was guilty of using the internet to dupe her parents, which made her just as bad as the slime balls she'd seen using the internet for deceitful purposes online.

Her mother started out the conversation by telling her what they'd been up to in Arizona—your typical card games, fifth wheels and trips to the desert. The whole time, she was desperately trying to think of a way she could confess to having read Maren's letters without telling her parents that she'd become involved in an internet romance with a man from Denmark.

She should have known she'd end up spilling her guts.

She'd known how her mother would react. Her father didn't say a great deal, but Jensen could almost feel his disapproval. Her strategy for damage control was simple but surprisingly effective—lure them away from the topic of her personal life by getting them interested in Maren's letters.

Her father retained his skeptical attitude (Jensen could only assume he saw through her ploy) whereas her mother took the bait immediately. Jensen wasn't the first to wonder if the mysterious letters Maren had written to her cousin Sophie contained the secret of why their ancestors had immigrated to the United States. They'd all been curious ever since Sophie's daughter Boyda had hinted of a scandal.

"You always did have a special bond with your great-grandmother," her mother said. "I suppose I'm more like Frederik."

Her mother's analytical, down-to-earth personality did seem to have been molded from Frederik's genes, not Maren's.

"Grandpa Frederik was like a father to me," Jensen's mother said. "My daddy died when he was a very young man. Grandmother Victoria took me back to the homestead in Blooming Prairie to live with Frederik and Maren after he died."

That was all she said until Jensen had finished recounting what she knew of Maren's feelings for Leif, and Frederik's decision to move the family to America.

"So as far as you know, nothing improper ever happened between Maren and Leif?" Her mother asked anxiously.

"Not as far as I can tell." Jensen could have predicted her mother's reaction. "The last letter I read hinted that Frederik believed he'd found them in a compromising situation. If I had to guess based on what I've read thus far, I'd say it sounded more like Leif had rescued Maren and the baby, Grandma

Victoria, if you can imagine, from some calamitous situation."

"I wonder why that would have upset Grandpa Frederik so much," her mother pondered aloud.

"Hopefully the next letter will give me a better idea."

"You say this other man's name was Leif?" Jensen's father asked from the telephone extension he'd been listening from. "Do the letters mention his last name?"

"I think they do, Dad, but to be honest, I don't remember. I'll have to go back and reread some of the earlier letters to see if I can find out for you. It must not have been a name that was familiar or I'd remember it."

"Why do you ask, dear?" Jensen's mother asked her husband.

"I think I remember seeing the name Leif mentioned in some of my father's papers from the old country."

Jensen smiled. Her parents were notorious for talking—even arguing—on opposite sides of the wall, each on their own extension, while their long distance charges multiplied. Not that it bothered her; it was more amusing than irritating.

"Your father's family was Swedish, dear. The Leif Maren knew would have been Danish," Jensen's mother reminded him.

"Actually, Leif was Swedish," Jensen interjected. "He moved to Denmark and bought the bakery in Slangerup after losing his wife and baby in childbirth."

"My father worked at a bakery when he first came to America," her father added. "Olsen's Danish Village Bakery in Solvang. I think it's still there."

Jensen knew very little about her father's family except that her dad had been born in California and lost both of his parents before moving to Minnesota, where he'd met and eventually married her mother. Her father's parents had looked to be on in years in the photographs she'd seen. Her father rarely spoke of them.

"You don't suppose this Leif was some relation to your father, do you, honey?" her mother said. "There were several sons from your father's family who were bakers."

"Anything is possible. The whole reason I came out to Minnesota looking for work that first summer after Dad died was because he'd told me about a family he'd known in the old country who had settled in Blooming Prairie. I'd never been east and decided I wanted to see the country."

She'd heard the story but she listened to the tale with renewed curiosity.

"I packed up the Buick and headed to Minnesota. The Jensen place was only a mile out of town, so it wasn't hard to find. Who knew I'd meet a sweet young thing like your mother and end up settling down in Blooming Prairie for good?"

Jensen picked up the tale. "Great-Grandma Jensen was sitting out on the front porch sipping on some lemonade when you pulled in the driveway."

"Ja, the men were out in the field cutting hay. And Maren's command of the English language was nothing to brag about. But as soon as she understood that my father was a friend from the old country, I was welcomed like family. Next thing I knew, I was out baling hay and had a place to bunk for the summer."

Jensen interjected the next segment of the story. "Mom walked out to the field dressed in a blue and white polka dot sundress to offer the baling crew some cold lemonade. The second you laid eyes on her you knew she was the one you'd marry."

"Your father waited patiently until I'd graduated from high school before he asked Grandpa Jensen for my hand."

Jensen could almost see the two of them glowing at each other through the walls that divided their separate telephones.

"I'll have to have a look at those old papers in Dad's chest when we get home in the spring and see if I find anything about a Leif. They're up in the attic, aren't they, dear?"

"Yes, sweetheart. Right beside the old steamer Grandma Jensen brought over from Denmark."

Jensen didn't have the heart to tell them that Peder and

Tara's attic was now full of Baratono memorabilia. And Peder had promised he'd keep the trunks safe.

"I'd like to take a closer look at these translations. Maybe something will jog my memory," her father speculated in his cautious manner. "If you don't mind making photocopies and mailing them to me, I'd like to read them, too."

"This gentleman who's been helping you certainly has gone to a lot of time and effort to translate all those old scripts." Her mother had seen the original letters and knew her grandmother's handwriting must have been hard to decipher.

"How old was Grandpa when you were born, Dad?" Reminiscing about the past was so much nicer than dealing with inquiries about the present. She'd been so sure she'd get a lecture when her parents found out she'd been hanging out with some stranger in a chat room, even if he was Danish. Maybe this was her lucky day.

"He was forty-eight," her dad said. "My mother was twelve years younger than he was. Why do you ask?"

She knew she'd made a mistake, but by then it was too late to backtrack. "No reason."

She could hear her mother's exaggerated sigh.

"One of these days you're going to have to quit living in a fantasy world, Jensen. I feel badly about what Ed did, too, but the bottom line is that if you want to have a family someday, you need to stop dreaming, get down to business, and go find a man who wants the same things you do."

"Oh, let the poor girl be," her father chided her mother.

"I'm being practical," her mother insisted. "She's almost forty. If she doesn't stop dreaming about Prince Charming, settle down and start having babies, it's never going to happen."

She didn't know which was worse, her mother's scorn or her father's pity. Regardless, she wished they would stop talking about her like she wasn't listening to every word.

Her mother gave up trying to convince her husband she was right and focused her attention on Jensen. "Just promise me you won't do anything rash like running off to meet the man. It's dangerous. You have no way of knowing who or what he really is."

Jensen spent a few minutes trying to defend Anders before saying her good-byes, but it was futile trying to convince her parents that anything good could come from an internet relationship. On that much, her mother and father agreed.

*****

Anders was midway over the Atlantic when he realized he was going to be within a few hours of Jensen's location once he arrived in Halifax. He hadn't thought of the journey as a trip to the United States, but he was crossing the Atlantic, and Minnesota did border Canada, and no matter how far a stretch it was from the eastern seaboard to the Great Plains, he was certainly going to be closer to her than he had been before. His mind was whirling with possibilities as he drifted off to sleep.

They were over Greenland when he next opened his eyes, tried to sit up in his seat, and found he was wedged between the window and Laila. He tried to contain his irritation. But there was no need to worry about fooling the renowned psychologist. Laila was sound asleep, snuggled tightly against his shoulder.

A grinning Erik caught his eye, pointed at Laila and winked. Anders shook his head. If the circumstances had been different, he might have welcomed someone to talk to, better yet, someone to snuggle up to during the long flight. But today his mind was with Jensen. The last thing he needed was Laila draped over his shoulder. He didn't need that kind of aggravation. Not today. Not ever.

21.

Jensen fastened her seatbelt, located her car keys in her purse, and started the engine with a surge of satisfaction. Ed had predicted that the weight of all the unnecessary keys on her key ring would ruin her starter. Well it hadn't happened. Not that she should be gloating. Ed had been right about her lilacs. He was probably right about a few other things, too.

Even her mother made a valid point. The risks inherent in an internet romance weren't the only disadvantage of love online. There was no one to eat dinner with, no hugs when you were discouraged, no shoulder massages when you were tense, and no one to help make decisions when you went shopping.

Replacing the things she'd lost in the break-in was not a task she was looking forward to. She half-wished she'd asked if Ed would come along to give her some advice. From the time she was small, her father had been there when she needed to buy anything auto or electronic related, her Grandma Victoria and her mother's cousins when she'd needed new clothes. The horrors of being with her younger brothers aside, she was a huge fan of her family's legendary shopping expeditions and the joint decision-making process the Christiansens utilized.

She smiled, thinking of Blooming Prairie and wondering if word still spread like wildfire the way it had when she was a kid. Back then, you could expect to find half the town gathered by the time you arrived at the fabric store to make a purchase, each one ready to give advice on what color looked nicest with your eyes or which fabric was less likely to wrinkle.

The size and shape of your breasts or hips and which style would be most flattering to your excesses and deficiencies had been discussed as openly as which items were a good buy and which were overpriced. Once decisions were made, there was no need to doubt their validity or second-guess oneself. The tribe had spoken.

She sighed. The sunshine wafting into the car from the

south hinted at warmth, but in reality, the heat was a brittle facade that threatened to crumble at any minute. The farmers were taking advantage of the dry weather to harvest their crops. Row upon row of cornstalks awaiting their fate, dried and shriveled by the autumn air, rippled by her window on one side. On the other side, naked hills lined up, punctuated with plumes of chaff where corn pickers ate away at the rows still left.

Her thoughts went back to Ed, then Anders. Great. The last thing she needed was to start thinking the grass-was-greener on the other side of the fence, or in this case, the world. Sure, the physical companionship when she was dating Ed had been nice, but she'd ached for someone to share her thoughts with. Anders was a gifted listener, but now she was starved for the simple sensation of touch.

Lately, even the satisfaction she'd felt initially when she and Anders had talked had diminished. He was still a willing confidant—if she managed to remember the plethora of things she stored up to tell him at the end of each day, and if her musings could be squeezed into their limited time together. Her thoughts rattled around in her head all day long like rocks in a cement mixer until they crumbled to dust and disappeared into the gray matter that filled her cranium. Sometimes there was nothing there by the time she met Anders online.

She applied the brakes as she topped the crest of the hill. Ed had always said this area was heavily patrolled. She felt a quick pang of regret. She'd known she'd miss the way Ed looked out for her, but she hadn't anticipated how much she would feel the loss of not caring for him—from thinking about what she would fix him for dinner to wondering if he'd slept well. Being with him had fulfilled at least a few of her maternal instincts.

She came over the rise of a hill and drove past a farmhouse. A golden retriever-looking mutt leapt from his perch by the porch and dashed out to meet her car, his legs pumping furiously, his hair flying backwards in the wind as he raced after her in the ditch that ran parallel to the road. She lost him after a few hundred feet. She was moving too fast for his short, stubby legs and they both knew it. Was it stupidity, hope, or love of a thrill that prompted the dog to jump up from the porch each and every time a car went by, engaging time and time again in such a futile chase?

Her mother's words echoed in her ears. Maybe the chances of finding the great love she'd always dreamed of were impossible. When she'd started dating Ed, she'd convinced herself that she could give up her dream of finding a man who was "perfect" for her and learn to be happy with what she had. Ed's only fault was that he was a typically stoic Midwestern man. In theory, she should have found everlasting bliss, or at least contentment, with him. But there was a crack in the premise somewhere. In the end, all she'd gotten from Ed was one more hole in her heart.

*****

Anders turned away from Erik's teasing glance and gazed stoically out the window. He stretched his free leg out as far as the cramped quarters of the airplane allowed and used the arm that Laila wasn't sleeping on to readjust his pillow.

He looked past the rigid countenance reflected in the window and watched the choppy, white-speckled waves disappearing into the distance, only to be replaced by a never-ending trail of stand-ins. It was common for those involved in a crisis situation to feel a sense of depression once the initial surge of adrenalin had passed. He'd counseled hundreds of trainees in the symptoms and recommended treatments, never dreaming he would find himself suffering from a classic case.

He felt a sense of tremendous loss, a sense of having been let down or deeply disappointed. Sitting helplessly, with nothing to do but think, was frustrating beyond words, even though he knew this was simply the lull before the storm. The true test of his grit awaited him in Nova Scotia. They would face emotional ups and downs over the course of the next seventy-two hours that would make the most terrifying roller coaster at Tivoli look like a spin around the merry-go-round.

Shivers ran down his spine as he recalled an air disaster he'd been called to help with years earlier. The pilot of that plane had been a close friend of his. He could still remember standing with his friend's widow at the cemetery when the call came to halt the pallbearers from lowering the casket into the ground; the horrified look in the widow's eyes as they were told the rescue crews had found and identified another piece of his friend's body. He closed his eyes against the memory.

Laila's hand moved across his lower belly in a subconscious caress. The slender fingers that clung to his shirt were soft and warm. He'd always believed it was better to live alone than with someone you didn't really love, but at times like this, when his body cried out for the comforting touch of a woman, he couldn't help wondering if he was wrong.

Maybe it was him. Maybe it was no accident that he always seemed to be attracted to women he couldn't have. Here he was, sitting next to a Danish woman who was perfectly beautiful, clearly interested in him, and logistically speaking, an ideal candidate for a life mate. Anders looked down at Laila and felt nothing but bone-numbing coldness.

On paper, the two of them were a perfect match. Things would be much simpler if he could forget about Jensen and fall in love with Laila, or any other Danish woman, for that matter. He'd never been one to take the easy route just because it was convenient, but the limitations of love online seemed impossible to overcome.

The relationship he had with Jensen, for all its loosely defined edges and uncertain future, was totally unique and unlike anything he had ever experienced. The things he'd told her, he had shared with no one. The depth of emotion that he felt for her was unrivaled. Comparisons were not only irrelevant, but impossible. Sometimes a man had to follow his heart, even when the heart made no sense.

He was going to have to deal with the maelstrom of

emotions she drew forth in him, to somehow find a way to bring their desire for love and companionship to fruition. He wanted, needed, someone to share his dreams with—in the flesh.

*****

Jensen knew that both Ed and her father would have checked the latest issues of "Consumer Report" before they set foot in Best Buy. Both men would have haggled for the best possible price, the longest warranty, and the highest quality before they spent a dime. She took it for granted a store called Best Buy would have the best buys and left the rest up to her instincts.

She was almost ready to check out when she noticed a cluster of customers with their heads tilted up. Her stomach twisted as she followed their eyes to a wall of television screens showing scenes from an airplane crash, each outlining the horrible aftereffects in a slightly different hue.

The plane had been on its way to Denmark. Her heart went out to the families of the people involved in the crash. She thought of Anders, and appreciated him all the more as she visualized the scope and impact of his work for the first time.

The ride back to Welch flew by quickly. How could she bemoan the fact that she had no one to hug her when she was blessed simply to be alive? How could she pity herself when she was lucky enough to have her whole life ahead of her?

*****

She was unpacking her new television when the phone rang. It wasn't the time of day she might have expected to hear from Anders, but it seemed very natural to pick up the phone and find him on the line. The first surprise came when she found out he was calling her from Canada. The second, when he invited her to meet him on Prince Edward Island at a country inn called Dalvay-By-The-Sea.

"The flight leaves from Minneapolis and flies non-stop to Nova Scotia, where you'll go through customs and make your connections to Charlottetown," Anders said. "If this is agreeable to you, you'll need to call the airline within the next twenty-four hours to confirm."

"Just promise me you won't do anything rash like running off to meet him." Her mother's voice echoed in her ears. "It's just too dangerous." Words she'd read in a newspaper article raced through her head. *One clue that your online lover might be married is the old "let's meet someplace neutral where we'll both feel at ease" line. Beware if they want to meet you some place other than their hometown. It could mean they have something to hide.*

How do you know he's telling you the truth? How do you know he's even from Denmark? A voice from quilting class jumped in. *If she'd gone out to meet him she could have ended up catching some disease, or committing adultery without even knowing it...*

She was terrified, exhilarated, scared out of her wits, and so excited she could barely contain her jubilation. This is what she'd been wanting, wasn't it? To take the fantasy she shared with Anders online and make it reality?

She was so used to spelling out her thoughts to him one word at a time on her keyboard that she couldn't find the voice she needed to speak the million and one things that were rushing through her mind.

"Are you there, Jensen?" Anders asked quietly. It had been a hell-of-a twenty-four hours. He was exhausted and stressed to the point of breaking. He was wearing the same clothes he'd thrown on in his bedroom in Danemark; he didn't know how many hours ago. "Will you come?"

He heard her take a deep breath. "I'll see you on Friday."

He couldn't muster happy, or even relieved. His whole body felt flat and expressionless. "I don't know how closely I'll be able to keep in touch over the next few days. I'll call when I can." Apologetic didn't work either. He was just too tired.

"Can I email you if I need to reach you for some reason?"

"Yes. I'll check at the internet bar at the airport."

"Be careful, okay?"

"I've got good reason to stay safe now that I know I'll be seeing you." His voice broke.

"I love you, Anders."

"I love you, too, sweetheart."

*****

Jensen corrected a typo in the last line and decided she ought to proof the letter one more time before she pressed send.

> *Okay, I'll admit it, Anders. I'm scared. Extremely scared. Nothing will ever be the same once we meet. If we feel the way we think we will, one or the other or both of our lives will have to change drastically to sustain the happiness we find. If we feel nothing, our hearts will break with disappointment. It will be even worse if one of us feels love and the other indifference. Yet all I want is for you to press yourself so closely to me that you can feel my heart beating. All I want is the very thing I am afraid of.*

She left that one in the drafts folder and wrote a second.

> *It's almost embarrassing to think of meeting you face-to-face and looking you in the eye—you, with whom I have been so intimate. You, to whom I've said the things I have. Yet it feels perfectly natural, as I've shared my heart and gotten to know you, that I would want to share other aspects of myself with you, too... to be honest about everything I think and feel. The level of intimacy that's developed*

between us makes me happy even though we're miles apart— despite the fact that it would probably take a miracle to overcome the geographical differences between us. I can also feel a part of me starting to distance myself from you; subconsciously trying to prepare myself for the fact that from here on out we are raising the stakes and doubling the ante and increasing the odds that one of us will end up hurt or disappointed or heartbroken. I know you have felt this too. If we meet, we pass a point of no return, and that scares me tremendously. That same fear makes me want to feel your arms around me, hear your voice and curl up safe and sound in your arms. I want to run to you, not from you.

She didn't send either one, but worked double-time finishing a quilt that was under deadline, corresponding with the Amish women who did her quilting, and taking packages to the post office. She came home with a burgundy lace bra and panty set from the lingerie boutique beneath the St. James Hotel, feeling a little like a modern-day mail order bride. She located her passport and moved on to the nitty-gritty of what clothes and shoes to take, and the all-important decision of what she would be wearing when she stepped off the plane.

She wanted to be comfortable, but she knew Europeans tended to think that Americans dressed down to the point of being sloppy. She didn't want Anders to have that impression of her. Eliminating her denim jumper, skirts, and blue jeans ruled out half of the outfits she'd pulled out of the closet. Nothing in her closet rivaled the suave, haute couture of the European women she remembered from her travels.

She considered a sage-colored, cotton sundress and a hand-knitted sweater dotted with sheep she'd purchased in Wales until she discovered a grease stain on the back of the skirt, which is what she got for riding her bike in dresses on windy days.

She went online to recheck the current temperatures on Prince Edward Island before finally deciding on a dress she'd made for a class she'd taught called *Fabric Art for Fashions.* The main body of the dress was a sultry plum challis that had enough give to be comfortable. The colors complimented her eyes, the style was sleek but not stuffy, the feel of the fabric was soft and sensual. What she loved best was the low, sweetheart neckline. The fitted bodice was a patchwork of moss green velvet, brown satin, and a floral print that combined the three colors. She'd used coordinating velvet and satin ribbons to define the quilted segments and accented the patches with a smattering of antique buttons from her great-great-grandfather's button box. She could definitely see herself floating into Anders' arms wearing the plum challis.

The last thing she remembered before her head settled into the soft cloud of her pillow was the feeling of his mouth on hers, his tongue dancing inside her mouth in a mating ritual as old as the sea. She fell asleep dreaming of his hands running over the silky fabric of her hand-quilted bodice, cupping her breasts, kissing her.

*****

Anders knew she'd be a bundle of nervous energy, waiting to hear from him, getting ready to go, making her plans. He wrote her from the airport on the evening of the night before she was due to fly into Charlottetown.

> *It's been a living hell, Jensen. I'm sure you've had indications from the media coverage as to the conditions here. I can't wait to see your face, to start to forget the images of sorrow and carnage and destruction, to feel your arms around me.*

Anders hesitated. A flight had just arrived from New York

City, and a myriad of people lugging suitcases and cameras pressed by him on either side. He needed to write this letter. If his words changed her perceptions or clouded the illusions she had about their first meeting, so be it. What he had to say was part of the process two people ultimately have to go through to achieve intimacy or an honest relationship of any kind.

Jensen, I want you to know that you will dictate how we proceed when we meet. If the endearments we have expressed for each other on-line do not feel right, you need not say them. Feel no pressure to do anything you don't feel so inclined in your heart. Whatever happens, we will be better people for having shared this time together. I know it is intimidating to think about seeing me in the flesh. We are invested in one another, we have the power to hurt and disappoint each other. We also have the power to bring much joy. That is the price of honesty. That is the risk that comes with love. I think you know that it is your vulnerability, your imperfections and your candidness that have endeared you to me. This weekend will not change that, even if our 'fantasies' are not fulfilled. Rest assured that I will always want to talk to you, hear from you, and see you as I may. The only thing that will continue to unfold and change over time is what we will be to each other. That is the book we are writing. No one knows what the final chapter will say. But whether you be friend, an occasional sharer of thoughts, confidante, lover, or all, I will not put the book down until we have finished writing. Do you understand? I love you, no matter in the flesh or from afar. I love you forever, no matter in my arms or in my heart.

He did not reread the letter. He simply pressed send.

22.

Jensen double checked her fanny pack for the tenth time that morning—passport, ID, cash, credit card, e-ticket, lipstick, comb, a paperback novel to read on the airplane, and a miniature quilt she could work on if she needed something to keep her fingers busy. She wanted desperately to look calm and collected when she met Anders. Sleek and sophisticated would be nice, but she wasn't counting on it after a long flight.

She wouldn't be flying halfway across the continent to meet Anders if she didn't trust that he loved her. So when the last thing she did before she left for the airport dressed in her plum challis dress with her new brown leather fanny pack wrapped around her waist was to make a copy of all the information she had about Anders, from his phone numbers and photograph to the Inn where they'd be staying on Prince Edward Island, it really didn't mean anything except that her mother had taught her to use the brain the good Lord gave her.

Her fingers trembled as she sealed the information and a brief note in an envelope addressed to Peder and Tara.

The sun was darting in and out of a cluster of clouds when she locked each of her doors and tucked her key chain into her fanny pack. She dropped the letter in the mailbox in front of Welch's tiny post office on her way out of town.

*****

Anders pulled away from the curb of a car rental office just outside Charlottetown Airport. He'd felt somewhat guilty saying goodbye to Erik and Helmut when they'd boarded their plane for the trip back to Copenhagen. They'd been through hell together—even Laila had turned out to be a valuable member of their counseling team.

His explanation of why he was choosing to stay behind had been brief. Erik knew the truth, but he'd told Laila and the others only that he needed a break and had always wanted to see more of Canada. He had plenty of vacation time built up, so no further questions had been asked. Laila seemed to have known that he wasn't letting her in on the rest of the story, but while he may have regretted being less than honest with her, his conscience was clear. He had never led her to believe his interest in her was anything other than professional.

It wasn't going to be easy setting aside the stress and horror of the last few days. He was feeling everything a person was expected to feel after dealing with an air disaster—a sense of helplessness, a generally depressed mood, and deep, penetrating fatigue. News of the plane crash had already been relegated to page two. While its aftershocks would ripple on for years as the legal and logistical ramifications were explored, the contents of the black boxes deciphered, and the public relations damage to Viking Airways addressed, the crisis was officially under control.

The quaint countryside he'd heard so much about started to come into view as he left Charlottetown and headed north. He'd been cooped up so much over the course of the last few days that he'd decided to check out the lay of the land and then double back to get Jensen.

The island was sixty-four kilometers across at its wide point and two hundred twenty-four kilometers long. He'd picked up color brochures at the airport and was keeping his eyes open for fun things to do. Options seemed plentiful, from beaches and sand dunes to light houses and art galleries, Celtic music and antiques to rustic lanes and historic sights.

He headed west toward Cavendish. Less than an hour later he was walking along the grass-tufted sand dunes at Cavendish Beach, a lobster roll and a cup of Cow's Ice Cream in one hand and a beach towel and his brief case in the other. He'd bought the beach towel at Cow's because the design had featured a helmet-clad cow riding a bicycle, not knowing it would come in handy.

He stood with his back to the wind. The towel caught like a

sail, then fluttered to the sand. Anders sat cross-legged and ate while the waves and wind danced merrily around him. When he was done, he opened his briefcase. He had only a few more lines to translate and the letter he'd been working on would be ready to share with Jensen. If all went well, he hoped to read it aloud to her while she lay in his arms.

*****

Jensen thanked the stewardess and closed her magazine before anyone could see the glaring headline, "Romance, or Naked and Alone on the Internet?" by Shane Wesley. She took a second to reassure herself that no one was paying attention and opened it again, this time at a discreet slant.

You've heard what can happen. It starts out innocently enough: a nice, single woman who's lonely and hasn't been successful meeting men in traditional ways, decides to enter a chat room and see what happens. What can it hurt? Before long, she's met the man of her dreams. He makes her laugh, understands her deepest desires, and is always there to listen. Soon, they're chatting every night and sharing everything about themselves, no matter how intimate. No subject, no secret is too personal. Eventually, they move to a private chat room and partake in cybersex. Soon, she is head over heels in love, and wants to meet in real life. But instead of making her fantasies come true, she ends up with a broken heart when she discovers that the love of her life is actually married with six kids, a she, or a twelve-year-old boy who thinks the whole thing is funny.

Jensen sucked in her breath and hoped she wasn't going to be ill. In her worst nightmares she'd never envisioned that Anders might be a teenager, or, God forbid, a she.

For the briefest of seconds, she pacified herself with the thought that she could turn around and fly back to Minnesota just as soon as she reached Halifax.

Then she listened to her heart. There was no way Anders

could be a teenager. His words were too eloquent, his thoughts too insightful. If he were married, he certainly wouldn't have conducted their relationship in full view of his son. As for the possibility that he was a she... there was no way. He was too good at describing what it felt like to be "thick". She could feel her face heating to a red flush as she read on.

Despite the horrible scenarios that can and do happen daily, internet dating is far less scary than most people believe. In fact, relationships that begin online often have a greater chance of success than do face-to-face meetings in the real world.

Rebecca and Gus met in a Yahoo! chat room two years ago. Although they felt instantly comfortable conversing, neither one was impressed by the other's profile or photograph. But as they got to know one another, they grew to care for each other so deeply that they finally decided they had to meet face-to-face and see if there really was a physical spark. By the time they met, neither cared what the other looked like. When they finally saw each other in the flesh, they were pleasantly surprised to discover they shared a very deep, very real attraction... and a love that may never have materialized had they met before they'd gotten to know one another online. Rebecca and Gus were engaged six months later and plan to be married next year.

The rest of the article was very positive. If it hadn't been for the mention of cybersex, she might have tried to get a copy for her mother.

"Virtual relationships can and do result in old-fashioned love affairs for many people who may never have met their match without a little help from modern technology."

She closed the magazine, then her eyes, as she leaned back in her chair and tried to doze. If communication was the key to a good relationship, she and Anders had it made.

*****

The hair on Anders' forearms tingled with pricks of sweat as the sunshine beat down on him. There was no shade except for a few shaggy tufts of marram grass. He focused his eyes on the photocopied image, squinted until his eyes adjusted to the glare, and continued to read the words Maren had penned. He reread the passage a second time to make sure he hadn't misread her archaic penmanship or mistranslated a key sentence. But there was no doubt. He wiped his brow and exhaled loudly. Maybe he was thinking too much like the man he was; maybe his impending meeting with Jensen was resulting in a surge of testosterone that was influencing his perceptions, but for the first time he could readily understand why Frederik had felt compelled to bring his family to America. If he had been in Frederik's place, witnessed what he had, he would have done everything in his power to make sure his wife never saw Leif Unterschlage again.

*****

Jensen peeked at her reflection and wished Anders could have seen her six hours and two airports ago. She never had been able to figure out why air travel was so tiring. Her neck was cramped from trying to get comfortable, her hair had wilted hours earlier, and she felt stiff all over.

The flight from Halifax to Charlottetown was short and flown at low altitudes perfect for viewing the details of the panorama below. Steeply slanted rays of sunlight filtered through the thick underbrush of the woodlands below while the blue waters of Northumberland Strait sparkled in the distance.

Thick. The word rippled through her memories until she was tingling with sensation. A sudden surge of energy flowed through her veins. This was no stranger she was meeting. This was a man she knew and loved.

The tide looked high as they neared the island. She could see the water licking the supple shores that curved in and out of each estuary, inlet and bay. The Indian name for Prince Edward

Island was Abegweit. *Land cradled on the waves.* The red sandy shores did seem as though they were caught in the ocean's embrace. It looked magical, from the pristine buildings and trees lining Charlottetown's streets to the wildly primitive patchwork of flowering fields, grass-tufted beaches and hilly red roads that creased the countryside.

The plane alighted with a touchdown so smooth she hardly realized they had landed until she saw the terminal approaching. She stood the second the plane stopped, took her carry-on bag from the overhead compartment, and waited impatiently as the people ahead of her disembarked.

She couldn't have been more nervous if she'd been blindfolded and walking a gangplank. What if Anders didn't recognize her? What if he took one look at her and left?

Her eyes scanned two men who might have been him, then stopped on a man leaning against the wall at the far side of the room. His lanky legs extended out in front of him, his hands were in his pockets, and his face was friendly but wary.

His eyes sought hers as she came closer; deep brown eyes, liquid pools filled with an intimate awareness that left no doubt to his identity. He smiled and nodded once, holding her glance as she moved toward him.

She could feel herself blushing as she let her eyes roam over him. He was only a few feet from her now. She shivered with a mixture of hesitancy and anticipation.

He gulped and took his hands out of his pockets. "Jensen?"

"Anders?"

He looked as dazed as she felt.

Her giggle just popped out. "I feel so silly all of the sudden."

"You are too beautiful," he said accusingly, then joined her in laughter.

Her mirth faded in the space of a second. "Keep talking," she pleaded. "You look the way I imagined, and then you don't. Your voice is familiar."

"You're staring," he whispered, chastising and reassuring her all at once.

"Is it really you?"

He stepped a little closer and stretched out one arm. "Maybe this will help." His hands urged her closer and closer until her neck was snuggled into the heat of his skin, her forehead touching the smooth expanse of his cheek, his arms wrapped around her.

She melted into him.

"I want you to get used to the way I look and feel." He kissed her temple.

"You feel heavenly."

"So do you."

She pulled back from his embrace. "I still want to look at you."

"We'll have plenty of time for both." Anders took her suitcase with one hand and gripped her arm possessively with the other. "Come with me, my shy one."

Was he as taken with her as she was with him? She loved the look of him; his tanned, muscular arms, the way his shirt clung to the shape of his chest, the sturdiness of his legs, the curve of his hips, the sparkle in his eyes. She continued to eye him covertly as they walked down the concourse, turning her eyes away each time he looked back.

He took her elbow. "You've nothing to feel shy about. You're everything I dreamed you'd be and more."

They were words she might have doubted coming from another, but from him, she believed every one. She adjusted her pace to his long-legged gait as they proceeded to claim her baggage and wind their way out of the airport, feeling more confident and at ease with every step they took.

*****

Anders watched her breasts rise and fall as she took a deep breath. He loved it that her body's expressions were transparent, that her face was true to the emotions she was experiencing, yet he saw in her eyes so many facets that he knew he would never tire of looking at her. He loved the fact that she laughed easily, that he could make her smile with little or no effort. Her eyes shone with pleasure as she looked up at him. She looked at once bemused and enthralled. He'd waited his whole life to see someone look at him that way.

She was sexy but sweet, silly but savvy, and he was more convinced than ever that she was the intriguing balance of sass and spirit he'd always searched for.

An hour later they were driving through the country-side, chatting like long lost friends. She pointed out things he hadn't noticed—a small cluster of flowers growing in the ditch by the roadside, an iron fence silhouetted against the sky behind a house on a hill, a Gothic, stained glass window shimmering in the sunlight. She appreciated what he admired; the unique slant of a church steeple, harvested potato fields bumpy with clumps of red clay, coves filled with sailboats and lobster traps. Their conversation flowed as sweet and smooth as honey.

They drove along the sea for the last link of their short journey to Dalvay-By-The-Sea. Red barns and white farmhouses silhouetted against the blue ocean made a picturesque fairy tale of an ordinary sight for Jensen, who was used to farms ringed by corn fields. The entire island seemed magical, every tiny lane quaint and charming, every house a whimsical storybook tale come to life.

She'd grown more and more quiet as they drove. What was she thinking? Was she simply mesmerized, or afraid of being alone with him? The inn where he'd made reservations loomed on the horizon, its size all but hidden by dunes until they rounded the last curve and saw its timbers and stone, stucco and gingerbread rising from the sand. Yards of spindle-railed porches wrapped around the perimeter and a grassy yard strewn with whitewashed lawn chairs and geese sloped down to a pond.

He ignored the trembling in Jensen's hand as he helped her from the car and escorted her into the lobby. Thick, stone walls whispered their greeting with a hushed, old-fashioned charm, their very breadth bespeaking sturdiness, endurance and fortitude. A wood staircase wrapped its way to the guest rooms on the right; a banquet room filled with linen-covered tables beckoned to the left. The succulent smells and savory decor promised the best in tasteful dining. Anders had no desire to taste anything but the woman at his side.

*****

Jensen's last thought before she completely blocked her family from her mind was that her mother would have been utterly and completely impressed with Anders' courteousness and old world manners. She felt like the belle of the ball—an opened door, a hand at her elbow, a whispered remark— Anders' every movement evidenced a quiet confidence and grace.

He'd barely touched her, yet her emotions had reached such a crescendo that it was hard to keep her wits about her. *There's no harm in being safe—no reason to rush into anything.* But there was. They only had a few days. If she wasted them being overly cautious or thinking about what her mother would do if she knew where she was, she'd fritter away half of their time together.

His choice of accommodations seemed thoughtful enough—a suite of adjoining rooms, hers with a canopy bed, his with a sitting area flanked by a trundle bed. But his intentions were far from gentlemanly, and she knew it. He took her hand the second they'd closed the door, pressed her palm to his, and twirled her around to face him. His eyes met hers for one searing second before his lips met hers. There was no caution in the way she melted into him, nothing demure about the way she rubbed her hands across his back, nothing shy in the way she kneaded his muscles with her fingertips and tipped her head to meet his mouth.

She couldn't say whether it was his tongue that touched hers first, or her his; but the jolt of energy that flew between them was ripe with promises.

His hands found their way from her cheeks to the strands of hair framing her face. He pulled her closer, his hands braided in her hair, his fingers massaging her temples and the base of her neck. His contours filled each hollow, pressing indelibly into her form where there were none.

He spoke to her between kisses, whispering endearments, caressing her with his lips and then his words. She murmured back to him with utterances unintelligible to anyone but one who knew her heart until the air was thick with primitive moans and insinuations, each whimper understood as clearly as though they had been spoken.

The evening passed like a blur; a walk along the beach at sunset while the sand was still warm from the day, a sumptuous dinner delivered to their room, served while they sat cushioned in wingback chairs at a table skirted in flowing moiré and topped with a pottery vase filled with wildflowers. She felt like a princess. In her heart she knew her prince was more gallant than those found in any fairy tale.

*****

Anders was fine until dinner was done, until she went in to take a bath. Listening to each tantalizing drop of water pour over her body was agony, pure and simple. Being with her was no different than being alone in that sense. He had a vivid imagination, and he had tortured himself many times before with images of water droplets beading on her throat, dripping from the tips of her areolas, caressing her skin. But this time he could smell the scent of almond and strawberries and peach, hear each splash of water as she rinsed herself, see the mist rising from under the door. Having held her only fueled his already poignant thoughts to heights of painfully acute awareness.

It was all he could do to maintain the decorum he had promised himself he would adhere to—at least on their first night together. His self-imposed condition went from bad to worse when she returned, wrapped in the same robe she had described to him online. Words typed on a screen held no magic compared to the sight of her walking across the room, her long, slender legs soft and gleaming with lotion, the swell of her bosom spreading open the folds of the robe, the tiny triangle of silk just visible between her breasts, her hair still damp.

No words, no matter how colorfully typed, could describe the pleasure that surged through him at the sight of her freshly scrubbed cheeks, her finely turned ankles, her soft ivory hands, so tender and expressive. Every facet of her was tantalizing, from the few parts exposed to his view to the hidden places he could only imagine. For now.

Maybe it was the cloud of steam swirling around her when she came out of the powder room; all Jensen knew was that she could hardly catch her breath when she saw Anders in his robe, that eerily familiar, hunter green and navy plaid robe she had seen him in as she sat at her computer. She gazed longingly at his strong, muscled legs and the curve of his thighs under the form-fitting fabric, then forced herself to divert her gaze. She finally let her eyes linger on the slit of bare chest visible under his robe, which was somewhat safer, but barely.

He was hard and lean from riding his bicycle; the toning gave him a gracefulness of movement that was uncommon to a man of such stature. She could hardly wait to touch him, to familiarize herself with every ripple and swell.

He backed away from her as though it took every ounce of willpower he possessed to move those few inches. "We think alike, sweet Princess of the Night."

"Yes," she whispered shyly, and continued to peruse him.

"You must stop looking at me that way, at least for a minute, or I will not be able to tear myself away from you."

"Whatever you wish, Prince Charming," she murmured, her eyes locked on his.

He laughed, a resigned chuckle that nonetheless broke the spell just long enough for him to make his escape.

23.

Anders' shower was driven by such intense impatience that he was still more than half-damp when he slipped his legs into his pajama bottoms. The feel of them was unfamiliar, but not altogether uncomfortable. He was used to being naked under his robe, in his bed, and in his house a good deal of the time. While the thin layer of fabric would hardly do the job of a chastity belt, if he were sincere about not wanting to rush things, he could hardly wander about their suite in the nude.

She was sitting up in the canopy bed when he returned, a mound of pillows tucked cozily behind her back, her legs crossed primly under the covers. A second mound of pillows awaited him.

His heart throbbed, looking at her there, so trusting, so beautiful, her hair so soft and shiny, her adoring eyes shimmering from the dusky twilight like twin blue sapphires. She shifted her legs, smiled and patted the pillows beside her.

He joined her, sitting crossed legged on top of the quilt, and bent to kiss her forehead. "Ready for a bedtime story?"

"Yes." She looked surprised.

"I've finished translating Maren's last letter. May I read it to you?"

Her eyes shone even brighter. "Oh yes! Please."

He took the manuscript and a pair of wire rimmed reading glasses from the pocket of his robe and looked at her tenderly over the top of the rims. He unfolded the papers and began to read in a hushed voice.

My dearest cousin Sophie,

Greetings! I must first impart my joyful news—much has happened since our letters crossed on steamers somewhere in the Atlantic. No talk of the past is important enough to overshadow the birth of my new baby boy, Wilfred Henry Jensen, born August first! He

243

is a big baby; long and wide in the shoulders like his father. (I wanted to curse the doctor for insisting I spend those long weeks in bed, fearing the baby would come too soon. Surely if we had left him to his own devises, he would not have grown so large nor been so hard to birth!)

Please don't take my jesting as a complaint, as the birth was free of complications and I am feeling more spry with every day that passes. The young neighbor girl who was such a godsend when I was forced to my bed has stayed on to help with the new baby and see to the older children since my mother cannot be with me. Truth be told, however, little Wilfred is a gem, and rarely makes a peep except to let me know he wishes more to eat. (Another trait he shares with his father.)

Mathilda has been a good helper to both me and Anna Marie, and Karl is delighted to have another male in the house. I guess he does not like being alone with all the women. I thought perhaps baby Victoria would be jealous, but she loves to cuddle the baby and sits by him for hours, cooing and giggling to him while Little Freddie gurgles and smiles back at her in a language only the two of them understand.

Jensen was beaming up at him when he lifted his eyes from the letter.

"I can't tell you how fun it is to hear her speaking of my Grandma Victoria as a baby, and in her last letter, to know that Maren was working on the quilt I have hanging in my bedroom. I feel such a connection to them," she said.

"I know." He leaned closer and kissed her on the head.

I am sorry my last letter was so ambiguous, Sophie. It is so painful for me to even think on these things that my thoughts come out only half formed when I hearken back to those days. Frederik was so afraid that his

244

humiliation would become public, that in my mind, I started to believe it had actually happened, envisioning that people discovered why we left Danemark and talked amongst themselves about the truth of what had happened at the farm that day.

I should have known that Leif would not say a word. He is the only other one who knew what happened beside my Mama, and even she knew only half of the story. At any rate, it is a relief to know that our secret has been so carefully guarded. I know you will do the same.

It all started the morning of the day that Victoria was born. It was a hot day, and the air was unusually thick with moisture.

He squeezed her leg suggestively as he let the word roll off his lips, knowing full well the effect it would have on her.

"Stop it." She giggled.

"Me? What did I do?" He smiled, trying to look innocent.

"It's not what you did, it's what you said."

"What? I am just reading what Maren wrote," he said.

"You're reading your translation of what Maren wrote." Jensen said. "You could have said humid or muggy or oppressively damp. You chose to say *thick with moisture*. Don't tell me it just happened to pop out."

Her laughter turned to a sigh when his mouth closed over hers.

"Be careful, Jensen, or something *thick* will pop out."

"Promises, promises," she whispered in a husky voice.

"Shhhh… be a good girl like your Great Aunt Mathilda. Sit back and listen." Anders cleared his throat. "Let's see now, where were we? It was unusually *humid...*"

He watched as the lilt in his voice lulled her back to a muggy day in Danemark almost a hundred years ago.

The breezes from the sea had disappeared and all was still. Remember the etching Mama has hanging above the sofa in her parlor called Vindstille? It pictures a woman with a baby in her arms standing at the end of a pier watching her husband's boat, trapped at sea because the winds had vanished. It was that kind of day. When Frederik left for the hay fields, I was feeling somewhat tired, sapped of energy and a little sick to my stomach—nothing to give any indication that I was in labor, and everything to suggest that I was hot and sticky, as big as a whale and tired from waking up every few hours to either make a trip to the outhouse or use the chamber pot.

It was still early when Frederik left with his lunch basket tucked under his arm. I went back to bed. When I heard the children, I set about dressing Mathilda and Karl. I had made a wedding cake the day before and knew that Leif would be arriving to pick it up; the last I had agreed to make until after the baby was born, as I was due in three short weeks. Other than that I had no plans for the day but to rinse out some clothes in the washtub, hang the laundry out on the line and fix a nice dinner for Frederik. The last thing I remember was sitting down for some breakfast with the children. Karl was clapping his hands and Mathilda was humming to herself.

The next thing I knew I was laying on the floor in a pool of water, the children were crying hysterically and I hurt all over. My head ached; my shoulder throbbed where I had hit the floor. The doctor had warned us that this baby might come faster than the other two, as it was the third I'd had in a fairly short time; still, nothing prepared me for the sharp intensity of the pains I felt or the quickness with which they came on.

I realized my predicament immediately, but there was little I could do but pray, grip the legs of the chair

*near the spot where I had fallen, and try not to push.
My goodness, I prayed. I was able to quiet Mathilda by
talking to her calmly between my contractions. She was
scared silly, poor thing. First she brought me a pillow,
then she found the little quilt my moder gave her to
wrap around her baby doll, spread it on the floor and
lay down beside me, her thumb in her mouth. Karl was
in his high chair putting up such a din that, had the
wind been blowing, might have carried out to the field
where Frederik was working. As it was, he was left to
his misery, for I was so cumbersome I could not right
myself to tend to his needs.*

*I must have floated in and out of consciousness the
whole morning, passing out from the heat and my
malaise and coming to with the intensity of each new
labor pain. The heat was more stifling, the air more
oppressive than anything I remember. I simply could
not seem to get my breath. I could feel the baby coming,
hear Karl's hysterical screams and feel Mathilda's little
body snuggled up beside me each time I came to. I
remember thinking that it was providence that Karl was
in his highchair, at the very least safe, even if he was
unhappy and in need of dry pants.*

*I must have faded out again. When I awakened, Leif
was standing over me. Oh, Sophie, I have never been so
glad to see anyone in my life! He might have been a
knight in shining armor for all the heroic implications
of his arrival; at the very least an angel sent by God at
the precise moment in time I was most in need of a
helping hand.*

*His face, as it looked at that moment, is still etched
in my mind. Leif had confided in me some weeks earlier
that he had lost his wife and firstborn in childbirth. I
could see that he was frightened for me, that he was
reliving the terror of his wife's death, but quite
honestly, I was in no position to reassure him. Friendly*

concern, modesty, decorum, and my ladylike sensibilities all flew out the window.

The baby was coming quickly. My skirts were around my waist, Leif was telling me to push, and my beautiful Victoria was sliding into Leif's outstretched hands. Leif opened her little mouth with his fingers and she started to make the daintiest little mewing noises.

That was when we both started to weep. Leif cut the cord with a clean knife, put the baby on my stomach, wrapped in Mathilda's little quilt, and then crouched down beside me and gathered the both of us up in his arms. We simply lay there, Sophie, holding each other and weeping. It all came flooding out as we lay there in each other's arms—the pent up grief he'd been holding in since his wife died, the fear I'd felt, laying helpless on the kitchen floor, wondering what would become of my baby, our mutual relief that the baby was safe and healthy, and yes, the trust and adoration we shared for one another. Every emotion we held for each other came to a searing climax in those minutes we lay together, oblivious to my half-naked state, the pain of the afterbirth, the pool of water still staining the floor.

And then I was brushing the tears from his eyes, he was kissing the tears from my cheeks, while we laughed and cried and clung to each other, our hands clasped together over Victoria's tiny body.

I will never forget the look on Leif's face as he knelt beside me, nor the expression on Frederik's as he stormed in the door and stared down at the two of us, giddy as children and crying unabashedly in each other's arms.

While Leif's expressions lingered in his eyes throughout the whole ordeal, changing only from fear to joy to regret as the sequence of events progressed, the look on Frederik's face left as quickly as it came, masked within seconds of the time the emotions surfaced. He could not say what he thought, or show what he felt, so instead he stomped around the house and acted as though the timing of the whole occurrence was my fault, when the truth of the matter was I would have still been laying there alone if it hadn't started to rain. He never even looked at Victoria, Sophie. Not until after Leif returned with the doctor and everyone had gone home, and I lay sobbing upon our bed.

You asked if I loved Leif, Sophie. The truth is, I did. I loved him and will always love him as a trusted friend and confidante. I loved him as a kindred spirit—the kind you never even know exists until you have found them. I loved him as a man, from the depths of my heart.

Leif whispered his feelings to me seconds before Frederik came bounding through the door, in a flood of tears and emotion so sincere, so pure, that it makes me shiver to think of it. There was nothing lurid or unseemly about it, Sophie, both of us covered in blood and sweat, our faces streaked with tears. It was the most honest emotional exchange I have experienced, before or since... the love of two human beings joined by the most precious experience on earth. I can only hope that my eyes conveyed my feelings for him as clearly as his words did to me, since I was never to have the chance to share what I felt in my heart, never to see him again after that day.

Anders looked up from his notes. There were tears glistening in Jensen's eyelashes. Without thinking, he reached up and wiped the moisture from her cheeks with his fingers.

That was when he felt the tears in his own eyes. "Sorry."

"For crying?" she said. "How could you read something so touching and not?"

Anders didn't know. But obviously, other men did. He'd be willing to bet Ed wouldn't have cried. "I feel like I know her."

"So do I. I mean, I did know her, but I feel like I knew her when she was young. I felt like I was there."

Anders set the letter down and looked into her eyes. He'd gotten to know both Maren and Jensen through their words, words plainly spoken, words that tugged at his heart so powerfully he could hardly bear it. He'd thought he might never know Jensen except through her thoughts. But she was here, in the flesh, full of life, blushing with anticipation, bursting with passion.

She was his. All his. "Let me make love to you."

She answered by climbing onto his lap and straddling his legs; placing her palms flat against his chest, and lowering her head to kiss him. God, she felt good. And then she was taking his hand and guiding it to her breast. He'd told her he'd dreamed of feeling her skin just after she'd climbed from her bed; still silky and warm from the cocoon of covers she'd been tucked in. His hands cupped her breasts through the lace of her teddy until he discovered the buttons that held the straps in place and lowered the bodice to her waist.

She was beautiful, looking up at him, her eyes hazed with love. He could hear the water lapping against the shore in the distance, the tide coming in or going out; he didn't know— didn't know what day it was, what year it was, what time it was in Danemark or Minnesota or Seattle or on this precious island. Only that she was warm and soft and in love with him.

He let his fingers graze the center of her breasts, teased her nipples shamelessly, and kneaded the buoyant flesh with the palms of his hands. Her nipples were as hard as marbles. He refocused his attentions on her waist, moving his hands up and down the sides of her breasts as he went. He found her belly button, slipped the fabric of her teddy a few inches lower, and dipped his little finger into the recess. He twirled his hands over her stomach. He wanted her naked. He looked at her and let the lust burn in his eyes unfettered. She hadn't said a word, but her hands spoke volumes; caressing, kneading, stroking, learning the surface of his face, the texture of his hair, the feel of his arousal.

He stumbled upon the snaps that connected the bottom of her teddy by accident. Who would have thought? He blessed whoever had thought of such a wonderful invention, peeled the fabric from between her legs, and bared her innermost secrets to his fingers. Oh, God, she was wet. She moved against his hand. She trusted him. He held her and watched as she stiffened and sighed against his fingers, so ladylike, so wanton, so willing.

He clung to her when she came, rubbing the small of her back until the pleasure radiated to every pore of her being.

"Go to sleep, my love," he crooned to her, feeling like the luckiest man on earth.

"But you..."

"Shhh... It's after midnight in Minnesota. The sun will come streaming through those lace panels you like so much at what will feel like an unearthly hour to you."

"It must be nearly daybreak in Denmark."

"Wake me up after you've slept awhile. If I open my eyes to see you gazing at me from across the bed, my fantasy will have come true."

*****

The time on Prince Edward Island felt early by three hours to her; to him, late by four. But scrambled schedules were no deterrent when it came to two hearts determined to find middle ground. Their early morning, middle-of-the-night-to-her, lunchtime-to-him tryst was only the first of many surprises Anders had for her that day—the second being tickets to *Anne of Green Gables* at the Confederation Centre of the Arts.

It was off-season on the island. They'd been warned that many activities were only available on the weekend. So they cram-packed their Saturday with events, knowing they could wander down Lover's Lane, see Anne's Haunted Wood's, or wander the beach any day that week.

They had soup and salad at an old Irish pub for lunch, and

lobster rolls and Cow's Ice Cream before the concert. By the end of the day, Jensen's mind was so full she wondered if she could take in one more thing. But the Rankin Family's melancholy melodies and toe-tapping, foot-stomping, Celtic folk music topped off the evening, and her mood, perfectly.

Anders squeezed her hand as the lead soprano's voice floated effortlessly over the night air. The big open-air barn at the fairgrounds was filled to the rafters with locals and off-islanders alike. Some, of Scottish and Irish descent, sang along to the melodies in Gaelic. Others joined in when the lyrics were in English. Even Jensen found herself singing on those choruses where the lines were easy to pick up.

Some danced on the area squarely in front of the stage, others jigged along the sidelines. Some sat, others milled about, nodding companionably at the neighbors and friends who crossed their paths. Jensen felt absolutely at ease both with Anders and the throng of revelers surrounding them. It was the kind of evening she'd dreamed of, sharing a scintillating experience with someone she loved, trying something new, learning, stretching and growing. She stood on her tiptoes and kissed Anders soundly as the melancholy strains of a fiddle wafted through the courtyard. The song was one she'd never heard, an original introduced as *Borders and Time* by Jimmy Rankin. She listened intently as the words enveloped her in their meaning.

You have drifted so far from me.
The winds of change
Have swept you away.
Night and Day;
It seems like eternity.
Borders and time have kept
You from me.

Blue are the ocean waters
Along a lover's shoreline.

You will not be forgotten,
But now that you've gone
The heartache lives on.
Oh borders and time,
The heartache is mine.

Chills ran down her spine as she listened to the words. She touched Anders' arm. "It makes me think of Maren and Leif."

He wrapped his arm around her waist. "It's a long way across that ocean. Even longer in the early nineteen hundreds. Leif and Maren must have known they'd never see each other again when Frederik brought her to America."

She nodded and looked off into the night. "It's so sad."

He responded by taking her arm and urging her onto the makeshift dance floor, twirling her with a spin and a flourish. She was laughing at his antics in no time, although she had to admit he did a fair impression of what she could only assume was some sort of Irish jig or highland dance.

"'Tis me Gaelic blood," he whispered, winking at her secretively.

"And here I thought you were a stubborn Dane through and through."

"Stubborn and marauding. The Scots don't like to talk about it, but centuries ago the Vikings conquered their bonny land just like they did Sweden and Norway. The Gaelic language and culture are a combination of Norse and Celtic traditions. Likewise, the intermarrying that occurred during that time introduced Celtic blood into the lineage of many Danes."

"Seriously? I didn't know that."

"It's the truth, though it was kept under wraps for centuries. I've been told that the period is glossed over to the point that it's almost ignored in Scottish textbooks. Only recently have the Celtic peoples started to acknowledge and embrace that part of their history. In the end, you can't deny what's in your blood."

"I can understand why the Celts might be a little bitter about that period of history," Jensen said sympathetically.

Sherrie Hansen

"The Danes aren't any more eager to talk about it than the people whose lands they conquered. The Vikings were great warriors and explorers, but in today's society it's not exactly politically correct to brag about the way you plundered and ravaged the lands and women of other countries."

"I suppose a lot of countries conveniently rewrite their history to protect whatever interests or image they deem worthy," she said when the music came to a momentary halt.

"Except the United States, of course," he commented, sounding a trifle facetious.

"That's not what I was implying."

"Obviously," he said. "That's why I implied it for you."

Anders seemed to think he was being cute, but she didn't see it that way. "Didn't they cover the Thomas Jefferson story in Europe? They discovered he has a whole line of descendants born to him by one of his slaves, a black woman who became his mistress. That's the only example I can think of, but I'm sure there are a lot of incidents from American history that are glossed over in our history books."

"Touché." Anders said. "At least you're honest."

She tried to bite her tongue, but she couldn't help but bristle at his implications. "It sounds like you think that's a rarity where I come from."

"Well, if your last two presidents are any example..." Anders let his words trail off but his meaning was clear. "I'll never understand why Americans repeatedly reelect men for a second term, knowing full well they've lied about everything from their sex lives to their reasons for invading Iraq."

"Or how they could elect Hillary to public office," she said, playing devil's advocate for a moment.

His eyes were twinkling when he looked down at her. "We're having our first argument. Over politics, no less."

"All countries have periods of history that their people aren't proud of," she said. "That doesn't mean every person in the country is a flawed individual or that the country as a whole is rotten."

"I'm sorry, sweet." He kissed the top of her head. "Old habits are hard to break. I'll try to keep my anti-American thoughts to myself from now on."

She gave him a seething look and shook her head. "Do you really think so poorly of America or are you just trying to get my goat?"

"Just when I think I've heard every silly American expression there is to hear..."

She glared at him.

"You're cute when you're mad."

She let out a long huff before she allowed her lips to curve into a smile.

"The way your nostrils flare is downright adorable."

"My nostrils do not do any such thing!" She smiled up at him as the music started and they began to twirl amongst the other dancers, in perfect step with the rousing beat.

"Be careful how you look at me, my bonnie lass, or I'll plunder your hidden treasure and ravage your body." He winked. "I can't deny what's in me blood."

She simply snuggled closer in response, wondering to herself whether the fact that they shared so many of the same stubborn Danish genes was a good or bad thing.

The music changed to the heartrending tones of a ballad and she lost herself in her thoughts once again as she laid her head on his shoulder and swayed to the music.

Borders and Time. The song's words continued to haunt her. The thought of Maren being separated from her true love by borders and time was enough to make her cry. She felt Leif's grief at losing a second love, Maren's bitterness at being torn from her country, her family, and her love more keenly than she could have imagined was possible.

A deep fog had settled over the landscape by the time they left the concert. The air was so warm and balmy the fog took on a life of its own, creeping down the little red lanes and clinging to the bottoms of the fir trees that hugged the hills. They would never have known the sea was nearby but for the sad blare of the fog horn or the lapping noises it made as it pounded the shore.

It was a slow trip back to the Inn, first caught in a string of headlights, winding their way through the white of the night, then creeping along at the mercy of the fog and the narrow, winding roads. But the time was as pleasurable as any they had spent together. They talked as they went, reliving their favorite moments from the day, sharing their observations and trading their perceptions of all they had seen.

The banter they shared was pure pleasure. His every word made her body hum with anticipation of what was to come, yet she had the strange sensation that she would be just as happy snuggled up in his arms, whispering back and forth through the night as she would be making love with him. He stimulated her mind as acutely as he did her body. Any journey she embarked upon with this tall, sexy, Dane would be one of constant exploration, discovery, growth and renewal.

It was her idea to walk down to the beach. The fog was so mesmerizing that she couldn't be content experiencing it from behind the windshield. She wanted to be a part of it, one with the white sand and fog as they merged together in the moonlight.

They could see only a few feet in front of them, but the sound of the surf beckoned to them and they followed. She felt like Gretel with Hansel at her side, except that they had no black pebbles or rye bread crumbs to help them find their way through the monochromatic mix of sand and fog. They walked hand in hand along the narrow strip of beach between the highway and the water, knowing if they strayed off course they need only turn their back on the sea to find their way back to the road.

It was impossible to know how far they'd walked when they stopped to spread Anders' beach towel on the sand and sat down to watch the waves rolling against the shoreline. They watched as one foamy wave appeared out of the white nothingness, then another, one at a time, from a sea swallowed in fog.

She thought Anders was teasing her when he eased her denim skirt over her knees and started to stroke her thighs. The fog shrouded them like a cloak, still, she felt scandalous when Anders stretched out on his belly in front of her and raised her knees to allow himself access to what he desired.

It never occurred to her to protest as she leaned back on her elbows, her knees pulled up, her head thrust back. The sensations were so heavenly that she couldn't have imagined such feelings could exist—a gentle wind, a quiet mist, the rhythm of the waves, his tongue teasing her, his hands touching her. She gave herself to him with abandon.

24.

If she thought the surprises Anders had in store for her were at an end, she was mistaken. First there was breakfast in bed, then a bicycle built for two awaiting them on the veranda. She couldn't have been happier if the mode of transportation he'd arranged had been a coach shaped like a pumpkin with six tiny doormen. The basket mounted on the front of the bike was even packed with a picnic lunch. It seemed Anders had an innate sixth sense as to what would please her.

The fog had lifted and left a gloriously sunny day in its wake. They found a little church just down the lane—square, with a tall, narrow steeple and thin, Gothic windows. The church appeared to be shadowed until they got close enough to realize the building was only painted on three sides. The reason for leaving the fourth side untouched became obvious when they saw the gardens lining the wall without paint. She could see Anders was touched by their reluctance to ruin the flowerbeds with ladders and tarps until the plants had stopped blooming.

She saw him in yet another light as she stood with him, singing from a shared hymnbook, placing his donation in the offering basket, yet another as they poked through art galleries and craft shops, admired a collection of locally made quilts, and wandered through the rooms of the famous *Anne of Green Gables* house near Cavendish. They pedaled back to the Inn along the scenic Blue Heron Drive at a leisurely pace, enjoying what was left of their picnic lunch along the way.

The day was so idyllic she felt almost sad, knowing it couldn't last, that this precious interlude was only a temporary respite, that Anders would soon fly off in one direction and she in another. But he kissed away any remnants of melancholy she might have felt later that night when they finally returned to the privacy of their room.

He made her body sing like no one ever had, but it was the

astounding clarity with which he touched her mind that left her senses reeling. It was as though the planes of her body were the vehicle by which he touched her heart and soul.

When he finally joined his body to hers, sometime deep in the night, it was as though she had finally met her match. Primitive. Wild. Wanton. He saw a side of her that she'd hardly known she had, a side she had never shown to anyone.

The way she touched him, the places she tasted, the parts of him she savored... she had never experienced desire so intense. Loving the lover made a difference so profound she couldn't have known such feelings existed until she had experienced them.

She felt total freedom and acceptance, a complete lack of inhibition. There was no need to feel shy, no thought or encumbrance from the past, nothing but hot, wet, hard, slippery. Each sensation was new. Thrusting to meet him, arching her back, clinging, gasping, panting... his touch did things to her; changed her in a way she couldn't have imagined. He anticipated what she wanted seconds before she knew it herself. It was as though he knew each secret fantasy and hidden desire she harbored in her sub-conscious.

She melted into him, caressing his backside, reveling in the feel of his muscles rippling under her fingers. His teeth nipped her lips as he pounded into her, his hands holding her firmly from behind, spreading her wide and pulling her to him, his chest crushing her breasts until they were one in form and mind. She could feel him growing thicker and thicker inside her body and knew he was close to coming; his mouth plundered hers with long deep kisses. With a sigh of anticipation she brought her legs up around his waist and crossed her ankles until she heard his cry, felt the hot, sticky torrent.

He chanted her name reverently, rubbing the small of her back, nuzzling her breasts with their bodies still joined. She loved the look on his face, loved knowing she was the cause of the pleasure reflected in his eyes.

"I love you, Jensen. The more I know of you, the more I love you, from the look on your face to the perfect maturity of your body to the beauty of your soul. I never want what we have together to end."

She looked up at him in a daze. Had she heard him speak or had she simply known that he loved every facet of her being for all of eternity? She felt an overwhelming need to kiss him again. It was a dream come true, the simple act of feeling him there beside her in bed; touching, stroking, breathing deeply of each other, knowing what the other thought and felt without uttering a word.

He looked down at her bare breasts and ran a finger around the pink areolas. "Now you have evidence of what the images you paint in my mind do to me physically."

"I wasn't sure what would happen when we met. You knew all along, didn't you?" She rubbed his belly absently.

"Yes."

"Is this a real-world fantasy, or fantasy-world magic?"

"Both." He cupped her breasts in his hands and massaged the sides with a tenderness she had already grown to love.

She signed contentedly. "Your hands are so warm."

"It seems like a lifetime ago that we were talking on the internet, Jen. I feel like we've been together forever."

She nuzzled her chin to his shoulder. "Being separated by all those miles, typing our hearts out, trying to imagine how you look and feel — it seems like a distant memory now."

"One I hope never to relive," he said.

*****

The next three days flew by in a dizzy blur of adventure, conversation, and frivolity. The knowledge that their time together was almost at an end was always lurking in the back of Anders' mind. If Jensen felt the stress of their impending separation as strongly as he did, she didn't show it.

The morning of their last day together dawned clear and

sunny after two cold, rainy days spent cooped up in their car or snuggled up in their suite. They decided to ride the tandem at Jensen's request, who knew her riding days could well be over by the time she returned home to Minnesota's harsher climate. She claimed the temperatures on Prince Edward Island, where the ocean currents kept the winters milder and the temperatures warmer, felt almost balmy compared to what she'd gotten used to at home. He'd been quick to tell her Danemark had the same advantage.

They'd set out riding at a leisurely pace in a new direction, intent on exploring another corner of the island and making the most of their last full day together. They found the quaintly renovated bungalow that housed the art studio totally by accident.

The high ceilings and generous windows framing the rooms made it the perfect backdrop for a bevy of distinctive pottery, watercolor paintings, and hand-hooked rugs. Jensen scanned the room and went directly to a display of tiny wall quilts made from velvets pieced in crazy quilt designs decorated with vintage buttons and charms. He supposed this was what Maren had called "fancy work" in her letters.

Jensen's fascination with the quilts gave him the chance to explore the vintage-looking jewelry in the back room. Even before they'd met, he'd contemplated asking Jensen to marry him. But he certainly hadn't tried to second-guess how and when he would go about it.

Jensen seemed deep in thought when he approached her from behind and put his arms around her waist. "Finding some new inspiration?"

"The woman who designed these pieces is very creative." She held up a long narrow piece made of three squares, one on top of the other. "Look at the way she's integrated the embroidery stitches into the design. Isn't it wonderful? It reminds me of some pillows my Grandma Victoria made for my mother when I was a little girl."

He kissed her behind her ear. "You're so beautiful when you're excited."

She leaned back into his embrace. "Then I'm sure I've never looked lovelier, given your perpetual knack for keeping me hot and bothered."

"Now there's an American expression I can relate to. Want to go find a little stretch of beach and get naked?"

"You Danes," she teased him back. "Not a modest bone in your bodies."

"Hey. You're the one who was half-naked on the beach the other night if I'm remembering correctly." He grinned wickedly. "And I'm sure I am."

"It was dark. And foggy." She turned her head and kissed his jaw. "Although if you keep looking at me that way, I'll be doing it in broad daylight in a heartbeat. I think it's your aftershave."

"There's a nude beach not far from my house in Danemark." He nuzzled his chin to the crook of her neck and whispered, "Just think of the fun we could have."

She turned in his arms and met his lips.

"If I was going to make love to you outside, I'd rather find that hidden creek you told me about in your email," she said. "The one where we were going to have a picnic."

"I knew there was a reason I liked you."

She said nothing, but rubbed her head against his throat.

He took her hand and turned her toward the back room. "Come with me."

"To Denmark?" She teased him.

"To the other room, silly." He tugged at her hand. "I want to show you something."

Her face lit up when she saw the delicately strung necklaces and earrings in the wooden display case. "What lovely jewelry."

"I thought you'd like it."

"You know me well."

He stood behind her with his frame pressed to her back. With a slight turn of his head, he nodded to the woman sitting at the desk on the far side of the room.

"Is there something I can get for you?"

"The ring on the left." He spoke in a calm, quiet voice.

The woman removed the ring from the case. Burnished gold filigree set with two perfect diamonds surrounded a shimmering opal on a raised mount. The stones shimmered in a rainbow of colors in the sunlight streaming through the windows.

"May I?" He took the ring from the woman's fingers with one hand and reached for Jensen's left hand with the other.

The woman smiled and walked discreetly back to her desk.

Jensen's eyes grew misty the moment his eyes met hers.

He leaned forward and kissed the nape of her neck, then whispered in her ear, "I love you, Jensen. I love waking to the sound of your breathing, the aroma of our love, the heat of your body, the keen workings of your mind. Your presence in my life has made me very happy, and I want more than anything to make you as happy as you've made me. Will you marry me, Jensen?"

"Oh, Anders."

"I can't offer you the moon, but I can give you what's in my heart."

"You already have." Her eyes were shining brilliantly; her face was wreathed in a smile.

He slipped the ring on her finger ceremoniously. "Consider this a promise."

"I will."

Anders looked across the room and nodded at the clerk. "Let's take care of the details and head back to the bicycle, shall we?"

She smiled and twirled the ring on her finger. "It's a perfect fit. Just like us."

*****

She knew it was time to go when the gray and moss green walls swallowed up the coral tones that made their room so warm and homey. Jensen listlessly placed a sweater in her suitcase, closed the lid and zipped the bag shut. The bed where they had shared such tender intimacies suddenly seemed as sterile as that in any hotel room, the cozy abode they had made so personal, no longer theirs. Their relaxed moods grew more melancholy by the moment.

They'd spent the night holding each other, saying little. When they'd finally made love, it was by the light of dawn—a slow, tearful, almost reverent merging of their hearts and souls. But the emotional urgency they felt changed nothing. They were scheduled on the same short hop to Halifax, where her flight would take her to Minneapolis and his to Copenhagen. The chiasmic ocean between them seemed to grow wider and more significant with every minute that passed.

Anders lifted her suitcases into the trunk of the rental car and made his way to the driver's seat as though his slow gait could delay the inevitable.

"We've been here for so long that in a strange way I've started to think of this as the real world," she said.

"As opposed to the fantasy world we shared online?" Again, he seemed to know what she was thinking before she spoke. "When in reality, this has been just as much of a fantasy world as the other."

She looked at him knowingly. "More so, probably. It will hit hardest when we get home. I'm afraid occasional emails and periodic online interludes aren't going to satisfy either of us much longer."

He rubbed her thigh and grudgingly removed his hand to shift the car into reverse.

They spoke almost simultaneously.

"I wish you could come back to Minnesota with me right now."

"As soon as I get back to Danemark I can start looking into getting you a permanent visa."

She met his stare halfway across the car. "Anders..."

"You didn't think..."

"But my family is... and your son... I thought..." She felt her face turning red. "I can't just leave everything dear to me and move to Denmark."

"You thought that I would move to Minnesota?"

A chill ran down her spine. "Yes."

Her eyes filled with tears at the implications of his words. She loved everything about her life except that it didn't include Anders. She loved him, but she couldn't turn her back on her family legacy, her career, her beautiful little bungalow.

Her face must have looked as dejected as she felt because Anders looked frantic. "You want to have your cake and eat it, too," he jested, failing in his attempt to lighten the mood.

"I guess I do." She didn't know how to explain what she was feeling. The fact that she wasn't willing to let go of everything she was and run to Anders was discomforting. She didn't want Anders to doubt her love, but he had to realize she wasn't some silly young schoolgirl without a care. She'd spent half a lifetime putting down roots and watering and nurturing the life she'd given birth to. Her house, her art, and her career were all she'd ever had. She loved Anders, wanted him to be a part of her life—"in her life" being key.

Anders' voice sounded firm, but she could tell his confidence was a facade. He was shaking. "Your roots are in Danemark, Jensen. You have a connection to the land that we've only just begun to explore. I have no such ties to America. Forgive me for making an assumption that I had no right to, but surely when you consider the pros and cons with logic, you will come to the same conclusion I did."

"Logic?" She blurted from her dazed state of disbelief. For the first time, Anders seemed like a stranger. "How can you weigh the options when you've never even been to Minnesota?"

"You've said many times that you love Danemark."

"I do. I loved visiting..." Her voice trailed off.

Anders' jaw looked tense despite his obvious efforts to maintain calm. "You said you envisioned my garden in a dream, that you took it as a sign that it was part of your destiny."

First logic, now fate. Her head started to reel. "Your English is flawless. You could adapt to life in Minnesota far more easily than I could to life in Denmark. It would take me years to learn Danish. I wouldn't even be able to read the directions on the back of a cake mix, say nothing about being able to pursue my career or handle a million other day to day necessities."

"My friends all speak at least some English. They'd love to have a chance to practice. And to help you learn Danish."

"I'd always be an outsider." She gulped down tears. "You don't know me, Anders. I take great comfort in familiarity. I surround myself with things that are a part of my heritage. My link to my family and our traditions is very precious to me."

Her heart started to pound; her words echoed in her ears. A few minutes ago, she had thought Anders knew her as well as she knew herself.

"You can bring your treasures with you. Your family will come to visit. I'm not asking you to give up anything, Jensen, just to move a few degrees to the east."

"Thousands of people have emigrated from Denmark to the United States. I've never heard of anyone leaving the United States to move to Denmark unless they were forced to because whatever company they work for..."

"Typical American arrogance," he muttered. "You're letting it color your thoughts. Even you have to admit it."

"It may be arrogant, but it's true!" she said, her voice just as passionate as his.

"It used to be true," Anders said softly. "America was a port in the storm for many generations. Now people risk their lives trying to reach your hallowed shores in crowded little fishing boats that are barely seaworthy only to be turned away and sent home. Americans adopt babies from war torn countries but leave thousands of injured adults behind to starve or perish. Guards patrol your border with Mexico. Innocent young oriental women, still virgins, are smuggled in to your country by the hundreds, promised the dream of good jobs, a better life, a chance to earn enough money to buy their family's safe passage to America, only to find themselves enslaved in prostitution rings. The immigrants who do manage to get into the 'promised land' are faced with lives of poverty in crime-ridden cities."

So she held a slightly idealized view of the United States. Anders was right—day in and day out, millions of people lived with horrific aberrations of modern day miracles gone wrong. Maybe that was the reason she found comfort in the quaint, historical, old-fashioned quality inherent in her work and home.

She wasn't blind. She read the newspapers, watched *60 Minutes*, heard the discussions after church. What Anders was saying was all too true. It didn't mean she wanted to abdicate the country she loved and move halfway across the world.

"Denmark must have its own set of social woes to contend with, doesn't it?" She said, her eyes cast downward. Unlike Anders, she didn't have the benefit of a press core that routinely aired its country's dirty laundry to rely on for news of Denmark's current situation.

"Danemark has a huge labor problem," he shot back, his eyes filled with sudden hostility. "There aren't enough Danes willing to work at low paying positions requiring manual labor, so we import foreign laborers to fill the positions. Pair that with the fact that we have one of the most comprehensive welfare systems in the world, and the imported laborers only have to be in country six months before they qualify for worker's compensation, socialistic medical care, and full welfare benefits, and you have all kinds of problems. All but the most principled ones work six months and find a reason to quit, or feign some minor injury, and we are stuck supporting them. It's a vicious circle and a tremendous drain on our society."

Jensen examined her fingernail and waited for Anders to continue, which he didn't. "That's one bad thing. Surely you can even things out a little bit more."

The car surged forward as Anders plunged his foot down on the accelerator. "Danemark is certainly not a perfect place to live, but I love living there. You won't find better people anywhere on earth." The car glided into a smooth outpouring of energy as Anders shifted into high gear. "When I was in Halifax last week I read an article in a *Reader's Digest* about a test the editors commissioned involving hundreds of wallets randomly dropped in cities around the world. Each wallet contained fifty dollars in cash and an I.D. with the owner's phone number. The test was whether or not the finder would return the wallet."

She could feel her shoulders slumping in defeat. And then her famed, Danish, stubborn genes kicked in. She set her jaw. "Go ahead and gloat. I read the article, too. Danes and Norwegians were deemed the most honest people in the world because they returned the wallet one hundred percent of the time. Although the results of the test varied by region, Americans as a whole failed miserably by comparison."

She turned her back to him and pressed herself against the far side of the car, looking not at him, but out the window.

"I can see I'm only making matters worse," he said gently.

She said nothing.

Anders cleared his throat. "I'm not saying that Minnesota is a bad place to live, or that Danemark is God's gift to earth. It's just a matter of perspective like everything else in life."

Jensen sighed forlornly from her side of the car. "We're alike in many ways, but so very different when it matters most."

"So it would seem."

They rode in silence for several minutes. The outskirts of Charlottetown appeared on the horizon—the rooftops of a new housing development, a large new shopping mall surrounded by gas stations and convenience stores. The real world loomed closer.

Anders gave her a sideways glance. "Even before we met, we shared something more intimate then a lot of people experience in real life. You can't throw that away."

"I just can't reconcile the idea of abandoning the life I've made for myself and moving halfway around the world."

"I understand your reluctance. But please do not let your obstinacy keep us from being together," he said. "I cannot believe it is all going to come down to this, after the wonderful time we have had together."

"*This* happens to be a major issue. And how dare you call me obstinate?" Her eyes implored him to say the words she wanted to hear. "The things we have in common count for very little if our opinions on where to live are as different as night and day."

Jensen leaned away from the door so her shoulder wasn't touching the windowpane. There was a chill radiating from outside the car that was making her cold all over.

What if she gave up everything, as Anders was asking her to, and then lost him, too? She'd have nothing. She'd always guarded the things that were precious to her. She couldn't just walk away from the people and places she loved.

"Damn it, Jensen! Up until now, I have not felt angry. Stunned, yes. Disappointed, definitely. But how can you say *the things we have in common count for very little?* I can't believe you can reduce the intimacies we have shared a statement so calloused and impersonal."

"I guess this is what happens when you try to merge two stubborn Danish wills into one," she said.

25.

The finality of the words they'd spoken was still echoing through her brain when she finally boarded her airplane. She couldn't even remember who had said what. In the end, it didn't matter—they'd both known, with painful acuity, how impossible it was to be together when neither of them was willing to move.

He was still on her mind when she unlocked the door to her house late that night and let her eyes roam over the parlor, then the dining room. The corners of both rooms were still stacked high with boxes from Peder and Tara's attic. Everything looked exactly as she'd left it except for a light sheen of dust, but for some reason, the whole place smelled musty and unfamiliar.

She locked the door behind her, carried her suitcase into her bedroom, and switched on the light just outside the bathroom door. Her claw-footed bathtub and the peacock feathers she loved so dearly were shimmering in their raspberry, teal and royal blue glory. She ran the water a minute in case there was rust in the pipes, then put the stopper in and watched as a torrent of water hurried to fill the bottom of the tub.

She had gained three hours flying home to Minnesota, arriving just in time to enjoy a full night's rest. Anders had lost four hours and would arrive home to a new day. She hoped he'd managed to sleep on the airplane. Anders had said he planned on stopping at his office before he headed home to shower and change for work. She was sure he would have millions of messages waiting for him.

It would be hard for him to catch up on his sleep once he'd returned to Copenhagen. She should have insisted he get more rest while they were on the island. He had to have been exhausted from the ordeal of the airplane crash even before she'd arrived. Instead of being sensitive to his needs and taking care of him, she'd kept him awake all hours of the night. She should have realized that he was emotionally depleted even before she'd arrived. Instead of helping, she'd sapped him of his remaining energy.

It had been all too easy for her to fall into the pattern of letting him pamper her. Anders had taken the lead from the start. He'd found their rooms at Dalvay-By-The-Sea, made her airplane reservations, and gotten their rental car. From now on she was going to start thinking of his needs. She was as strong and capable as he was.

She looked over at the flat, square computer monitor that sat silently on her desk, and wanted to scream, which good girls like she and Mathilda just didn't do.

Resigned, she added some strawberry scented bath gel to the tub and, per her usual routine, waited to give the hot water heater time to rejuvenate before she got into the tub. Her old claw footed tub was so large that filling it drained the hot water heater of water. In about twenty minutes, there would be more hot water for washing her hair or adding a fresh round of steamy water to the tub in case she decided to soak.

Her mother had once told her it was a good thing she hadn't married and had children because there was no hot water heater in the world big enough for Jensen and a family. Jensen herself had once told Ed that if they ever moved to a house big enough to hold both of them that her bathtub was coming with her. Ed had assumed she was teasing, but she'd been dead serious.

It was like her to get attached to things. It wasn't just her bathtub. She envisioned herself stepping off a steamer at the dock in Copenhagen, surrounded by porters laden with trunks and crates filled with her possessions; trailing behind, a bevy of beleaguered attendants struggling to push her cast iron bathtub up the boarding ramp.

She went to her computer to type a brief note to Anders letting him know she'd arrived safely at home, then checked her email.

The letter from her mother came as no surprise. She'd known Peder would call her parents in Arizona when she'd sent the letter telling him she was flying off to meet Anders. At least her mother hadn't called Dalvay-By-The-Sea and demanded she come home. Jensen had to give her credit for that.

She scanned the letter quickly, knowing her tub full of hot water was waiting, accepted her mother's chiding, and resolved to call her parents first thing the next morning. She was almost done with the letter when a line caught her eye. She paused and reread the sentence at a slower pace.

I've been thinking ever since we talked about Grandma Jensen's letters the other day, Jensen. I believe there's another letter tucked away with some things of Maren's that I left up in the attic at the farmhouse. (So who knows where it is now. You'll have to dig. Oh, how I hope Peder didn't throw it on the burn pile!) Anyway, I don't know why this letter wasn't with the others. It was also addressed to Sophie, but it was written at a much later date. If I remember correctly, it was dated sometime after you were born. Grandma would have already been an old woman when it was written. To tell the truth, I never even looked to see if it bore a postmark. It may be nothing more than a birth announcement she intended to mail to Sophie, or perhaps it was mailed and returned with the other letters after Sophie died and got tucked in a different drawer. At any rate, I thought you might as well see if it contains anything important as long as you have a translator at your disposal. Tell Peder and Tara to look in the trunk with the brown leather straps that used to be at the west end of the attic. (If it's Tara who helps you, tell her to make sure she shuts the door at the bottom of the stairs if you have to go up to the attic. There haven't been bats in the attic since you were a little girl, but after your recent experience, I don't want Tara to take a chance, squeamish as she is about living out on the farm.)

She'd forgotten that Tara and Peder had been at odds over where to live when they'd first gotten engaged. The two had met at a college in Illinois. Peder had always intended to come home to run the family farm. Tara, who hailed from Philadelphia, was born and raised a city girl. Although she hadn't really wanted to live on the densely populated eastern seaboard, she hadn't wanted to live on a farm in the middle of nowhere in Minnesota either. For a time it had seemed as though their romance was doomed, since Peder had been unwilling to give up his dream of taking over the family farm.

Looking back, Jensen thought her sister-in-law had adapted pretty well. Tara might not be thrilled with Maren's house, but she'd kept the perennial gardens and rosebushes Maren had planted decades ago in prime condition and added a huge vegetable garden. For the last two years she'd grown pumpkins and Indian corn to sell commercially. She'd made friends with the neighbors and volunteered to teach Sunday school at the church she and Peder attended.

Jensen felt a momentary pang of guilt before she brushed the comparison from her mind. Tara may have had to get used to a few Nordic inflections when she'd moved from one part of the country to another, but she hadn't crossed an ocean or left the English-speaking part of the world. Besides, Tara had had four years at college to get used to living in the Midwest.

Jensen disconnected from the internet and peeled off her clothes. People were pliable as putty when they were in their twenties. They simply grew into the mold life's events cast for them. Anders certainly couldn't expect her to exhibit the same malleability given the fact that she'd had almost two decades to grow set in her ways.

*****

Damn it, Anders thought. Jensen wasn't the only one with sentimental attachments. There were times when Anders took comfort in the familiar, too. In fact, he could almost hear his mother telling him to *slå koldt vand i blodet*, or 'Put some cold water in the blood'.

Anders shut the door to his office a little too firmly and dropped unceremoniously into the swivel chair behind his desk. He was angry—angry at himself, angry at Jensen, angry at their situation. He was angry that he hadn't seen it coming, that he had let himself be lulled into believing that there was such a thing as happily ever after.

He might not have been blissfully happy or even moderately sexually satisfied before he'd met Jensen, but he'd managed to find a certain contentment in his day-to-day existence. He'd been comfortable in the knowledge he was better off being alone than with the wrong person. Jensen had stolen that peace, and it made him damn mad to think he'd stood by like a naive fool and allowed her to do it.

The pile of messages and documents stacked on his desk was almost a foot high. He paged through the forms listlessly until he was satisfied there was nothing that needed his immediate attention. If he was going to face Erik and the grilling he was bound to get and come out with any shred of his dignity still intact, he needed to hit the showers and doze for at least a few minutes before he returned to work. That was when he saw the sticky note stuck to his monitor.

Hope your vacation was relaxing. Call me when you get home ~ I'd love to fix you dinner one night. Laila

Anders gazed out the window of his office longingly. There was no reason in the world he shouldn't dial her number and accept the invitation. He'd be damned if he would sit around feeling sorry for himself because Jensen didn't want to share his life with him. Being with her had reawakened his emotions in more ways than one. If Jensen didn't love him enough to be with him, then he would find someone who did.

He slammed his briefcase shut. Thank God he wouldn't have to look far. For once, it seemed the answer to his problem was practically in his own back yard.

*****

Jensen yawned sleepily and snuggled back under the covers. The schedule she and Anders had kept for the last week had been so erratic that she didn't know whether it was time to wake or sleep. Not only was her body clock out of kilter, the season was changing, daylight savings time had confused her, and she was so tired that for a moment, she didn't know whether the sun that was probing her eyes so persistently was rising or setting.

Her body sought his instinctively. First, her fingers, wiggling toward his side of the bed, then her leg, in search of his to twine around, at last an arm, groping and patting until she was awake enough to realize his side of the bed was empty. The sun hit her full in the face the second she rolled over to lie on her back. She locked out the image of Anders' sultry grin and focused on the ceiling.

Her parents had helped her wallpaper the ceiling when she first moved into the house. The ceiling had been pocked with holes and crisscrossed with cracks. Wallpapering it from the picture rail that hung a foot down from the ceiling on all sides had seemed like an easy way to cover the damage. She smiled, remembering her mom and dad on their respective stepladders, one on each side of the room, a fifteen-foot long strip of wet wallpaper stretched out between them. Jensen had manned the center court, using a wallpaper brush held high over her head to anchor the strips while they all struggled to match the pattern.

She'd put a lot of elbow grease into making the house her own. Anders had most likely done the same, if not with his house, then his garden. When relationships came and went like sunrise and sunset, and you could never count on your current dating situation to last beyond the immediate future, inanimate objects like your house or your bicycle or even your quilts had a funny way of becoming the anchors in your life. Jensen's house had become her constant. Realizing it didn't change it. These four walls and the cherished mementos within were her security.

She groaned and rolled out of bed. A pile of new mail, a blinking light on her answering machine, and a lengthy list of emails all vied for her attention. She had a sneaking suspicion that once she dove into the vortex of work awaiting her, she might find it hard to tunnel her way out. At least that was the rationale she used to convince herself that she should drive to Peder and Tara's house before she embarked on the task of catching up with her work.

She learned via a quick phone call to Tara that both her brother and sister-in-law would be out in the fields by the time she arrived in Blooming Prairie. But Tara said their door was always open, and insisted Jensen was perfectly welcome to make herself at home and help herself to the trunks' contents.

She cut across country to Zumbrota and drove west to Wanamingo on the hilly roads that bisected the area. She'd driven every conceivable route there was between Welch and Blooming Prairie over the years; still, she saw the scenic landscape through new eyes every time she drove down the familiar byways. It took her nearly two hours to get there.

How she loved this place! She remembered sitting at the table, crowded with relatives and farm hands, like it was yesterday—the way they'd teased her when her face puckered up after her first taste of fresh-from-the-cow, unpasteurized milk. She remembered playing checkers and dominoes in the parlor on holidays, the flurry of activity when her great aunts and second cousins had gathered to make mincemeat, rolapolsa or apple cider. Her memories of watching her great-grandmother quilt, helping to pick out fabrics and learning to thread a needle for the first time were the most precious of all.

She found the cedar-lined trunk her mother had described

in her old bedroom, covered with a sheet. The wallpaper she'd loved hung in tattered shreds, soon to be stripped from the walls forever. The ruffle-edged curtains she'd sewn were gone; the walls above what was left of her wallpaper splotched with red and yellow paint samples.

She opened the trunk. She could hear the fabrics crinkling under her fingertips as she moved them aside to sift through the contents. The letter was tucked between an old dress and a hand-tatted handkerchief. Touching it, she felt the same familiar connection to Maren that she did when she handled her quilt, but today the feeling was shrouded with a sense of cold finality.

She didn't understand. Reading Maren's letters had made her feel closer to her namesake than ever. Being in the house Maren and Frederik had built should have sharpened the bond she'd always felt. But today, all she could think of was Anders—the way his skin felt when it was warmed by the sun, or soft and smooth from being under the covers. As hard as she tried to forget the lingering images of their time together and dwell on the mysterious images from the past she had always loved, she could not. The scent of his aftershave, the sigh of his breath, the smell of his arousal—none of it would give way to the musty contents of the trunk.

When she left, she barely slowed down enough for the cloud of dust at the end of the driveway to catch up with her.

She took the lengthier but faster way home, up Highway 218 to Interstate 35, intending to stop at Medford Mall, a factory outlet strip mall. She was halfway across the parking lot when she saw a huge sign in the window of a popular bath and bedroom store.

HANDMADE DESIGNER QUILTS IN ANY SIZE ONLY $69.95. HUGE VARIETY OF PATTERNS & COLORS.

The worst part was that she'd always loved shopping there. She sat in the parking lot for several minutes, staring at the banner, trying to decide what to do.

She'd been raised to appreciate a good bargain as much as the next person. Danes were known for their thrifty nature, and her pockets were not so deep that she didn't need to maintain a somewhat frugal budget. Until she'd seen the sign and stopped to think about its ramifications to her livelihood, she hadn't had a qualm about shopping for discounts.

She knew the quilts inside were not made in the USA, were certainly not hand-stitched, unless it was by underpaid, underfed child laborers in third-world countries. They most definitely did not have the artistic quality her quilts did. But the fact remained that it cost her twice, even three times as much as they were asking for these quilts to even buy the fabric to make one of her quilts, say nothing about the cost of her time and the labor of the Amish women she paid to quilt them.

There were times in one's life when a line had to be drawn. Trade relations with China be damned—a person had to stick up for their own at some point. She threw the car into reverse and wove her way out of the crowded parking lot. Let the mall cater to people who would sooner trade their heritage away than pay a fair price for good quality, durable goods made by their brothers and sisters in America. Let the masses buy their cheap, imported goods for a little bit of nothing. Let them do whatever they wanted. She didn't have to join in.

Jensen flicked on the radio station as she drove down the on ramp and rejoined the thousands of people streaming down the interstate. There were times she found it hard to be proud she was an American.

*****

Anders let his body slump down into one of a pair of matching leather lounge chairs sitting in Laila's living room and swiveled around to face the North Sea. The floor to ceiling windows provided a panoramic view of the ships moving through the main channel separating Danemark and Sweden.

He slid his hands down his thighs, gliding along the ribs of his slate blue corduroy pants as he attempted to ease the tension from his limbs.

"Enjoying the view?" Laila rubbed her hands over the lightweight sweater covering his shoulders and traced the Nordic pattern that was woven into the design with her fingertips. When he didn't respond, she kissed the top of his head and sat down facing him on the footstool that matched his chair.

She was dressed in a sheer caftan whose layers of fabric flowed gracefully from her seductively squared shoulders to her scantily sandaled feet. Her hair was draped over one shoulder.

"I'm glad you came."

"I am, too." Anders marveled at the effect the trip to Nova Scotia had apparently had on Laila. He'd had a sense of it as they'd worked together in Canada, but he felt it even more acutely here in her native environment. The experience had humbled her.

"Put your feet up." She scooted over to one side of the footstool and motioned to the spot she'd vacated.

He complied. She slipped his shoes off one at a time and used her thumbs to massage the balls of his feet.

"Ja, right there," Anders moaned. He'd started to relax the moment he walked through the door. The combination of the soft lighting that was prevalent throughout the house, the glass of wine she'd poured for him, and the courtly strains of Handel's Water Music in the background all merged to produce a mesmerizing effect. It was a distinct contrast to the sharp-edged rancor he'd felt since he left Prince Edward Island.

Even if she hadn't been plying his feet like putty, the sound of her voice speaking soothingly in the familiar strains of his native tongue would have been enough to make him smile after a week of forcing himself to think and speak in English.

Laila needed to talk. She'd put names and faces to the people lost in the air disaster, and it had changed her entire demeanor. Her hands continued to work their magic on his feet as she spoke of counseling the mother-of-the-bride who had lost her daughter and son-in-law, newlyweds who had gone to see Niagara Falls on their honeymoon; a man from Helsingor who lost a wife and two young daughters who had dreamed of seeing the *Ann of Green Gables* house on Prince Edward Island; the wife of a businessman from Odense who had just found out he was going to be a father.

Anders looked down at Laila with a wistful look on his face. She'd shed the cocky self-assuredness she'd had when they'd first met. He liked her this way, her eyes solemn and respectful. He leaned back in his chair and closed his eyes, speaking only to compliment her on her handling of whatever situation she was describing. The night was young, dinner smelled divine, and he hadn't felt so relaxed in a long time. He determinedly thrust any remnants of Jensen's face from his mind and promised himself he would enjoy his evening with Laila to the fullest.

*****

Jensen looked down at her ring and watched, mesmerized, as the opal shimmered in the moonlight. It was unlikely the newly discovered letter contained anything of importance, but she was glad for any excuse to contact Anders. They hadn't made a conscious decision not to stay in touch, but there was no denying something had changed when they'd realized their dreams took them in opposite directions. In her mind, the letter was a way to back up and start over again, to recapture the simple, uncomplicated emotions they'd felt when they first met online.

But Anders was nowhere to be found. Except for the short message he'd left to confirm his safe arrival in Copenhagen, there was no sign of him in any of their online haunts.

She went ahead and faxed the letter anyway. If he contacted her after reading it, it could break the ice. It was bad enough having an ocean between them; the last thing they needed was the treacherous sheet of ice that seemed to have glazed the lane leading from her heart to his.

When she was done she turned to the stack of messages on her desk and started returning phone calls, starting with the owner of the shop who'd run the *View from Your Front Porch* promotional that had brought Jensen so many special orders.

"You're sure?" There was no reason for Jensen to hide her disappointment given the fact that she was alone.

"Please don't take it personally," her friend said. "Current trends ebb and flow. The stock market is down and Bloomington alone has lost over 6000 jobs. When people feel the pinch, they cut back on anything that's not a necessity. Handmade quilts are a luxury."

"I understand," Jensen said.

"It's a compliment to you that sales remained as high as they did for so long. People started to feel the effects of the recession last year, but our promotion was so successful that it masked the effects until now. If I thought a similar campaign would produce the same results a second time around, I'd be happy to try again, but under the circumstances I think we've milked as much recognition from the idea as we're going to. Now if you could find another fabric store in another city to sponsor you, the same thing might be accomplished with the limited number of patrons able to make this kind of investment given the sagging economy."

Jensen's mind reeled. Not only had she been spoiled this last year, doing ninety percent of her business locally, she'd let her other accounts slide. With the exception of a handful of clients like the woman from Aspen whose quilt she'd been working on, she'd had her hands full filling the orders she'd taken at the Minneapolis shop.

It wasn't that she couldn't start doing shows and hawking her goods again. She had the means, the wherewithal and the savvy to do what needed to be done. She just hated the thought of being away from home. Visiting Vail, San Francisco, and

Santa Fe had been fun the first few times, but the thought of rental cars, airplanes, suitcases, restaurant food and hotels beds was not appealing at this stage of her life.

She'd appreciated the simple blessing of being free to pursue her art without having to divide her focus between marketing, advertising, and selling.

You want to have your cake and eat it, too. For a second, she thought the shop owner had voiced the words. But it was Anders who had made the teasing accusation. Or had it been Ed?

Jensen thanked the storekeeper for her candid appraisal and told her she'd be in touch. She hung up the phone and stared at Maren's quilt. Chalk one up for Anders. Or Ed. Maybe they both knew her better than she'd given them credit for.

26.

Anders pushed his chair back from his plate and pulled his sweater closed. It was starting to get chilly on the deck. "The roast pork and watercress sauce were delicious. You're an excellent cook." There seemed very little Laila didn't do well.

Laila picked up a basket of dishes she'd cleared from the table and lopped the handle over her arm. "Let's go inside by the fire."

"I'll help with the dishes."

"I appreciate the offer, but it's not necessary. My housekeeper will be here first thing in the morning."

He took her glass and went to the bar. "The least I can do is freshen your drink."

"Thank you."

He poured the wine and met Laila inside. He held her wine glass while she slid to the floor in front of the sofa, then handed his to her while he sat. He leaned his back against the couch, his legs stretched out in front of him, slung his arm around her shoulders, and scooted down until his head was the same height as hers.

Laila turned her head expectantly. Too late, he realized his mistake.

The fire spit embers into the air.

He cleared his throat. "The log is ready to split in two."

Laila smiled and tucked her hand under his arm. She splayed her fingers slowly, subtly searching his muscled chest. Her finger settled on his nipple and started to swirl around the outer edges.

Anders stiffened and cleared his throat, more loudly this time.

"I'm sorry," she said. "I thought you wanted the same thing I did."

Anders stroked her face with the back of his hand. "You've been a wonderful friend."

She turned her head and kissed his fingers. "Does the woman who's stolen your heart have a name?"

"Jensen," he stammered.

He felt Laila's sigh through his sweater.

"She's from Minnesota. I met her on the internet one night when I was online talking to Bjorn."

"You rendezvoused in Canada."

"Yes."

"For the first time?"

He nodded.

"And?"

"It was perfect."

"Except?"

"She doesn't want to leave her home and family in Minnesota."

"And you don't want to leave Danemark."

"No."

Laila looked at him intently. "Why?"

"I don't really know. I don't want to live in the United States."

"So move to Canada, Germany, Ireland."

Anders shook his head. "Why make both of us suffer? She wants to stay in Minnesota, I want to live in Danemark. One of us may as well be happy."

"But if you won't move to Minnesota and she won't move to Danemark, neither of you will be happy."

"I guess not."

"So you've resigned yourself to being unhappy for the rest of your life." Laila looked at him expectantly.

"If that's the way it has to be." He turned his back to her and rose.

She gave him a few moments before she followed. He was looking out at the cold gray waters of the North Sea when she found him, his fists clenched at his side as he gazed out over the fading light.

He could hear her bare feet padding quietly against the

ceramic tile. "Oh, Anders," she whispered, cradling his waist in her arms and laying her head on his shoulder.

He turned to face her and took her in his arms without saying a word.

*****

The first light was shimmering in the eastern sky when Anders pulled into his driveway and climbed out of his car. He swung the car door closed with the same gentle force his mother had claimed pervaded so many of his mannerisms.

His brain was overflowing its banks as he unlocked the front door to his house, hung his jacket in the closet and went to his desk. The muscles along the length of his back rebelled as he slipped his sweater over his head. He pulled off his shirt and unbelted his pants. It had been a long night. The massage Laila had given him had helped, but his shoulders were still tight as a drum. All he wanted was a few hours of good sleep before he had to report to work that afternoon.

He spotted the papers jutting out from the tray of his fax machine on his way to the shower and stopped to read Jensen's cover letter. Placing the papers on top of his desk, he walked toward the shower, his shoulders slumped in defeat. He was beginning to understand Jensen's reluctance to move away from her family. There were many times he wished his own mother or father were still living so he could indulge in the simple pleasure of calling them on the phone and asking for a bit of advice.

*****

Jensen snuggled under the covers and listened as hundreds of ice-covered lilac branches scratched across her windowpanes like fingernails on a chalkboard.

It was barely past ten, but without electricity, the only option open to her was to go to bed. She couldn't see to read—

the night was as black as ink without lights and streetlamps to penetrate the darkness. She'd tried to do some hand quilting by candlelight. Historically apt as the experience had been, her eyes had been bleary with fatigue after only a few minutes of straining to see the tiny stitches in the dim, shimmering streams of yellow.

The ice storm had hit with little warning. The temperature had hovered just above freezing all afternoon. A steady rain had doused the Cannon River Valley until there were an extra 10,000 or so lakes dotting the Minnesota landscape. It had still been raining at dusk when autumn lost its hold and the temperature slipped a mere degree below freezing.

The rain clung to the branches in sheets, glazing and re-glazing each lacy twig with an ever-thickening coat of clear, shiny ice. It was the first time she'd actually seen fall turning to winter, looking out the window, watching the rain turn from wet and slippery to thick and sleek. She turned her head away from the window and fought back thoughts of Anders. She could not stop thinking about him. Her emotions filled her with wonder one minute and threatened to overwhelm her the next.

It was still sleeting. She could hear the syrupy moisture slathering itself against the west side of her house, sliding down the window panes and slapping the already fragile trees with the heavy force of its weight, coating everything in its path.

She used her arms to tuck her quilt under her chin and stared into the night. The faces of her new clock radio, microwave and VCR blended into the black abyss that was her room, but she had batteries in her new boom box thanks to the salesman at Best Buy. Her telephone service was intact thanks to underground cables.

Her body melted into the soft valley in the middle of her bed. At least she was warm. It was the first time she'd turned the furnace on that fall and the radiators smelled slightly of hot dust and mildewed water. It wasn't cold enough outside to endanger lives or freeze pipes in the homes of people who didn't have gas hot water heat; Minnesota homes were too well insulated for that. Still, she was glad to be warm and cozy.

The phone rang—Ed.

"Just checking to see if your pilot light is lit," he said. "I figured you hadn't had your heat on until now."

"Thanks. Mr. Finnegan checked it while he was here."

"Good. I don't think I could make it over there if I wanted to. I barely made it home from work without going in the ditch. The roads are glare ice."

"I don't think there's been an ice storm this awful since I was a kid," Jensen said.

"I remember an ice storm back in 1971 when the wind was so bad it bent small trees in half and glued their branches to the ground. It cracked telephone poles and snapped brittle power lines in half."

"I remember that one, too," she said. "My mom and dad and the boys and I toughed it out for two days before the cold forced us into town. Mom had us bundled up like Eskimos in long johns topped by layers and layers of winter clothes. It was almost a week before the power was restored out in the country."

"Is that the time Peder's goldfish froze to death in their fishbowl?" Ed said. "I think you told me about that."

It was weird being reminded of the history they had. "The ground was frozen solid by the time we got home, so we couldn't bury them."

"Didn't your mother flush them down the toilet?"

"As soon as the water in the basin of the commode had thawed. I was really heartbroken. I wanted to keep them in the freezer until spring when we could bury them outside. They were Peder's fish, but I was more attached to them than he was."

She'd always felt lucky to have such clear memories of her childhood. Sometimes it was a pain being the oldest, other times, it was nice. Her younger brothers had been so young when Maren died that they barely remembered her.

"I haven't seen my brother or my sister since my folks' funeral. We didn't get together all that often even before they died," Ed said.

"Things have changed in the Christiansen family since my parents started spending half the year in Arizona. Peder calls and tortures me on a regular basis, but I talk to Karl only once in a blue moon. Tara and Melody are both nice, but living almost two hours from them makes it hard to be a part of their day-to-day lives. I've just never gotten to know either of them all that well."

"They'll probably have kids sooner or later. That would give you an excuse to go over and visit more often."

"I'd like to be an aunt someday." She wiggled her toes. "Brr, it's cold. I hate to think what it's going to be like when it's fifty below."

"The first storm of the season always feels the coldest," Ed said. "It takes a while to adjust after being spoiled all summer."

"I should go find an extra blanket," Jensen said. "Thanks for calling."

"Sleep tight. I'm glad you're okay."

She got another quilt from the cedar chest and squirmed back under the covers, then groped for the flashlight and switched it on long enough to see the controls of her radio. She knew she should conserve what battery power she had, but she couldn't stand the sound of branches screeching, the wind moaning, or the sound of molten ice slinging itself against her windows any longer. She lined up the beam of her flashlight with the knob and spun the dial to Minnesota's Public Radio station. The soothing strains of a Celtic melody encompassed the room.

It had to be close to midnight. She calculated the time difference between her time zone and Anders' and tried to imagine what he was doing. Anders didn't keep a tight schedule like Ed always had, so it was harder to envision what he might be doing. Several images came to mind. Dreamily, she focused on the one that was the most erotic and slipped her hand under the covers.

She remembered the feeling of his lips on her breasts with painful acuity. How she missed him. Not just touching him, but talking and sharing and just spending time with him.

"That was Fiona Blackburn's *When Your Daddy Comes Home From the Sea* from her debut recording, *Land of Passages*. The next selection in our salute to Canadian musicians takes us from Vancouver to Nova Scotia for *Borders and Time,* from the Rankin Family's *North Country* CD."

The words washed over her heart and filled her veins with a cold substance much like the sleet that slicked her windows. A haunting soprano voice rose above the moans of the wind and resounded through the room in a husky, almost mournful tone.

> *I think of you all the time...*
> *I can't free you from my mind.*
> *It seems so these days –*
> *I've tried every way.*
>
> *You have drifted so far from me.*
> *The winds of change*
> *Have swept you away.*
> *Night and Day;*
> *It seems like eternity.*
> *Borders and time have kept*
> *You from me.*
> *Blue are the ocean waters*
> *Along a lover's shoreline.*
> *You will not be forgotten,*
> *But now that you've gone*
> *The heartache lives on.*
> *Oh borders and time,*
> *The heartache is mine.*

The voice floated through the heartrending strains of the

final chorus; the tones of a mandolin and then a fiddle fluttered through the room in a melodic panoply of song. Jensen shivered under her quilts, suddenly and irreparably chilled to the bone.

*****

Anders read and reread the letter he held in his hands. Although the style of the prose was a little different, her Danish a little rustier, the penmanship more careless and mature, Maren had clearly written the letter.

Unless Frederik had put two and two together at some point, Anders was the first to know the secret Maren had carried in her heart—and very probably taken to her grave. Why she had never finished the letter, sealed the envelope and mailed it off to Sophie, Anders could only guess. At any rate, he felt quite certain Jensen's father did not know the truth of the matter, or surely he would have told his daughter.

Anders looked at his watch and did a quick mental calculation. It was nighttime in Danemark - he'd been home from work for about an hour. He usually didn't call Jensen during the day, but he assumed she would either be at home or out doing errands. The chances were good he could reach her, and maybe even her parents. Jensen would want to know, her parents, too.

He dialed the number from memory and without thought to the distance between them—or the uncertain terms of their relationship.

"Hello?"

"Jensen?"

"Anders?"

"Yes. Is something wrong?"

"The electricity has been out for almost a whole day. We're in the middle of an ice storm."

"Do you not have heat?" He felt the same familiar frustration of knowing she needed him, knowing there wasn't a damn thing he could do to help.

"I have heat. It's so cold and dreary, there's ice on everything, and the sky is terribly gray. I hardly slept last night. I just can't seem to get warm."

"You could be coming down with something. Can you get to the doctor's?"

"They're not advising any travel. I'm sure they've salted and sanded the major roads, but they never do the road to and from Welch until it stops snowing, or in this case, sleeting."

"Can you put some more clothes on or do some jumping jacks to try to get yourself warm?" He asked.

"I tried riding my bicycle earlier but the wind the wheels generated spinning around just made me colder."

She had told him about the device that enabled her to ride inside the house all winter long when they were on Prince Edward Island and expressed her concern about how she was going to attach the mechanism to the axle of the back wheel by herself. *Ed had probably helped her out.*

"I just made myself a pot of tea. I'm lucky I have a gas stove and furnace. Hundreds of people are without electricity."

The vulnerability in her voice tore him in two.

"If I was there I'd snuggle you warm."

"I wish you could."

"Me too." He paused, hoping she understood that he didn't really wish he were there; he wished she were in Danemark. "I read the letter you sent."

"Oh."

With that one word, he could tell she'd thudded back into the same pit of despondency she'd been wallowing in when she first picked up the phone.

"I hope it wasn't a waste of time," she said. "Mom was just curious. I mean, since we've come this far. I assumed maybe this letter was an update on how Maren's children were doing, how many grandchildren she had, that kind of thing, but my mother couldn't help wondering." She gulped. "This letter was written over fifty years after the others. Surely Maren wasn't still thinking about Leif after so many years had passed. Was she?"

There. Her voice was sounding warmer. She laughed; a lighthearted, feathery laugh that twinkled over the phone lines and gladdened his heart.

"Anyway, nothing could be so climactic as the letter we read together on Prince Edward Island, could it?" She said.

"Actually, I think you're in for a surprise," he said. "Are your mother and father somewhere where you can reach them, Jensen? This really involves all of you."

"You're scaring me, Anders."

"It's not bad news." He hesitated. "It's going to be a bit of a surprise, that's all."

"Mom and Dad used to have conference calling so they could talk to all us kids at once. I think they still do. If you're not in a big hurry, I can call them and see if they're home, then have them redial my number and yours so we can all talk."

"Perfect. Don't forget to give them the international access code."

"I'll do my best to set it up," she said. "Please be patient if it's awhile before you hear back from me."

"I'll be waiting."

She got her parents on the first ring, brought them up to date on the ice storm, and told them about Anders' request.

"I've been wanting to meet this young man anyway," her father said in his don't-think-you're-going-anywhere-with-him-until-your-mother-and-I-have-had-a-chance-to-talk-to-him-about-a-few-things voice.

Lovely. The scary thing was that she could actually see her father saying something that would put Anders on the spot. She gave her parents his number and made them promise to dial her number first, then bring Anders into the conversation. A few minutes later they were on the phone exchanging pleasantries.

Her father finally took the bull by the horns. "Jensen tells me you've read Maren's letter and wanted to speak to us about some information that you discovered."

"Yes, sir. That's correct," Anders said. "I haven't taken the time to write out an exact translation like I did with the other letters, so I'll be paraphrasing Maren's words the best I can. The letter was written the year Jensen was born, but Maren starts the letter by telling Sophie about the day you walked up to the Jensen's front porch and introduced yourself, Mr. Christiansen. She thought she was seeing an apparition, you looked so much like your father."

"My father always claimed I was his carbon copy. I never saw the resemblance. Of course, I was a cocky young kid who wasn't eager to admit my father and I had anything in common. I thought he was absolutely ancient and didn't know anything."

"Well, your father was older when he married and started a family." Jensen's mother spoke up.

"Still, we're a quarter of a century older now than my father was when he and my mother had me, and I don't feel ancient by a long stretch." Jensen's father chuckled.

"I've never even seen a photograph of your father when he was young," Jensen's mother said.

"If any were taken, they must have remained in the old country with his family," her dad responded.

Anders cleared his throat and continued. "Maren said you looked so much like your father that it took her breath away. She said it was like seeing a vision from the past or a dream come to life, you standing there in front of her, the spitting image of your father. Then she looked down and saw her wrinkled hands, and realized you could not be who she thought you were. The man she'd known in Danemark would have aged just as she had."

"We have photos of Grandpa Christiansen taken in California, Dad," Jensen said. "You look just like him in that photo where he's standing beside his '57 Chevy."

"You really do, dear," his wife agreed.

"Does no good to argue with the two of them, Anders," her father said. "I'm telling you that much right now."

"Dad," Jensen warned him, then laughed. "Let Anders finish."

Anders resumed his tale while he had an opening. "Maren knew your father had immigrated to the United States and settled in Solvang, California. Sophie heard the news in Slangerup and passed it on to Maren."

Jensen's father cleared his throat. "So my father never got in touch with Maren and Frederik after he came to America?"

"Not so far as I can tell from the letter," Anders responded. "From the tone of the letter, I would assume at the very least that Maren didn't know your father had married or had a son. Thus her surprise at seeing a younger version of your father standing on her front porch."

"I remember that she got tears in her eyes when I told her that Papa had passed on," Jensen's father added. "I'm sure I was the first to tell her of his death."

"Maren mentioned that in the letter as well. Meeting you, and then finding out in the next breath that your father was gone was very difficult for her."

Anders' words hung in the air for a second while the three of them contemplated his meaning.

"You make it sound like they had some unfinished business. Did Maren say how she and Frederik knew my father?"

"Your father was Leif Unterschlag, the baker from Slangerup who delivered Maren's baby," Anders said.

"Leif Unterschlag? But how can that be?"

"According to Maren, Leif's complete name was Christian Leif Unterschlag. It would seem each of his four brothers was named after their father, but each one was given a different middle name. Taking your father's name with 'sen' tacked on the back if you were a man, or 'datter' if you were a woman was common. Maren could only speculate on Leif's reasons for changing his name. Many did it because their original names were hard to pronounce or because they wanted their names to sound more American. For whatever reason, Leif listed his name on his immigration papers as Christian Leif Christiansen and was known as Chris Christiansen from that time on."

Jensen could hardly take it in. "Leif was my grandfather?"

"My father was the Leif who was in love with Maren?"

"So it would appear."

"You said you remembered the name Leif appearing in some of your father's documents, darling," Jensen's mother reminded him in a shocked voice.

"What else does the letter say, Anders?" Jensen said.

"Maren was only able to put all of this together because she knew Leif was his middle name and that his father's name was Christian," Anders said.

"She might never have put two and two together if you hadn't looked so much like your father, Dad."

"She probably kept the knowledge to herself all those years to protect Grandpa Frederik," her mother said.

"In the second part of the letter Maren talks about the two of you getting married, Mr. and Mrs. Christiansen," Anders continued.

"Leif's son and Maren's granddaughter," Jensen said incredulously. "Oh Anders, will you translate the rest of the letter?"

"In Maren's eyes, you were the grand finale of a miracle that took almost fifty years to come to fruition, Jensen. Maren spun a fanciful dream about you from the moment she found out your mother was expecting. She felt Leif's presence very intensely on the day you were born. Especially in light of the fact that you were Victoria's granddaughter."

Jensen knew her shivering had nothing to do with the ice storm. Maren had believed she was a connection to a man she had loved very dearly. No wonder there had been such a special bond between her and her Great-Grandmother Maren.

"Maren told Sophie you had her dainty fingers and Leif's eyes. She wrote that she felt a sense of awe every time she heard your name. Jensen Marie Christiansen—her name and Leif's, joined into one."

"Oh, my." Jensen's mother sighed. "It's so romantic I want to cry."

"It's a very touching tale," Jensen's father admitted in a gruff voice. "It makes me sad to think that my father died when I was so young. There's so much about him I don't know and never will. I was too immature to appreciate him like I should have."

"I'm sure your father loved you very much darling," her mother said gently. "Grandma Jensen always had a soft spot for you, too. Now we know why you were so special to her."

Anders scanned the hand-scripted letter once more. "The fact that Jensen was Victoria's granddaughter made the situation all the more extraordinary to Maren, who credited Leif with saving her life and the life of her baby the day he delivered Victoria."

Anders' eyes darted around the four walls of his bedroom as he listened to Jensen and her mother swooning over the implications of the information he'd revealed. It was hard for him to comprehend the ease with which Jensen and her father and mother bantered back and forth. Half-formed thoughts and half-completed sentences floated freely between the three of them. Each seemed to comprehend the other's thoughts before the ideas were even fully formed.

It had been several years since Anders had lost his parents, but he didn't remember having that kind of rapport with them, ever.

Anders suddenly understood why Jensen had been so discontented with a man like Ed. Being raised as she had, she was bound to carry the expectation of this kind of communication into any relationship she entered. The reason she'd been so taken with Anders was suddenly just as obvious. He and Jensen shared the same open candor, the same knack for knowing what the other was thinking before it was said that her parents did. They had each sensed it immediately. It was the reason he had gravitated toward her even though she was from the United States. What he shared with Jensen was a gift too precious to toss aside. They had both understood that. Despite the odds against them, they had both seen the merit in giving their relationship a chance to flourish.

Jensen and her parents proceeded to discuss each and every innuendo and facet inherent in the startling news Anders had just imparted. Anders listened with a vague awareness of the conversation that swirled around him. Mr. Christiansen shared pertinent tidbits about his father he had previously thought unimportant, while Jensen and her mother tried to compose a dateline by aligning birth dates. Their voices were rapt with enthusiasm as their thoughts echoed back and forth. Little by little they started to make sense of what they had learned.

There was poetry in the lyrical conversation that passed between the three of them. Anders could hear the doggerel flowing as he listened from his unique vantage point. For the first time Anders understood how strong and impermeable the bond between Jensen and her family was. And it made one thing painfully clear. He couldn't ask her to give it up. Not for him, not for anyone.

27.

Anders looked out the window to his garden and watched the shadows play over the wilted fronds and faded blossoms. The cabbage roses along the stone wall hung their tattered heads in shame and the cinnamon basil in his herb garden was a dried-up network of shriveled branches. But the sun danced as though nothing was wrong, oblivious to the fact that the delphiniums it was flitting across were the color of a brown paper bag instead of their usual brilliant blue.

In years past Anders had dried his herbs to use in cooking or to give as gifts to the hostesses who included Bjorn and him in their Juletide celebrations. He'd prolonged the life of his flowers by covering the blossoms with tarps on nights when frosts were predicted. This year they'd had a heavy frost while he was in Canada.

He'd had plenty of time to work in his garden in the weeks since he returned home from Prince Edward Island. He just hadn't had the heart.

Except for a couple of lunch dates with Laila and a disastrous evening spent at Erik and Helle's in which they'd tried to cheer him up and failed, he'd had very little contact with anyone. Mr. and Mrs. Christiansen had sent him an e-card, thanking him for all the time he'd spent translating Maren's letters and helping them piece together the missing chunks of their family history.

Jensen had sent a thank you note through the mail, reiterating how much she'd enjoyed their time together on the Island, and expressing her appreciation for the gift he'd given her family. Except for forwarding an occasional joke or story via email, they'd had no other contact.

He hadn't spoken to or chatted with Bjorn either. He shook his head. Like it or not, his son was becoming more American with every day that passed. The last email Bjorn had sent was a stupid tongue-in-cheek story about the top ten things Bill Gates had to be thankful for. As if he cared.

Anders stared out at his yard. He couldn't put off telling Bjorn about his decision any longer. He located Bjorn in a private room talking to SweetYoungThing. Much as he hated to disturb his son when he was engaging in God only knew what, he was determined to tell Bjorn of his decision before he lost his resolve.

Bjorn was not pleased at being interrupted by a message saying his father needed to talk to him immediately, especially when he learned why.

Boy_Wonder: You called me out of a private conversation to tell me that you cancelled your flight?

Ugly_Duckling: I'm sorry to disappoint you.

Boy_Wonder: Christmas is only a month away. I can't request enough vacation time to come all the way to Copenhagen at this late date, and I've turned down three different invitations, including a ski trip to Aspen.

Ugly_Duckling: Can't you tell them you'd still like to go?

Boy_Wonder: They asked Jeremy when I said no.

He'd known Bjorn would be disappointed, but he hadn't anticipated his anger.

Boy_Wonder: You could still come by yourself even if Jensen doesn't want to.

Anders looked guiltily at his screen, and hoped Bjorn wouldn't put two and two together.

Boy_Wonder: You have told her you're not coming, haven't you?

Ugly_Duckling: I will. I assumed she would know.
Boy_Wonder: Damn it, Dad! Assuming things is what got this relationship in trouble in the first place. Haven't you learned anything?

Bjorn left another message saying he had to let SweetYoungThing know what was going on, but he made no move to rejoin her until he had told his dad a thing or two.

*****

299

Jensen braked at the stop sign on the outskirts of Red Wing and looked down at the list she'd propped on the empty car seat next to her. She wanted to make sure she didn't forget any of her errands, and at this point, it was likely she would if she didn't keep close track of her list. She was still reeling from the news she'd just received.

She'd started her Christmas shopping early this year. Her parents had decided to fly home for Thanksgiving instead of Christmas since most of their children would be spending their holiday elsewhere. It was Peder and Tara's year to spend Christmas with Tara's family in Philadelphia. When Jensen had announced she was going to Seattle, Karl and Melody had decided to fly to Arizona to spend the holiday at her parent's place.

She hoped she was still going to Seattle. She had started to wonder given Anders' silence the last couple of weeks. Fortunate or unfortunate as the case might be, she was as stubborn as he was, and she was not going to miss meeting Bjorn for anything in the world short of specifically being asked not to come.

She pulled into the parking lot of the old Red Wing Pottery factory; a unique brick building that had been converted into a shopping mall. She checked her list once more: Victorian stationary for her mother's computer from the paper goods store, a pair of Red Wing boots for her father to wear hiking in the hills around Phoenix, and wool socks and scarves from Minnesota Woolens for her brothers and their wives. She had one gift for Anders; a Rankin Family CD she'd ordered from Amazon.com. She hoped to find a unique piece of Red Wing pottery at one of the antique stores to round out her gift to him.

She left the shopping gallery two hours later with an armful of packages. The daylight hours were already so short that it was pitch black by the time she finished.

It was out of her way to go past Ed's, but she hadn't seen him since he'd helped trim her lilac bushes and she thought it might be nice to stop by and say "happy holidays" on her way out of town. These days she didn't even get to Red Wing very often.

When she got to his house, it was ablaze with light. Warm glows emanated from every window. A vehicle she didn't recognize was parked in the driveway. She slowed as she neared the house, thinking for a second it wouldn't hurt her feelings to see Ed with someone new now that there was a little more water under the bridge. But after hesitating for a second, she drove on.

*****

Thanksgiving Day dawned clear and cold. Clear roads and the lack of snow were right up there on her top ten list of things to be thankful for. Still, her heart was heavy as she drove to Peder and Tara's house. Ed had celebrated the last two Thanksgivings with her family—and one very special Christmas when she'd thought she would get a diamond and hadn't.

Maren's house held no bad memories, but it did hold a few good ones gone sour.

The dreams she'd had of Anders meeting her family, seeing the farm and Maren and Frederik's house, spending the holidays with her were no more than that... dreams, a wild imagination run amok... once again.

She was at Peder and Tara's by half past eleven, right on schedule. Her parents had been at the farm for two days already and she was eager to see them. Jensen lifted the basket of garlic bread she'd been asked to bring from the back seat and walked up the sidewalk to the back door.

Tara's pink petunias were withered and brown, frozen in a killing frost that matched her litany of failures a little too perfectly. Jensen raised her hand to knock, forced a smile and tried to shake off the feeling that she was already a stranger in the one place on earth she should feel most at home.

Her mother and father were at the door waiting to give her a hug. Tara took her breadbasket and hung her coat in the hall closet. She looked around. At least Peder hadn't gutted the living room.

For a second, she felt guilty. Thanksgiving was a time to be thankful and she certainly had been blessed.

When she was a little girl, Grandpa Frederik had played a game with her called Count Your Blessings. They had gone back and forth, each saying something they were thankful for until one of them couldn't think of anything else, or she had fallen asleep trying. She had much to be thankful for, and she knew it, but it was hard to be joyful about the last Thanksgiving she would ever spend in the house she had grown up in.

She walked into the parlor. Her brothers were clustered around the coffee table, oohing and aahing over some blueprints and a small, made-to-scale model of what she supposed was the new house. No use pretending it wasn't going to happen...

That was when she caught a whiff of garlic. Jensen sniffed, her nostrils flaring in an attempt to determine what was baking. It seemed funny that she couldn't smell the turkey roasting. They were rolling both holidays into one this year—perhaps Tara was serving Swedish meatballs with mashed potatoes and gravy, their traditional Christmas dinner, instead of turkey and the trimmings. Whatever it was was spicy, but she didn't detect the distinctive nutmeg or cloves her mother used in her Swedish meatballs.

Jensen shot a worried glance at her father. Surely Tara hadn't used someone else's meatball recipe. Jensen's mother's were the absolute best in the world. Hmm.... whatever was cooking smelled more like garlic and tomatoes than any of their traditional holiday meals.

Karl looked up, stood and gave her a quick hug. Peder nodded from where he sat on the floor. She looked around the room, face to face with reality for the first time. This wasn't sentimental nonsense, it was the cold, hard fact that this time next year, their home would be filled with strangers.

"Maybe I should move back to the farm." The words were out in the open before she could think about how to put them, guesstimate how people would react, or talk herself out of saying them in the first place.

The room grew quiet and six heads turned to look at her.

"You have a house," Karl said.

He was right. She'd poured so much of herself into her house, done so much to make it hers, that she and it were intertwined in not only her mind, but everyone else's.

Tara and Melody wisely said nothing.

"You've always hated riding your bike on gravel roads." This from her father.

"Maybe the county will blacktop it."

"If they do, it'll be tax money they take out of my pocket to pay for it," Peder said.

She reached for a piece of celery and a carrot stick. "Well, at least I know where I stand." She stared Peder down while she snapped the end of the carrot off with her teeth.

Peder looked away. "If you're trying to make me feel guilty, you can forget it. It won't work."

"I thought maybe you'd be moving to Denmark," her dad said.

Jensen nearly choked on a chunk of celery.

Karl started to laugh raucously. When no one joined in, he stopped, and the abrupt silence lingered in the confined space like a sky about to erupt before a storm.

"She wouldn't be happy at the farm for two minutes," Peder said.

"It's not just a farm. It's our family home."

"Well, families change." Peder glared at her.

"They do?" Her mother said. "Because hearing the two of you fight is like reliving the 1980's all over again. If I didn't know better, I'd think you were a couple of grade-schoolers."

"Peder might as well be, the way he's acting," Jensen said.

303

"She's the one who started it." Peder's neck muscles clenched and unclenched.

"C'mon now, kids." This from her dad. "No need to spoil a perfectly nice Thanksgiving Day."

"Jensen?"

Her mother didn't have to say another word. Jensen knew the drill.

"Sorry," she mumbled in a sarcastic, near whisper.

"You can do better than that, can't you, sweetheart?" her dad said.

Talk about déjà vu. "I'm sorry I've been giving you a bad time about moving, Peder."

"There now. Doesn't that feel better?" her dad said. "Peder?"

"I owe her an apology for wanting to live my life where and how I see fit?" Peder's eyes flashed black.

"No," Tara said from the kitchen door. "You owe her an apology for being an insensitive oaf. One that I love."

"Thanks," Jensen said, overlooking the fact that Peder still hadn't apologized.

No one said anything for a second.

"Dinner is almost ready." Tara smiled brightly. "Peder, I could use some help in the kitchen."

"Sure."

"Hey, Jenny," Karl said. "Melody and I have been meaning to ask you about making us a quilt for our guest room."

Jensen smiled and watched Peder disappear through the door to the kitchen. "Sure! Do you have some colors you're trying to match or do I get to play?"

Her mother cornered her the second she and Melody finished talking.

"So what do you hear from Anders these days? Your father and I so enjoyed talking to him on the phone. I wish we were going to meet him at Christmas, but I suppose meeting the whole clan might have been a bit overwhelming at this point."

"We've talked a few times since we were in Canada." She turned toward the kitchen. "Is that Tara's vegetable casserole

I'm smelling?" Jensen asked her mother, ignoring the suspicious look on her face. "Funny how one odor can be so strong it overwhelms all the others."

"Your father and I were certainly impressed by your Anders," her mother reiterated pointedly. "We thought the world of Ed, so it's no wonder we were skeptical that you'd ever find a man who would measure up in our eyes, especially when we heard you met him on the internet. But I have to admit that this Anders seems like a perfect match for you. Your father and I are just thrilled that you found each other."

As always, the same things she could hide from her mother over the phone or in emails was impossible to cover up once they were face to face. "The last time I talked to Anders was the day we found out about Leif."

Her mother put her arm around her. "I didn't pick up any negative vibes when we were all on the phone. Did you argue about something or has he just lost interest?"

Jensen winced. Leave it to her mother to get right to the point. "He wants me to move to Denmark."

Her mother looked at her. "Then you'll go."

"I will not."

"Have you really thought this through? Weighed the pros and cons?"

"No." Jensen stared at her mother like she didn't know her. "You know how I am. I can't just up and leave. Everything I've worked for is here. My roots are here."

Her mother raised an eyebrow. "It's not as though he's asking you to move to Timbuktu, darling. It wasn't that long ago that our family's roots were in Denmark."

Jensen stood her ground. "I guess this is one more way that I take after Maren. Except that I live in the twenty-first century and no one has the right to drag me off to somewhere I don't want to go."

"Dinner's ready!" Tara's voice echoed through the parlor.

Jensen stood and slipped into the powder room. She waited just out of sight until her mother had taken a seat, then seated herself at the opposite end of the table.

Karl went to the kitchen door. "Say Peder, you want some help carving the turkey?"

"I thought Dad told you. Tara made her special vegetarian lasagna," Peder said.

"Oh." Karl responded with a bit too much cheeriness.

"You mean we're not having mashed potatoes and gravy and stuffing?" Jensen said.

"I'm sure the lasagna will taste great with the turkey," Melody said.

"It's wonderful," Jensen's mother promised. "Tara got the recipe from her Grandma Baratono."

"There's no turkey," Peder said. "Tara made two huge casseroles of lasagna."

Jensen's mouth dropped open and hung wide for a second before she regained her wits and snapped her jaw shut.

"Chocked full of several kinds of cheese for all you dairy farmers," Tara said proudly as she came through the door carrying a steaming dish.

"And fresh vegetables Tara grew in her own garden," Peder added. "She's been storing the cream of the crop down in the root cellar, just waiting until Thanksgiving."

"Looks delicious." Jensen's father grunted appreciatively.

"Help yourself," Tara urged them. "We've got Caesar salad with homemade croutons and Jensen's garlic toast."

Jensen swallowed and forced herself to smile. She felt like she was in the middle of a bad dream. Not only was there no turkey, there was no Grandma Jensen's sage stuffing, no Aunt Mathilda's Lime Jell-O Salad, and no Grandma Victoria's famous mashed potatoes and giblet gravy.

Her father said the blessing before they passed their plates to Karl, who heaped each one with a generous serving.

"Look at those vegetables," Jensen's mother cooed. "The strips of zucchini and summer squash are just lovely with the tomato sauce. It's so colorful."

"That tomato sauce is made with fresh Roma tomatoes

from the garden. It's been simmering on the stove since yesterday." Peder said enthusiastically. "Roma's have much more flavor than the old Beefsteak variety Grandma always grew."

"So does this mean we get homemade pumpkin pie made with one of Tara's own pumpkin's for dessert?" Jensen asked hopefully as Peder passed her plate back to her.

Tara giggled and met Peder's eyes across the room, "Well, we did talk about what fun it would be to make a pie out of one of my pumpkins, but it didn't seem like it would go with the lasagna very well. So we stayed with the theme and made my family's traditional Thanksgiving dessert."

"Tiramisu," Peder said, his pronunciation cocky with the promise that they would love the dessert.

Tara blushed. "Peder calls it *Taramisu* because I make it with a few of my own special touches."

Jensen smiled politely and took a bite of lasagna. The meal was surprisingly tasty, but it certainly didn't feel like any Thanksgiving she remembered.

Karl dropped the next bombshell. "Speaking of original recipes," he said, after his third helping of lasagna. "Melody and I have an announcement to make."

Everyone in the room turned their head toward him expectantly.

"There's going to be a new little Christiansen next summer," Melody said, her round face beaming. "We're going to have a baby."

It went without saying that Jensen was very happy for them. Really, she was. The day had been cram-packed with surprises. What more could she have asked for in the way of a memorable family affair?

Try a lecture from her mother.

Jensen offered to help with the dishes, confident her mother wouldn't continue to ply her with questions or opinions about Anders in front of her siblings. She'd obviously underestimated her mother's tenacity.

"You can't get out of talking to me that easily, Jensen Marie Christiansen," her mother said from her watchful perch.

"I wasn't trying to."

"You were too. Now get in here and shut the door." Her mother tugged her into a small room off the kitchen that Maren and Frederik had used for an office in their later years.

"Mom," Jensen protested. "I'm not a child."

"You're acting like one." Her mother met her stare head on. "Now I want you to set aside your father's stubbornness for just a few minutes and listen to what I have to say."

"My father's stubbornness?"

"Yes."

"You don't think I inherited any of it from you?

"No. Now sit down."

Jensen had only heard this particular tone a few times in her life, but she recognized it loud and clear. She sat. And listened.

Her mother started to pace as much of the floor as the narrow room allowed. "I know you've always idolized your great-grandmother, Jensen, and I'm not saying you should stop, but you need to know that Maren wasn't perfect. I know you sympathize with Maren's side of the story in all of this, but you need to know what Frederik felt too."

Her mother's fists were clenched but her face was almost serene. "I knew Maren for many more years than you did, Jensen. I was there through many more stages of her life. I saw and observed first hand things that you never did, thus I've been able to piece together a few thoughts based on my knowledge of the portions of the story you were never privy to."

She'd never seen her mother behave so passionately.

"Maren was creative and whimsical and beautiful. As you know, she was a very lovely young woman. She was also stubborn as a mule. She lived in the Blooming Prairie area for over seventy years and never learned more than a few words of English. And it wasn't just the language she resisted.

"You know how much Grandma Jensen loved to bake.

Well, she stopped the day Grandpa Frederik bought an electric stove from Sears. If she couldn't cook on her old cook stove, she wasn't going to cook at all. Time after time, she refused to adapt, clinging to the old ways to the consternation of all the people around her. You'd think she would have been thrilled when Grandpa Frederik traded in their old wringer washer for a brand new electric washer and dryer, but she wouldn't go near the machines. I finally taught grandpa how to do the laundry himself. Grandma simply would not learn.

"What Maren said in those letters is true. Frederik dragged her kicking and screaming all the way across the Atlantic. And she never forgave him for it. Sure, they made their peace, raised a family and made a happy home for their children, but on some level Frederik always knew Maren resented him. Maren may have lost her family and a beloved friend that day so long ago when Frederik walked in and saw his wife in Leif's arms, but what Frederik lost was much, much greater. He lost the love of his life. Maren held herself at a distance from him. From that day on, he never had her heart."

Her mother paused and took a sip of coffee from the mug she'd been nursing since dinner. "Okay. I'm done lecturing you on Maren and Frederik the way I see it. Now let's talk about Leif. You have his genes too. Let's think about what would have happened if Leif had had Maren's attitude.

"Leif lost his wife and his firstborn. But he didn't bury himself along with them. He moved to Denmark, bought a bakery, started over again. Then, however unintentionally, he found his soul mate in Maren and found himself falling in love with a married woman.

"He was in love with someone he couldn't have. Only a cruel and very unfortunate twist of fate would demand that any man face that kind of loss twice in only a few short years. But through no fault of his own, that was Leif's lot."

Her mother's voice grew soft and sympathetic. "Leif was alone for many years, I assume mourning in his own way. But at some point he moved on. No one dragged him to California,

Jensen. He went there of his own volition. He followed his heart. And then he found it in himself to love another woman, a woman who wanted nothing more than a child of her own, a woman who needed to be loved. He gave her many happy years, and a child. He made her dreams come true, Jensen. Had Leif not followed his heart, you wouldn't be here today."

Jensen was only vaguely aware that her father had slipped into the room.

"While we're on the subject of the Christiansens, let's talk about your father," her mother continued, oblivious to the fact that her husband was listening. "Your father was an only child who had lost both his father and his mother by the time he was twenty-one years old. Any surviving members of his family were back in Europe. Did he refuse to adapt? Did he stagnate in a pool of grief? No! He followed his instincts. He set out on the adventure that destiny set in his path. He came to Minnesota on little more than a whim and made a new life for himself.

"You're right, Jensen. No one's dragging you anywhere. You have a choice. You can be like Maren and refuse to adapt to the course fate has laid out for you. You can sink in your heels and be stubborn. You can refuse to learn Danish, refuse to leave Minnesota, refuse to go where your heart leads you. Or, you can be like Leif. You can find the strength to say goodbye and move on when the time is right. You can follow your heart, take a new name, embrace a new home, learn new customs."

Jensen choked back a sob. "Oh, Mom."

"Come here, baby," her mother said, reaching out her arms. "Do you know how much I'm going to miss you?"

"Can an old man join in on this or is this strictly a mother - daughter moment?" Jensen's father asked, laying a hand on each of their shoulders as they hugged.

"Go ahead, dear." Jensen's mother sniffled. "Do you have something to add?"

"Two things," Jensen's ever-pragmatic father said. "You knew Maren for almost two decades longer than I did, but you told me some years ago that you thought Maren changed after Jensen was born, that she finally seemed to take an interest in learning English, that she seemed to appreciate Frederik more. You said you were glad your grandparents finally made their peace before your grandfather died."

Her mother sighed. "Now that we know the rest of the story, it makes perfect sense doesn't it?"

She wiped away her tears. "You said there were two things."

"Yes, I did. I was just thinking that I'd like to take a trip to Denmark and Sweden and try to find the Unterschlags. Wouldn't it be fun to see if any of my father's family is still living? The only problem I see is that a research project of this magnitude could take some time. We'd need to make several trips, say over the course of the next few years. Oh—and we'd need an inexpensive place to stay."

Jensen looked at her father and smiled.

28.

Jensen followed Anders' directions and logged on to the internet—just as he'd requested. Her assumption, based on what he'd said in his email, was that he was logging on to tell her he'd had a change of heart about spending Christmas in Seattle. She'd logged on to tell him she'd had a change of heart about how she wanted to spend the rest of her life.

They spent their first few minutes chatting about the cold turn the weather had taken and telling each other what they'd been up to. Then, an uncomfortable silence settled over them. Jensen sat at her keyboard, feeling unsure what to type. If the pauses between their messages were any indication, each was hoping the other would warm to the occasion and say something to break the ice.

Ugly_Duckling: Bjorn tells me this is a holiday weekend.

The_Little_Mermaid: Thanksgiving. I forget it's strictly an American holiday.

Jensen twirled her mouse to untwist the cord.

The_Little_Mermaid: Christmas is right around the corner.

Ugly_Duckling: Yes. Um. About Christmas...

The_Little_Mermaid: Yes?

Ugly_Duckling: I've been thinking about Juletide—how we made our plans to meet in Seattle before we knew we'd be meeting each other in Canada.

She rapped her knuckles against the edge of her keyboard.

The_Little_Mermaid: True.

Ugly_Duckling: I just thought, in light of the fact that we've already met, that perhaps you'd rather spend the holiday with your family.

The_Little_Mermaid: You needn't worry about me. Peder and Tara are going to Philadelphia to see Tara's family, and since I planned on being in Seattle, Karl and Melody decided to fly out to Phoenix to be with my folks. Christmas without snow sounds strange to me, but they're looking forward to playing golf and soaking up some rays. We actually exchanged presents yesterday since we knew we wouldn't be together again for the holidays.

She was no dummy. She suspected the reason Anders was pussyfooting around the subject of meeting in Seattle and had from the beginning—all the more reason not to make it easy for him.

Ugly_Duckling: I wasn't sure whether or not you'd want to come to Seattle, now that...

The_Little_Mermaid: Well, actually, I was thinking I might rather have you come to Minnesota for Christmas, that is if Bjorn wouldn't be too disappointed. Of course, Bjorn is more than welcome if he'd like to join us.

Ugly_Duckling: I thought your family was going to be gone.

The_Little_Mermaid: They are. And I would like you to meet them one day soon. But the activity I had in mind doesn't involve them so it really doesn't matter what their plans are.

Ugly_Duckling: I see.

She could almost see him grinning, and then trying not to.

Ugly_Duckling: Jensen? Much as I want to make love to you again, I'm not going to keep torturing myself by indulging in something that holds only pain and disappointment.

Her heart went out to him.

The_Little_Mermaid: Is that why you don't want to meet me in Seattle for Christmas?

Ugly_Duckling: Do they have a saying in your language that talks about a carrot being dangled in front of your face? A carrot you can never have? I love you, Jensen. I've been absolutely miserable since we left the Island. Seeing you now would only make things worse.

The_Little_Mermaid: Well, if you're sure... but the two of us could really get a lot of packing done if we both worked at it over the holidays.

Jensen knew she had him thoroughly confused, but she kept typing anyway.

The_Little_Mermaid: There are a few things around the house that I could use your help with. I'm not very good with a screwdriver, but it would be wonderful if I could get some of those things done before I list the house. The realtor told me houses sell for a lot more if they're in A-1 condition.

Ugly_Duckling: Are you saying what I think you're saying?

The_Little_Mermaid: I've been a fool, Anders. According to my dad, I've been complaining for years about wanting to do more traveling, not having anyone to go places with and do things with, and wishing I had more opportunities to be adventurous.

Ugly_Duckling: I can give you all that and more.

The_Little_Mermaid: I know you can. I'm just sorry I didn't see it before now.

Jensen's fingers hovered over her keyboard as she tried to put her feelings into words.

The_Little_Mermaid: My mother helped me see that I've been clinging to something that doesn't even exist anymore. Everything changes. The memories I hold so dear are just that. Memories. They're not and never will be my reality.

Ugly_Duckling: Memories are with you wherever you go, Jensen. No matter where a person lives or what a person does, memories are always there to be shared with the ones you love.

The_Little_Mermaid: Things haven't actually been the way I remember them, or wish they still were, for years. I've been living in a fantasy world.

Jensen stopped to wipe a tear from her eye.

The_Little_Mermaid: It's time I moved on and made some new memories with the man I love.

Ugly_Duckling: God knows I love you, Jensen.

She was weeping openly by then. Sitting in front of her computer and crying.

The_Little_Mermaid: I went to Thanksgiving dinner at Peder and Tara's house expecting turkey, or at the very least Swedish meatballs, Copenhagen cream and Aunt Mathilda's melting moments. All I wanted was for our family traditions to be upheld. And Tara fixed us Italian food. Vegetarian lasagna.

Jensen started to giggle as the absurdity of the situation finally became clear.

Ugly_Duckling: It's almost as though someone up there is bound and determined to bring us together, no matter what it takes. I've been stubborn, too. I was no more willing to give up my life than you were yours.

The_Little_Mermaid: We're two of a kind, all right.

Ugly_Duckling: You don't know the half of it. I was offered an early retirement package last week, Jen. The new owners want to trim out the "middle management glut" and replace me with one of the young punks I did such a good job of training. They made a lucrative offer that would have freed me to move wherever I wanted to. I ruled out the possibility before they'd even finished enumerating the benefits. Erik told me I was crazy, that this could be the opportunity of a lifetime, that guys with my experience can write their own ticket anywhere in the world if they're willing to be flexible.

The_Little_Mermaid: Neither one of us has demonstrated much flexibility lately.

Ugly_Duckling: I'm just as much to blame as you are, Jen.

The_Little_Mermaid: Well, I'm done clinging to my stubborn ways. I really would like to come and live in Copenhagen. That's why I want you to come to Minnesota for Christmas. Having you here would be a chance to see and know this part of me, your last chance if I sell the house. Maybe I'm being silly and sentimental, but that's important to me.

Tears started to stream down her face again.

Ugly_Duckling: Oh, sweetheart. Of course I want to see your house.

The_Little_Mermaid: When I reminisce about my cottage or the bike trail or my favorite childhood haunts, I want you to be able to see the landscape of those places in your mind's eye. I want you to know the part of me that's been happy here, to appreciate the life I've built for myself.

Ugly_Duckling: I understand. And I'd love to come. I've got enough vacation time coming to spend all the time we need.

The_Little_Mermaid: Thank you, sweet man.

Ugly_Duckling: I've been doing some thinking these past couple of weeks too, Jen, and I can honestly say the only thing that really matters to me anymore is being with you. We can live anywhere we want to live. For the time being, Copenhagen would be wonderful, if you're sure you're willing to give it a try; but for all we know we may decide to move back to Minnesota, find neutral ground in another country, move to Seattle to be closer to Bjorn, take a job in a less heavily populated part of Danemark, retire to Arizona, or win the lottery and move to a secluded tropical isle someday. All I care is that we make the decision together; that you're here to make the decision with me.

The_Little_Mermaid: You'd actually consider living in the United States?

Ugly_Duckling: How can I continue to hate America when I love one of its native children so very much? You may be Danish by design, but it was America that made you the woman I love.

His words raced across her computer screen. The sensation his words evoked in her made her tingle with a heat the coldest temperatures couldn't thwart.

The_Little_Mermaid: I never want to be without you again, Anders. You're the only thing that matters.

Ugly_Duckling: Do you know how happy you've made me, Jensen Marie Christiansen?

The_Little_Mermaid: I have an inkling.

Ugly_Duckling: I'll check at the American consulate, but I think our children will have dual citizenship. Just think, Jen. Our offspring will be true children of the world. We can send them off to spend their summers working with your brothers on the farm or find them a summer internship in Seattle so they can get to know their big brother Bjorn. We'll teach them both languages and the history of each of our countries. They can decide where they want to live when they grow up, and we'll go to visit them wherever they are.

The_Little_Mermaid: Please don't tease me, Anders. Not about this.

Ugly_Duckling: I'm not teasing, sweetheart. Ever since you told me about Ed deciding to have a vasectomy, I've wanted to give you the opportunity to be a mother. That was when I barely knew you. It would be such a shame if someone as lovely and talented as you didn't have at least one child to share their memories with.

The_Little_Mermaid: You're going to make me cry, Anders.

Ugly_Duckling: Think about how happy we're going to be.

The_Little_Mermaid: You make me feel so loved.

Ugly_Duckling: I'm very moved by your willingness to give up everything else you love to be with me. Thank you for accepting me for who I am, Jensen.

The_Little_Mermaid: A stubborn Dane through and through. And I adore you for it.

Ugly_Duckling: I don't want anything to come between us ever again, Jensen. From now on I want to share every secret, each desire, even in those instances when we see things from a different perspective.

The_Little_Mermaid: Oh, I've missed you, Anders. I feel so drowsy and content I just want to close my eyes, snuggle against you and fall asleep. Even my second wind seems to be gone.

Ugly_Duckling: Don't close your eyes for too long, beautiful. I want to see the pleasure my love brings you.

Jensen's lips curved into a smile.

The_Little_Mermaid: How will we ever wait until Juletide?

Ugly_Duckling: I finally finished the word for word translation of Maren's last letter. I know I've already shared the general contents, but I'd like to read a few passages to you before you go to sleep. If I give you a couple minutes to turn your computer off and get into bed, may I call you?

The_Little_Mermaid: Talk to you in a few minutes!

The nightgown she slipped into was long sleeved and had a low, scoop neck trimmed in delicate white lace. The bottom was short, leaving her legs unrestrained while keeping her shoulders warm and protected against the nippy air.

She had just burrowed under the covers when the phone rang.

Anders' voice was soothing and sensual as he read the words Maren had penned so many decades ago.

> *My dear Sophie.*
>
> *My how the years have flown by. It seems like a lifetime ago that we were little girls in Danemark. It comes as a shock to realize that it was more than two generations ago—until I look in the mirror, that is. I suppose it is a good thing that I don't feel nearly so old as I look!*
>
> *You and I have seen many changes in our lifetimes, haven't we, Sophie? From horses and buggies to auto-mobiles; from steamers to airplanes; from high Victorian fashion to mini-skirts and halter-tops. My how things have changed.*
>
> *My Mathilda started teaching school in a one-room country schoolhouse southwest of Blooming Prairie during the depression. She is now at Austin High School teaching flower children and hippies who listen to rock and roll music and smoke marijuana. I often wonder if Danemark has such problems with its youth, or if it is just America.*
>
> *But enough about that! (I know we cannot solve the problems of the world in our letters to one another, Sophie, but I find it comforting to swap stories from the good old days and share my bewilderment with the new-fangled ideas that make up the modern world with someone who understands how things used to be!)*
>
> *You asked how Karl was doing in your last letter—*

although his allergies continue to bother him, he leads an active life in California, where he has moved from designing transistor radios to working with a team of engineers on a new piece of technology called the computer. He tells me they will be used by businesses to make things run more efficiently in the offices and manufacturing plants.

I still have to shake my head when I think about poor Frederik's plight—only two sons out of eight children, and neither of them the least bit interested in farming. Thank goodness Victoria and her daughter Mary married men with a passion for the land so there was someone to take over the farm when the time came.

That brings me to the real reason for my letter—the most miraculous thing has happened, Sophie!

The letter went on to detail the happenings surrounding Maren's realization that the young man who had appeared at her door that summer day was Leif's son. Anders skipped over some of the specifics he had already relayed to Jensen and her parents and went on to the part of the letter that concerned Jensen.

Much to my delight, they've named the baby Jensen Marie Christiansen. My namesake is such a sweet looking little thing, Sophie. How I wish you could see her!

She has Leif's eyes, wide open with curiosity and the adventurous spirit I so loved in him, while at the same time vulnerable. I can see his indomitable spirit raging unchecked in her when she cries, as though she is raging against the world's inequities. I could watch her for hours on end, Sophie, and hold this warm little bundle forever. One minute so taut with displeasure, the next, so snuggly sweet, so wide-eyed and innocent.

Her nose is mine, as are her long, slender fingers

and that adorable little mouth. She will be a beauty someday, just like her mother. And if her personality truly is a fabrication of the best things from both sides of her linage, she will be a charmer to equal no others. (And very likely stubborn as a mule, although we won't wish that upon the innocent little thing at this point!)

I have grown to appreciate Frederik in many ways over the decades, most especially in my later years, when we finally forgave each other for the misunderstanding that had smoldered between us.

Still, I never forgot the love I felt for Leif. No matter how far life's twists of fate kept us from one another, we were truly kindred spirits. You may think me a sentimental old fool if you wish, Sophie, but I feel in my heart that God himself conspired to bring Leif and I together. Across borders and time, oceans and obstacles, some heavenly design brought us together at last in the form of this precious little gift from God.

"That's the end. Are you still there, sweetheart?"

"Yes," she sighed happily. "I feel so loved; by you, by Maren, by my whole family. It's a glorious feeling."

"Then that's the way I'll leave you."

"Until tomorrow night?"

"Until daylight dawns in Copenhagen," Anders promised. "Sweet dreams until then."

"Sleep tight, my love," she whispered.

She touched her fingers to her lips and threw a kiss across borders and time, on the tails of the night wind, to the dawning of her dreams.

Also by Sherrie Hansen
Available at Indigo Sea Press
indigoseapress.com

Stormy Weather ~ Maple Valley Book 1

An ill wind is brewing up a storm and as usual, Rachael Jones is in the middle of the fray. If the local banker succeeds in bulldozing the Victorian houses she's trying to save, she's in for yet another rough time before the skies clear. The only bright spots on the horizon are her friendship with Luke... and her secret rendezvous with Mac...Is Rachael meant to weather the storm with Luke, who touches her heart and soul so intimately, or with Mac, who knows each sweet secret of her body?

Water Lily ~ Maple Valley Book 2

Once upon a very long time ago, Jake Sheffield and Michelle Jones graduated from the same high school. Jake can't wait to take a trip down memory lane at their 20th class reunion. Being with his old friends is like guest starring in a favorite episode of Cheers. Everybody knows your name. Everybody's glad you came. The last thing Michelle wants to do is dredge up a lot of old memories and relive a part of her past that wasn't that great in the first place. Will the murky waters of the past destroy their dreams for the future, or will a water lily rise from the depths and bloom?

Merry Go Round ~ Maple Valley Book 3

Tracy's supposedly perfect life as a pastor's wife and mother of three is turned upside down when her husband leaves her for a man.

Clay Alexander's charmed existence starts spinning out of control when his father threatens to shut down Maple Valley 's woolen mill - unless Clay conforms to his family's expectations.

Is Tracy and Clay's love meant to be, or will they forever be on opposite sides of the merry-go-round?

Her children. His parents. Her pride. His honor. The welfare of an entire town.

MERRY GO ROUND... Hang on for dear life.

A Gentleman Never Tells - Book 1 of the Wetherby Brides series
By Jerrica Knight-Catania

An honor-bound lord and a destitute debutante think they've found what they want in one another. But will secrets and lies shatter their dream of happily ever after?

Hand-Me-Down Bride
By Juliet Waldron

Innocent, beautiful Sophie is a proper German girl who becomes a mail-order bride for an older American farmer of German descent in the early 1870's. The unexpected death of her aged groom on her wedding night puts Sophie in the unexpected position of literally becoming part of an estate, inherited by the mercurial, rugged, handsome Civil War veteran Karl. All the more astounding because the story is based on fact.

Lacey Took a Holiday
By Lazarus M Barnhill

Lacey Took a Holiday is the story of a desperate act of love and the cascade of irrevocable changes it begins. Lacey, the most unlikely heroine, has been betrayed and abused by the men in her life. Andy has lost everyone he ever loved tragically. This 1920's mountaintop romance breaks every rule.